Praise for *The Silent Bride*

"If you're already a fan of detective April Woo, one of the New York Police Department's sharpest and funniest, all you need to know is that her latest—*The Silent Bride*—is just out." — *Chicago Tribune*

"The author's flair for capturing idiosyncrasies and developing quirky characters is highlighted by her cast of supporting characters. . . . With its rich characterizations and well-drawn setting, this rollicking mystery is a plentiful source of comic thrills and suspenseful chills." — *Publishers Weekly*

"Excellent. . . . The strength of the series continues to be the characterization, especially the details of April's dilemma in trying to reconcile her Chinese heritage with her American way of thinking." — *The Mystery Reader*

"Leslie Glass humanizes her protagonists so that readers understand what the heroes feel. . . . An intricate puzzle with tantalizing clues sprinkled throughout the story line." — BookBrowser

"Woo comes across as wonderfully human . . . likable and believable. Her relationsips with Mike and Ching—and the real feelings and fragile egos these characters display—prove charming and true to life. . . . Plenty of suspense and enough red herrings to make it interesting." — *Crescent Blues*

"Suspenseful. . . . [A] riveting, romantic, high-adrenaline read." — *Romantic Times*

continued . . .

ALSO BY LESLIE GLASS

Leslie Glass

A
KILLING
GIFT

AN ONYX BOOK

ONYX
Published by New American Library, a division of
Penguin Group (USA) Inc., 375 Hudson Street,
New York, New York 10014, U.S.A.
Penguin Books Ltd, 80 Strand,
London WC2R 0RL, England
Penguin Books Australia Ltd, 250 Camberwell Road,
Camberwell, Victoria 3124, Australia
Penguin Books Canada Ltd, 10 Alcorn Avenue,
Toronto, Ontario, Canada M4V 3B2
Penguin Books (N.Z.) Ltd, Cnr Rosedale and Airborne Roads,
Albany, Auckland 1310, New Zealand

Penguin Books Ltd, Registered Offices:
80 Strand, London WC2R 0RL, England

First published by Onyx, an imprint of New American Library,
a division of Penguin Group (USA) Inc.

First Printing, June 2003
10 9 8 7 6 5 4 3 2 1

For Nancy Yost

ACKNOWLEDGMENTS

For six years I had the honor of serving as a Public Member of the Middle States Commission for Higher Education. In that capacity, I worked with many university provosts, professors, deans, and presidents. It was a remarkably collegial group, and as is often the case in my not-for-profit work, I was the only novelist at the table. For years, my colleagues entreated me to write a novel about them and their fund-raising dilemmas—but Dear God, please not anything specific or identifiable about their particular school.

A Killing Gift is for them and for the wonderful supervisors and Glass fellows from Columbia Psychoanalytic Institute, CUNY Graduate Center, NYU Schools of Law and Social Work, the New School, Adelphi, Derner Institute, Boston University, Emory, and the New York Psychoanalytic Institute, and for others who have been grant recipients over the years of the Glass Foundation. In every case, we at the Foundation always receive far more from our research projects, our students, and their professors than we are able to give to them.

At NAL, thanks to Kara Welsh, Claire Zion, my wonderful editor Audrey LaFehr, and all the good people in publicity and production, and on the sales force who work on and sell my books. And to the art director for the great covers.

And thanks to my children, Alex and Lindsey, to Judy Zilm and Dorothy Harris, and to my friends in the New York City Police Department and the Police Foundation, who give me so much inspiration every day. And last but not least, the York U of my story and its people bears no resemblance to any university or university personnel I ever met. This is fiction.

God answers sharp and sudden on some prayers,
And thrusts the thing we have prayed for in our face,
A gauntlet with a gift in't.
Elizabeth Barrett Browning, *Aurora Leigh*

One

"That's it. I've had about all the nostalgia I can take." Lieutenant Alfredo Bernardino's retirement party was still going strong when he abruptly pushed away from the bar at Baci and called it a night. "I'm outta here."

"Hey, what's the rush?" Sergeant Marcus Beame, his second whip in the detective unit of the Fifth Precinct, protested. "The night's young."

"Not for me." Bernardino raised two fingers at his famous protégé, Sergeant April Woo. Woo had her eye on him while sipping tea with Inspector Poppy Bellaqua, another girl star. It made him sad. He was going. The girls were taking over. He snorted ruefully to himself about the way things were changing and how he wouldn't be there to gripe about it anymore.

Poppy didn't look up, but April nodded at him. *Coming in a second.* Her body language told him she wasn't walking away from an inspector for nobody. Bernardino snorted again. He hated this girl-ganging-up thing. They were getting to be a pack. Then he smiled and let up on the resentment. So what? It was April's turn. Even if she didn't jump for him now, he knew she was a good girl. She'd planned the event tonight, had chosen his favorite restaurant, made sure that the invite was up all over the puzzle palace so anybody could buy a ticket. Made sure enough brass was there. It was a nice party, and she hadn't even worked for him in five years! Yeah, April was a good girl, and she had a good guy, too.

Bernardino glanced over at Lieutenant Mike Sanchez, April's fiancé for going on a year now. The good-looking CO of the Homicide Task Force was having his third espresso with Chief Avise, commander of the Department's six thousand detectives, who never hung around anywhere for more than a minute or two.

Bernardino was aware that a lot of important people had shown up to give him a nice send-off, but he was feeling drunk and more than a little sorry for himself. He couldn't help feeling that it was all over for him—not just the job to which he'd devoted his whole life, but his life itself.

What does a man think about when he has a premonition that he's on his very last page? Bernardino was a tough guy, a bruiser of a man. Not more than a hair or so over five-nine, he was barrel-chested. Always an enthusiastic feeder, he had quite a corporation going around his midsection. He still had a brush of gray hair on top, but his mug was a mess. His large nose had been broken a bunch of times by the time he was thirty, and his face, deeply pitted from teenage acne, was creased and pouchy with age. He was sixty-two, not really old in the scheme of things. His father had lived past ninety, after all. The lieutenant wasn't as old as he felt.

"Thank you guys for everything. That's about all I can say," he muttered to the detectives nearest him. Charm was not exactly Bernardino's middle name. He was done. He was goin' home. His working life was over. No pretty good-byes for him. He took a quick survey. The dark Greenwich Village hole-in-the-wall where he'd spent many happy hours was so full of old friends that he actually had to blink back his emotions. Thirty-eight years on the job could make a man a lot of buddies who wouldn't want to call it a day, or a lot of enemies who'd barely stop in for a free feed. Bernie had been surprised to see that he'd collected the former. At eleven forty-five on a Wednesday night the speeches were long over. His awards were sitting on the bar, and the buffet of heavy Italian favorites— the lasagne and ziti, the baked clams and calamari fritti, the eggplant parmigiana—had been picked clean and cleared away.

A lot of the guys had gone to work or gone home, but the pulse of the party was still beating away. More than two dozen cronies—bosses and detectives and officers with whom Bernardino had worked over the years—were eating cannolis, drinking the specialty coffees, the vino, beer, and Sambuca. They were hanging in there as if there were no tomorrow, telling those stories that went back, way back to when Kathy and Bill were just kids and his wife, Lorna, had been a beautiful young woman.

Bernie shook his head at what time had done to him. Now Kathy was an FBI special agent, working Homeland Security out in Seattle. She couldn't make the party. Bill was a prosecutor in the Brooklyn DA's office. He'd come and gone without either stuffing himself too much or drinking more than half a beer. With Becky and the two kids at home and court tomorrow, Bill was out the door in less than an hour. A real straight arrow. But what could he expect? Bernie couldn't blame his son for turning out to be a grind just like him. He'd wanted to take off with his son. The party was like a wake—everyone reminiscing over his life as if he were already dead and gone to Florida.

"Hey, congratulations, pally. You watch yourself in West Palm." His successor, Bob Estrada, patted him on the back on his way out. "Lucky bastard," Estrada muttered.

Bernie snorted again. *Yeah, real lucky.* Lorna had

won the lottery, literally, then died of cancer only a few weeks later. You couldn't get any luckier than that. Lorna had finally gotten the millions she'd prayed for all those years so they could retire in the sunshine and spend time together. Then she had to go and die and leave him to do it alone. What was Florida to him without her? What was anything?

He slipped out the door, thinking about all the others who'd passed before they should have. In thirty-eight years as a cop he'd seen quite a parade of death. Each former human who'd passed away too soon had been a little personal injury for him that he'd covered with macho humor.

The worst of all were the officers and civilians, the bodies all over the place in the World Trade Center attack. Smashed fire trucks and police cars. And the fire that had gone on and on. You couldn't get the smell of smoke and burned flesh out of your nose in Chinatown for months. Refrigerators in apartments down there had to be replaced. Thousands of them. The smell wouldn't fade. And that was the least of it.

When the unthinkable happened, Bernardino had been CO of the detective unit in Fifth Precinct on Elizabeth Street in Chinatown for over a decade. Too close to Ground Zero for comfort. Everyone in the precinct worked around the clock because nobody had wanted to go home or be anywhere else. They'd stayed on the job twenty-four/seven for weeks longer than absolutely necessary. People who'd retired years ago came back on the job to help. And they came from other agencies, too. Retired FBI and CIA agents manned the phones, directed traffic. Whatever had to be done. He shook his head thinking about it.

All through those long, long days, the cops who worked the front lines waited with the rest of the world for the second shoe to drop. They'd responded to hundreds of bomb threats a day, telling themselves they were fine. Doin' okay. But the truth was none of them were okay. The worst for Bernie was that he'd let Lorna down. He'd been out fighting a war on New York and hadn't been home for her in her last year of life.

Amazing how one thing could tip a person over. He hadn't been there for Lorna long before she'd gotten the cancer. That was what ate away at him. He hadn't been there when she was well. Then as soon as things were back to "normal," people were out the door. Retiring left and right. And now he was out the door.

Bernardino was a retired cop on the street on a humid spring night, and he was immediately enveloped by a deep warm fog. He looked around and was startled by it. You didn't see real pea soup in New York that often anymore. The thickness of it was like something in a movie. Downright dreamy. While he'd been inside, the haze had dropped low over the Washington Square area, blurring figures, lights, and time. Maybe that was what got to him. Bernardino dipped his head, acknowledging to himself the spookiness of the night. But maybe he was just drunk.

He shuffled his feet a little as he headed north on a side street he knew as well as his own home. He'd parked his car on the other side of Washington Square. He walked slowly toward it, muttering his regrets to himself. Lively, funny, rock-solid Lorna had faded in a few short months. He remembered a social worker's warning to him at the time: "Denial isn't a river in Egypt, Bernie."

But he just didn't believe she would die. The smell of Italian cooking followed him down the block. He was a warhorse, a cop who'd always looked over his shoulder, especially on really quiet nights. But tonight he wasn't a cop anymore. He was done. His thoughts were far away. He was feeling sluggish, old, abandoned. All evening his buddies had punched and hugged him, told him they'd visit. Told him he'd find a new honey in Florida. He'd be fine. But he didn't think he'd ever be fine.

Out of the fog came an unexpected voice. "Hey, you're number's up, asshole."

Like a blind dog, Bernie turned his big head toward the sound. *Who the hell . . . ?* Then he burst out laughing. Harry was pranking him. *Ha ha.* His old partner from years ago following him to his car to say goodbye. His number *was* up—his retirement number.

"Harry, you old devil!" Bernardino had been unnerved for a moment but now felt a surge of relief. "Come out here where I can see you." He spun around to where he thought the sound originated.

"Nopey-nope. Ain't going to happen." An arm snaked around Bernardino's neck from behind and jerked hard.

Bernardino didn't even have time to lean forward and flip the guy before the grip was set. Despite his size and heft, he was positioned for death with very little effort. After only a very few panicked heartbeats, his neck was broken and he was gone.

Two

It took Detective Sergeant April Woo only a second to realize that Bernardino had gone. The plaque from the Department for his wall and the watch from his cronies for his wrist were still sitting on the bar. He hadn't said his formal good-byes. But April was always finely tuned to what was going on around her, knew him, and knew he'd slipped away. She clicked her tongue. No doubt he was sad and hated to part, but there was no need to be rude.

"What?" Poppy Bellaqua followed her gaze to the bar, where her new driver, Martha Ciciatelli, was ostentatiously avoiding alcohol, downing San Pellegrino in a wineglass.

"Bernie took off," April murmured.

The inspector lifted her shoulder. The movement caught Martha's eye. *Want to go, boss?*

Poppy raised five fingers for five minutes. "Maybe he's taking a piss," she said.

"Uh-uh." He'd have to pass the two of them to get to the men's room. Bernardino was a real old-school cop. He would not have been able to resist stopping to heckle the inspector, who was CO of the Hate Crime Unit, and the Chinese officer he'd promoted to detective who'd made good. Bernie would have tried to disconcert Poppy with his teasing. He would have called April *cara*. Nothing offensive, just guy stuff.

"Miss me, *cara*?" he'd say. And, "When are you

going to marry that bum?" Then something about her becoming an inspector herself someday. Yeah, he'd have done that.

A familiar chill feathered the back of April's neck. Something was wrong. She knew it for sure. Sergeant April Woo was an ABC, an American Born Chinese, as far from old China as a New Yorker could get. She had thirteen years in the Department—nearly twelve as a detective, and three of those as a sergeant. She'd solved a number of major homicide cases with her former supervisor, now fiancé, Mike Sanchez. Recently she'd been studying for the lieutenant's test and would take it in a couple of weeks. Everybody said April was a comer, a big boss in the making. But the magic of old China was formed in the foundation of her soul just like fossils were preserved whole in prehistoric stone.

Sometimes that ancient superstition informed April that vengeful ghosts from another age were about to wreak havoc on a human life. The ghosts and demons couldn't be banished. They had a life of their own. April didn't exactly believe in Chinese magic, and certainly didn't talk about it, but the supernatural was in the air nonetheless. The unexplainable happened. All the time. There was no way to hide from it.

"I'll be right back," she said, already on her feet and trailing her words behind her. Her handsome *chico* turned his head from his conversation with Chief Avise when she rose. He had his own radar. All cops did.

Time to go? In cop talk there was body language for everything. She pointed at the forgotten gifts. *Be right back.* He nodded and returned to the shop talk.

April tapped Marcus Beame on the shoulder. "Looks like the lieutenant forgot his toys."

"He was just here a second ago. Did he leave already . . . ?" Marcus seemed surprised to have missed it. April raised a delicate eyebrow. Marcus was too busy flirting with Martha to pay attention to his old boss.

"Anything you need, Sergeant?" Martha jumped in quickly. "Want me to go after him?"

"No, I'll do it." April scooped up the two gifts and was out the door without further discussion.

Then, like Bernardino hardly a minute earlier, she was stopped by the unusual fog. In a few hours it had blanketed the street like smoke from a deadly fire.

Rationally she knew a cold front must have hit a warm front. But the gray cloud clinging to the ground was creepy all the same. There would be many crashes on the roads tonight. Bad things would happen for sure. She shivered at the thought.

A chain leash chinked ahead of her as a man curbed his big furry creature. "Good girl," he said as the mastiff peed a noisy lake into the gutter.

A car's ghostly headlights moved slowly down the narrow side street toward Washington Square. No sign of Bernardino. She turned toward the square. Behind her, a young man and woman walked slowly arm in arm. Ahead she could just make out another figure, no, two figures. She frowned. No, it was one figure bent over. Her heartbeat spiked with the strong feeling that someone was sick. Maybe it was Bernie and he'd had way too much to drink. Hard to believe, but possible.

She was wearing the kind of shoes that defied haste, fashionable slides with really thin heels and no backs that made her mince along like one of those women who never had to walk very far. As she moved toward him, the blurry figure straightened up, glanced her way, then walked in the other direction toward Washington Square.

"Bernie?"

She hurried after him, her eyes pointed ahead, not down. She bumped into the thick bundle on the sidewalk. Her foot struck it; then she looked down and saw the leather sleeve with the hand at the end.

Air sucked into her mouth with a hiss as she dropped the retirement gifts and went to her knees.

"Bernie! Oh, no!" She knew instantly that it was him. She recognized the old jacket he'd worn for years. She knew the hand, and she knew by the way he was lying there, his face pointing over his shoulder, that no natural disaster had occurred. He wasn't drunk. He hadn't had a heart attack. His neck was broken. Her old boss, her rabbi, her friend was gone, and there wasn't a thing she could do for him.

Rage and adrenaline shot through her system. Her purse with her gun in it was on the chair in the restaurant next to Inspector Bellaqua. The restaurant was full of cops, but at the moment she wasn't thinking about them or what she was supposed to do: Sound the alarm. Get help. A cop was down. There was no more serious crime than that. Instead she was up again, running to catch the man who'd killed her friend. Her party shoes flapped against the soles of her feet, clacking on the concrete as she ran. She'd caught a glimpse, only a glimpse, of a figure in the fog, and didn't see him now.

Shit! Where did he go? People in the square were just forms in the mist. But she had a feeling he was heading straight through. She crossed the street and picked up speed. Her heel caught in a crack in the concrete, and her own arrested momentum almost brought her down. She twisted, wrenching her back, but didn't fall. The shoe stuck, so she left them both behind. The cold of wet cement bit into the soles of her feet. But she was a fighter from way back, centered and fast. She didn't mind the wet.

Just ahead of her she sensed motion in the mist and heard footsteps. A man was walking, not fast enough to be in a hurry. She didn't want to yell, *Stop, police,* at someone she couldn't see clearly, someone who could take off. She didn't want to declare herself a cop without any backup, any muscle to protect her. Double stupid to leave the scene with no gun. Now it was too late to sound the alarm. She was running. The man ahead was walking fast. Useless strategies spun in and out of her head until some words spilled out of her mouth.

"Sir, you dropped something," she called.

"What?" He stopped, turned around, and took a few steps toward her, then crouched down, as if looking for whatever he'd lost. In that position it was hard to tell how big he was. April approached, automatically thinking she could take him.

"Beat it. I'm not interested." The voice was low and confident. The man thought she was a hooker. All she saw was a baseball cap pulled low. He seemed to be tying his shoes.

She moved closer. "It's right there. I think it was a credit card or something."

The rule was never to let them get close enough to stab or lunge at you. April was wary. She was thinking things over. He couldn't see that she didn't have a gun, but still she didn't want to take the risk of saying she was a cop and having him run. She wanted to engage him in conversation to keep him there. Her brain was spinning like a car wheel in sand.

"Where?" he asked, laughing.

"I'm not sure, I think near that bench." Under the light. April had both feet on the ground. She was balanced and sure of herself. The man was talking to her, way too calm to be Bernie's killer. But it felt odd, wrong. She was frozen, couldn't leave and didn't dare attack.

He crouched down as if to take a look. He wasn't acting like a killer, but she'd learned a long time ago to take nothing for granted. Then, soundlessly, he sprang at her with the full force of his coiled legs. His right shoulder tried to catch her in the stomach, and had she not moved backward a quarter step, she would have been driven to the ground. Instead his shoulder glanced off her side and she spun away. When he came back at her she kicked him, spun around a tree, and kicked him again. But he didn't go down. On her third kick he grabbed her foot and flipped her into the air as if she were a matchstick. She flew, and although she turned as she fell, she did not miss crashing into the trunk of the same tree that had shielded her before. Red blotches of pain filled her eyes. He was on her, pulling her to her feet, before her vision cleared. Helpless, she could feel the arm closing around her neck and another coiling around her shoulder. In a sickening instant she knew that this hold would leave her with a broken neck in a heap on the sidewalk like Bernie. She raised her right leg and smashed her shoeless heel down on his instep with all the force she could muster. The blow startled him, but did not ease the pressure of his arm against her throat.

"Arrgh." Her arms and legs tried to find a target as he held her from behind. More colors exploded in her own private fireworks behind her bulging eyes. This was what it felt like to die. Pure panic filled her as her throat was squeezed like a sponge. She could not call for help. She could not use her brain or her training. She didn't hear the screams from across the street or the sound next to her of a dog barking, or even the male voice that called, "Hey, cut that out."

Another cop was down.

Three

Mike Sanchez had been preoccupied all evening, but not with murder. Homicide numbers in New York had hit their lowest level since 1962, when murders first started to be recorded in the city. Although there were still too many gun-related deaths in the tough sections of Brooklyn and the Bronx, there hadn't been a high-profile Manhattan homicide in months. Mike had watched the love of his life socialize and thought about police politics. A few years ago he never would have dreamed that he and his fiancée would be a Department power couple, invited everywhere the top brass went.

To the chief of detectives Mike had appeared to be wholly focused on the conversation. But actually April's every gesture had drawn his eyes to her. He couldn't help it. April was so changed from the way she used to be, he hadn't been able to keep his eyes off her.

When they'd first met in the detective unit of the Two-oh, April had kept the lowest of low profiles on the job. She worked hard, kept out of sight, and interacted with superiors only when she had to. She had not approved of dating colleagues in the Department—or, indeed, mixed marriages—and tried to keep their relationship low-key and unofficial as long as she could. But after they'd gotten engaged everything changed.

The two famous case solvers were perceived as comers, and now it seemed that every few days they were invited to some Department function they couldn't avoid. April's shyness fell away with the higher expectations for her, and she was thriving in her new identity. Tonight she'd looked good with her sleek longer hair and silk wrap dress. Classy, and no longer afraid to show off her figure a little. She had been talking easily with Inspector Poppy Bellaqua.

Mike liked that. He never hung by her side, but he enjoyed watching her negotiate the new territory. Not that socializing with the chief of detectives was exactly old hat to him, either. He'd been a street kid from the Bronx who'd run with a gang and could have gone either way. In fact, it had been a young cop who'd turned him around after stopping a knife fight in which he had participated. The scars from it would stay with him forever.

"Yes, sir," he responded when his boss gave him a look.

Chief Avise was nursing a diet Coke and brooding about old times. "Back in the day" was always a big topic of conversation at retirement parties. And this was their third retirement party in ten days. March and April were bad months this year. It seemed as if good people like Bernardino were throwing in the towel every day. Even before 9/11, things had been bad. Experienced bosses with more than twenty years in had been falling away like hair on a cancer patient. Bye-bye to grubby precincts, bad guys, frustrations of the job. Bye-bye to risking their lives in the toughest neighborhoods.

The accrued overtime of 9/11 and the huge shakeup of a new mayor after eight years of triumphs in law enforcement with the last one brought about even greater upheaval and defections. The Department was still reeling from its losses. The new commissioner brought in retired CIA terrorist experts to reinvent security in New York. And comers in the middle ranks, like Mike and April, were moving up to fill the gaps.

Mike had done well on his captain's test—the last test for promotion he'd ever have to endure. Henceforth all promotions would be discretionary. For him job openings were coming up. Any day he would receive the promotion and change of command that would put him back in uniform as commanding officer of a precinct, or head of a special unit, and bring him up the next step in the ladder of his career. He was not thinking of the old days. He was thinking of the new ones to come.

"Chief, we've got a problem." Sergeant Becker's face was white. He didn't shout across the room. He'd come inside the restaurant, passed the people sitting and standing at the bar, and now spoke softly into the chief's ear.

Avise tilted his head slightly to listen. His face didn't change. Only the tone of his voice. "Jesus," he muttered.

Mike waited silently for his cue. Avise gave it to him. "Shit. Bernie's dead," he said softly.

"Heart attack?" he asked Becker. It wouldn't be the first time a warhorse died the minute the pressure was off. But the COD didn't matter. Avise was moving his heavy body before the answer was out, and Mike was right behind him.

Mike might have been finished for the night, full of food and thoughts of love with his *novia* later on, and far from thinking of disaster. But a cop was never really off duty. Tragedy always got sluggish blood going. He and Chief Avise joined the brass in suits hurrying down the block to the place where a clot of partygoers had instantly formed around the fallen man. Circling them, uniforms were already organizing

with the efficiency that made it plain that Lieutenant
Alfredo Bernardino was no more.

This was the moment when lightness usually broke
the tension among cops. Corpses of former human
beings always elicited inappropriate remarks because
no one ever wanted to give in to emotion and weep.
Tonight, however, no jokes were forthcoming. Aware
of the chief's arrival, the recent revelers parted silently
for Avise. One quick glance at Bernardino's body told
him the one thing he didn't want to know.

"Aw, shit. What the hell happened here?" he muttered angrily.

Fog blunted everything but his voice. He was already barking out orders to people who didn't know
any more than he did.

"What do we got here? You got any witnesses?
Close this street now. Get every name. Everybody!"
Avise shook himself and backed away, rattling off the
to-do list as Mike took his place near the body.

"It's a homicide. Mike, you're it," he said, pointing
his finger.

"Sorry, sir." Somebody shoved Mike from behind,
inadvertently offering him an even better view of Bernardino's staring eyes and twisted neck.

Oh, no. Mike took the punch and groaned without
sound. Violent ends always told the most pathetic stories. Bernardino's eyes in his startled face made him
look as if he'd been caught in some embarrassing faux
pas. A bad finish for a tough and loyal soldier. *Poor
Bernardino. Poor guy.*

"Mike, you're it." Avise's words hit like a hammer
in his head. Mike's promotion to captain was immi-
nent. His days of test taking were over. No more
hands-on homicide. No more knocking on doors to
find out what made victims magnets and who were
the killers.

But now he was tagged and It again. He had to find

out who wanted Bernardino dead only days after his tenure in the Department was over. *Jesus.* Why Bernardino? Why now? What had been his last case? What had he been into? Who might be out on the streets that he'd put in the slammer five years ago? Ten? What was the story? *Shit.* Already the questions were roiling around in Mike's head. The last thing he needed.

A quartet of sirens were howling now. Blue-and-whites coming, an ambulance. He snapped to, thinking he had to find April and get organized. As he stepped aside, the toe of his cowboy boot caught the hard edge of the plaque that applauded Bernardino's thirty-eight years of service. His first thought was that April had been first on the scene and must have sounded the alarm. Bad luck for her. Bernie had been her old boss, her rabbi before she'd moved out of Chinatown. He wanted to push the weather away so he could see her, go to her side. He began searching the crowd for the familiar figure in the pretty dress.

"Anybody seen Sergeant Woo?"

Poppy Bellaqua touched his arm. "What happened?" she breathed into his ear.

"Some bastard broke Benardino's neck," he said tersely.

"Jesus!"

"Where's April?" His voice sharpened as he scanned the crowd and didn't see her. His second thought was that she might have been on the scene when it went down.

"She followed Bernie out," Bellaqua told him. "She must be here."

Mike knew she wasn't there and was rattled. He couldn't hear her voice, couldn't see her through the smoke, couldn't smell her or feel her presence. He felt the panic rising. He was a cop, but it didn't mean he didn't get scared. At the best of times he didn't like having April out of his sight. Times like this he was no better than her crazy mother, who wished she'd do practically anything else for a living.

"Mike, you okay?"

"April may have seen Bernie's killer." It hurt to spit the words out, but he had to move. April had gotten too close to a fresh kill. Way too close. She might have tried to prevent it. In any case it wasn't like her to leave a scene. Anxiety crawled all over him as screams broke out in Washington Square. He and Poppy locked eyes, then started running.

Four

"You did a good job. Don't move. An ambulance is on the way."

Jack Devereaux heard the command and obeyed. Frankly, he couldn't have gotten up if he tried. His whole right side was a fireworks of pain. He couldn't feel his feet and couldn't lift his right arm at all. Not even the hand. He knew without even seeing that particular hand that he'd need a cast. This was a disaster for a person who lived his life by computer. But that was the least of tonight's disaster. His body was on hold, but his brain kept going without it, bumping along over relevant and irrelevant subjects like a jeep on a dirt road.

"Is she all right?" he croaked out. He was pinned to the ground and no one would give him an answer.

People were screaming. Sirens were going. And there might be a dead person a few feet away from him. He couldn't tell when he'd tried CPR on her whether it had worked or not. He'd been pulled away too fast, and now no one would tell him if the girl was dead. If she was dead, he'd never forgive himself for not moving fast enough, for not making enough noise. Sheba seemed to think she'd done something wrong. She was on her belly, trying to crawl closer to him. Whining deep in her throat. *Sorry, sorry, sorry, boss. Please forgive me.*

"It's okay, baby." He tried to reassure her that she

was a hero, she'd done right, but the words came out more like a moan.

Pain cut through his body, and anxiety cut even deeper. He'd failed again in the saving department. Then his thoughts switched over to smells. He couldn't help being aware of odors. When he was happy, when he was sad, when he was making love to Lisa they could distract him. During disasters especially, his emotions could easily be derailed by his olfactory sense. When his mother was dying of liver cancer three years ago, he'd rushed to the hospital hoping to make it in time. When he got there and saw that she was gone, he couldn't feel the terrible loss because the sheet covering her body had the incongruous odor of wet rubber. So wrong for her, who'd always smelled of the delicate tea rose. After a lifetime of wearing it, she had had the perfume lodged so deep in her pores it seemed part of her. And yet it was the odor of wet rubber that stuck with him. He was like a dog that way.

Now, lying on the damp cement and fearing another death, Jack was aware only of the agony of broken bones, and the smell of strong garlic and stale cigarette smoke. The mountain of a man who was holding him down had breath that could kill. But the sidewalk under his body also had a smell. So had the girl he'd tried to save; so did the bark and new leaves of the venerable Washington Square trees. Right at that moment Jack Devereaux could have named all the smells of flat-on-the-ground Washington Square. A faint odor of urine, too, from the dogs. What else? Something about the guy struck a chord. He couldn't pin it down. Then his thoughts spun back to the woman surrounded by cops on the ground near him. Dear God, he didn't want to have hesitated and been too late.

"Please . . . is she okay?" His voice was like ashes in his throat. Everything in his life had changed two weeks ago, but he still sounded pathetic, like someone who had no control over his life.

"Whose dog is this?" The question did not come from the mountain with the horrific breath. A new person had arrived. This one smelled of leather and bay rum aftershave.

"Mine." Jack tried to reach out with his other hand, his left one, but Sheba was beyond his reach, too. The chocolate lab also had a strong smell. It was always comforting to him. Now, restrained by a stranger holding her leash, she whined from the bottom of her soul. *Boss, boss, boss. Get over here.*

"How are you doing?" The new person squatted by his side. Jack saw his mustache and thought cop, not doctor. "I don't know," he said honestly.

"Looks like your arm is broken. I'm Lieutenant Sanchez. We're going to move you in a minute. Can you give me your name and address? Someone to call?"

"Is she all right?" Jack asked about the woman.

"Yeah." The word came out curt. "She's all right. Your name?"

"Jack Devereaux."

There was silence for a moment. It was always like that these days. As soon as people heard Jack's name, it hit the famous-name register. *Yeah, know that one. A celeb.* New York was full of them. But Jack was a recent celeb. He wasn't used to it.

"*The* Jack Devereaux?" the lieutenant said after a beat.

"Which would that be?" Jack might be paralyzed for life, but he couldn't resist playing out the famous-name game.

"Creighton Blackstone's son?" Already amazement was sounding in the officer's voice.

Jack and the rest of the world were pretty much with him on that one. Shock had echoed around the

globe. It was difficult to believe that one of the found-
ing fathers of the Internet, a man with a large empire,
whose life had been written about and dissected a
hundred times, had actually died leaving an heir no
one knew he had. Including and especially the heir
himself. Jack Devereaux, a perfectly ordinary young
man, nobody of note, was suddenly immensely wealthy.
Or soon to be wealthy. Who'd have thunk?

"Yes, sir, I am," Jack admitted. Until two weeks
ago he'd been a young entrepreneur struggling to
build his own Internet company. And his mother, bitter to the end because her husband had left her long
before making his fortune and having to share it with
her, had never told him.

Lieutenant Sanchez's response to the news was a
low whistle. "Well, you've got another feather now.
You just saved a cop's life," he said.

"That woman was a cop?" Jack was shocked. "She
wasn't in uniform."

"She's a sergeant. Did you get a look at the attacker?"

Jack searched his mind, and the moment of chaos
flashed back. He'd been walking in the fog with Sheba.
He'd heard indistinct noises, like shuffling, scuffling.
It had sounded like dancing on leaves until Sheba stiff-
ened and began to whine and pull on the leash.

Despite his unwillingness to go in that direction,
she'd dragged him closer. At first the blurred silhou-
ette of two bodies moving apart, then together gave
him the impression of a modern dance of some kind.
But he heard grunts, and finally realized that what
looked like an embrace was in fact a judo hold. Sheba
was lunging on the leash and he dashed forward without thinking of anything more than to stop what he
and the dog knew was a mugging.

He called out, reached out. The man dropped the
girl and spun around behind his body so fast that Jack

could not see his face or even get an impression of how tall he was. He turned blindly with no plan at all, just turned to where the danger was. As he turned, the man grabbed his arm and used his own weight to flip him. He didn't know if it was the hold or the fall that broke his arm. All he knew was that Sheba lunged at his attacker with her powerful teeth bared, and the man took off. It all happened in seconds.

"No. I didn't see him," he said finally.

Two medics interrupted the questions. Lieutenant Sanchez stepped back to let them do their work. Jack wanted to hang onto him, but a woman with a crew cut took his place, crouching down to talk to him. Another paramedic with the same hairstyle followed her, wheeling the gurney. *Oh, no.* He wanted to go home and hide out with his girlfriend, Lisa. Whatever happened, he couldn't take any more reporters.

"Could we keep this out of the news? Please!" he called after the lieutenant with all the strength he could rally.

"Press is here already, but I'll do what I can," he promised. "First we're getting you to the hospital. Later we'll talk. We'll be sending a few uniforms with you. You won't be alone."

Jack didn't have time to figure out what that meant. What did it matter if he was alone or not in the hospital? He gave the officer their home number, then turned his attention to the medic who was sticking a needle in his arm.

Five

April's eyes were closed. When she'd gone down like a wet noodle, the back of her head smacked the sidewalk hard. Two explosions went off at once. Her skull, like a baseball connecting with a bat. Her lungs, already screaming for air, further deflated on impact. April was no character out of a cartoon flattened by a steamroller who bounces right back. Uh-uh. All her training went for nothing that night. She didn't fight right. She didn't fall right. And when she fell, an evil dragon snatched the breath right out of her and flew away with it.

Seconds passed. She wanted to say, "I'm okay," get up, find her shoes, and get out of there. But her chest didn't rise. Her lungs didn't fill. There was commotion all around. She also had the sensation of a large animal, some beast from Chinese mythology, circling her body, breathing on her hotly. Marking her. She would have avoided that beast at any cost. But the grip of death held her as strongly as if her attacker still had her by the neck. She could not catch that breath the dragon had stolen.

The weight of defeat crushed her, and she could feel herself letting go. The next thing she knew was the screaming agony of air forced into her lungs. And Mike was talking her back into the world.

"Come on, *querida*. You're okay. You're okay." He said it over and over. "You're okay. You're okay."

Irritation filled her. What the hell did he know about that? She was not okay.

"You're okay," he said again.

A memory filtered through the black. April had heard those words her first year on the job when she'd been in uniform on foot patrol in Brooklyn. She'd just come on duty when there was a radio call of a shooting nearby. There, at the improbable hour of eight A.M., a young mother and her child on their way to nursery school had walked into a *dispute* between two males—what cops called a fight. April and her partner had been the first uniforms on the scene. They'd found the woman sitting on the sidewalk cradling her dead child in her arms, crooning, "You're okay. You're okay."

"You're okay," Mike told her in the same voice, then *"Mirame."* Look at me. As if he needed proof.

She didn't want to look at him. She wanted to float away on the cloud that had come for her. But her mother, the Skinny Dragon, reminded her that the heavens were the territory of angry ghosts and dragons. If she died right now, she would not be so lucky as to fly away with the harps and angels.

Did you get him? She formed the words, but no sound came out. The dragon that stole her breath had kept her voice.

Mike whispered in her ear. "The ambulance is here. We're moving you. You did good, *querida;* he didn't break your neck. You're going to be fine."

That line they always used finally opened April's eyes, and she came back to the horror of being a vic, lying on the ground. Somebody's jacket under her head. Probably Mike's. Poppy Bellaqua was holding her hand. She may not have a broken neck like her boss, but she knew she hadn't done good, not at all. Chief Avise was standing above them, arms crossed over his chest, shaking his head at her. She'd messed up.

Six

"Aieeyyee." Sai Yuan Woo hit the ceiling when Mike came to tell her that her only child was in the hospital again. The shriek said it all. *Last time shot in head. What now?*

The skinny dragon that was April's mother could wake the dead with that scream. She wouldn't stop long enough to listen when Mike tried to explain what happened or why he'd come at the early hour of five A.M. He'd come at that time for multiple reasons. He'd wanted April to benefit from a few hours of sleep before the assault of her parents. But he had to come before anyone in the sizable Chinese extended family claimed by the Woos was up watching TV. They didn't have any actual blood relatives left, but the large circle of friends and acquaintances from the villages of another world called each other sisters and uncles and cousins and thought of themselves as such. This prodigious fake family watched the local news twenty-four/seven, always on the lookout for trouble.

Skinny Dragon Mother would never have forgiven Mike if she'd heard that April was in the hospital from someone who'd seen the story on the morning news. It was his job to tell her before anyone else. He'd let them sleep as long as possible, but he himself had pretty much worked all night.

Mike had a reason for staying up all night. Alfredo Bernardino had been overweight and in poor condition. The attack on him was bad enough. But a second nearly fatal attack only a few minutes later on a black-belt champion in the middle of Washington Square added a few lethal details to the story. The killer was not just lucky. He was highly skilled and fearless. The man was a trained killer who could break a man's neck in the blink of an eye. Damn right he'd been up all night talking to Bernardino's children and getting organized.

Now he wasn't in the mood to listen to Skinny Dragon Mother yell bloody murder at him in Chinese. Never mind that he was telling her April was fine. Skinny screamed so loud she woke her husband, Ja Fa Woo, a chef in a fancy Manhattan restaurant who'd just gone to sleep a few hours ago.

Muttering in Chinese, he stumbled out of the bed-room wearing shorts and a T-shirt with the logo of Midtown North on it, April's precinct.

Skinny, who was dressed in black pants and a thin padded jacket, spun around to her husband and screamed at him for a while. He screamed back. At least he could understand her. Mike didn't interrupt what sounded to him like a dogfight. Finally Ja Fa Woo acknowledged him.

" 'Lo, Mike. What happen?" he asked.

In the early days of their courting, whenever Mike came by to see April, her father used to lean over and spit on the ground. But now he bobbed his head in respect. Mike was an important man. Almost son, so he gave him an almost bow in the middle of his wife's tirade.

Mike bowed back and went through the story again, because Skinny always got her facts mixed up.

"Somebody dead?" Ja Fa asked.

"Yes, somebody is dead. But not April." Some other cop. Her old boss. Mike left that out. "April is fine. Just a little shaken up."

"Then why in hospital?" Ja Fa demanded.

"Aieeeyee!" At the word *hospital* Skinny's wail went up again.

"Something wrong?" Gao Wan, the Woo's upstairs tenant, padded into the kitchen. He, too, was wearing a T-shirt and shorts.

Mike repeated his sanitized version of the story. The three of them conferred in Chinese while Mike stood there trying to reassure them. As expected, his worst fears were realized when they insisted that he drive them to St. Vincent's immediately because they had no other way of getting to the hospital fast enough to suit them, then drive them back to Queens when they were ready to come home.

Mike nodded. "I'll get you there and back," he promised. Of course he would. And April would kill him for bringing them. With the Woos he couldn't win. Either the parents would be furious because he didn't do enough, or April would be furious because he did too much. Today, because he'd almost lost her, he would err on the doing too much.

Mother, father, and tenant ended their discussion and disappeared to get dressed and collect important items for April. Immediate action for them took a long time. The minutes spun out into a very long wait. It was an hour and a half before they squeezed into his wheezing Camaro for the trip into Manhattan.

Seven

By two A.M. Thursday, April had been examined, X-rayed, and admitted for the night. But once she'd returned to life she was too wide-awake to calm down. She'd dozed and thought about Bernardino, how he'd promoted her. She'd thought about the search for the poor little girl who'd been held for ransom by a neighbor, then murdered. Her first kidnaping and homicide. April had been the one to see the little sneakered foot peeking out of a half-zipped sleeping bag in a pile of garbage behind a Chinatown building, years ago. Now Bernardino was gone, efficiently executed by what appeared to be a professional. But why Bernie?

April had been in a lot of fights over the years, but only practice fights. Competition. Nobody had ever tried to kill her. Last night a man had tried to kill her. Now she knew what it felt like, and it didn't feel good. She wouldn't forget that iron forearm pressing into her neck. Her defensive moves kept playing in her head. Pathetic. She'd resisted, but not well enough. A little more pressure and he would have crushed her voice box—and maybe ended her life as well. He could have snapped her neck like a twig, as he'd done to Bernardino, but he hadn't. She was lucky. But she didn't feel lucky; she felt shamed.

All through the night her privacy curtain was pulled all the way around her bed, and the faint glow of the night-light beamed ten thousand questions at her. People didn't usually kill cops on purpose. Sometimes they got in the way when something bad was happening, like a cop walking into a particularly violent domestic dispute and getting knifed while trying to break up a fight. Or someone responding to a radio call for a DUI and ending up shot in the face when he approached the driver's side of the car. Nothing personal. Accidents.

Cops didn't get assassinated after their retirement parties. This was personal. April knew Bernardino. She'd worked with him and known his cases, but that was years ago. She had no idea what he'd been working on lately. She worried about it, drifted off to sleep, was awakened when a new patient was brought in at four-fifteen. She could hear the nurses whispering. It was an old woman with death-rattle breathing. April didn't want her to die right next to her. One death that night was enough. She wanted to go home.

She was up with the light and getting dressed in her torn party dress when her mother appeared suddenly, pulling open her curtain with one yank.

"Ma!" As usual, April was horrified to see her mother.

Ja Fa Woo stuck his bald head in to get a look at her, too. No such thing as privacy.

"Dad!"

Then her replacement, Gao Wan, the substitute son she'd offered Skinny to get her mother off her back about marrying Mike, pushed into her space as well. Gao was the one carrying the bulging plastic shopping bags. April knew they contained the emergency medical supplies, stuff Skinny knew the hospital wouldn't have on hand. Ghastly fake medicine to cure whatever was wrong. Usually April didn't even have to be sick to be treated by her mother. Imaginary illnesses were enough.

She eyed the bags with dismay. She had managed to get her underwear on under the hospital gown (modesty in case someone came in), but the torn silk dress was still over her arm. And she had no shoes. Gao Wan, about her age with no known girlfriend, stared at her excellent legs sticking out of the hospital gown.

"What's wrong with you?" Skinny demanded in Chinese, as if she couldn't see perfectly well that April's jaw and neck were bruised.

Ma! I'm fine.

"Aieeeyeee!" Skinny screamed because no sound came out of her precious daughter's mouth.

Ma, be quiet. People are sleeping. April's mouth moved, to no avail. Her voice was still gone. She put her finger to her lips. "Shh."

Skinny Dragon didn't care how many sick people were trying to get some rest. She grabbed her daughter by the shoulder and gave her a little shake.

Ja Fa Woo told his wife to be quiet. Couldn't she see that April was on her feet? Almost fine.

Help!

Mike stepped in to regain control. "*Querida,* where do you think you're going?" he demanded.

To work. Did you bring me clothes? Still trying to get some sound out.

"What?"

"What's wrong with her?" Skinny screamed at Mike in Chinese, unaware that he could not understand her when she lapsed out of English.

"Don't you know you can't come in here at this hour?" A nurse in a pink uniform came to shoo them out. "Visiting hours start at eleven."

Mike flashed his badge.

"I don't care who you are."

"I'm getting out of here." April pulled on the nurse's sleeve to get her attention.

"What do you need, dear?" The nurse turned to her.

Skinny grabbed a shopping bag from Gao and pulled out some clothes. While the nurse's head was turned, she gestured April toward the bathroom. *Go get dressed. We're going home.*

Eight

Only a few hours later Officer Greg Spence gave April his usual line with an encouraging smile. "You don't need to think about this today, but it would help if you could get your impressions out while they're fresh."

Greg was thirty-five, tall and attractive, with a more boyish look than Mike, who was only two years older than him and sitting on the other side of the table. April studied the two cops. Greg had married a few years ago, and his wife, Judy, was pregnant. April knew he'd make a good father. He was patient with witnesses. Patient with uncertainty. She was sorry she couldn't help him out now.

"Okay?" he said, fiddling with his equipment. "You look a little shaky."

Shaky? No, she wasn't shaky. She was angry. The last thing she wanted to do right then was go over the details of her failure. She took a painful breath and tried to calm down. She was a captive of the system just like every other victim of a crime. Like it or not, she had to go through the process.

Actually, she had only herself to blame that she was there with the police artist instead of home in bed. She'd walked right into it. After escaping from Skinny and her father, she and Mike had gone back to the apartment they shared in Forest Hills. He expected her to sack out for the day, and she could have done that. Instead, she'd followed her plan. She'd swallowed three cups of strong green tea and a handful of analgesics. She'd bathed in a hot bubble bath for half an hour and then had to lie down to nap off a heavy case of dizziness from the hot water. She almost lost her day right then.

Mike was just about to leave her and to go to work when she sensed his departure and popped right up again. Well, she didn't exactly pop. She dragged herself out of bed and rummaged around looking for something easy to wear. Mike heard the noise and came into the bedroom to investigate.

"What do you think you're doing?" he demanded, catching her getting dressed for the second time that day.

She couldn't get out an answer and tried some sign language. *Got to go to work.*

"What?"

I'm going to work!

Mike shook his head. He could hardly argue with a mute, so he fried up a bunch of eggs and resteamed some of the dim sum left over from the weekend. He was so hungry himself after the long night that he didn't notice the problem she had getting solid food down. Every painful swallow reminded her that she was lucky to be alive and that Bernardino, who'd loved to eat, had had a different fate. Her resolve to get on with it deepened. She knew what she had to do. She had to go to his autopsy even though she dreaded being close to dead bodies. The ghost factor.

Chinese believed that violent deaths led to angry ghosts. And angry ghosts were like invisible devils that caused every misery known to man. Keeping far away from the dead was no insurance against ghost revenge, but it made people feel safer. April, too. Despite the possibility of attracting Bernardino's negative afterlife attention, she needed to be there with him. Maybe it was loyalty. Maybe it was the ghost factor itself that encouraged her to stay with him. If there was the slightest chance that his unsettled spirit was still lingering around him, she wanted that spirit to be assured that she would not abandon him. She would find and punish his killer. She would return his care of her during his lifetime by helping to free his spirit for a happy afterlife with the wife who'd preceded him. She wanted to attend his autopsy.

Her determination to be with Bernardino drove her past Mike's objections and back into the city to follow her own path, but other people had a different agenda for her. Mike took her to headquarters downtown.

First she was questioned by Chief Avise himself, then Poppy Bellaqua. They wanted to know if she had spoken with the man, if he had said anything. She couldn't remember. They'd asked if she'd seen him. She couldn't remember that either. Now the artist who sketched the faces on the wanted posters that the police distributed to the newspapers and TV had the assignment of getting a description from her. And they all used the same words. They were all talking to her the way they talked to civilian victims: as if she'd gone deaf and stupid as well as mute.

She was ensconced in Mike's airless, windowless office in the Homicide Task Force on the second floor of the Thirteenth Precinct on Twenty-second Street, close to the Police Academy, where she'd been trained to remember a lot better than this.

"You up for it?" Greg asked again gently.

April had worked with him many times before, helping witnesses remember details buried deep in their subconscious. It was an iffy business. Nothing these days was proving to be more unreliable than eyewitness testimony. A lot of people over the years had been falsely accused and falsely convicted of crimes they hadn't committed on the basis of what people said they had seen, sometimes just to help the police close the case. That would not happen here. She had not seen the man's face. She hardly saw his shape. She did not remember talking or fighting with him, only the grip around her neck.

"You up for it?" He repeated the question a third time.

She swallowed some cold tea from the bottom of her cup, testing her throat. Then she wrote on the pad in front of her what she had written before. *I didn't see his face.* Then, *Tea?* Stalling.

Mike got up and disappeared out the door to ask someone to get it.

The features Greg used—noses, mouths, eye and eyebrow shapes, foreheads, jawlines, head and hand and limbs and body shapes—could be manipulated in a computer program, but he also could do it manually, creating faces and forms from laminated flip cards that he sketched into his own more lifelike portrait. Naturally, he ignored her denial. "We'll start on the shape of his head and his body type then, okay?"

April closed her eyes, trying to conjure an impression of size from a blocked memory. Why were they bothering with this? They knew she'd gotten hit on the head in her fall. For how many seconds she'd lost consciousness she didn't know. What she did know was that lost consciousness also often meant a loss of memory of precipitating events as well. Sometimes it was a merciful thing that those minutes of actual violence disappeared forever, but it was not good for law enforcement.

What April remembered was her annoyance at Bernardino for leaving without saying good-bye, the wet blanket of fog on the street when she left the restaurant to follow him. She remembered hearing the sound of the metal leash. A man had been walking his dog, some kind of big dog. She didn't remember now what kind. The two had passed her. Now that she thought about it, it seemed odd. How could they have missed Bernardino when she had almost tripped over his body?

As she waited for her tea, she puzzled over this. Somehow she had gotten into Washington Square. She'd been barefoot. She didn't remember either of those things. When she first regained consciousness, Mike had been holding her head, talking to her. She remembered that. She'd assumed that Mike was the one who'd had saved her. But later in the hospital Mike told her a man with a chocolate lab had intervened. If it was the same man and dog, how could they have avoided Bernardino's body?

Dogs were very sensitive to human states: injury, sickness, fear, anger, death. Even if the man hadn't seen Bernardino, the dog would have known. Something was wrong about the story. She had to talk to that guy. That hero who'd saved her. She made a mental note and checked her watch. How long would it take for them to catch on to the fact that she was not going to be any help in identifying the killer? One hour, two? Seventy-two?

Mike came back with a fresh cup of tea. April sipped at hot water that was just beginning to streak with the brown of a tea bag. She read *Lipton* on the tag at the end of the string. Stalling. She had no impression of any body shape. No head shape. No features. And now she didn't even remember how the man had gotten his hands on her. The whole thing was a blank. She wasn't being difficult. She really didn't remember.

She drew breath and coughed experimentally, aware of how investigators felt about this kind of thing. For once the shoe was on the other foot. Usually she was the one trying to help a witness remember. She was the one who felt frustrated because so often they seemed to be holding something back. She drank some tea to warm her throat. It didn't help.

"What about his size, the shape of his body, April?" Greg fiddled with his shapes as if April didn't know the difference between a wiry build, a medium build, and a heavy build.

"There you are!" Bill Bernardino opened the door and pushed into the small space. His suit was a rumpled mess and his face was flushed an angry red. He looked as if he'd been crying. "What the hell happened?" he demanded as if he hadn't spoken to Mike several times last night.

"Bill!" Mike jumped out of his desk chair, offering his hands for condolence.

Bill put his own hands up to reject the gesture. "He was fine when I left. Jesus!" he spit out angrily, as if it were their fault his father was gone, as if it were brand-new news to him.

April's eyes welled up. "Oh, Bill." The words didn't come out loud enough to qualify as a whisper.

He glared at her. A few days before the party April had called him personally. Prosecutors were very busy, and she knew from past experience that Bill would need a reminder to make it to his father's party. She also wanted to be sure that his wife, Becky, knew she had an invitation and that Bernardino wanted her there. Becky hadn't come, and Bill had kept his appearance short. From long habit, April kept her face stripped of her feelings. But her heart hammered out her anger so loudly she was afraid he could hear it across the room. Skinny Dragon Mother would be very vocal indeed about a son like Bill.

What kind of son doesn't stay to the end of his father's retirement party? What kind of son doesn't take his old widowed father home when the party is over?

A busy son? A careless son? No, a bad son. Skinny would say Bill Bernardino was a no-good son.

"I'm sorry for your loss." Now Greg Spence was on

his feet. "I'll catch you guys later," he murmured to Mike and April. Then he was gone, right out the door as fast as he could get away.

A real prosecutor, Bill raised his hand a few inches to acknowledge his triumph in getting the floor. Then he went right to the point. "What the hell was going on there, April?" he demanded, singling her out as the focus of his rage even though they'd met only a few times over the years. And he'd heard what happened already!

She blinked back the tears in her eyes, put off by the way he was behaving. No respect. Her tears dried out of her eyes as quickly as they had flooded them. She understood that he was upset. They were all upset. But this was no way to talk to his father's old friend.

"For Christ's sake. The least you can do is talk to me, tell me what you guys were up to. Or are you going to cover this up like everything else?" he went on bitterly.

Oh, that was it. April and Mike locked eyes, and Mike intervened. "Hey, take it easy, Bill."

"Take it easy! My dad is murdered at a Department party where the top brass was skunk drunk, and you expect me to take it easy. How do I know one of them didn't do this? Huh?"

"Oh, no, no, no, no. Don't talk crazy," Mike said softly. "You know that's not right." He glanced quickly at April a second time. She knew he wanted to move to her side of the table to protect her. An almost imperceptible shake of her head told him she was fine.

"I know that she's responsible for this." Bill pointed an angry finger at her. "She was there on the scene. She let this happen! You'd better believe I'm not taking it easy. I'm not letting it go. Someone's going to pay."

"Okay, sure. Fair enough. Why don't you sit down

now? You need a cup of coffee, something to eat."
Despite her warning, Mike instinctively reached out
to April.

She was wondering how Bill knew who was on
the scene.

"Don't give me that cop shit! I don't want coffee.
My dad is dead. I want some answers." His face was
almost purple with rage. April figured he'd had
enough time to start feeling guilty and almost felt
sorry for him.

But even if she could have found her voice, she
would have remained silent throughout the tirade. Bill
was threatening them, and it was a little scary. She
knew how these things could be tilted and turned
around. Police investigations came up with all kinds
of explanations and skewed answers to cover up mistakes. It wasn't good, but it happened. Bill was a prosecutor and she could see where he was going.

There had been incidents in the past of cops par-
tying just before they went on duty, then having fatal
car crashes as they sped to work. Each time drinking
was implicated as a factor in a tragedy involving cops,
a lot of people went down. Supervisors were trans-
ferred, demoted, or lost their jobs. Now the possibility
of scandal because a bunch of high-ranking cops had
been drinking at the retirement party of a distin-
guished lieutenant who was murdered on the way
home was not beyond possibility.

Dozens of friends only a few feet away and all too
drunk to do anything to save him. Oh, it was so clear
where Bill was headed.

"Sit down, Bill. I was there and you weren't. So you
listen to me for a minute before you get yourself and
everybody else in a flap. Okay?" Mike pointed at the
chair. April could see how angry he was but knew that
Bill could not.

Bill hesitated.

"I said, 'sit down.' Let's be civilized here," he said softly. "I'm not going to bite you."

"Fine. She was there, too; why doesn't she tell me what happened?" Bill took the chair Greg had vacated and looked to April.

April was not feeling so good. But her hair covered the lump on her head, and her turtleneck hid the bruises on her shoulder and neck. Maybe he didn't know what had happened to her.

"She can't," Mike said, real steel coming through in his voice for the first time. "She went after the guy. The bastard almost killed her. The man who killed your father is some kind of martial-arts expert."

Bill's mouth opened. "A what?" He stared at April, stunned. This bit of news hit a nerve.

Stony-eyed, she stared right back. She remembered that Bill happened to be a judo expert himself. Then her eyes went furry on her, and she took a little nap.

Nine

Birdie Bassett got in from her meeting with her husband's estate lawyers before noon and went straight to the phone in the library.

"You have ten new messages," the flat-toned female on voice mail reported.

Birdie sighed. It had been three weeks since Max's sudden death, and the phone was still ringing off the hook. Ten calls already, and she'd been gone only a few hours. She was still in shock, dizzy from hunger, but not yet up to eating. People told her she was depressed, that there was a book she could read about the stages of grieving. But she didn't think there was anything in the book about being a really prominent widow whose husband had taken care of everything.

She took a few deep breaths to calm herself after the unpleasantness in Silas Burns's office. Max's lawyer of thirty years had informed her this morning that Max's two kids were going to contest the will. They were going to hold her up, fight her for a bigger piece of the pie. And that did depress her.

"You have three options, Birdie." He put up three arthritic fingers to emphasize them. "You can fight, you can make a deal, or you can try to wait them out. You're young, and you have your allowance." He lifted his shoulders. "They could hold you up for a very long time, but so could you. Why don't you take a few days to think about what you want to do and let me know."

She opened her mouth to speak, but he stopped her. "There's no hurry, dear. Take your time."

Birdie had left the office and headed uptown. Back in Max's favorite post in the paneled library of his fifteen-room Park Avenue apartment, she picked up the last photo taken of him, taken only a few months ago in Palm Beach. He'd looked strong, healthy, and a good fifteen years younger than eighty-one. He was still a handsome man with a full head of hair. "Max, what do you want me to do?" she whispered. "Fight or flight?"

Max's desk was a huge *bureau plat* of the Louis XIV period with lots of ormolu. The desk was genuine. The large leather chair behind it was of a more recent vintage. The library table and club chairs were English. The rugs were two complementary Persian garden carpets with blue borders. The curtains that framed the eight-foot French windows were made of shimmering red-and-gold silk damask and edged with two varieties of silk tassels and braid. Everything was too ornate and grandiose for her taste, but had suited Max perfectly.

Birdie still couldn't believe he was gone. She'd expected him to remain vigorous for another ten years, then fade slowly for another five. She'd fully expected them to scale down during his lifetime. Simplify. She had no interest in the three houses he'd left her or the antiques his children thought belonged to them. Max didn't give her a sign, so she began listening to her messages.

"Mrs. Bassett, this is Carla in President Warmsley's office at York U. President Warmsley asked me to call you to confirm for Monday night. Could you give me a call at nine-nine-five-six-four-eight-two. Thank you."

Birdie punched three for delete, then listened to her next message.

"Birdie, this is Steven Speel at MOMA. I'm calling to set up a lunch with you and Marilyn. She's available Thursday of next week. Would you give me a call when you have a moment? Seven-five-one-four-four-eight-nine."

Steven Speel reeled off the numbers at twice the speed of the rest of the message, and Birdie got only the first three. She had to listen to the message again and again before she got them all. She hated it when people did that.

The next two were personal requests that she take tables at forthcoming benefits to which Max had supposedly pledged his support. But how would she know if he really had? Twenty thousand for the Emerald Dinner at the Museum of Natural History sounded possible. They'd gone before. But fifteen thousand for BAM? Birdie could not recall ever seeing the Brooklyn Academy of Music on Max's foundation's donor list.

Another call was from the Psychoanalytic Institute. What the hell was that? She listened to it with Max's heavy pen suspended over his ornate message pad. The pleasant voice of a Dr. Jason Frank invited her to lunch so that he and the foundation chairman could personally thank her for Max's generous bequest last year and encourage her to consider taking his place on the board. What? Birdie hadn't even known that Max had been on such a board. She shook her head at the latest revelation.

Max had been retired, but he'd been busy every day, running his own sizable foundation with virtually no staff and no board members to keep track of his activities. The foundation had no brochure, no guidelines for grant proposals, no procedure for donors, and far fewer documents than there should have been.

While he'd sent out letters with his foundation checks, the terms for the use of his sizable grants were often vaguely stated. Worst of all, Max had left her the reins of his foundation but no mission statement, no written pledges, no clues to his intentions. He hadn't bothered to groom her for this. All Birdie had ever done for the foundation was attend the functions of organizations he supported. She'd never been asked to participate on the board of any of them. Even on the occasions when Max had been honored, or had served as honorary chairman, all she did was lend her name. And she'd always understood that she had taken the place of a first wife with whom she could never compete. Her predecessor's name had been Cornelia, pronounced *Cornelllya,* and Cornelllya had never gone anywhere without a hat and gloves even in the summer. Forty years her senior, after all. The original foundation had borne her name. The Max and Cornelllya Bassett Foundation. Now Max's name stood up there alone.

As sole trustee, Birdie could rename it the Birdie Bassett Foundation, and the thought of that made her smile for the first time all day. She'd been snubbed and overlooked so many times for so many years, it was bittersweet to think of the power she had now. But she didn't know where to start.

Birdie Bassett was thirty-seven years old. She'd married Max when she was only twenty-six and he was seventy, a crazy thing, but not unheard of. For the eleven years they were together people would talk over and around her at dinner parties, as if she were still the temp who'd filled in at his home office after his previous secretary went on vacation with a handful of his dead wife's jewelry and never came back. Birdie's stepchildren, both older than she, had loathed her from the start and never tried to hide it. Still, she would never have dreamed of begrudging them their wretched houses and wretched furniture.

The Bassetts lived on Park Avenue, in Palm Beach, and Dark Harbor, off the coast of Maine. Max's bequeathing her the Bassett family enclave in Dark Harbor was a truly appalling move. In Florida all types mingled with relative ease. Even among the social set whose roots in Palm Beach predated air-conditioning, May–December relationships between the socially unequal were common. Lovely blond women of any origin, the young second wives of ancient gentlemen, were part of the scenery, a social set of their own. But Dark Harbor was another story. The houses were handed down from generation to generation, and new people just weren't welcome. Next message.

"Hi, Birdie, it's Al Frayme. Just calling to reschedule our lunch. By the way, the funeral was beautiful, and I thought you were very dignified in a difficult situation. Do you have time for lunch this week? I'll take you anywhere you want to go. Sweets. Paris. Tahiti. You name it."

Birdie smiled again. Sweets was downtown in the Fulton Fish Market, close to the Wall Street lawyer's office where she'd been earlier. The phone rang, distracting her from the rest of her messages.

"Hello, this is Birdie."

"You're next," a soft voice said.

"What? Hello? Hello?" A dial tone buzzed on the other end.

Jesus. Birdie felt so ill. She couldn't eat a thing. Nothing appealed and nothing stayed down. She was almost paranoid enough to believe she was being poisoned. Max's kids hated her; that much was clear. And people with money were always at risk. She glanced around the elegant room, wondering which things could hurt her. She knew that people could be poisoned by their clothes, by their toothpaste, by the air they breathed. Again she had that nagging worry. Max had not been sick. He'd died without warning. Everybody, including his doctors, had thought he was just old. But she wondered. The voice on the phone unnerved her. She wasn't sure anymore. She just wasn't sure.

Ten

As far as catastrophes for April went, second only to not witnessing what went down between Bernardino and his killer and not being able to save him was not being able to ask any questions about it. She'd recovered quickly enough from her exhaustion to tackle Bill Bernardino with a pad and pen. He wasn't answering her questions any better than she'd answered his.

Bill, what had your father been working on these last weeks? she wrote and passed over for him to read. As with the earlier questions she'd posed to him, this one sat heavily on the page, giving Bill ample opportunity to twist his mouth into any number of disgusted shapes while he pretended to decipher her perfectly legible handwriting.

There was no nuance to the written word, no tone of voice to temper her line of questioning. The questions looked like something out of a survey, not a personal exchange between two people who'd lost a loved one. With April's side written down, the interview was between Bill and the page, not between her and him. So he was having an easy time avoiding her.

His eyes looked down, away from her, when he tossed back, "How would I know what he was working on?"

He might have said something. You two talked,

didn't you? There was a time lag while she wrote this. There was another time lag while he read the reply.

Worse than using sign language, this was like instant messaging with both people in the room. And one of them was determined not to help. April knew that Bill's mind was still on the blame track, but she wasn't going to stop trying to engage him in a dialogue.

Her expression was neutral as she strung her questions out like beads on a necklace she would never get to wear. Several times she exchanged glances with Mike. April could read in his face that, like her, he was annoyed and hiding it well. Whether or not Bill had meant his threat of a scandal, it was on the table, putting the cops and prosecutor on different teams. It was clear that neither Mike nor Bill was going to share information, so she had to do the talking, because she was the one who'd been close to Bernardino. Too bad. Now the investigation might have to go needlessly deep into the grieving family's private affairs. Unless they found the killer soon, Bill was going to get less happy as the days went on. He certainly wasn't making it easy on himself now by dismissing her queries.

"Yeah, we talked, but not about business. Look, I have to go." He tapped his watch and got to his feet, looking at them angrily as if one or both of them might try to keep him there. But neither Mike nor April made a move to delay him. He had come to them, after all. He could go when he pleased.

"Look, we're going to have to go through his things at the house," Mike said as he opened the door.

"Fine. The place is a fucking mess, though. He was getting ready to move." Bill paused long enough to shake his head. Then he made a point of checking his watch again. "Kathy will be here in a few hours."

"I'm really sorry," Mike murmured.

Anger flashed in Bill's face. "Yeah, well, something's wrong here. To get through thirty-eight years on the job and die like this." He shook his head. "It shouldn't happen."

April agreed with him. It shouldn't have happened. She gripped the pen in her hand, wanting to add something, but Bill glared at her, triggering a guilt she didn't want to feel. It wasn't her fault that his father left the party alone. It wasn't her fault that she'd followed him too late. It wasn't her fault that he was dead, and she was still alive.

She didn't want to feel it, but the guilt was there. Bernardino had been her boss, her friend. A part of her couldn't help believing that the timing of the events tonight and her position in them had some special meaning. And without her being aware of it, somehow the fault really was hers. Chinese guilt made for an extensive menu, and numbers one through a hundred were weighing her down at the moment.

Her cell phone rang almost immediately after Bill left, and she forgot that she couldn't speak. She punched talk, but only the sound of air came out of her mouth when she tried to say hello.

"What the hell happened to you?" It was her boss at Midtown North, Lieutenant Iriarte.

"Hahhhh," she answered.

"What? Where are you?"

"Pshhhh."

"For Christ's sake, speak up; I can't hear you." Iriarte's usual irritation sounded in his voice.

April rolled her eyes at Mike. *Iriarte,* she mouthed at him.

"April, I know you're there," the lieutenant said crossly. "What the hell is going on? When are you coming in?"

April passed the phone to Mike. "Hey, Arturo, it's Mike Sanchez. How ya doin'?"

"Mike. I heard about Bernardino. Terrible thing. What's with April?"

"Ah, she got into a little fight trying to apprehend the suspect."

"What! Nobody told me that. Where are you?"

"Well, she bolted from the hospital a while ago. Didn't anybody tell you she wasn't coming in?"

"She's supposed to call in. Let me talk to her, will you?" He barreled right ahead as if he hadn't heard the words *hospital, fight,* and *suspect.*

"Really sorry about that, Arturo, but I told you some asshole tried to wipe her last night and she's lost her freaking voice."

"Huh?" For a second April's boss was speechless himself, not sure whether or not Sanchez was pranking him to get April a day off. Pranking was not uncommon. Finally he said, "No kidding."

"No kidding. She's lucky he just knocked her voice out. It's a woman's nightmare, right?" Mike winked at April.

"Jeez," Iriarte said. "Anything I can do?"

Thanks, April mouthed at him. *Thanks a lot.*

The rest of April's day was just as frustrating. Bernardino's daughter, Kathy, arrived in the afternoon, but April was not able to call with her condolences, to inform her that she and Mike would be out to talk to her and to look at the house soon. Mike had to make that call, and it was a tough one. In less than two months Kathy and Bill had lost both their mother and father. Bill needed someone to blame. So heaven only knew what ideas the prosecutor would pour into the ear of his sister the FBI agent over dinner tonight. Both were trained investigators. It was almost enough to make a person paranoid. April didn't want to be paranoid, and she didn't want the Department to be blamed.

Chinese philosophy for health called for the consumption of no less than twenty cups of tea a day. For once April was following it. Hot water and Lipton's tea bags were all she had, but she downed some every twenty minutes. She was wired with all the caffeine and desperate for the return of her voice.

In her early years as a cop, April had followed orders and kept her thoughts to herself. Silence had been a choice she'd made to stay out of trouble. Now all her thoughts were trapped inside, but it wasn't like the old days, when silence was her comfort zone. She wanted to talk to Mike, but she had no voice and she could tell he was shutting her out.

And sure enough, just before two P.M. Mike glanced at the clock on his wall. "Ready to go home now, *querida*?" he asked, trying hard to sound neutral.

April shook her head. She wasn't going home. She had things to do. She wanted to see Marcus Beame, who'd been standing next to Bernardino at the bar before he left, probably the last person to speak to Bernardino. Beame had the same job in the Fifth Precinct that April had in Midtown North. He was second in command in the detective unit. He'd know what Bernardino had been working on.

"*Querida*," Mike said slowly. "I want you to go home now, rest up." He said it *suavemente, con cariño,* but there was steel behind the sweetness.

She shook her head.

"I know you want to stay on this, but you know you can't."

She shook her head some more. She didn't know why she couldn't. Anger flashed in her eyes.

"You've got to move over," he said softly.

Victims didn't investigate their own cases. It was clear that was what he meant. She wasn't being asked to the dance.

April's anger came and went quickly as she considered her options. For every rule deemed unbreakable in the Department, there was always an exception. Long history had proved that nothing was set in stone.

Homicide investigations were like construction sites. In the beginning there was the body and the physical evidence that included everything the perpetrator left behind of himself—fibers from his clothes, hair from his head, saliva from a cigarette butt or a piece of gum. A footprint, a fingerprint. A weapon. The shape of his hand on the victim's body. And everything he took away from the scene that could later prove he'd been there, had had contact with the victim. The cause of death itself could be a signature. The principal investigator on the case was the architect who had to construct the murder from the crime scene backward to precipitating events that might have been set in motion days, weeks, or even years before.

In easy cases the plan of the house could be read right in a crime scene that told the whole story almost from beginning to end. Man came home, surprised his wife/lover/girlfriend in bed with another man, shot them both, then himself. The lovers were naked. The perpetrator was clothed. Double homicide/suicide. Case solved in a matter of hours. In hard ones the physical evidence didn't lead to the perpetrator. They called the hard cases mysteries. April moved over to Mike's desk and nudged him out of his chair.

"I knew the day would come when you'd try to take my place." He laughed, but a little uneasily. April was nothing if not hard to manage.

"Look, *querida,* I got people waiting for me," he told her.

She blew air out of her mouth and started typing on his computer. *Is IA investigating?*

Mike read the words as they came up on his screen and nodded. *Of course. So?*

Are they going to talk to me? She typed some more.

"Probably." *So?*

Who's on it?

"I don't know," Mike said. "What's your thought?"

Just thinking dirty, she wrote.

"Any particular reason?" Reflexively, he lowered his voice.

Bill jumped on it, she typed.

"That doesn't mean anything." But Mike shook himself like a dog shaking off a hurt. Then combed his mustache with his fingers. "One of us?" He said it softly, doubtfully.

April took a few seconds to go through the list of people who'd been there at Baci's last night. People they'd known for years. People Bernardino had known for *decades.* Friends. But that wasn't where she was going with it. She was thinking about all the posters that had been up on every floor of the puzzle palace. Must have been hundreds of people who knew about that party and didn't go. People on the job, but also people coming in and out of the building for dozens of reasons. Civilians could read, too. Everybody who could read knew about it. Everybody who'd ever worked with Bernardino knew about it. It hadn't been private. And probably a poster had been up at the Fifth Precinct, too.

I'm not suggesting it's one of us. It was just an odd time and place to make a hit, she typed.

"Yeah." *So, they already knew that.*

Anybody talk to Beame yet? April changed tack.

"I'm sure. Why, do you want to talk to him?"

All this time he'd been standing next to her reading the screen. She swung around in his chair and looked at him. *Yeah, I want to talk to him.*

Shit. He sighed, shaking his head.

April turned back to the keyboard and typed some more. *Well, what do you think?*

He put his arms around her and breathed into her hair.

"I feel lucky, *querida.* I could have lost you." He

said this seriously. He didn't go so far as to blame her for what she did. But it was in the air. For a second she felt a deep chill.

"Look, April, even if you can't remember what he looked like, he knows you. He has an advantage. You don't know him, but he knows you. He knows Devereaux, too. Are you listening to me?"

Her face had become like stone. She was listening. He pulled over another chair so they both were facing the computer.

"Do you know who Devereaux is?"

Yeah, they'd told her who he was. April typed, *My hero turns out to be one of the richest men in America. What do you get a guy like that for a thank-you gift?*

A little joke to make Mike laugh. He didn't laugh.

What was he doing out there anyway? she tapped out.

"Walking his dog. You asked me what I think. Well, it doesn't have the look of a robbery gone bad."

April touched his hand. No, it didn't. And it didn't have the look of a stranger murder.

Mike echoed her thought. "If it's a stranger murder, what would be the motive?" He ticked off a list of possible motives. "Jealousy? Revenge? Money?" He scratched his chin. "That's about it."

Fear of discovery? April typed. *Maybe Bernardino knew something.*

"Or maybe he just did something to tick the guy off. A spur-of-the-moment thing."

April shook her head. The perpetrator hadn't run away. He'd attacked her, too. *I knew Bernardino,* she typed, then wondered.

Jealousy? Or had Bernardino just pissed someone off big-time, someone who felt this was his chance to get even. Someone he'd put in jail. Somebody he'd demoted. Somebody he'd hurt in some other way. Or was it about money? That led to the question, Who else stood to gain by his death? Anybody other than his kids?

"Sorry, *querida*. It's time for you to go home."

Mike had already arranged for a car to take her home. April had her own plan. She didn't resist.

Eleven

Bernardino's autopsy took place between two and six P.M. that day. Dr. Gloss, the medical examiner, liked to boast that he could do an autopsy in two hours if he was pressed. But in this case, he'd taken his time.

Mike got him on the phone at six forty-five.

"Sad thing," was the first thing the ME said.

"Yeah. What do you have?" Mike cut to the chase.

"Believe it or not, the guy was in pretty good shape. He had some shrapnel wounds that healed pretty good. Was he in 'Nam?"

"I don't know," Mike said. But he'd check. In cases like this, surprisingly often Vietnam was a factor.

"Three pieces of metal were still in his back, one in his left leg. Did he walk okay?" Gloss asked.

"Bernardino walked fine," Mike assured him. He wouldn't have been accepted in the Department if he couldn't run. Mike did a quick calculation. Thirty-eight years ago was what? 'Sixty-five. Early sixties, anyway. That was before the big action in 'Nam, but it would work as a time frame. Plenty of special forces in there back then. Gloss interrupted his note taking: *Check out military service.*

"And he must have snored like a horse. What a schnoz," Gloss went on. "He had a deviated septum. Let's see; it's an interesting case. His arteries were not too bad considering his weight and what he must have

eaten in his lifetime. You cops. But . . . he had the
heart of a thirty-year-old."

That didn't help. "What else?" Mike asked.

"He was missing a few teeth. He had two hernias
that he'd probably been ignoring for a long time. A
common enough thing."

"The COD?"

"He had no defense wounds. No bruises on his fists
or palms. No foreign tissue or skin under his fingernails. We didn't get lucky there. Looks like he didn't
have time to put up a fight. It must have happened
very fast. I'm thinking maybe he knew the guy. He
wasn't expecting it."

"COD?"

"Asphyxia. Not strangled. Looks like he was yoked,
probably by a forearm. He couldn't breathe, but the
spinal cord was . . ." Gloss paused to slurp up some
drink out of a straw.

"Yeah, yeah, yeah. Spare me the medical terms. I
saw him. His neck was broken." Mike inhaled and
exhaled to let out some tension.

"By you, his neck was broken," Gloss agreed. "Bernardino was a hefty guy. He weighed one ninety-
eight," Gloss went on. "It's not so easy to yoke someone his size. Forty-eight inches around. He was like a
tank, not tall but big. You're looking for someone
with arms like a gorilla. I'll have the preliminary by
tomorrow, maybe the next day."

"Thanks. We'll talk again."

"One other thing." Gloss hesitated.

"Yeah?"

"Did Bernardino chew gum?"

Mike drew a blank on that. "I have no idea. Did
you find gum on him, or in him?"

"Well, he'd eaten within the last two hours. Must
have been some party. Lasagne, ziti, eggplant, baked
clams. Cannolis. He'd pretty much stuffed himself.
And he'd probably had quite a bit to drink, too."

"I'm sure. A couple of beers, maybe some wine. Where are you going with this?" Mike asked.

"I don't have his alcohol levels yet so I don't have that piece . . ."

"But you're suggesting Bernardino was impaired at the time of his death." Mike tried to remember how intoxicated Bernardino had been. He certainly hadn't had that manic affect, talking too much or too loudly. He hadn't looked or sounded drunk. He hadn't stumbled around or anything like that. But Mike didn't know how much he could hold. Maybe April or Marcus Beame would know. They'd both worked with him.

"Maybe drunk. He'd reeked of garlic, of course," Gloss went on, unperturbed in his musings.

"I'm sure he did, but how does it play?"

"You know, we smell them first."

The corpses. Yes, Mike knew the medical examiner sniffed his customers like a dog for the presence of drugs and poison and powder in the case of gunshot wounds.

"Yes, and?"

"He smelled of spearmint."

"As in spearmint gum?"

"Yes."

"The body or his clothes?"

"Both."

Mike pulled on his mustache. *Hmmm.* "Gum wouldn't make his clothes smell," he murmured.

"Well, it would if there was an open packet in his pocket. I just didn't see one. Did you find any gum or gum wrappers at the scene or remove them from his pockets?"

"Not that I know of. But I'll check. Any other ideas about what might have caused the odor?" Mike asked.

"Well, it might be nothing. Did they have those puffy mints at the restaurant, you know, by the entrance?"

"No. Wrapped M-and-M kind of things. Chocolate mint." Mike had left with a handful.

"Well, no then. Chocolate was the one thing Bernardino hadn't eaten."

"Well, maybe he was a gum freak and had it in his pockets, his car. I'll check it out."

"Well, let me know."

"Anything else?" Mike asked. He had a feeling there might be.

"Not at the moment."

Mike hung up. The case was being handled downtown. It was time for him to join the party.

Twelve

"Jesus, April. I'm sorry about the mess." Kathy Bernardino was an attractive woman about April's age and size who didn't look her best as she confronted the chaos in the house where she'd grown up.

She was wearing jeans and a black turtleneck speckled with what appeared to be white towel lint. It was clear she'd made no effort to dress for the trip east, just grabbed her purse and come as she'd been when she heard the bad news. Her thick dark hair looked as if she'd pulled it back into a ponytail without brushing it first. Her nose and eyes were red.

April knew that Kathy had returned to New York several times during the year her mother had fought her cancer, and had been with her during the last week of her life. Now, only a few months later, she was back for another death, this one a total surprise. The chaos was unexpected, too. Kathy seemed mortified that she couldn't find a sofa or a chair to offer April that wasn't covered with the detritus of her late father's and mother's lives.

"What a fucking mess." She shook her head, the tears coming at the way her father had left the world and his house.

"He told me he was getting someone to help him. God knows, he could afford it. His sister, I don't know . . ." Her sentence trailed off.

April touched her shoulder. *Don't worry about it.*

"Fucking mess," Kathy repeated. She dragged a box filled with a hodgepodge of books and papers to the edge of the sofa and let it drop to the floor, then shoved it out of the way.

April scanned the living room that Lorna had decorated with such loving care. It truly was a mess, but not the kind of mess a burglar would leave, things tipped over and flung in all directions. Here it looked as if Bernardino had begun the process of moving but hadn't known how to go about it in an orderly fashion. The house seemed to be disgorging its contents from the inside, as if the disparate items had just tumbled from their cupboards, dressers, and closets all at once.

A whole lifetime's collection of stuff was out of the hiding places, covering every surface. Clothes, books, photos from every stage of their lives, a jumble of female house accessories in every category—statues, vases, needlepoint pillows with cute sayings on them. Kathy and Bill's artwork from years ago. Porcelain, colored glass, mugs. Decorative watering cans in graduated sizes. Linens. Artificial flower arrangements, dead and dying plants, housewares, lamps, long-ago-abandoned sports equipment. Maybe Bernardino had just begun the sorting process prior to packing and giving away. Maybe he'd just given up. It was hard to tell.

Kathy, it doesn't matter, April beamed at her. They could go outside into the backyard. The patio furniture was still covered from winter, but April could see a stone bench out there in the green lawn that needed cutting. She pointed at the bench. It was just six. The dense fog of yesterday had departed with the morning sun. At six P.M. it was still light and pretty out there, the sun dappling through the new leaves on the trees. An unseasonably warm evening.

Kathy followed her gaze. "No, I used to read there when I was little. My escape. I don't ever want to sit there again. We'll stay here." Kathy pointed to the space on the sofa she'd made, then pushed some more stuff onto the floor. The pile hit the rug with a muffled thump. "Sit here, okay?"

April nodded. Whatever. This was tough. The fact that Bernardino was gone was bad. Kathy's seeing her parents' house like this was bad. Bill lived in Brooklyn and was coming over to get Kathy in an hour or so. That was bad, too. April thought it through. The whole situation was rough.

Four hours ago she'd decided to leave Mike to his thing and obey his order to go home. She'd accepted a ride out to Queens from a uniform, but had stayed only long enough to get a neighbor who was always home with her baby to make a few calls for her.

Missy Yu had called Kathy Bernardino to tell her that Sergeant Woo was suffering from laryngitis, but wanted to offer her condolences today. At that time Kathy must not have heard Bill's suspicion. Her reply had been to come as soon as possible. So April had grabbed her laptop and zip drive, settled her bruised body into her car, and driven from Queens to Westchester.

Now she sat down on the red-and-blue flower-print sofa and looked around for a plug. Before she could locate one Kathy threw off her mantle of grief and went professional on her. She gave April the shrewd look of an FBI special agent, and April knew right away what was coming.

"I heard you got hurt. Is that why you can't talk?" Kathy asked.

From long habit, April shrouded her eyes and shrugged. *I'm okay.*

"You don't look so okay. What happened?"

April considered the question. She didn't want to be paranoid. Kathy was the daughter of a cop, after all. They'd known each other slightly and had always been friendly before Kathy became a Feeb. Right now they were supposed to be on the same side, but maybe Bill had shared his suspicions with her after all. April wondered how much trouble she could get into by sharing information. She hadn't spoken to Internal Affairs yet, but there was no question the unit was going to be all over this. April would certainly be called on the carpet and maybe have to clean it for almost getting herself killed last night. And Kathy was first and foremost an FBI special agent. It didn't really affect the situation except that NYPD liked to keep things in the family. Things were getting complicated.

April felt herself being sucked into the dangerous currents of Department politics. Could she trust Bernardino's daughter? Should she hint at the trouble Bill might be creating for himself by crying scandal? DAs could easily be investigated and disgraced. They got shunned. They got fired. She coughed to test her sore throat. A little sound came out but not much of one. The cough did produce a decision, though. April realized that she had only one story to tell and she would tell the same one to anyone who asked. She opened her laptop and typed the short version.

When she was finished, Kathy read it and sighed. "My father didn't like strangers crowding him even in bars. If anyone got close enough to take him, it would have to be someone he knew."

So Bill had talked to her. April lifted a shoulder and wrote, *Any ideas?*

Kathy covered the bottom of her nose and mouth with a hand as she thought about it. "You know, I could go way back on this. Dad was an MP in the army before he became a cop. Over in Vietnam. Before I was born. He's always been in law enforcement. He was a damn good cop, and good cops make enemies. You know that."

April guessed she did know. She had a few enemies

herself. *Did he have some special buddies from then that he kept up with?*

"Yeah, I heard stories. I never met any of them, though."

Helpful. *What about pictures? Do you have pictures?*

"Oh, yes, there are a lot of pictures. Do you suspect one of them? Someone from then?"

I don't know. Just the way he was taken down suggests a military angle. Every killing tells a story; you know that. So what could it be here, revenge from an old gripe? A new one? Any ideas? she asked again. It took a while to type it all.

"No," Kathy broke in before she was done.

What about his cases. Did he ever talk to you about anything special? April tried something else.

"Oh, sure, all the time. Dad wasn't one of those guys who kept work and home separate. A lot of them do, you know. They pack up the gun and take off for work and you never know where they are or when they're coming back. And when they do get back, they give you that look that says, 'No questions, please.' That puts up a wall no one can get through."

Kathy seemed proud of the way her father had been. "Dad liked to talk about his cases. Not the gory stuff, but the puzzles, the personalities. He liked what he did. He must have, or Bill and I wouldn't do what we do." She paused for a minute, refocusing on April's question, then shook her head.

"Enemies . . . I just don't know." Then her expression hardened. "He had that money, that lottery money. What was it, fifteen million after taxes?"

Really? April had no idea it was that much. She'd never asked.

"It was all in the newspapers. His name, his profession. Pretty much everything but his phone number. What about that angle?" Kathy asked.

Yeah, we'll look into it for sure. Kathy, did he give

you any of it? Did he promise it to you? How was he handling it?

"Oh, jeez. The truth is he wasn't much interested. Mom was the one who wanted to strike it rich and move to Florida, you know. She probably spent more on lottery tickets over the years than she did on food. It used to piss Dad off big-time." Kathy let out a short laugh at the old family conflict. Her father the cop. Her mother the gambler.

"After he got that money I'll bet a thousand people called him. Money managers, stockbrokers, bankers. Every neighbor. And the causes—oh, God! Cancer, heart fund, starving children. Police Foundation. Half of Chinatown. Maybe more than a thousand requests. There's a stack of grant requests in here somewhere. He was collecting them."

Did he have a plan?

"Yeah, get out of town. That was his plan."

A spending plan, I mean, April typed.

"Well, he was a shrewd guy. He wanted a simple life. A little room somewhere. Nothing special. We thought he'd get over it." Kathy gave April rueful smile. "And he thought it was our money because it was Mom's money. He wasn't going to give it away to strangers anytime soon."

But what about you? Didn't your mom give some of it to you before she died?

Kathy shook her head. "Too sick to care. She left it to Dad. He didn't want to deal with it. End of story."

April found this hard to believe. Bernardino won millions and was holding out on his kids? Why? And Kathy didn't seem upset about it. Wouldn't she be upset? Nobody couldn't use money. She and Mike could use it. They wanted to buy a house. Her stomach began to churn as the scope of the investigation needed began to sink in. Somebody had to trace every one of those thousand calls to Bernardino, check out who sent him e-mails, who sent him letters. What they all wanted and who got what. For indeed Bernardino must have promised or given away some of it. He must have. April thought back on all the times Bernardino had helped out his buddies one way or another when things got tough. Whatever Kathy said, Bernardino would take requests for money seriously. But she was right about one thing. Her father wasn't just a murdered cop. He was also a murdered lottery winner, a lottery winner who hadn't shared with his kids. Weird.

Are you going to keep working now? April typed. She meant at the agency, now that she stood to inherit half of that money.

"I'm going to work on *this*," Kathy said angrily.

Your dad was a friend of mine, April reminded her.

Kathy read the words on the screen. "I know. You risked your life for him."

April's chin moved from side to side. There hadn't been any heroism involved. Just reflex. *He promoted me. He was my rabbi. He brought me along when other people wouldn't. Lot of people thought I was a wimp, a girl. A lesbo Chink.*

April finished typing the last two words and flushed. There hadn't been many Chinese cops even in Chinatown a decade ago, but no one had thought very much of them. They were small of stature, insecure in the white culture, had a nerdy look. She'd never revealed her feelings about this to anyone before. Out loud she always said that people were fair, that the old guard was fair. You didn't have to be a guy, and a white guy at that, to get ahead in the Department. But when she was coming up it hadn't been true. Not at all.

"I know how much he admired you," Kathy murmured. "He might have pretended to be a chauvinist, but he wasn't really. He had his prejudices. He didn't like the agency, but he was proud when I was accepted."

April nodded. *I'd like your help. . . .* She typed in the dots, hinting without asking outright.

"I understand," Kathy said.

April typed some more. Her fingers were beginning to feel the strain. *Look, I don't want anything to disappear from here. Who knows what's here. We need the materials, all of them. His old notebooks, whatever files he has, everything in the computer, in the e-mail file. We can zip it right out. The letters and requests he got. I need to go through everything. We don't want any problems down the line.*

"I understand," Kathy repeated. April could see her considering her brother's take on it. There might be things he'd want to hide. But finally she said, "Okay, you have a good resolution record. A hundred percent. I'm glad you're working the case."

April flushed at the misconception. Not a hundred percent at all. Occasionally she didn't solve one.

Kathy sniffed and went on. "At least he wasn't a creep. He wasn't into porno or computer dating or anything like that," she said about her dad.

How do you know? April typed.

"I checked. He had no funny names for the chat rooms. His on-line buddies were all cops, retired cops. He had no girlie files. Probably the only man in America . . ." Her eyes teared up again.

Bernardino's on-line buddies were all cops. April shivered. She'd have to check them out, every single one of them. Every old army buddy. It was getting late. Bill would be arriving soon. She had a headache. The typing was getting her down.

Zip his computer now, okay? she typed. *I'll be back for the written stuff. You could identify his regular contacts. I may need photos. Who knows . . . maybe we'll get lucky.*

Kathy nodded and got up to lead the way. April followed with her laptop and the zip drive.

"He turned Bill's room into an office. You're welcome to it," Kathy said as she picked her way up stairs that were littered with piles of women's clothes and shoes, probably Lorna's. "I'm really sorry about this."

The upstairs hallway looked like an attic, but Bernardino's office was another story. All signs of Bill's adolescence were long gone except for the red-and-green-plaid curtains on the windows and a matching spread on the single sleigh bed. Everything else was perfectly neat. The large office-type desk showed that a tidy adult had worked here. The phone had a blinking message light and caller ID with eighty-three calls stored in it. April's heart thudded with excitement. His whole world was opening. The computer was a Micron with a flat screen. April punched the on button and Windows 98 came up.

Good old Bernardino. Everything on his desk was labeled and arranged just so, his notebooks, stacks of old files, the proposals Kathy had mentioned. Boxes of photos. It looked as if he'd trashed his home life, but had been carefully cataloging his work life. As if for some future reference. Amazing.

"He was a good guy, right?" Kathy said.

April sat down at the desk, cleared the screen, and typed, *The best!* Then she got to work.

Thirteen

Jack Devereaux's right arm was bent at the elbow, frozen in a cast that pretty much immobilized him right down to the fingertips. Eighteen hours after he'd been treated, assured that he'd be fine, and sent home, pain started chewing him up again. Home was a one-bedroom apartment on the parlor floor of a falling-down town house in the heart of Greenwich Village. It wasn't even the whole floor, just half of it. Twenty-five feet long by sixteen feet wide, broken up into a tiny kitchen, a tiny bathroom, and a tiny bedroom, all without windows to the outside, and a living room that faced the street. Jack, Lisa, and Sheba had been living there for a year and a half. Until two weeks ago the couple had felt very lucky indeed to have found a place in such a great neighborhood that they could just about afford.

Now, with an unimaginable fortune heading his way, Jack's concept of the bare essentials was only starting to change. What does a person dream of acquiring when suddenly he can have anything at all in the world he wants? A week ago he'd been thinking of a bigger apartment and a new printer. Now all he wanted was for the pain to stop.

He was settled uncomfortably on the sofa. The sofa had been his mother's, and was a restful tan-and-white tweed number that was long enough to sleep on. It fit snugly in the handsome bay windows with an excellent view of the street, the only windows they had. And even after years of continuous service the sofa still didn't show its age. Jack's computer and desk chair were placed outside the curve of the windows where the room widened. The computer sat on what might have been the dining room table if they ever actually dined, which they didn't.

Until last night, Jack's task had been to accept the gift of sudden enormous wealth that would come when the estate lawyers got through with whatever it was they did. Tonight, as he fought the pain in his arm and shoulders, he tried to adjust to this new twist in his life. He didn't know which made him more uncomfortable, the unexpected riches or the unexpected role of hero. He sat awkwardly on the sofa, propped up by all the pillows off the bed, watching the TV version of his valor. Every word a lie.

Nobody in the hospital had told him that two cops had been attacked, that one was dead and he'd saved the life of the other. Lisa hadn't known it either. But now, despite that cop's promise last night to keep Jack's part in the incident out of the news, the whole world knew it anyway. His picture was on the screen, the same photo they'd used before. And his personal story was back on the front page. Lisa sat beside him, watching with pride and delight.

"Jack, this is so cool. My boss is all over me to sign you," she said excitedly. "You know, he's been talking TV movie. But now it's much bigger than that. You're a phenom."

Jack didn't feel like a phenom, but he cracked a feeble smile for her.

"What can I do for you?" She sat on his left side and squeezed his good hand. "I love you so much."

"Well, just don't leave me," he said. And actually meant it, as if his new persona might actually put her off.

God, my boyfriend turns out to be rich. What a bummer. She smiled at the joke. "Why would I leave when I love the dog?" she said seriously.

Lisa was a petite, dark-haired girl with a pretty face and a knockout figure. They'd met in Washington Square two years ago when she stopped to play with Sheba, the puppy he'd gotten to keep him company and attract pretty girls. Lisa always said she'd fallen for the dog first and him much later. And it was true that he wouldn't have dared talk to her without a subject and certainly wouldn't have fallen in love with her if she hadn't been smitten by the subject, the dog in question.

In fact, Jack loved everything about Lisa but her job. Lisa worked for a top literary agent who screamed at her all the time and wouldn't let her take private phone calls or go to lunch in case an important call came in while she was out. Kingsley Bratte wasn't just a literary agent; he was a famous one, and his name suited him perfectly. Bratte had fired his last assistant just for habitually being five minutes late, so Lisa was always early and never dared to take a day off. Because Jack was in the hospital she'd taken today off, but Kingsley had kept constantly in touch. He'd called her on the cell he'd given her. He'd left messages on their home phone, too, tasks and reminders for things she had to do upon her return tomorrow. He called as if it hadn't sunk into his selfish brain that she didn't need his job anymore. And of course he called constantly, asking to speak to Jack: possible new client with a great story to tell.

"What can I do for you? There must be something," Lisa teased. "Anything, really."

Quit your job and get away from Bratte, Jack felt like saying. He didn't say it, though, but only because he wasn't up to a fight. She read his mind.

"Are you at least *thinking* about doing a book? We have a great ghost for you to work with." Lisa kissed the back of his hand. She couldn't help being loyal to Bratte. That was the kind of girl she was.

Jack shook his head. He didn't want to work with a ghost. He hated Bratte. Six months ago he'd allowed Jack to come to the agency Christmas party but hadn't condescended to speak to him once. Now the tables were turned. Bratte was all over him, trying to be his best friend. Funny how fame and fortune changed everything. If he weren't so groggy and miserable, Jack would crack up laughing.

"I made you soup. Would you like some?" Lisa changed the subject, and for a minute the sun came out.

Lisa's soup, which she called Jewish penicillin, appeared like magic with every little ailment. Have a headache, chicken soup. Have a cold, chicken soup. Feel lonely, chicken soup. They'd eaten it every day during the anthrax scare. And they hadn't gotten the disease, proof enough for Lisa that chicken soup cured everything. That and potato pancakes were the only items on her menu. But she did them both well, and since his mother hadn't cooked anything well, two dishes seemed like a lot. Tonight, however, chicken soup wouldn't cure him. He wanted peace and quiet. If he were a drinker, he'd be dead drunk by now. But he wasn't a big drinker.

"What's the matter?" she said. "Was it something I said?"

Didn't she get it yet? A blond TV announcer was mouthing the familiar words about his father's legacy to him and now the unfamiliar words of his new status as a cop saver. Jack was lost. He felt his life was being stolen from him. Even Lisa had been writing about it. Before all this happened, she'd been working on a novel about a man who didn't know who his father was. Her version of his life. Jack's mother also had her version.

Ever since he was old enough to know he was missing a father, he'd blamed only his mother, because she was the one who'd kept him from the knowledge of what had happened between them. Only she knew why his father never called him, never wrote letters, never gave him a birthday present. Many years ago Jack made up a reason for this: His father was a lifer in prison, or maybe even on death row, a man who had committed some huge and heinous crime worse even than abandoning him and his mother. His mother was only protecting him from the immense and unreconcilable shame of being sired by a criminal. It was the only answer that made any sense to him. Certainly his mother had thought of his father as a criminal.

But even with such a big secret at the core of Jack's life—a secret he had to admit he'd never tried very hard to penetrate—he thought he knew who he was. Just a simple, regular guy, raised by a single mom who'd been abandoned long ago, loved him a lot, and hadn't had much to give him in the way of material goods. Not an uncommon story. But it turned out to be not the right story. Jack's father had a plan of his own.

Creighton Blackstone's philosophy was plainly spelled out in his books. He believed that wealth corrupted, that the children of the rich were selfish and spoiled. He'd declared that he didn't want children because he didn't want to raise them with the burden of wealth and a famous name. He'd been so committed to this view that even when he did have a child, he'd covered his tracks so no one knew it. Jack's mother had died with the secret because telling it would have cost Jack his legacy. His father didn't want him to know. A social experiment, as it were. And even after she died he'd kept his silence, letting his son think he was an orphan three years before the fact. He kept the secret to the end. He'd been a hard man, giving his only child a sad lesson in cold calculation. Money had corrupted. It had corrupted *him*. Jack shivered.

"Honey, I can tell you're uncomfortable. Why don't you take a pill for the pain." Lisa felt his forehead. "You're hot. Come on, it would take the edge off," she urged.

When his segment of the news ended, he shook his head and surfed to another news program to see how far the story was traveling. Would he make national news? The phone rang, and Lisa checked the caller ID.

"Private," she told him.

"Don't answer it."

"What if it's the police again?"

"I've already told them everything."

"It might be my mom."

"If you want to answer it, answer it." He often wondered why her mother had to be a private caller.

He watched her pick up and an uneasy look cross her face.

"What is it?" he asked.

She hung up. "It was that guy again."

"What guy?"

"The one who says, 'Tell Jack not to forget his promise.'"

"Oh, jeez."

"What promise, honey?"

"I have no idea." But the unknown caller was making him uneasy, too. It was about the tenth time now. He shifted painfully so he could see out the window. The detectives this morning had told him a plainclothes cop was out there watching them. Jack wondered if it was the guy dressed in blue jeans and a sweatshirt who'd been pretending to read the newspaper for the last two hours at a front table in the espresso bar across the street. He hoped so.

Fourteen

April's cell phone rang while she was in the car on her way to her parents' house in Astoria. Glad to have an excuse to ignore it, she didn't even bother to search for it in her purse. For a second or two she did worry that maybe by now Mike had guessed she wasn't at their place in Forest Hills. But it didn't have to be him; could be a lot of people calling. Woody Baum, the detective who drove for her and served as her gofer at Midtown North, would definitely be trying to reach her to report on the day she'd missed. But there was nothing she could do about it. Being mute had its advantages.

Driving back from Hastings on Hudson, April had time to think. She took the Cross Bronx Expressway, then the Whitestone Bridge to avoid getting caught in Manhattan traffic. She didn't feel guilty about visiting Kathy Bernardino without telling Mike. There were a lot of things Mike could do to influence her, but he couldn't tie her up and keep her at home. He wasn't her boss, she told herself. She still had her own mind and wouldn't give that up for anybody.

Still, she was already justifying herself, working on ways around whatever restrictions were in store for her. Back in the day when Bernardino used to hold forth, he liked to describe the difference between Asian and Western thinking this way: An American told not to cross a line in the sand would cross it anyway. But an Asian told not to cross the line would rub it out to avoid disobeying an order. April was like that. Since she would not willfully disobey an order, she'd been forming a plan ever since Mike sent her home.

Conscientious to a fault, she almost never took sick leave, and never just took a day off for fun. Fun was a foreign concept to her, an idea that flickered from time to time like a faltering lightbulb. It couldn't beam out steadily in a world where disaster too often intruded on good times. Even fun like last night's had a way of turning to tragedy without warning. Life threw its little curves, and April was schooled in an ancient culture in which bad luck was always an expected guest.

Across the Whitestone the traffic on Northern Boulevard was heavy heading west through Queens. She had plenty of time to catalog a collection of aches and pains worthy of a week off. Her head and neck hurt. Her shoulders. Both knees had been skinned on cement and were now weeping through their bandages. She could embroider.

As the temperature dropped steadily, chilly evening air pelted her from the cracked car window. The sky was quickly darkening to the NYPD blue she loved, and she felt the rush of freedom in her wheels. She'd always liked traveling on her own. Her plan was to take some sick leave, to stay out of sight long enough to figure out if Bernardino's killer was someone close to him, someone who might know her, too. A cop. An ex-cop. Not that she believed for a second that Bernardino's killer was a cop, but cops did funny things when their heads got screwed up. Just this year two police officers in separate shooting rampages within a six-month period killed ten people in a small New Jersey town. And cops had weapons. All Bernardino's killer needed, however, was his forearm. For all

April knew he was back at work somewhere today. The last thing she wanted to do was scare him.

She figured as long as she couldn't speak, no one would bother her. She could sleep at home with her mother for a few days. With her mother she was impossible to reach. Skinny was the world's best gatekeeper when her daughter wanted to hide. April smiled to herself as she pulled up in front of the brick house that was her official residence, the place she used to call home.

As soon as the engine was off, however, Skinny Dragon Mother wiped the smile right off her face. She must have been sitting by the window turning the red envelope over and over in her hands, watching and waiting for April, because she started screaming in Chinese before April even had her key out of the ignition.

"What took so long? I wait all day." Skinny was out the front door running down the cement walk in her red-for-luck padded jacket, her red-for-heart look-like-silk blouse, her loose black pants, and soft black canvas peasant shoes. Tightly curled into a fried seaweed frizz, her thinning hair was jet-black and looked freshly dyed today. Oh, and there it was, the ultimate message. The red envelope ready for delivery in her hand was not the kind used for special occasions, an exciting *Hong Bao* printed with gold designs and stuffed with money. This was something else. For once April could not ignore it and say, "Hi, Ma. How ya doin'?"

So Skinny kept right on screaming until she was close enough to scream right into April's ear. "*Ni*, you sick. You supposed to come home."

As usual, she reached over as if to give her daughter a hug but instead tugged angrily on April's arm, shoving the red envelope into her hand. April didn't protest. Protesting never helped.

"Still can't talk?" her mother yelled, as if she couldn't hear, either. A common misconception.

April shook her head.

"I fix," Skinny screamed, thrilled to have something useful to do.

She started right in, quickly making the mind-calming mudra with her thumbs touching and her hands cupped one over the other. She kept her posture with the slight bow for all of two and a half seconds because she was incapable of calming her mind, or anybody else's. Then she moved right along to the ousting motion. She stuck out the index finger and pinkie of her right hand and started flicking her middle two fingers with her thumb.

Flick, flick, flick around April's head that was now lowered in deep humiliation for what her mother was doing. Flick, flick, flick, they walked the sidewalk leading to the front door. For April it was like walking the plank on a pirate ship. Flick, flick, flick. She knew what was in store.

Flick, flick, flick around the door of the house. Skinny was ousting in the unspoken message of the Speech Secret Mantra. After that she began the Three Secrets Reinforcement Blessing. This would go on for a long time.

"Gete Gete Para Gete Para Sum Gete Bodhi Saha!" Skinny chanted the heart sutra. It meant something like: Get smart, hurry up and run to the other shore a whole bunch of times.

Impatient for results, Skinny started the Six True Words Mantra. *"Om Ma Ni Pad Me Hum."* She yammered just like the bald guys in the orange robes who turned up to dance through Washington Square and Chinatown sometimes, but Skinny did it without the finger cymbals.

I bow to the jewel in the lotus blossom. I bow to the jewel in the lotus blossom. I bow to the jewel in the lotus blossom. In other words, I bow to the god I see in you. Something like that.

Shit. April clutched the red envelope that was guaranteed to keep her spiritually and energetically protected during Skinny's ousting of bad *qi* and request for positive results in her attempt at the Black Hat feng shui cure. April wanted to sink through the sidewalk and disappear under the Earth's crust.

Actually Skinny's personal meaning of the mantra was a little different: *Almost dead daughter, again returned to life by constantly vigilant, all-powerful mother.* That was Skinny's mantra.

She pushed April through the front door and took a bow at the changes that had been made to the entry and living room. The left wall just inside the door was covered with a huge mirror where there used to be just a little one. Must be borrowed. Wind chimes hung on the light over the door. And wow! Surprise, all the corners of the foyer and living room were hung with colored strings tied in knots at intervals. The strings were stuck on the ceiling with tape and puddled on the floor. April knew that the blue strings at the top represented the part of her body that was injured, the throat. They hung up there closest to ceiling where the higher power resided. Next the red string at eye level represented April, the human in need. When April had been a child, eye level had been much lower. And last was the yellow string puddled on the ground representing Earth. Thus April was bound to heaven and Earth, yin and yang, as her mother tried to transform and release her newest health problem.

Bowls of oranges and other symbolic gifts were evidence of the day's visitors. So much trouble to get the energy right, to balance yin and yang in the body and in the room. April could not help but be touched by the effort Skinny and her friends had made. And April could tell by the strong aroma of simmering ginger that Skinny had been brewing her cures, too.

Sniff, sniff, sniff. Skinny stopped chanting and was smelling her now. "Let me see tongue," she demanded. She was ready to play doctor.

April knew what was coming up and backed away. She didn't want nasty Chinese fake medicine. Boiled-for-five-hours mung sprouts and green food for sore throat wasn't so bad, but disgusting snake broth and some of the other crazy shit made her gag. April was not going to stand there and let her mother pinch her nose tight with iron fingers to get it down. She was too old for that.

"You want to talk?" Skinny screamed. The woman didn't know how to keep her voice down.

April nodded, bowing almost as a joke with as much respect as she could muster to the jewel in the lotus blossom, the god in her mother.

"Then open up mouth. Can speak by morning. *Hao bu hao?*" Okay or no okay.

"*Hao.*" April opened her mouth. It was worth a try.

Fifteen

"**D**r. Frank, this is Birdie Bassett returning your call." Birdie's voice was soft, almost a whisper. She spoke to an answering machine, but the doctor came on before she finished.

"Yes, this is Dr. Frank. Thank you for calling back so quickly."

Birdie did not jump into his pause.

"I want you to know that we at the institute are deeply saddened by your husband's passing," he went on.

Birdie was sure he was.

"Your husband was a wonderful man." The doctor's voice was pitched to soothe, but she wasn't soothed by it. She'd been studying the foundation's tax returns all afternoon and knew that Max had given the Psychoanalytic Institute of New York a whopping five million dollars over the last several years. It hurt her that she'd never heard of it.

"The funeral was very moving," Dr. Frank went on. "And there was a wonderful turnout. I couldn't get anywhere near you to pay my respects," he rattled on.

"Yes, the line was very long," Birdie acknowledged, and she hadn't known a quarter of the people who'd shaken her hand. It had made her feel horrible. So much of her husband's life had already been lived decades before she was even born. But the funeral was three weeks ago; enough about it.

"Dr. Frank, how well did you know my husband?" she asked.

"Oh, very well. He'd been deeply interested in psychoanalysis for many years, as you know. And, of course, he served on our board. I was privileged to know him personally for over twelve years."

Birdie exhaled silently. A growing complication of missing Max desperately was her increasing fury at all the things he'd done without her.

"He was a very astute businessman, very helpful. We will miss him a great deal." Dr. Frank's voice droned on. It sounded more unctuous than sad to Birdie, and she hated this shrink already. He'd never get any more money from her.

"How was he helpful to you?" She said the words slowly, trying to get a handle on her feelings.

"Your husband advised us on the reorganization of our institute, helped us with our business plan. He donated to our building renovation. He was very active." He sounded surprised that she didn't already know all this.

"I wasn't involved in the foundation. Your call came as a surprise to me. I'm playing catch-up," Birdie admitted. In fact, Max had treated her like one of his children. He hadn't told her anything.

"I'd be delighted to help you. What would you like to know?"

There was a subtle change in his tone. Birdie hesitated. She needed a translator, someone close enough to Max to explain his state of mind, his decisions, even the cause of his death. If she didn't know whom she could trust, how could she go about finding out if he'd died of natural causes? *You're next.* She couldn't get the words out of her mind. Next for what? Finally she answered.

"Dr. Frank, there are a lot of things I need to know, including everything about you. I never heard of the Psychoanalytic Institute until your call today."

A long silence suggested Dr. Frank's continued surprise.

"That's the reason I asked how well you knew him," she added. "The truth is, I have some questions about the way my husband died."

"What do you mean?" the shrink asked cautiously.

"He was a very healthy man," she said.

"Yes, he was lucky. He did not show any vulnerabilities. He hadn't slowed down yet."

"He was a healthy man. He had the heart of a forty-year-old," Birdie said flatly.

"I understand, but surely your doctors have told you that it's not uncommon for older people—"

"He was in good health. I would know," she insisted.

"Well, healthy people can have hidden vulnerabilities."

Dr. Frank still sounded smooth, and Birdie realized that he was arguing with her. She didn't like that.

"I thought shrinks were supposed to listen," she said sharply.

"Ah . . ."

Silence. She'd stopped him cold. But now she didn't trust him and didn't want to go in that direction. "Why was he interested in psychoanalysis?" she asked.

"Oh, he was interested in the human mind, why people behave the way they do."

"This is news to me. Did he talk about his children?"

"Ah . . ."

"Dr. Frank, you called me for my support of your organization. If you want my support, there are a great many things I need to know."

"Of course, would you like to come to my office? I'd be happy to fill you in. . . ."

"Tell me now," she insisted. "Why was he so interested in the human mind?"

"Max didn't tell you about his wife's history?"

"Dr. Frank, my husband was from the old school. He wanted life to be pleasant all the time. As far as I was concerned, his wife was perfect, his children were perfect, his life was perfect, and psychology simply didn't exist."

Now she heard him sigh.

"Max was a very private man," he murmured.

"Are you telling me that Cornelia Bassett had a history of mental illness?"

"She had problems," he said hesitantly.

"Problems? What kind of problems?" This was news to Birdie.

"I'm surprised he didn't share this with you."

"What about Max's children? Do they have problems, too?"

"Everybody has problems, Mrs. Bassett."

This was not what Birdie expected to hear.

"Dr. Frank, were you my husband's doctor? Did you treat him or his wife or his children? Is that why he gave so much money to your organization?"

"Mrs. Bassett, I met Max after his wife died. He felt he hadn't given her the right kind of support and didn't want to make that mistake again with you or his children."

"Oh, really." Birdie was stunned. Once again, he hadn't shared his issues with her.

"We talked, but he felt he was too old for therapy. That was how he came to be involved with the institute. He wanted to learn more. He was an interesting person," Dr. Frank finished up.

He was indeed.

"Well, I need to know a lot more. Would you mind coming to the apartment?" Birdie said.

"No, of course not. Would you like me to bring the president of the institute? He knew your husband very well, too."

"Not at this time. When are you available?"

It was Thursday. Dr. Frank was not available to see her until the following Thursday. They made a date, but Birdie Bassett wouldn't live to keep it.

Sixteen

The Bernardino task force was working out of the Sixth, the precinct where *NYPD Blue* was filmed. At eight P.M. Thursday—twenty hours after the killing—the second-floor squad room was no quieter than it had been at noon. The priority case had sucked in ten of Mike's detectives from the Homicide task force, plus eight detectives from the Sixth. Plus a half dozen more from downtown. That didn't count the number of detectives from Internal Affairs, which was running its own parallel investigation, the hot line that had been established, or the Crime Stoppers van that had been cruising the area all day. They were looking for witnesses. A man with a big dog. So far, nothing.

In some cases, no matter how many detectives and uniforms fanned out to canvass an area for witnesses to a crime, they weren't the ones to get information. The anonymous channels out to the public sometimes caught it. Hot lines and Crime Stoppers numbers were flashing on the news, and the nuts were coming out.

Since two P.M. Mike had been supervising the collection of data from people working the streets. He was also organizing the time charts. Where Bernardino had been in the twenty-four hours before his death. Whom he had seen and talked to. What he had planned for the next day. And Mike had to manage the delicate task of mapping the movements of everyone who'd been to Bernardino's party and what they'd done after they left.

No strong leads had emerged yet. But it was impossible to know which bits and pieces that were coming in from many sources might be useful down the road. Only the scope of the investigation was clear. It was going to be wide. By eight-thirty Mike had done all he could do and needed a break from the noise. Before heading home for the night, he decided to visit Marcus Beame, Bernardino's closest associate. He knew that Beame was working the second tour that day—four P.M. to midnight in the Fifth Precinct. Mike headed over to see him.

The Fifth was one of the oldest police precinct buildings in New York, built before the turn of the last century and renovated twice during the tenure of the last three police commissioners. Finally completed for the final time with the typical second-class workmanship precincts were known for receiving, the building was already looking like the dinosaur it was.

Mike parked his dirty red Camaro in a no-parking spot on Elizabeth Street, walked into April's old precinct, and climbed the steep, old-fashioned staircase to the detective unit on the second floor. He found Marcus at his desk, talking on the phone. Here it was quiet. At just before nine P.M. on a Thursday night there was no one in the holding cell. Two broad-faced Chinese women were talking loudly to a Chinese detective who chewed on a toothpick. Two other detectives, neither Chinese, were yakking into their headsets. Everyone else was out. The CO's office was empty. A quiet night.

Mike entered the CO's glass-enclosed office with its window that overlooked Elizabeth Street. Unlike Mike, who stared at four solid walls and had no glass in his office door, Bernardino had been able to view the comings and goings of a busy Chinatown street. For fifteen years he'd watched the uniforms arriving and leaving the precinct, vendors going in and out of their stores, residents doing business on that block every day, and the tens of thousands of visitors who traveled to Chinatown from the tristate area and beyond on weekends to shop.

Every time he came in here, Mike couldn't help being reminded that April had grown up only a few blocks away, had gone to school and high school here, and had returned as a patrol officer after eighteen months in Bed-Stuy. She'd been promoted to detective here, and stayed more than six years. Those facts swam in and out of his thoughts, as everything about April did: where she came from, what she was doing and thinking, her health at the moment. April was the sun and moon that waxed and waned around him. She was his yin and yang. He thought about her all the time, the way some people obsessed about work, and he knew that she was pissed off at him. She wanted to be there right now. Too bad. She needed a rest.

He was bone tired, too. Day one of the investigation was gone, and they didn't have a clue who Bernardino's killer was. Some maniac out there in the wind didn't know that April couldn't remember his face. That was too close for Mike. He was glad she was living with him, where she was safe. Not even insiders knew that address. While Mike waited for Beame to get off the phone back in the bigger room, he took a look around Bernardino's old office. The usual precinct business was posted, but there were no personal photos on the walls or surfaces. He checked the desk drawers one by one. Some used tissues, pencil stubs, forms. But no computer disks or notebooks, nothing resembling the stack of important calling cards—the bigger the better and in two alphabets—that were so prevalent and necessary in Chinatown. Bernardino's stuff was gone.

Mike sighed again. The old wooden desk that was centered right in the window over Elizabeth Street

that Bernardino had occupied for nearly fifteen years
no longer housed a single item he'd owned. The desk
chair was also a relic. A wooden rock-and-roller. Mike
leaned back and closed his eyes. The chair creaked
noisily. After a few minutes Beame came in.

"How ya doin'?" Mike said before he opened his
eyes.

"Okay."

Reluctantly he opened them. He was the one who'd
been up all night, going on thirty-six hours without
sleep, but Marcus was the one who didn't look good.
Mike noted the bad color, kind of graying out, as if
Beame had been pickled. His skin sagged around the
eyes and chin. No tone at all, and his meager lips
looked thinner than usual. Mike frowned at the wrinkled tan shirt, the knot of his tie pulled down to the
middle of his chest. Beame's tawny sport jacket was
still hanging on the back of his chair. He hadn't bothered to clean up for the interview.

He settled in the chair opposite Mike, thrusting out
his pelvis and legs. Already defensive. Mike didn't like
the show of disrespect.

"You don't look so great," Mike observed. Neutral.

"Four hours of interrogation, you'd look a little rag-
ged yourself," Beame shot back.

Mike sniffed. "So?"

Beame lifted a shoulder. "They've got everything
I know."

Mike let go of a small smile that couldn't be seen
under his mustache. "That's good. That's very good."
He made a steeple with his fingers, rocking in Bernardino's creaky chair. "Let me in, Marcus. You were
the last to hear Bernardino speak. What did he say?"

"All he said was he couldn't take any more nostalgia. Period. He was out the door."

"Anything else?"

Beame wagged his chin, then glanced down at the

desktop where Mike was twiddling his thumbs. "I'm way behind here." He was chewing gum, showing his teeth. Being a shit.

Mike wondered if the gum was a cover for beery breath, and looked closer at Beame's face. His blue eyes were bloodshot, sheepish. Maybe he was a drinker. But maybe it was guilt about something else.

"What do you have?" Beame asked after a moment. It was clear his four hours with Internal Affairs hadn't yielded *him* any information. Too bad.

Mike put his index finger to his lips as if he were considering sharing. He stroked his mustache. A lot of cops had good mustaches. Mike had a great one. Not too bushy, not too in-your-face with the machismo. He trimmed it every day for discipline. He had a good strong mustache over the kind of nice, full, smiling lips that made women feel safe and didn't threaten men.

"A canvass of the area hasn't come up with much," he said slowly. "We're waiting on the COD." A lie. "When did Bernardino clear his stuff out?"

Beame lifted his shoulders in an exaggerated shrug. "I don't know. One day last week."

"What day?"

"Maybe Thursday or Friday. I was off."

"Who was here?"

"You can check with Patti."

"That the secretary?" Mike pulled out his notebook, found a clean page, and started scribbling in it.

"I wouldn't call her that. She does what she can, goes home at six. Her number is posted." He jerked his head at the clipboard where it might be found.

"What about ongoing cases? Anything specific to Chinatown?"

"Small stuff. You can go through it. They did."

IA again. Mike nodded.

"Don't you guys share?" Beame demanded.

"Sure we do." Mike changed the subject. "Was Bernardino working anything on his own?"

"Look, I liked the guy. He was tough, but I liked him. I knew him for years, okay?" Beame said. Now he was washing his hands of it.

So what? They all liked him. Mike prodded a little. "What was he into? Come on, was it gang stuff?"

Beame shook his head. Over the years there was always a variety of criminal activity in Chinatown. Extortion and protection, both Chinese and mob-related. Illegals working in sweatshops and restaurants. Back in the early nineties an influx of immigrants from Fujian had brought in unusually vicious gang members who didn't play by Chinatown rules. After a shooting in a restaurant, the unofficial officials of Chinatown stopped it. Chinatown had its own way of dealing with things. Mike was looking for a connection, a string leading anywhere.

"You're interested in the karate. Well, they don't kill that way down here. Gang members cut with big knives, shoot with big guns. They need a lot of blood to send their messages. What was the message here, huh?"

"Anything . . ." Going on ten P.M. Mike was getting impatient. And it didn't have to be a karate thing. Bernardino was yoked. Any cop, anybody in the military, any corrections officer knew how to do it.

"I'd say nothing, Mike. But what do I know?"

"You were close to him. You saw him last," Mike reminded him.

"Yeah, but after his wife died, it was like someone pushed his off button. He went somewhere in his head." Beame twirled his finger around his ear.

"What do you mean?"

"Oh, he was treading water here. Grumpy-old-man shit, didn't have a good word for anyone. He'd lost his fight, know what I mean? He was going through the motions. Just did the administrative stuff. He wasn't investigating shit."

"But he was a good cop . . . ?" Mike let the question trail off.

"Yeah, he was a good cop." Beame lifted his shoulder again. "But somebody popped his bubble."

"But not about work, you'd say?"

"I don't think so." Now it was Beame's fingers beating a little number on the chair arm.

"You got a hypo?" Mike asked finally.

"A hypothetical?"

"Yeah, a theory? This a stranger thing? You know the area."

Beame drummed his fingers, reached into his pants pocket with his other hand, blew his nose on a dirty handkerchief, chewed his gum. "You got anything pointing in that direction?" he asked finally.

"Oh, sure. We got stuff. We got a lot of stuff. You think about it. Call me tomorrow. Okay?"

"Yeah, will do."

Mike left unsatisfied. He felt as if a giant gnat were cruising back and forth in front of his face. That gnat was Internal Affairs, taking this case very seriously. *So what?* he told himself.

Back in the Camaro and finally shutting down for the day, he punched automatic dial for his home number. The answering machine picked up, telling him no one was available to take his call. He shook his head, feeling uneasy. If April was at her mother's, he was going to be upset. He couldn't help thinking she might not be safe there, but since he'd already shut her out of the case it didn't seem like a good idea to interfere if she wanted to go home.

Seventeen

Gao Wan rented what used to be April's apartment, so April could not go upstairs to sleep in her old bed. There used to be two bedrooms on the second floor. April had made the other bedroom into a living room, but Gao sometimes let a friend stay there for months at a time. A friend was there now, Wei Fong, a dental student. April's old pink tufted sofa was only forty-eight inches long but curved like a bean and was hard as a board. Wei, who didn't even have enough money to buy a bed, slept in a sleeping bag on the floor.

Downstairs there was just one bedroom, a tiny dining room, living room, kitchen. April made her headquarters on the sofa bed in the living room, where the feng shui was good because the *qi* could get around easily and she had excellent visibility to all the entrances. Because there were no bars on the open window, her cell phone and gun shared the pillow with her head in case Bernardino's killer knew her address and wanted to finish her off. Despite the lack of real security, however, the *qi* felt good. She wasn't really worried. It was a quiet night on a quiet block. The whisper of a breeze through the screen was hardly enough to stir the bamboo wind chimes. She felt she was home—in a place of safety where no one could reach or bug her, or tell her what she shouldn't do. Only Skinny, and Skinny was too busy mumbling her healing mantras and brewing her fake medicine.

Worm daughter's old boss had been killed for nothing. Just showed how no-good the job was. That was Skinny's take on the situation.

April fell asleep and stayed that way until noon, right through the constantly ringing telephone. Unlike the day before, when she'd been full of anxiety in the hospital, on Friday morning she had no question about who or where she was. Steam from an infusion boiling in an electric teakettle on a table nearby filled the air with the familiar aroma of eucalyptus and other chest-opening flora and fauna. In the dining room incense was burning on the altar that was permanently decorated with Buddhas and other gods in varying sizes that sat on plastic lotus blossoms and were surrounded by the usual colorful symbolic adornments in red and gold. The smells were conflicting and strong, but the *qi* was still very good. April stretched, and before the sleep was gone from her eyes, Skinny padded in with a cup of hot water.

"Ni xingle ma?" Are you awake? Then in English, "Mike called last night. Want to know you okay."

April sat up. She wanted to ask if he was mad, but she put up her hand at the sight of the dreaded cup.

"Drink. Don't say anything." Skinny muttered a little Chinese mumbo jumbo to speed the healing process.

April inhaled and exhaled a few times, drank the hot water, and did not say a thing.

"Better?"

April wasn't going to say.

Skinny frowned pointedly at the gun and cell phone on the pillow. She wasn't going to elaborate about Mike. She went away for a few minutes, then returned with the nuclear weapon, a large cup of something in which April hoped lovely golden ginger juice would be the primary ingredient. Shinny shoved it into her face. Just off the boil, the liquid fumed disgusting vapor up her nose. She flinched. *Eeww*. This pungent brew was greenish brown and smelled as if it had snake bladder or snake liver or deer penis in it— maybe all of the above. It looked like pond scum.

"He, he." Skinny flicked her middle fingers at April, ousting the bad *qi. Drink!*

April gestured to her dangerous mother to back off.

"He," Skinny intoned ominously.

Okay, okay. But back off. She'd drink it without having her nose pinched. April took the cup, closed her eyes, and swallowed quickly. *Whoooo.* Old memories of many past tortures competed for first place. Scalding the roof of her mouth and throat. Rising gorge trying to expel the boiling liquid. If it came out as vomit, she'd burn her tongue and lips. She clamped her jaw shut to keep it down, then waited with tears squeezing out of her closed eyes for the heat to hit her stomach.

"Hai hao ma?" the Dragon demanded.

Tears course down April's cheeks. *Shit.* Scalded again.

"Hai hao ma?" Skinny's voice rose with her anxiety.

No, she wasn't okay. April held her breath to contain the agony.

"Ni?" Skinny screamed.

Oh, for God's sake. Hao. April opened her eyes. The room with its canopy of strings was still there. Her panicked mother was only just refraining from punching her back into consciousness. The weeny Dragon looked small and terrified. Typical Skinny, she always forced the medicine down when it was too hot, then got scared because it was too hot.

But April always took it almost boiling because she, like her mother, believed that merely warm wouldn't work. Her throat burned like hell as she crawled out of bed and padded into the bathroom. Then exactly the right heat hit her stomach with a jolt and she felt sick again. The downstairs bathroom was a putrid avocado color that must have been popular back in the 1950s. The floor and wall tiles matched the tub and toilet, and everything was pretty badly cracked and chipped with age. In fifty more years, however, the Woos would never spend a single unnecessary dollar to update.

April assessed herself in the tiny medicine cabinet mirror. *Shit.* The bruises on her neck were still a deep and ugly purple, not even beginning to yellow around the edges. Through her tangled hair, she could feel the lump on her head, still huge and tender. Scabs were beginning to form on her throbbing knees. They protested when she bent them to sit on the toilet. Oh, yeah, she was just fine.

"*Ni,* talk to me," Skinny screamed through the door.

April ignored her and took a long hot shower. She was heavily into heat.

"*Hao?*" the Dragon said anxiously when she emerged.

April made a face and shook her head. First time in her life she had no interest in saying a word. She was ready to listen, but not to talk. She lifted a shoulder. *Sorry.*

By then it was one o'clock and she was wondering where the world went. No word from Mike yet today. No word from Iriarte. She was a little annoyed. She pointed to the telephone, and Skinny made as if she didn't understand that April wanted some clarification on her calls. It took her a while to figure out that her cell phone hadn't rung all morning because her mother had turned it off. She checked her messages.

Eleven P.M. Thursday. "*Querida,* I talked to your mother. She says you're sleeping. Love you. *Hasta mañana.*"

Eight A.M. today. "*Buenas, corazón.* Your mother says you're still sleeping. *Te quiero. Hasta más tarde.*"

Eight-fifteen A.M. "Hey, it's Woody. Your mother says you're very sick. Iriarte is driving me nuts on the Stilys case. He wants some word on your court appearance Monday. If you're still with the living, call me. . . . If you're not with the living give me a call anyway. Ha, ha." A real card.

Nine forty-five. "Lieutenant Iriarte. Mike says you're not doing so good. Call in. I'm worried." *Ha, ha.* Another card.

There were seven more in that vein, two more from Mike. In the last one he threatened to come over. Nothing useful until she got to Kathy's. Eleven-seventeen A.M.

"It's Kathy. Look, this is going to be a long message. The funeral is set for Monday. The Department doesn't want to do it. This is an outrage. Is something going on? They said the reason was they don't do big funerals out of the city unless it's a line-of-duty death. Too many people off from work. This is terrible. Dad deserves the whole honor thing, the PC, the brass, the bagpipes, soup to nuts. What am I going to do?" She sounded close to tears.

"And something else . . . the ME's office won't give us the death report. Bill's getting the deep freeze. What's going on? It's pretty crazy what's happening here, and I don't like what I'm hearing. If you still can't talk, for God's sake get in touch somehow. Smoke signals. I don't care. You know the number. The hordes are here. I'll be around all day."

April took a few minutes to throw on yesterday's clothes and try swallowing a few spoons of her mother's *jook* (rice gruel) garnished with minced beggar's chicken, ham, and boiled-until-melted vegetables (only deep green ones for throat).

Skinny's face fell when she started gathering up her things. "You didn't eat anything, *ni*. Where are you going?"

April didn't answer.

"You can't leave. You're not finished. Are you leaving? *Ni!* You can't talk yet. Are you coming back?" Skinny had a whole one-sided conversation as she followed April to the door.

April didn't want to say she'd be back later in case she wasn't. She didn't want to say anything. She gave Skinny a little smile. *Once again you almost killed me, Ma*, the smile said. Xiexie. *Thanks.*

Eighteen

At two P.M. Birdie Bassett was having lunch at York U and receiving more of a giving lesson from Al Frayme than she had bargained for. He was in the alumni office, and as soon as Birdie had became a widow, he pressured his boss to add her name to the list for the last president's dinner of the year, which was coming up Wednesday.

"Gee, Al. I'm not sure I can go," Birdie said.

"Look, you need to learn the ropes. The one thing the president doesn't want is negative donors. So don't get any off-the-wall ideas in your beautiful head."

Birdie didn't like the way he was talking, as if she were a sure thing. Just barely, she decided to let pass the possible put-down of the "beautiful head" remark. Perhaps she was just overly sensitive. "What's a negative donor?" she asked.

"A negative donor is someone with big money who wants to build a building or start a program or new school that the university doesn't need or want just to get their name on something."

"Give me a for-instance," Birdie said.

"Okay . . ." Al dropped his head back and rolled his soft gray eyes at the ceiling. "Ah, here's a good one." He focused on her again with a grin.

"Say you loved the sea, loved it, and wanted to start a marine biology center here at the university to rival the one at Wood's Hole."

Birdie laughed, relieved finally to be with someone who didn't make her feel stupid or uncomfortable every single minute. For the first time since Max died she was actually having fun.

"See, I told you I could cheer you up." Al looked pleased.

"Thanks, this was a good idea." She liked the restaurant he'd chosen, 103 Waverly Place, where Fifth Avenue met Washington Square. A small restaurant where university people from all the schools in the area went. Birdie was pleased to be in such a place.

At the very next booth sat the latest star that John Warmsley, York U's new president, had lured from Harvard with an endowed chair of her own. Angela Andersen was a skinny, salt-and-peppering, wild-haired woman with no makeup who'd cracked the code on the psychology of girls. Birdie had read her book a few years back and nodded all the way through. And there she was sitting only a few feet away with an angular wild-haired man who could have been her male twin. The close proximity to such high-powered brains was enough to give her goose bumps.

Al caught her staring over his shoulder. "Do you want to meet them?" he asked in a stage whisper.

"Maybe later. Go on with the marine biology." Birdie focused on Al again, someone who'd circled in and out of her life over the years who suddenly resurfaced as a potential friend with Max's death. She was glad he'd called.

"Okay. This is a really good one. Let's say you're an environmentalist and want to study the Hudson and the East rivers and all the tankers' impact on the harbor, blahbity, blahbity blah. This is a huge concept, right, and you have fifteen, twenty million to give. That's a lot, right?"

Birdie nodded. A whole lot.

"Wrong. That's nothing. It wouldn't cover a little

building, let alone the research boats, the pier, and the faculty that would be needed to support such a program. You'd need hundreds of millions for that."

"Oh." Birdie sipped some San Pellegrino from her water glass. *Excuse me.*

Al's face took on an intense expression as he explained it. "A negative donor gives the big hit for name recognition, then moves on, leaving the institution with a white elephant it can't support. A lot of institutions get burned that way because they think the donors will stick with them and keep on supporting the new whatever-it-is that bears their name. We won't do it. Warmsley is adamant about that. Got it?"

Birdie nodded.

"You have to offer something they want, not something you want, okay?"

She nodded again, beginning to see how Max's mind had worked. Al was going to be useful, very useful. She smiled at him, pleased that someone benign was around to guide her. Max hadn't used a foundation consultant, and she didn't want to, either. How hard could it be? She was in charge of a seventy-five-million-dollar foundation. She'd never thought the sum was huge. She knew that to avoid tax consequences charitable foundations had to give away no less than five percent a year. But Max had habitually given away closer to seven percent, which put his giving level at about five million a year.

And he had his own style of giving, which was in some ways similar to the kind of giver that Al described, but in other ways very different. Max had liked to do big hits, like the two grants he'd given to the Psychoanalytic Institute. They were one-time deals. He didn't continue for years at the same level. After he helped an organization with something they needed to do, he moved on to something else. He wasn't a negative donor, by any means, but he was definitely a donor who didn't stick to giving the really big bucks to the same organization year after year. It meant he was always shopping, always meeting with people. To his very last day, he had been a vibrant man who loved his cell phone. What had happened to him? She shook her head.

Al watched her face. "Something wrong?"

"No, no. Just thinking of Max."

"You miss him?"

"Of course."

"Of course." Al sat back in the booth with the self-effacing smile he'd had ever since college. "You know, I've been telling you this ever since you married Max. You're in a wonderful position here as an alum. Wonderful. You can leverage this opportunity and who knows, maybe even get on the board. This is the *time,* Birdie."

"The time for what, Al?"

"Come on. We don't have a lot of time. Let's get with it and decide how you want to allocate your gift."

Birdie laughed. She didn't mean to, but she couldn't help herself. No one understood that she didn't want to leverage her opportunities. She didn't want to be on boards, couldn't think of anything more boring. Now that she was alone she didn't know what she wanted, but she knew it wasn't that.

"What are you laughing at? Are you laughing at me?" His voice sounded hurt. "You have no idea how it is here, being brushed off by people with *millions.* Some of them are so . . . dismissive."

She flicked her manicured fingers at him. "Well, don't be silly; I'm not dismissive. It's just the idea of allocating my gift." She giggled, then sobered when Al looked annoyed.

"Oh, come on, you think it's fun having a responsibility like this?"

"Yes," he said fussily, "I do. And what are you going to do about it?"

She snorted to herself. That was the question they

all asked her. The trophy wife with the size-two figure whom nobody ever took seriously now had the chance to be on the board of the ballet, the board of the museum—whichever one she wanted—also the board of the hospital. The Psychoanalytic Institute. Her eyes slid around the restaurant at the tweedy York U types lunching there. She'd wanted to be one of these thinkers, one of these intensely involved academics years ago . . . but not anymore.

"I don't know yet," she said honestly. "Maybe I'll develop my own board; we'll consider our options."

"What about York?"

She blinked. "Oh, for God's sake, Al. You have more money than God. You don't need any more."

"Birdie. We don't! And this is what I do for a living," he said hotly. "I raise money for this great institution. This is Harvard with heart, don't you understand? You can't disrespect us."

"Of course I understand, and I won't forget you. We'll find a slot for you." She smiled reassuringly. She hadn't been able to get down much of her salad, but she had liked the lunch and didn't want to hurt him.

"A slot! How much of a slot?"

"I don't know yet. . . . We'll have to see." One thing Birdie had learned already was not to commit too soon.

"Are we talking six figures, seven figures, what?" He gave her an exasperated look.

"Don't get excited. I don't know yet."

"Give me a ballpark then," he pressed.

She shook her head, wasn't going to do it. "Walk me to my car," she said. She didn't even glance at the check. One nice thing was they always paid.

Nineteen

Back in her Le Baron and on the road again, April started breathing easier. This time she didn't have to check her map for the way to Bernardino's house. As she drove through traffic, she imagined Bernardino taking this ride every day back and forth to the Fifth, going from one world to another. But no, he would not have traveled the Deegan. He'd have taken the Saw Mill on the West Side, then the Henry Hudson Parkway along the river. Nice drive. Nice life.

Forty minutes later she turned into Bernardino's heavily bowered suburban street and slowed down to a crawl. Circus time. Where yesterday the block had been quiet, today there were news vans, Westchester news, the city stations, too, and lots of cars, including Crown Victorias. One of them was Mike's. April's heart beat a rumba. She parked way back and walked slowly toward the crowd of reporters stalled in the front yard of Bernardino's house. How to hide?

The house next door had an arbor and a front gate. April opened it, sighed, and strode through it as if she belonged there. In the house a dog started barking; it sounded like a big dog. She ducked her head and skirted the house, not pausing to glance at the windows to see if anyone was watching.

In the backyard an in-ground pool was still covered for the winter that was over. She searched for a gap in the hedge, saw one at the end of the half acre, and plowed through. On Bernardino's side, the lawn was full of dandelions and needed mowing. She walked toward the house. Kathy was working in the kitchen. She looked up and locked eyes with April. They met at the storm door.

"What are you doing here? They tell me you're not on the case," she said worriedly, then opened up so April could come in. "Your husband's here," she added. "He's on the case."

Not her husband yet, but who was quibbling? Speak of the devil. Mike appeared with an empty glass in his hand.

"Mind if I help myself to some more water?" His bushy eyebrows shot up at the sight of his *novia*, not where he expected her to be. "Hello, what are you doing here?"

Caught, April gave him a weak little smile. Then he got it and turned to Kathy. "Oh, I see. Girls sticking together. Okay, let's go for a walk." He took April's upper arm and marched her outside. She didn't resist.

"April, you coming back?" Kathy asked at the door. She seemed alarmed by the brevity of the visit.

April nodded and let herself be taken away by the man of her dreams.

"You didn't come home last night. You had me worried. I don't want you in that house alone." Mike let the fire die from his eyes as they walked to the edge of the patio and turned their backs on the house so no one could read their lips.

Then what about her parents. Didn't he worry about them?

"You didn't call in. I missed you." He said this softly. Here was the truth, but he didn't give her a hug. He was working.

She touched her mouth, flipped up her hand. *I wanted my mommy. What can you do?*

"Yeah, I know. You didn't want to be alone, but

you've got to be careful." He touched her arm and she nodded again. She was always careful. Well, nearly always careful. Then she glanced back at the house to get off the subject. *What's going on?*

"You want to know what's going on?" he asked with a smile. "The autopsy came in. Bernie was yoked. I guess you knew that. But here's something you didn't know. About a month ago a check came in for his wife, Lorna, from the New York State Lottery. You know she hit the big one?"

Of course, who didn't? April nodded some more.

"Our Bernie deposited fifteen million in a new account at Fidelity. Lorna hadn't passed on yet. In an old will she left him everything and never changed it. But get this. As soon as she died, he withdrew four million, and no one admits to knowing where it went."

April registered shock, then turned around to catch Kathy's eye. She was working at the sink and didn't look up.

"Kathy says she doesn't know anything about it. We'll run a check on her accounts and of the banks out in her area, but the FBI does that routinely with their agents, so she would know not to hide any big money in plain sight. She might have used safety-deposit boxes. Other names. There are a lot of ways to hide money. She would know." He lifted a shoulder.

But why the need to hide it? It was their money. Oh, a tax reason? That would be so stupid and squir-relly. She frowned at Mike.

"Yeah, well, like I said, she claims Bernie told her he hadn't gotten the money yet."

That didn't make sense. Everybody knew the lottery paid off quickly. She tried to remember what Kathy had said about it yesterday.

"Maybe Bernie didn't want his kids to bug him. Maybe he had a different plan for it." Mike shrugged.

But it didn't sound like the Bernie April knew. She considered the time frame in light of yesterday's conversation with Kathy. Kathy had been out of town since her mother died. If Bernie had wanted to give his daughter a bunch of tax-free money, could he have gotten it out to Seattle without taking it there himself? Did he plan a trip later on? If he'd given a bunch of tax-free cash to Bill, would Bill have sent it on to his sister? If it went to the kids, it had to be about taxes, right? What else was there?

Possibly a whole lot of things. A woman none of them knew about? An illegitimate child. Through the window April could see Kathy washing dishes at the kitchen sink, carefully not watching them. Her hair was no different from yesterday, unwashed and unbrushed. Today she was wearing an old gray sweatshirt and jeans and had circles under her eyes that were visible from a mile away. She certainly didn't have the burnished look of a grieving millionaire.

One thing Kathy had told April was that her father used to discuss everything with them. If he hadn't told her about the money, maybe he'd told Bill and the two men were in some kind of scheme to avoid taxes. April shivered. Now she knew what had bothered her yesterday about the mess Bernardino had left. Bernie was a tidy guy who'd wreaked havoc on his house, so he must have had a reason. April hoped that the money was right there, somewhere under their noses in the house, and had nothing at all to do with his murder. She didn't want to suspect his son of killing him. That was too terrible to imagine.

The press outside the front door didn't know about the missing money, and no one would tell them anytime soon, but the detectives inside were looking for it, guessing that maybe something had gone wrong between Bernie and Bill, and the son had murdered his own father. No one was hoping for that. But they were praying for something simple; anything was better than a mystery.

Mike interrupted April's speculation on the missing money. "And what are you really doing here, *querida*?"

She considered her options. If she played the cripple, he'd send her home. If he thought she could be useful, he might let her in. It was a small chance that she decided to take. So much for her carefully thought-out plan to remain silent for at least a week. She cleared her sore throat and tried vocalizing for the first time since Wednesday night.

"Kathy wanted to talk." Her voice was a gravelly whisper that sounded like something a whole lot worse than Marlon Brando playing the Godfather, but at least it was audible. Score one for the Dragon.

"Did she tell you anything?" Mike showed no surprise that her voice was back.

"Not yet. Her mom is dead, her dad was murdered, and her brother is a suspect. I'd say she's scared."

Mike squeezed her arm. "You thought you could handle this on your own? Pretending you couldn't speak? How long did you think you could pull that off?"

April shook her head. "I was just helping out an old friend."

"That's what you always say. You have no idea what's going on here." He glanced back toward the house.

No, she didn't know what was going on. She changed the subject. "Why isn't Bernardino getting a full police funeral?"

"He isn't?" At this Mike registered surprise.

"Kathy's pretty upset about it. I would be, too. Thirty-eight years on the job. Lieutenant murdered on a city street . . ." April shook her head. "What's the reasoning behind it?"

"I don't know. This is the first I've heard about it."

"Well, I'm going in to talk to her."

Mike glanced at his watch. "I thought we settled this already."

"It's not a problem. I'm taking sick leave." She gave him a mischievous smile, feeling better in his presence.

"Oh, please." He snorted through his mustache.

"I am."

"Fine, if you're taking sick leave, you've got to stay out of sight. Get in bed. Don't attend the funeral. These are the conditions."

" 'Oh, please' yourself. The picture's changed. You need me."

"We got a lot of people on this case. What's so special about you?" But he said this with a smile, already opening the door a crack.

April walked through it and felt the fog of Wednesday roll back in on her. "What's special about me, *chico,*" she said in her chalk-on-the-board voice, "is that I don't make the answers up."

He laughed. Like he made them up. "Well, I guess you're feeling better."

"Look, Bernardino has to have a full department funeral. Bagpipes and everything. Tell Avise it would be a scandal not to. He has the muscle to get it done."

"I don't know what's up with that," Mike murmured, checking his back.

"Well, find out what's up with it. You're one of them now. The whole city is watching here. Don't let them act like asses just because they don't know the whole story. Okay?"

He didn't say anything, but she could read agreement in his eyes.

"I'll see you later, boss." She took his hand and shook it, rubbing his palm briefly with her thumb. "Nice working with you. By the way, where are you keeping the file, the Sixth?"

"Anybody ever tell you you're a piece of work?" Mike said.

"Nope." She let go of the hand and picked her way across the patio to the kitchen door.

Kathy was sitting at the counter. Mike followed April in, got the water he'd come in for, and disappeared without a word. Okay, it was up to her to get a few things clarified. April filled the kettle and put it on the stove to boil.

"I hope you have tea. I need it," she said.

"Oh, Jesus, what a voice," Kathy remarked.

"At least I have one." April sat on the other stool.

"Thanks for coming." Kathy looked pretty dispirited.

"No problem. I'm not officially on the case."

"Can you stop them from tearing up the place? Baboons."

"Nope. I warned you. Look, Kathy, when we talked yesterday you didn't really answer my questions about your dad's lottery money."

Kathy brushed her hair away from her face, looking fifteen years older than yesterday. "Is this an interview?"

"Very informal. No tape recorders, no cameras, no lie detectors at this time. As I said, I'm not officially on the case. We're just talking, okay? I want to help you."

"Jesus, don't creep me out. No one ever helps anyone."

"Try me. What about the money?"

"Dad said he'd let me know when he got it. As far as I knew, he hadn't gotten it yet. What happens now?"

"Oh, come on, Kathy, you expect me to believe that a dad who told you everything didn't tell you that he got a check for fifteen million dollars before your mother even passed on and he cashed some of it in even before the funeral?"

"What?" Kathy's whole body jolted with shock. It didn't look like an act.

"We have the time frames on his deposits and withdrawals. You didn't go through his files and find them?" April studied her. She must be a pretty lousy special agent.

"I did check," Kathy said slowly. "The recent statements aren't here." She passed a hand over her brow. "And the house was a mess. It looked to me like he was falling apart. That's how I saw it."

"You didn't have any suspicions that all was not right here?"

"I don't know what you mean." Kathy looked out the window.

"That something was out of whack. That nobody was talking about the elephant in the living room."

"I told you. Dad wasn't interested in money. He didn't like people chasing him around the block trying to get it. He wanted to run away from that."

"And he was a brick wall when he wanted to be," April added.

"Yeah," Kathy admitted. "He was a brick wall on certain subjects."

"Is that the reason you didn't come to his retirement party? Because he was holding out on you?" April rasped out.

"No! I was working a case. My supervisor wouldn't give you any more time off. I'll give you his number. You can ask the bastard yourself."

The front doorbell and telephone rang at the same time. They rang and rang. Nobody made a move to answer them.

"So, did you talk to Bill about the money?" April asked.

The wall phone had no caller ID. Kathy waited for it to stop ringing before she responded. "When?"

"Before Wednesday." April's face was empty of emotion. She didn't want to say "before the murder."

Then the kettle began to sing. This got Kathy up. Miss Hospitality. "What kind of tea do you want?"

"Whatever you have is fine."

"Mom liked chamomile." Kathy searched around in a cupboard for it.

"Chamomile is good."

Kathy fussed with a mug and tea bag. "Sorry, I don't have any cookies."

"Tea is fine." April took the mug and put her nose into the steam. Hot was best, but she'd wait this time.

Outside the kitchen, they could hear the noise of men going through the house, talking to each other from different rooms, not making any effort to be quiet or show respect. April guessed there were three or four of them, and Mike was one of them. They were still working the upstairs, hadn't gotten to the basement yet. The doorbell rang again. Nobody answered it.

"Let's get back to the money. How were you and Bill handling it between the two of you?"

Kathy pressed her lips into a thin line. "We didn't talk about it."

"Gee, Kathy, this is hard to believe. If my dad got fifteen million dollars, I'd have an interest in it."

"I never said I wasn't interested. I said we didn't talk about it. You don't get it, do you?"

"No, Kathy, I don't get it. None of this is playing for me. Why don't you help me out?"

"Look, just don't patronize me. Mom died. We were dealing with that, okay? The money was a perk we didn't want to mix up with grieving. Like, Mom died, but hooray, we're rich. That may not make any sense to you. But that's how it was with us."

"That's what you thought." But that was exactly how it wasn't. April sipped the chamomile. By now she was wishing for that cookie. For a whole plate of cookies, but she never ate when she questioned.

Kathy clammed up.

"Looks like you weren't in the loop. Your dad was cashing in the money big before he died. Four million of it. You said he thought of the money as yours. . . ." She watched Kathy register betrayal.

The doorbell rang again. A look of irritation crossed Kathy's face. She licked her lips. "Where's the money?" she croaked out in a voice almost as fractured as April's.

"That's what I'm asking you."

Kathy shook her head. "I don't get it." But her face said she did.

"So what about Bill? Does he need money?"

"Who doesn't need money?" She rolled her eyes, trying to cover her own growing suspicion.

Good. April had her.

"Is he the kind of guy who'd hold out on his sister?" she asked.

Kathy collapsed inside. April could see her world breaking down. Right then she looked as grubby, unkempt, and highly unfemale as a very attractive person could get. Her body language said it all.

"We weren't close. Dad made us compete when we were kids. Bill was the one who got to law school. He was married, had the kids, got the perks, but he always resented me. You know how it is. Whatever bothers them, they don't get over it, right?"

The doorbell kept ringing. Kathy ignored it. "Yeah, I guess he might cheat me out of millions if he could get away with it, why not? But kill Daddy? Uh-uh."

"Maybe Daddy found out."

Kathy clicked her tongue. "Like you said, April. It isn't playing for me."

"Well, we'll figure it out."

"Is this the reason the Department isn't giving him his funeral? Possible gift-tax evasion? Isn't there, like, a three-million-dollar exemption anyway?" She clicked her tongue again.

"Not my area; I wouldn't know." April's voice was going again, but she believed Kathy's story.

Four detectives plowed through the kitchen on their way downstairs to the basement. It was clear from their faces that they hadn't found what they were looking for.

Twenty

An hour later Mike got into the passenger seat of April's car and slammed the door. Down the street a reporter from a local station had spotted them coming out of the neighbor's yard and started yelling. April could see the girl's open mouth. See her hand raised. She had big red lips and the kind of straight streaky blond hair many Asian girls envied. The reporter was wearing a photogenic outfit, a nice heather-colored jacket and lilac blouse. The pants didn't match perfectly, but it didn't matter because on camera she would never be seen below the waist. April opened the window for some air and heard her plea.

"Officer, give me a second. Just one." The woman was clearly yelling at Mike.

April gunned the engine and took off. "You coming with me, *chico*? That would be nice."

"Only to the next stop sign," he said.

April slowed and cruised the next block of lovely brick houses with picture windows and pointy roofs. She wouldn't mind living out here, but who wouldn't?

"Okay, stop anywhere along here."

She slowed in front of a house with a good strong slate roof and a lucky red door. Too bad they were there too soon for the show of fat-budded peonies that were thickly bedded in little kidney-shaped plots, like commas, by the front walk. Next couple of weeks, in mid-June, they'd be out. *Nice house,* she thought.

She sighed. Six o'clock was always an in-between time. Not really day anymore, but not yet evening either. Today at six again it was still bright as morning. On her second day in Westchester she could feel the tug of the suburbs, where the backyards were large enough for whole suites of lawn furniture. Where attics and basements were big enough to hold extensive junk collections. And where every house had a garage to hide the car away. The Woo house didn't have a garage. Mike's building had only a covered area. April kept saying she'd buy a new car when she could afford a home for it. *Ha.*

She let the engine idle for a moment, then turned it off. The Le Baron was toasty from its long wait in the sun, but she really wanted to bask in the warmth of Mike's nearness. "Miss me?" She was desperate for a hug and didn't want to admit it.

"Why should I? You're always up to some trick." He shook his head. "This is why we can't trust the Chinese."

Uh-oh. She didn't like when he went global on her. "Oh, come on, you did miss me." She was determined not to bite back.

"You're not trustworthy. Why can't you just rest, take a day off for a change?" he grumbled, hitting all her buttons.

"Look, I don't like to be kept in the dark. I don't like to be pushed aside." *Not trustworthy. Jesus.* She sulked in the driver's seat, angry at herself for raising the issue. She should have known better than request a time-out for love when he was the primary on a case that was getting stickier by the hour.

"Left me alone, no message, nothing." Out of his window he studied the house she liked. "You didn't return my messages. How do you think I felt?"

"I couldn't talk," she reminded him.

"So now you can talk. Big improvement." He turned

to face her, and the bicker transformed itself into a slow, steamy smile.

Mike was never one for holding grudges. He had his priorities straight. His smile moved right on to the hug she needed. A kiss followed, a long kiss, uncomfortable to maneuver in the bucket seats, but a good kiss nonetheless. April didn't want to be the one to break it up.

"Mmmm." Finally he made the motions of disentangling.

She rubbed his neck and discovered muscles that were rock hard with tension. "How late will you be?" Now she felt bad because she hadn't been there for him last night.

"Few more hours. Are you going back to your mom's? You smell funny. What did she do to you?"

"Nothing much. I'm coming home." Eventually.

"*Que bueno.* I gotta go." He shifted in the passenger seat, refueled for the moment, but then didn't move to get out.

"I'm sure Kathy didn't know about the money," April said suddenly.

"Oh, yeah?" Mike raised bushy eyebrows as if he found that impossible to believe.

"What can I say? It was a dysfunctional family. Welcome to America." April's voice was breaking down again, but she'd already promised herself that she wouldn't go back to Astoria. She'd have to work on it herself.

"We'll find the paper trail. It won't be difficult," he said.

"Yeah, follow Bill. Where was he yesterday morning, anyway? Remember when he burst in on us all, Mr. Indignation? He didn't go to his office in the morning; I checked while you were tossing the basement."

"Yeah, I know. You're thinking that he came out here and took the files from the house, aren't you?"

April nodded. "And possibly some of the money. Maybe all of it, who knows?"

"You think Bernardino kept that much money in cash right here? We didn't find any signs of it."

"Yeah, but he was smart. I thought I knew him. Now I don't know. Where's his car? Did you check the trunk?"

"Crime Scene has it. And we're getting serial numbers of the bills Bernie had. He got money in thousands. If anyone starts spending, we'll know." Mike lifted his shoulder, answering April's unasked question. "We could get a warrant and search Bill's place."

"Well, sure. But he wouldn't put it in a closet, either. Did you talk to Chief Avise?"

"Twice. He told me to tread softly. He told *you* to stay out of trouble." Mike pointed a finger at her.

April gave him a Chinese blank expression that was full of meaning for anyone who knew how to read it. Mike shook his head.

"What about the funeral?" she asked.

"Working it." Mike shook his head some more and leaned close to her again. He kissed the side of her mouth and stroked her hair. "Don't get in any trouble between now and nine-thirty, okay? Promise me?" He gave her another look, then kissed her nose.

"Well, don't tell me to back off again. I can help you." April made an effort not to bristle.

"Play nice; be a team player, *querida*. Somebody knocks you off, I'll be the one in trouble."

"No one's going to knock me off. I want to talk to Bill."

"Not alone!" Mike shot back.

"Then come with me."

Moody, she stared out at that nice yard. She wanted to know what Bernardino had been up to. If it was just tax evasion, why would anyone kill him? Tax evasion was a national sport. There had to be something else. If Bill was innocent, she wanted to get him out of the way.

"Tomorrow. We'll talk about it." He brushed her lips one last time, tickling them with his mustache. Then he got out of the car. "Be a good girl," were his last words.

"Well, sure," she said.

But of course she didn't head home right away. How could she go home so early when she had things to do in Manhattan? She took the Saw Mill River Parkway to the Henry Hudson Parkway. At this hour all the traffic was coming out, and traveling was a pleasure. The route she followed brought back memories. As she crossed the toll bridge into Manhattan and drove south along the Hudson River, the old city views of the West Side reminded her of her years in the Two-oh when Mike had been her supervisor, always on the make. All his heavy breathing when they drove around together in the unit had driven her nuts. Why couldn't he just keep his mind on the job? she'd wondered back then. *Men!*

She smiled, remembering her irritation. *Shou zhu dai tu* was a Confucian saying: Change is the only constant. It was the primary incentive for a Chinese to hold his tongue. In police lingo the litany went, What goes around comes around. Just wait; things would change and maybe you'd get what you wanted. But lucky for April there were a few things that hadn't changed in her life. Mike's mind still strayed from the job to love whenever he was with her, even when the tight muscles in his neck betrayed the pressure.

Clearly someone high up was nervous about Bernardino. As long as the back story on his lottery money and his murder were a mystery, the Department didn't want to take the chance of giving him a hero's funeral. Politics was another thing that never changed. It was only the influence of the players that waxed and waned.

By seven-thirty P.M. she was driving east on Fourteenth Street, forming questions in her head for Jack Devereaux, the man who'd saved her life. She had not yet made a list of places where tae kwon do was taught, but it was on her to-do list. Mike had been right yesterday when he'd said she had a link with Bernardino's killer. But he didn't know that it was in the moves that almost killed her. The killer was a fan of unarmed combat.

People interested in the martial arts came in several categories. The shadow boxers, tai chi fans, did it to limber up and acquire balance. Some tae kwon do practitioners thought they could use it to protect themselves from muggers on the street. Others learned it as part of their military training and used a variety of fighting techniques: Thai boxing, karate, mix fight, Muay Thai, kata, and a whole bunch of others. All martial arts involved weight, core strength, and balance training along with spiritual elements as an aid to concentration. Many people who started training became obsessed with the fighting discipline of "empty hand" combat. April herself used to be one of them, working at it for hours a day from seven, eight years of age. She had been a girl child and a small one, and needed to even the odds against her. From long experience she knew the moves and the training it took to excel. She knew that those obsessed with mind and body control did a lot more than keep in shape, but no one she knew learned martial arts to kill the way a sniper kills.

She shook her head. She hadn't competed in this arena for a long time. She didn't have to even the odds anymore. She was in love and had mellowed. A person in love didn't need to live and breathe the mantra *"one punch, one kill."*

Full of remorse for faltering the one time her life was on the line, April told herself that the reason she'd been caught off guard was that she'd lost her edge. But the truth was that Bernardino's killer had to be a very strong man, an iron man. He had to be one of the obsessed. And he was probably younger, rather than older. Maybe someone around Bill's age. Bill was into karate, but if the killer wasn't Bill himself, maybe it was someone he knew or someone with whom he'd trained. Those guys tended to stick together. They needed someone to show off for. But why would Bill kill his own father for money when there was so much more on the come? It bothered her. The boldness of the hit and the possibility of a buddy thing. Who would be the buddy?

As the car moved through city traffic, April brooded again on the cop and former-cop theme. Even a crazy cop wouldn't thumb his nose at the Department so publicly. Too dangerous. An enemy would have followed him home and killed him on his quiet Westchester street, where a less experienced local law enforcement agency would investigate and never connect the dots. She felt certain that Bernardino hadn't been killed by a cop. But if it had been Bill, he would not have let him get home. She didn't like thinking dirty and switched to other possibilities.

She drove down University Place, thinking about it. University Place was a short street, only six blocks long. Where was the killer training? A search of all the martial-arts schools in the tristate area could take months. She peered out at storefronts, the cop's habit. She didn't remember a tae kwon do studio there, but the words were spread across three large windows on the second floor of an old building. The fourth window said *Tai Chi*. The fifth, *Aerobics*. Clearly the whole floor. Twelfth Street and University. She made a note of it, thinking she'd come back when she had an hour. Maybe she'd get lucky.

Then she concentrated on the geography of the area and found the brownstone where Devereaux lived on a busy block. She parked the car in front of a hydrant, too tired to worry much about getting a ticket. She was losing her steam and felt uneasy so near her old neighborhood and the site where Bernie had died. She decided to visit the spot before returning to Queens.

With this plan in mind, she rang the bell next to the name Devereaux and waited for what felt like a long time before a female voice answered.

"Who's there?"

"It's Sergeant Woo; can I come in for a few minutes?"

"A is in the front," was the reply.

A buzzer sounded, and April pushed the door open. Inside the foyer, the floor was worn stone, but the blue marbled wallpaper and runner on the stairs appeared to be of a more recent vintage. She followed the homey aroma of cooking chicken upstairs to the second floor and rang the bell of the front apartment.

The door opened on a chain.

"Sergeant Woo. I hope I'm not interrupting dinner," April said.

"Can I see your ID?"

April held her gold up to the opening.

"Sorry, we're a little paranoid these days." The girl who opened the door was short, not more than five-one, more cute than classically beautiful. She had chin-length almost-black hair, almond-shaped eyes a little like April's, and a nice apologetic smile.

April followed her into a small living room, where the girl suddenly broke into excited chatter.

"Jack, this is April Woo."

"What?" With a stunned expression, April's rescuer lumbered awkwardly to his feet from his place on a sofa in front of a TV. He was a regular-looking white guy, one of thousands of ordinary young people in the downtown crowd. Just under six feet tall, skinny, sand-colored hair, surprised blue eyes.

"Hi," April said a little uncertainly. "I'm sorry to bother you at dinnertime. I just came by to say thanks."

A chocolate lab with a mouthful of scary-looking

teeth closed the space between them to sniff and lick her while its fat tail lashed out at everything within reach. April made a point of patting its huge head only because she thought it would be impolite not to.

"You didn't have to do that." Jack took his time studying her, as if trying to match her with the barefoot girl in a party dress who'd stopped breathing in Washington Square two nights ago.

"Well, you saved my life. People don't do that every day." April stood there trying to smile, feeling like a jerk. She'd never had to thank someone for saving her life before. Well, only Mike. Now she thought she should have brought a gift. A big gift. Jack Devereaux didn't help her out. It was an awkward meeting.

"You look pretty messed up. How are you feeling?" she asked finally.

"Not too bad. I've never broken a bone before. This is my girlfriend, Lisa. This is Sheba." He introduced his dog. April concentrated on the girl.

"Pleasure to meet you. It smells like you're a great cook."

"Well, it sounds like you need what I made." Lisa laughed, happy under the praise. "Bronchitis?" she queried about the voice.

"Ah, it's on the mend." April downplayed the problem.

"Please sit down." Lisa patted the sofa, where a blanket bristled with itchy-looking dog hairs.

April avoided it by sitting in a nearby armchair that was too small for the beast.

"Would you like some Jewish penicillin?" Lisa offered.

"No, thanks. It's not an infection."

"Well, it's not real penicillin; it's just the soup. Very good for the chest, you know, the sinuses, the throat, and the fingernails. Practically everything. I know it's going to fix Jack's arm."

"Really?" April smiled. Another doctor.

"Absolutely. Would you like some?"

April hesitated, computing the time since she'd eaten Skinny Dragon's *jook*. Six and a half hours with only tea since then. Her voice felt and sounded horrible. She could use the soup.

"It would help, really. We were just going to have some, weren't we, Jack?" Lisa was pushing the soup hard.

"Oh. Yes, we definitely were." Jack flinched as the dog jumped up on the sofa and dropped its heavy head and shoulders into his lap, then added, "Don't worry; we have a lot," as Lisa disappeared to get it.

He rolled his eyes and changed the subject. "You don't look like a cop."

April heard this every day. She always wondered if people meant Chinese couldn't be cops, or women couldn't be cops, or just—how could she be a cop if she wasn't wearing a uniform? She always chose the last answer. "Detectives don't wear uniforms. I was hoping that you could fill me in on what happened that night."

"They've already asked me," Jack said vaguely.

April studied him. He was hardly huge—a young man not filled in yet, but he was taller than Bernardino. Definitely taller than she was.

"I'm sure they did, and I'm sure they will again. Sometimes new things come out. Right now I'm asking for me," she added.

"I was wondering how you lost your shoes," he said suddenly.

April didn't like the question. She'd taken off her shoes not only to run after the killer, but also to fight him. Really nuts.

"Let's do you first," she said. "What time did you go out with the dog?"

"No one asked me about Sheba. I always take her

out at eleven. We walk over to Washington Square and walk around the square a few times. She's a big girl. She needs her exercise." He patted the beast fondly.

April remembered hearing the sound of a chain leash when she exited the restaurant. She didn't think it was this dog but wanted to be sure. "What kind of leash do you use?"

Jack nodded at a doorknob across the room, which had a chain leash hanging on it. "She'd eat any other kind. Why do you ask?"

"The dining table is in use." Lisa returned with a large bowl of something that looked more like stew than soup. She put a spoon and paper napkin on the coffee table in front of April.

"Thanks, it looks great." April returned to her subject. "What route do you take?"

Jack looked surprised. "What route? We go downstairs and head straight to the square. We turn left and walk counterclockwise, north first, then east, then south."

"You did that Wednesday?"

"I always do it. I'm a creature of habit."

"You didn't walk down Thompson on Wednesday?"

"No, why do you ask?"

"Just trying to place everything. Did you see anything unusual?"

"Well, now that Giuliani is gone, the drug dealers are out again everywhere. Anything you want, and people are smoking right out in public."

April didn't tell him that the new mayor wasn't responsible for drugs being back on the streets. Priorities had changed after 9/11. Guarding against terrorists was number one now. She dipped her spoon in the soup and tasted it. Thicker than Chinese chicken soup, this version had rice and very thin spaghetti strings in it, carrot coins, celery chunks, chicken meat, and not even a hint of ginger.

Lisa sat down. "How do you like it?"

"It's really great," April told her. "Do you ever walk with anyone else?"

"I walk with him if I'm still awake," Lisa piped up.

"I mean other dog walkers."

"Oh, yeah. I know what you mean. Some people cruise with their dogs. They know each other and everything. I'm not part of that scene."

"You don't talk to anyone?"

"Just to say hello. The dogs know each other. I know some of the dog names, not the people."

April nodded. She didn't know the dog owners on their block because they always put Dim Sum out in the backyard. But Jack knew the local dogs. That was something. She took a moment to eat her soup and think about it.

"Do you know anybody with a mastiff?" she asked.

He rolled his eyes and didn't answer. "Who was the guy who died?" He couldn't balance the bowl with one hand but shook his head when Lisa tried to help him.

"He was a retired lieutenant from the Fifth Precinct. That's in Chinatown. My old boss," she added.

"Jesus. That's too bad. . . . The story is all over the TV."

"And you're pretty famous yourself," she said.

Jack shook his head. "The whole thing is weird."

April was curious, but she didn't want to embarrass him by asking about his father. "New Yorkers are supposed to run away from trouble," she said instead.

"Oh, that. Well, I didn't realize you were in trouble at first. I didn't see it. The fog was something. Why didn't you yell?"

Good question. The answer was, she didn't yell because she was fighting. You don't yell when you're fighting, only when you're losing. Then when you're yoked, you can't yell. She burned with shame. No wonder Chief Avise was angry at her. She would fire any cop who'd done the stupid things she'd done.

"Do you know anything about martial arts?" she asked.

Jack shook his head. "Only that it can kill you."

"Well, it isn't so easy to kill someone," April murmured. "How did you get out of it?"

"He flipped me, but I was screaming from the get-go. And Sheba got pretty loud. I don't think she would have bitten him, though."

"Can you remember anything about the man? How tall he was, what he was wearing? His face or hair. Anything?"

"He was shorter than me. He had to reach up."

"Five-eight, five-nine, five-ten?"

He shook his head. "You wear tea-rose perfume, right?"

"Yes." She was surprised that he could pinpoint her fragrance.

"He smelled of Icy Hot."

"What's that?"

"It's like Vick's VapoRub for the muscles. I think it has eucalyptus in it."

April ate more of her soup, considering that.

"Do you know Lieutenant Sanchez?"

She nodded cautiously.

"He told me a plainclothes cop is watching us."

"You're a witness."

"So are you; is someone watching you?"

April smiled. "I have a gun. What's worrying you?"

"A lot of things. We're getting phone calls. Hang-ups. And someone keeps saying 'Don't forget your promise.'"

"What promise?"

"I don't know. I didn't make any promises."

"Male voice?"

"Yes."

"Is it on your voice mail?"

Lisa glanced at Jack, then shook her head. "He doesn't leave messages, just hangs up."

April pushed her bowl away. "Did you tell Lieutenant Sanchez about this?"

Jack locked eyes with Lisa. "We didn't think it was a big thing."

"Do you have caller ID?"

"Of course."

"I'd like a list of the numbers of your incoming calls."

She took down all hundred of them. A large number of them were private callers. She thanked Lisa for the excellent soup. Then it was time to go home. She didn't want to overstay her welcome.

"Oh, one thing before I go. The person you know with a mastiff. Who is it?" she asked.

Jack laughed. "Oh, God. I wouldn't know a mastiff from a sheepdog."

Twenty-one

April's car hadn't been towed away yet, but there was a parking ticket on the windshield. She didn't even register annoyance. She was looking for a plain-clothes cop who might be surveiling Jack and Lisa. She didn't see anyone wearing the color of the day, the sign the Department used for plainclothes cops to recognize and avoid hassling each other on the job. Undercover cops in the subways, in housing projects, and the DEA especially needed it. An uneasy feeling shot through her as she left her car where it was and took Jack's route to Washington Square, a straight shot east.

The sky was night-dark now, but lights were on everywhere, and the streets of Greenwich Village were full of people, many with dogs. April had her eye out for a mastiff, she thought, that wore a chain leash. Jack had told her that he'd come east from Sixth Avenue and turned left at the square. He'd walked north, then east, then south. It was on his southern route that he'd encountered April fighting with a five-tenish man who smelled like Icy Hot. She vaguely remembered that she'd met the black dog going north on Thompson before they hit the square. As she walked the area, she figured they could do a house-to-house canvass of the neighborhood, to find the mastiff's owner, who must have walked by—and possibly seen—Bernardino's killer. Dog walkers often had a regular routine. They'd find him. But tonight April didn't have time to stay out until eleven to look for him. She'd promised that she would be a team player. All she could do was make suggestions. They could check vets in the area. It shouldn't be too hard.

As she walked Jack's route, she was aware of the pungent smell of marijuana, as strong as that of frying garlic from the restaurant on the corner of Fifth Avenue. Jack was right that people were smoking dope and dealing in the square again. She didn't go all the way around, after all. Instead she crossed in the middle and came to the place close to Washington Square South where she'd called out to the suspect. Her stomach clutched, and once again she felt the shame of messing up. It didn't matter if it had been foggy, if she'd eaten too much and had had a glass of wine. It had been stupid to play Wonder Woman, to throw off her shoes and run barefoot after a killer. Stupid. Double stupid.

But she knew what her instinct had been. In martial arts they always fought shoeless. Her legs and feet were very strong. Of course she would shed the high heels to be more effective in bare feet. It wouldn't go down well with her superiors, though. She shivered as her cell phone rang. She located the thing in the bottom of her purse and saw *private caller* pop up.

"Sergeant Woo." Her tired voice broke on her name.

"Hey, it's Marcus. You sound bad."

"Marcus. What's up?" April was glad to hear from him.

"I've been checking on some of Bernardino's old cases. You know those two guys you and the lieutenant collared eight years ago in that sweatshop fire? They got out last week. I just thought you'd want to know."

"Didn't they get fifteen?" April remembered the

case. A nasty one. Two owners of a run-down Chinatown building had been running a pocketbook sweatshop with a couple dozen illegal workers. They'd boarded the windows and locked all the exits so the employees couldn't wander in and out during the day. An angry ex-boyfriend of one of the workers had set the place on fire and killed five people on the top floor who'd been trapped inside. An unexpected consequence was the jury's decision to convict the two building owners for criminal negligence in the deaths.

"Yeah, white guys, they served eight," Marcus said.

"I remember them." April did remember them. Slimy guys, Ridley and Washburn had said they'd get even, but dozens of people who were put away said that. By the time the scum got out, they usually had other things on their minds. "Good going. Have you checked where the pair were on Wednesday night?"

"Well, it didn't have to be them. They could have hired someone," Marcus said. "But yeah, I'm all over it."

"Thanks for letting me know."

"How ya doin'? You sound like hell," Marcus said.

"I'm doing great. Keep in touch on it, will you?" April didn't feel like socializing.

"You bet." Marcus obediently rang off.

April turned back to where she'd left her car. Ridley and Washburn were jerks, but jerks who'd killed by accident because they were greedy. They were hardly karate experts, trained to kill in public places. As she faced west, the air behind her stirred in an uneasy shimmer from another dimension, predicting more trouble to come. Goose bumps rose on the back of her neck. She'd experienced the same sensation many times before, and much as she wished it were just a breeze picking up, she knew it wasn't a breeze. It was a chilly warning to watch her back. The ghosts and devils from Bernardino's past were coming alive.

Twenty-two

Friday night passed in an anxious haze of yin uncertainty. Together again by eleven P.M., Mike and April talked very little about the case and held each other tight all night, each hoping the other would get a few hours' rest from the case. By seven A.M. Saturday morning, however, April was up again, padding around in a T-shirt and bare feet. The twenty-second-floor, one-bedroom apartment they shared faced Manhattan in the west, and the first thing she did every morning ever since 9/11 was to reassure herself that the beloved skyline was still aligned the same as it had been the night before.

Today she opened the doors to the terrace, where the wisteria she had planted a year ago was now in abundant bloom. The flower sprays were her favorite color, huge and purple. They cascaded over the little trellis Mike had sunk into the pot for her. Neither she nor he had much interest in playing gardener, but the little time they'd spent on planting the cutting back then yielded a huge reward now. The magic of nature distracted her for a moment. She stepped outside into the chilly spring morning to smell her prize. Instantly the healing scabs tightened on her tender knees, and cold cement bit into her bare feet. She ignored the cold and leaned against the terrace railing to inhale the wisteria's sweet perfume. She was fully awake now, and despite her bruises and sore muscles, she felt clearheaded.

She gazed out at her wide view of the jewel Manhattan so tantalizingly etched against the sky. From across the East River in Queens, it always looked so tempting, like a magical city. But right now within the island's twenty-one miles Bernardino's killer might well be sleeping, eating, still walking around unchallenged. Then again, he might be somewhere else, far from their reach. Or the killer could be as close as a relative. It was too soon to know. Finally the cold got to her, and she went inside to put the kettle on.

As she waited for the water to boil, her brain began to gallop through the list. Bernardino was a retired cop, a Vietnam veteran, a father of two law-enforcement specialists, a recent widower, and the heir to a lottery fortune. Unconnected slivers of information bombarded her like parade confetti in a high wind. Where did the dots connect? She'd bet a year's salary the key to the murder was the fortune. But maybe it wasn't.

If she had to examine every aspect of Bernardino's life leading back the last few days, the last few weeks, the last few months, the last few years of his life to find where Bernardino had been headed and who had crossed his path before he got there, she would do it. Anything to release his soul for a happy afterlife. She moved to the sofa in the living room to start with the computer files that she'd copied into her laptop.

A decade ago, when April began working with Bernardino, he hadn't owned a computer, and neither had she. Then they'd done everything the old way. They'd taken notes by hand and banged out reports on manual typewriters. A couple of desks in the unit had been equipped with electric typewriters, but not the correcting kind. That had been back in the dark ages when they'd kept their files in boxes and stacked them up in corners because there weren't enough filing cabinets to contain them all.

When she'd copied Bernardino's files, April could

see that he hadn't been one of those older guys who hung onto carbon paper and Wite-Out and hated technology. Quite the contrary, Bernardino even had his PalmPilot hooked up to his Micron, so both his address book and schedule came up on his computer screen. April wasn't this meticulous. Her precious address book was a small fat loose-leaf that contained the phone numbers and addresses of nearly every person she'd ever used as a source, people from all over the country. She'd never gotten around to copying all of it. Periodically she'd forget where she'd left it and tailspin into a panic.

Bernardino was on the other end of the spectrum. He'd taken all the precautions. He also had Quicken, the accounting software that showed his deposits and itemized all his expenses. This degree of organization was initially surprising to her, because he'd always seemed like a sloppy kind of guy, not that disciplined. He'd eaten anything he fancied, didn't mind what hours he worked or who was inconvenienced by his schedule, and when he was investigating a case he'd been like an octopus. The tentacles of his mind had reached out in all directions.

Looking at his work more slowly now, April saw that organization had been his strong suit. His list of notes, detailing everyone he'd talked with and everywhere he'd gone every day, said it all. But the last three days of his life showed a change in this habit. Whatever activities he'd had, he hadn't recorded by this method. Or else someone had erased them.

She scrolled through his list of folders and found Jupiter, West Palm, Venice, Fort Myers, Bradenondon, Sarasota. West-coast-of-Florida cities. Opening them one by one, she saw that he'd been corresponding with real estate agents. The files contained dozens of photos of Mediterranean-style houses with exotic-shaped pools on canals and golf courses. The gorgeous-looking places listed at four, five, six hundred thousand dollars. That would be an unthinkable amount for Mike and April to spend, but much less than Bernardino could have afforded with his millions.

His correspondence with brokers showed that he'd been planning a trip to check out the towns and houses on his list. If his heart truly had been as broken as Marcus Beame had intimated to Mike, it certainly hadn't stopped him from planning his new life. April clicked to Quicken and scrolled through his checks. Not surprising, there had been a lot of medical bills. After the lottery money came in, he'd stopped playing the insurance game and simply started paying for private rooms for Lorna's hospital stays, for the lab tests, second opinions, private duty nurses. The list went on and on. The costs added up to such a large number that April began to wonder about Kathy again. Kathy was beginning to look way too naive for an FBI agent.

And then there was Lorna's funeral. Bernardino had put out some major bucks on that. April checked through to the funeral costs. Here was another surprise. Lorna had been cremated, an unusual thing for a Catholic. Another entry showed that Bernardino had bought a plot in a Queens cemetery. Calvary. But did Catholic churches accept cremated remains? She'd have to ask.

Another thing puzzled her. Would Bernie bury his wife up in Queens if he planned to sell the house and move away? The bank statements themselves were missing. This seemed inconsistent with his character, as did the mess in his house. It seemed highly likely that someone had erased at least some of the files they were looking for. But that was not a problem for a techie. The computer had been removed from the house. Their experts could find whatever had been in there. Crooks were often dumb. Their dumb moves always nailed them.

At ten past nine April heard the toilet flush, then the water in the sink run. A few minutes later Mike wandered in, shirtless and bleary-eyed, his face still wet from washing.

"You left me," he murmured. "Why couldn't you sleep in for once?" He came over to the couch and took her chin in his hand to review the bruises on her neck. He made no comment at the deep purple not yet beginning to yellow.

"I couldn't sleep."

"You sound bad. What are you doing for that?"

"*Te quiero,*" she said softly.

"Well, thanks. But that's not a response, froggy." He sat down beside her and followed her gaze to her computer screen. "What do we have here?"

"Bernardino's Quicken."

"You copied his files?" He looked impressed.

"When I went out there Thursday. Looks like some stuff is missing."

"I need a minute to wake up." He gave her a quick kiss and disappeared into the kitchen.

She heard the refrigerator door open and close, the coffeemaker percolate, the teakettle begin to sing. He returned four minutes later with a mug of coffee and a mug of tea. He was a nice guy.

"Thanks." She took the tea gratefully, put her face into the steam of her favorite brew. There was nothing in the world as wonderful as a useful man and a good cup of tea.

He drank his coffee thoughtfully, then got up for more. When he returned from the kitchen the second time, he was ready. "What have you got?"

She shook her head. "Nothing close to a clear picture of what was going on in Bernie's life. While Lorna was alive he paid her medical bills but made no other big purchases that are recorded here. It doesn't mean he didn't buy anything, though. The

Quicken software only has his Chase account recorded in it. He bought a cemetery plot in Queens, not here. He paid for a funeral. He was looking for a house in Florida. It's weird."

"What?"

"Just this little thing. Would you bury me up here if you were moving away?"

Mike snorted. "No, I'd take you with me in a little jar. Keep you in the car and drive you around with me." He combed his mustache with his fingers, laughing at the idea of April in a jar.

"Thanks. That's what I'm guessing. He had her cremated. He was taking her with him. I'll bet there was nothing buried in her plot. Just the marker. But why would he do that?"

"He probably didn't. There wasn't an urn in the house. What's your point?"

April sipped her delicious tea. "Just picking up strange vibes. Bernardino didn't mention any of this to me." She shrugged. Not that they'd been that close. She shook her head, sorry now that she hadn't asked a few more questions.

"What else?" Mike asked.

"He donated some money. Nothing big. I'm not all the way through it. A little here, a little there. If he hid big money in offshore banks or in Switzerland, those records aren't in here. And you didn't find any in the house. He was a fastidious guy. Where are they?"

Mike added a new point. "We located a bunch of files from old cases. It looks like he made copies of the ones that interested him."

"No kidding, which ones?" April was surprised. They weren't supposed to do that.

"We took about a dozen boxes of paper out of there. No recent bank stuff. You can take a look."

"I'd like to." She could probably guess which cases

from her time with him continued to niggle at him. But she returned to the money question. "Why move cash out of the country if he was relocating to Florida?"

"There's an explanation for everything. We've got Stevens working on the computer. He'll recover whatever was in it."

But that took time, a lot of time. April changed the subject again. "I went to see Jack Devereaux last night. His girlfriend gave me chicken soup."

"Always full of surprises. You didn't mention it."

April smiled. "I must have forgotten."

"Uh-huh. Did he give you anything?"

"Just that he had the impression the killer was shorter than him, and young."

"What about you? Has your memory come back with your voice?"

"No." She looked down at her hands. *"Lo siento,"* she said softly.

"Too bad." Mike's face remained neutral. He didn't say that sorry wasn't good enough. He leaned over and doodled on her bare thigh with one finger and didn't have to say what he was thinking now. April ignored it. There was going to be no love this morning. She felt terrible. How could she not remember almost dying? And they had work to do.

"Who's watching them?" she asked about Jack and Lisa.

"McBeel. He's good."

"Well, whoever he is, I didn't see him. If the killer thinks Jack got a look at him, he's at risk."

"I know," Mike said. "You, too."

"I carry a gun." April dismissed it. "Listen, this is important. Someone's been calling their house, bothering them."

"On what subject?" Now Mike was interested.

"Something about a promise."

"What kind of a promise?"

"Jack told me they have an unlisted number, so it has to be someone who knows them. So let's get started on the phone numbers right away."

"We're working Bernardino's phone, too. How about you? Anybody funny calling you?" he asked, draining the last of his coffee.

"No. You're unlisted." April finished her tea. "And Jack did remember one other thing. He told me the killer smelled like Icy Hot."

"What?" Mike let the mug clatter on the coffee table.

"It's like Tiger Balm, you know, that liniment for sore muscles. Watch that mug; it's going to go over."

Mike clapped his hands. "Oh, boy." He jumped up, almost knocking the mug over a second time. "Oh, boy. Get dressed. We're going to the labs."

"What about the viewing?" They'd planned to way-lay Bill Bernardino at the funeral home.

Mike brushed it aside. "When I talked to Gloss, he told me that Bernardino's body smelled like spearmint. So we've been looking for a chewing-gum connection. We checked his house, everywhere. We needed to nail that odor down, see how it fit. Way to go, *querida*!" He patted her shoulder.

"Why didn't you ask me? I could have told you that Bernardino didn't chew gum." Bernardino used to stick an unlit cigarette in his mouth and suck on the filter for hours at a time. A disgusting habit.

"Icy Hot is eucalyptus, camphor, that sort of smell. Spearmint is something else," she said slowly. She didn't want him distracted. He promised they'd take aim at Bill and Kathy at the viewing, try to get on the money trail.

"He's a medical examiner. His sniffer's probably all messed up," Mike said.

April lifted a shoulder. Bernardino's body smelled

of spearmint. The killer smelled of Icy Hot. Were they the same? She herself remembered camphor emanating from the skin of an old opponent over twenty years ago, when she was a little girl and regularly got slammed to the mat. That odor mixed with the intense feeling of shame at being knocked down again and again became her symbol of resolve: one punch, one kill. Memory of the karate mantra prickled the back of her neck.

"This may be our break," Mike urged.

"Okay." Even in the cleanest crime scene the killer nearly always left something of himself behind. It was worth a try. She took the mugs into the kitchen and dumped them in the sink, reminding herself to tell him they had to do a lot more to find that mastiff walker. And they had to start checking the dojos for people who liked to hurt. They had to get on it right away.

Twenty-three

They settled for April's aging white Chrysler Le Baron because the muffler of Mike's even more ancient red Camaro was making too much noise in the quiet Queens neighborhoods even for him. His pained surrender to the girlie car was not appeased even when she put the top down and insisted that he drive. Behind the wheel Mike looked like a movie star with his shiny black hair and dark sunglasses. They both needed new cars, but neither thought about it now. They were saving for a house of their own like Bernardino's in Westchester, also for a big wedding and maybe a baby. For months, on weekend days off they'd been house hunting. They were looking for just the right area, just the right place. But things came up, and lately they hadn't had the time they needed to finish the job. They didn't mention this lost weekend. The sun shone down on their heads and the air was sweet in their faces. They were detectives first. Murder took precedence over everything else.

April sat in the passenger seat, brooding about Bernardino's children. Her gut feeling was that Bill had taken, or been given, the missing money, and Kathy didn't know anything about it. The niggling certainty that the brother was cheating a trusting sister wouldn't go away. This kind of playing favorites happened in Chinese families, in Irish families, in Jewish families. In all families. Relatives ganged up against each other—and the IRS. Every time April thought of the way her own parents had tricked her into a thirty-year mortgage debt on their own house, her adrenaline spiked with rage. And she didn't even have a sibling to worry about. But was Bill a killer, too? Was he?

It was not a long trip from Forest Hills to Kew Gardens, where the state-of-the-art police labs were located in an unmarked brick building on the back side of a commercial street. At eleven on this balmy Saturday morning the facility that handled all the physical evidence from crimes in the five boroughs was not exactly abuzz with activity. Except for the CSU unit, which was open for business around the clock, it was always pretty quiet here on a weekend. These post-9/11 days, however, personnel was down to a skeleton crew. Retirement of specialists who hadn't yet been replaced had taken its toll.

April and Mike exchanged pleasantries with the sergeant on duty in the cage that kept people from wandering in and out with unauthorized materials. They submitted to a routine search, signed in, and were admitted. Inside, they threaded their way to the back of the building, where they knew Bernardino's car was in the loading bay.

"Anybody home?" Mike called out when they got there.

No answer, but the victim was a sorry sight. The late-model navy Ford Taurus was dirty and smudged from various fingerprinting and other tests. The trunk was open and the inside of it dismantled. The glove compartment was open and disassembled, too. The backseat was out of the car on the floor, and some car parts were missing altogether. Even the owner wouldn't have recognized his vehicle now.

The car had been parked several blocks away from the murder and was possibly unconnected to it, but it was being analyzed as part of the crime scene. Unfortunately, no one was around to enlighten them as to what clues, if any, it had given up.

Disappointed, April circled the wreck as if a visual tour alone could yield some useful information. "Let's go see if Duke is here."

"He's here," Mike said. "I called while you were in the shower."

She didn't say, "Thanks for sharing." She'd been afraid the trip was a waste of time. On their way back to the elevators they heard a familiar voice droning out a familiar lecture. They detoured down a long hallway to a classroom. There, Mike cracked open the door and saw Lieutenant Loeff of CSU doing his number with grisly crime-scene photos. He was challenging a roomful of people in plainclothes to guess how a bloody body in a kitchen told an exact story of how the victim had died. The audience could be anybody—uniforms who'd been promoted to detective, people from other agencies. A number of them turned around as Loeff pointed a finger at Mike.

"Yes, you over there. Thanks for stopping in. Catch you later."

Rebuked for interrupting, Mike nodded and closed the door.

"He's still using the same case," April remarked as they took the elevator up to Fernando Ducci's dust and fiber lab, with the million-dollar equipment that could help identify particles of just about anything except the wet stuff.

The elevator stopped and the doors slid open. Mike touched April's hand and they moved out. As they started down the wide deserted hall, a deep voice thundered out at them.

"Fee fi fo fum, I hear steps of the pretty one."

"Oh, Jesus," April muttered.

"Fee fi fo fum!" The disembodied voice came again, sounding like a cross between the Wizard of Oz and the giant in *Jack in the Beanstalk*.

April glanced at Mike. Fernando Ducci was not amusing even in small doses. He believed with complete certainty that he was at the very top of the food chain: the king of forensic magic, a true giant among men, maybe the most important man in the entire department. In fact he was small, shorter than April, and beefy from too many years of consuming half a dozen candy bars a day in addition to three sizable squares. Despite the weight, he was always dapper with his full, round choirboy cheeks, his fancy dress shirts in myriad combinations of blue and white, and his full head of slicked-down silver hair. If he wasn't already sixty, he was close to it.

"Pretty one, get in here and give me a kiss to brighten my day."

"What an asshole," Mike muttered. But pretty one smiled and shot back a response.

"Hey, Duke, stop that carrying on. You're going to ruin my reputation."

"You sound terrible. What's wrong with you?"

He didn't get up from his chair until she had passed through the outer room and was all the way into the inner sanctum. Then he was on his feet with open arms, blue-striped shirt with white collar, sleeves rolled up.

"Nothing catching." April crossed the space between them and gave him a quick hug.

"Is that all I get?" he complained. "Hey, Mike, thanks for stopping by." He thrust out a paw, and the two men shook.

"You're looking good, Duke. How's it going?"

"This is a terrible thing. Bernardino was a good man. What do you know?" Ducci tossed the hot potato right back.

"You first."

"Look, I don't know nothing. I get the clothes in a freaking box. Nobody says nothing about it. I have no death report. No briefing on what happened. What do you expect, miracles?" He lifted his arms with exaggerated exasperation.

"Absolutely. What do you have?"

He shrugged. "Not a lot. Dog hair mixed with the lint in his pants cuff. One grease spot and two coffee stains on his tie. Six grease spots on his jacket, shirt cuff, pants—right thigh. He must have been one messy eater. Or never changed his clothes.

"Let's see, oh, and a lipstick smudge on his shoulder. Might be yours, April. It's that Chinese red. I'm working on what kind. I think it's Revlon. His socks didn't match; that doesn't sound like him—"

"What kind of grease spots?" April interrupted.

"What happened to your manners, Pretty? I'm not finished." Ducci looked offended. "There's a long list here."

"We don't have a lot of time," Mike apologized for her.

"Bull-oney." He reached over and opened a drawer, then grabbed three Mars bars from the collection of candy bars stored in there. "Here, relax, have a snack. Didn't anybody tell you're going to have a stroke one day if you don't slow down?"

"Bernardino was my ràbbi," April said. "And red is out this season. Nowhere near my color." Especially with the purple dress she'd been wearing. But why was she arguing? Ducci was playing with himself. Bernardino hadn't been killed by a woman.

"Go on, take. I insist."

"Thanks." Mike palmed the candy bar, opened the wrapper, and bit in.

April frowned at him. Ducci stared at her until she relented.

"I'd prefer one of those," she said meekly, pointing to a Baby Ruth. She wasn't a fan of sugar but she was a sucker for those peanuts.

"Sure, sure. Whatever you want. Keep both, I have plenty. . . . Now, what do you want to know?"

"The grease stains. Where and what were they?" April watched Mike devour his Mars bar. Then she handed him hers. *There you go, piggy,* her face said.

"Marinara sauce on the underside right sleeve near the cuff of his shirt. Matching stain on the shirt cuff. He must have put his arm in it. Splatters of olive oil here and here." He touched his chest where his tie would have been, then lower down on the stomach.

"Tiramisu." Right shoulder. "Oil of spearmint." Left shoulder. *Ha ha.* He was making the sign of the cross.

"What about that oil of spearmint? Where did that come from?" Mike asked, deadpan.

"I'm still analyzing it. My guess is Tiger Liniment." April caught her breath as the long-winded explanation began.

Two hours later, April and Mike joined the large, sober group that had gathered around an open coffin in the white-painted colonial funeral home to which Bernardino's body had been released late Friday by the medical examiner's office. Many of the mourners looked like neighbors. Some were clearly cops with their spouses. It was always a tragedy when a cop was killed, but this group was still in mourning for Bernardino's wife, Lorna. Everyone who'd known Bernardino had expected him to remain a fixed figure in their firmament, a grumpy but steady friend, for years to come. There were some teary faces.

Kathy broke away from the family group as soon as she caught sight of April. She looked better today. She'd cleaned up for the company, was wearing a crisp white blouse under a dark gray suit that showed off her figure. Her hair was shiny and brushed, and her makeup had been carefully applied.

"Thanks for coming." She kissed Mike and April on both cheeks, very polite, then asked, "Are you working or paying your respects?"

"Half and half," Mike replied, already surveying the crowd.

"Well, thanks for helping out with the funeral. He would have appreciated it." She followed his eyes and helped him put names to faces. "A lot of Mom's family is here. That group is her sister's family." She pointed to an ancient woman with a stoical expression. "And that's her mother, my grandma.

"Dad's family is over there. His brother, nieces, and nephews. A lot of people are coming tomorrow. The cops you know." She turned to April. "How are you doing? Your voice better?"

"Much better," April croaked. She was watching Bill deal with a six- or seven-year-old girl who was hanging onto his leg. A cute kid. He was talking over her head and patting her on the shoulder at the same time. Kathy caught his eye. He detached from the child and stepped over.

"Thanks for coming up," he said, and then closed his mouth to discourage any further conversation.

"We need to talk," Mike told him.

Bill gave him a look. "How about later tonight? I'm busy now."

"Sorry, it can't wait."

Bill made an impatient noise and looked around for his wife, a pretty, worried-looking blond. Her eyes were already locked on his. He gave her a signal, then detached the child. "Okay. Let's go outside."

Mike and April followed him out of the room, out of the somber lobby, out of the building, and he didn't say a word until they hit the sunshine. Then he blinked as if he'd come into another world.

"Look, I'm sorry if I was rough on you the other day." He looked them straight in the face. Man-to-man. And woman.

"No problem," Mike said smoothly.

"Well, it is a problem. Somebody's causing trouble

for me. I've been put on leave from my office. You people are hounding me. It has to stop." He marched down the sidewalk so fast and furious that April almost had to skip to keep up.

Mike glanced at her, but all that showed was her stone face. All expression had gone to ground while she studied the subject.

"I was home by nine o'clock. My kids had the flu. They still do. Kitty has a fever. She should be home in bed right now. My wife has been questioned half a dozen times already. What do you want from us?" He stopped abruptly and let his body slump against a parked car.

"It's a complicated situation," Mike said, pulling on his mustache.

"What's complicated? My father was murdered at one of your parties. Why are you looking at me?" He addressed at April as he said it.

"You know why," she said softly. And he bit.

"Because I'm a black belt?" he said, exasperated.

"Hey, we're on your side," Mike interrupted. "We both are. No one's pulled a warrant on you. No one's brought you into the station. No one's searching your home. Come on, play ball. All we're trying to do is clear a few things up."

"Look, don't talk warrant to me, okay? I know what you're trying to do." Bill clenched his fists, trying not to lose it.

"Bill, we've had over a thousand calls to Crime Stoppers alone. That's a lot of tips. The street canvass has pulled in more leads than we can handle. Believe me, we're looking into every single one. But face it, this is no stranger murder; you know that. And we're going to find your dad's killer. You can take that to the bank."

Bill's eyes flickered at the bank reference. "No matter who it is?" he said challengingly.

"You bet," April said softly. "No matter who."

He turned to her as if she were an alien, not a longtime friend of his father's. "I don't know."

"Hey, if you want to get off the hook here, you're going to have to help." Mike prodded a little more.

"I was at home. I'm not on the hook," he responded angrily.

"Then let's talk money."

"I can't believe this." Bill pushed off the car.

"We're just looking for a motive here, and fifteen million is a lot of motive." Mike smoothed his mustache and smiled. "People kill for less. A lot less. For a dollar, a pair of sneakers. You prosecute them. You know."

Bill's jaw worked in tandem with his fists. He couldn't argue the facts. "I just can't believe this," he muttered angrily.

"What can't you believe?" Mike asked him softly.

"Don't you guys talk?" Bill demanded.

Mike shook his head. "Let's not get into politics here. I'm not asking what you told IA or anybody else. We're the primaries in this case, and for us the cash is a factor. A big factor. It may be missing, but it's not going away."

Bill was not an ugly bruiser like his dad. He was five-eleven, stocky, close to forty. He had a prosecutor's irritability in his stance, almost as if he carried a gun in his pocket. But his anger died away as he said, "I just don't know."

"What do you mean, you don't know? You don't know your dad had four million dollars in cash in his possession? Or you don't know where it is?"

"He got strange after Mom died."

That wasn't an answer. "What's strange, Bill?" Mike asked.

"He was distant, secretive." Bill looked away.

"How about sad? Would sad describe it?" April cut in.

"Did you go into the house Thursday morning?" Mike changed the subject.

Bill blinked. "You know I did. So what?"

Mike glanced at April. Now they did.

"What for?" she asked.

He didn't answer. "Maybe I should get a lawyer. Everyone says I should. I don't know what I'm waiting for."

"What did you go to the house for, Bill?"

He shook his head. "You guys are real shits; anybody ever tell you that?"

"Imagine that. We're the shits, and we're the ones on your side. Come on, what did you go to the house for—the files, the money. What?" April demanded. Her jaw was beginning to ache. A new pain.

"I went for Weenie," he said. His angry face erupted in a smile.

"Weenie?" Mike frowned.

"Oh, Jesus." April looked down at her feet. "Weenie was Bernardino's dog."

"I didn't see any sign of a dog," Mike said.

"Well, you don't see a lot of things." Bill snorted.

"What time did you go for the dog?" April asked.

Bill made some breathing noises. "I don't know. I remembered him sometime in the middle of the night. I went to get him early in the morning."

April considered the story for all of two seconds before rejecting it. "You know what it sounds like to me? Sounds to me like you got a lot of money from your dad, and maybe your sister didn't know about it." She watched his hands. He was a prosecutor, for God's sake. He knew how to tell a story.

"My sister was in California," he countered.

"Maybe she was going to get her share later." April gave him the benefit of the doubt.

"What are you saying? What are you implying here? It was Dad's money. He'd already paid taxes on it. Whatever he did with it was his business. Why can't you leave it at that?"

"Gee, Bill, we would have. But somebody killed him," April said flatly.

"I'd like to see Weenie," Mike said.

"Fine, toss my house. You're not going to find what you're looking for." His fist hit the car.

"How do you know what we're looking for?" April asked.

The prosecutor's face revealed that he'd been thinking money. He didn't know about the Tiger Liniment. For a change he was out of the loop. He didn't know what they were looking for. "Fuck you," he said softly.

Twenty-four

Marcus Beame called on Mike's cell phone at four-fifteen. "How ya doin'?" he asked.

Mike and April were in the Camaro, heading to Brooklyn to take a look at Weenie and collect some of his hair to see if they matched those Duke had found in Bernardino's cuff. Also to check on Bill's medicine cabinet and sports bag for muscle analgesics. They were supposed to be treading softly. If they tossed the house of an ADA while he was at his father's wake, they'd break every rule in the book. They'd been talking about it for the last hour. April was close to Kathy. That complicated things, too. Frankly, they needed a warrant or Bill's blessing, or both, to do the search, and April wanted to stay far, far away from it.

"Hey, Marcus. What's going on?" Mike asked, then put the cell on speakerphone so April could hear it.

"We're working about fifty tips down here, and we're not even on the task force. Everybody here is on it. How about you?" Marcus's voice was animated. It sounded as if the second whip in the Fifth Precinct had had a battery charge since they'd talked last. Maybe his hangover was gone.

"Same," Mike said.

"We've checked out Ridley and Washburn," he reported.

"Who?"

"April suggested we look at old cases. Those two went down for criminal negligence in five fire deaths back in—"

"Oh, yeah, I remember. What about them?"

"Bernardino handled the case. They just got out of the can last week and always said they'd get back at him. Is she with you?"

"Yes, Marcus, April is with me." Mike glanced at her. She didn't say anything.

"Well, tell her they've been in the Bahamas on vacation with their families since the day after they got out. We're still going with old cases, but we've got two people working the dojo angle."

Mike glanced at April again. "Who's on it?"

"A couple of guys in the unit are into it big-time—with the martial-arts magazines and the training equipment. The whole nine yards. They're taking the lead here."

"Were they at the party?"

"No, sir. They were working that night. I know the case they were working. I'm their supervisor."

"Names?"

"Wagner, Francis. Angelino, Fred. April knows them."

She shrugged and nodded. They were okay. "Hey, Marcus, tell them to check out where Bill Bernardino trains and who he spars with. Tell them to be discreet, okay?"

"Will do."

"And tell them you're looking for someone who has a reputation for hurting his opponents."

"You know something?" Marcus asked.

"There's always somebody like that. Maybe one of them went over the edge to see if he could get away with it. It's just a guess," April croaked.

"Good point. I'll tell them."

"Anything else?" Mike asked.

"Yeah, one other thing. Bernardino and his old partner had a falling-out last week. I didn't tell IA, but I thought you'd like to know."

"I do. Thanks. You got a name for him?" Mike asked.

"Harry Weinstein. Big talker, big with the horses. He's retired now."

April nodded again. She knew that.

"Oh, yeah. He was at the party. Tall guy, bald head, beard, yellow plaid jacket?"

"Yeah, that's the one."

"What's his story?" Mike asked.

"Oh, he's a gambler from way back, had some scheme he wanted Bernardino to go into with him. I don't know the details. I just know that Bernardino blew him off, and he was pissed about it."

"Has anybody interviewed him, Marcus?"

"I wouldn't know, Mike. The file's in the Sixth. I'm down here in the Fifth. We're working in the dark here."

"Well, we're not keeping any secrets on this case, and we need all the help we can get. Go over there and tell Peter Ashley you have my blessing. He'll give you whatever you need. Good to have you on the team. I won't forget it. And let me know what time Weinstein left the party and who interviewed him."

"Thanks, I will."

The call ended. "Looks like Marcus has had an attitude change," Mike said.

"Definitely looking for a way in," April agreed.

"Good for him. What do you know about Harry?"

April snorted. "A real loser. He used to come and bug Bernie for betting money, years ago. Two dollars, five dollars. Never won much, never paid anything back." After a stoical afternoon, April's features finally came alive as the lightbulb went off. Harry was a gambler, chronically in need of money, and his old partner had won the jackpot. Here was another recipe for trouble.

"Did you talk to him at the party?" Mike asked.

"Not me, I keep my distance there. I don't like him. I don't think Bernardino talked to him much, either. Who was he talking to?"

"I wasn't watching. The chief wanted to reminisce. You know how that is."

"No, I don't know how that is. He doesn't reminisce with me." April laughed without much mirth, and Mike changed the subject quickly.

"What about Harry as our killer?"

"He's a big man, and he's a loser. But Jack Devereaux and I didn't lose a fight with a sixty-year-old. I don't care what's wrong with my memory. That wouldn't be it. But he knows how to yoke, and maybe he has a friend."

"What put you into this buddy thing?"

"You always have a sparring friend, a kind of a coach," she murmured.

"No kidding." Mike swerved into the exit lane. "I'm thinking we shouldn't go to Brooklyn right now."

April opened the passenger window as relief flooded through her. Good—even if Bill was their killer, she didn't want to search the house of an old friend's son. The day was heating up as the BQE took them to the Brooklyn Bridge, which dragged them into the worst Chinatown traffic of the week. Then north to the Village, where things weren't any better. Mike finally pulled up in front of the Sixth Precinct, where they spent the next three hours reviewing the file and time lines with detectives there.

As in every case, there were pieces of information that weren't shared with everyone. Mike didn't share the medical examiner's remark about the odor of spearmint on Bernardino's body or Ducci's finding Tiger Liniment, which contained oil of spearmint as well as eucalyptus oil, on his jacket. Neither mentioned Jack Devereaux's memory of smelling Icy Hot—which contained some of the same ingredients, but not all of them—on the killer. And absolutely nothing about the yoking cause of death. These bits were not for general release. They didn't want the details leaked. April put the mastiff with the chain leash on the table to assign a dog-fancier detective to track his owner down.

The case was a big operation. The hacker was still working on Bernardino's computer down at headquarters. Crime Stoppers was still driving around Greenwich Village with the van, hoping someone would come forward. At the end of the day, something else emerged. A check of all the people who had tickets for the party revealed that Harry Weinstein had crashed. Nobody remembered what time he had left and nobody had bothered to interview him. As usual, he'd been freeloading, and as a freeloader, he'd been overlooked.

Twenty-five

On Sunday, four days after Bernardino's murder, the story dropped to the back of the Metro section of the *Times,* and Harry Weinstein could not be located at any of his usual haunts. He wasn't at home, or his local beer joint, or any of the racetracks in the area, Yonkers Raceway, Belmont, Suffolk, New Jersey. And he wasn't picking up his cell phone, either. At least he wasn't picking up for private callers. Harry was out in the wind.

Worked out of the Sixth Precinct, the Bernardino homicide was taking on that air of workmanlike organization that always settled in when a case was in for the long haul. Half a dozen major lines of investigation were being followed at the same time. Bank and brokerage canvasses searched for accounts. Neighborhood canvasses continued. The hacker in Bernardino's computer searched for the files that had been scrambled in its hard drive. Bernardino's military record had been obtained, and all the people he'd known back then were sifted through. The list of black-belt members and teachers in martial-arts schools, including the one Bill frequented, were scanned one by one. There seemed nothing unusual about him. He was a popular guy. The case file thickened with interviews that didn't go anywhere and tips that had to be checked out. One by one, people who had known and worked with Bernardino, his friends and associates, were being ruled out. There was still no luck with the dog.

Only a few members of the task force knew about the missing lottery millions, and they were told they'd lose their jobs if it leaked to the press, so it didn't come out. The lid was on the pot, but inside the water was on a hard boil. A deep probe was also prying into Bill Bernardino's personal and business life. And now, despite his size and age, Harry Weinstein was moving up the list of suspects. He had a motive.

On Sunday morning April called Bill and caught him just as he was leaving for the open house at the funeral home where his father's wake was still in progress in Westchester.

"I'm in a hurry. What's going on? Anything new?" he asked.

"Just following up on a few things," April told him. "Tell me about Harry."

Bill was silent for a moment. Then he said, "Harry who?"

"Harry Weinstein, your dad's old partner."

"Oh, Jesus, that crook. I haven't heard the bastard's name in years. Frankly, I was surprised that he showed his ugly face at Dad's party."

"He crashed," April said.

Bill blew air out of his mouth. "Cheap asshole."

"Yeah, well, what happened between them?"

"Christ, who remembers? Guy's a thief. He'd take money out of your back pocket while you're taking a piss. Anything, steal the shoes off your feet if you nod off. Dad gave up on him years ago. Why are you asking?"

"Just looking at everything, Bill."

"Jesus—Harry?" Bill sounded puzzled. Then he was silent for a long time, suddenly not in such a rush.

"What do you know, Bill?" April asked.

"Nothing. Not a thing. Look, I've got to go. You coming today?" He sounded almost hopeful.

"No." April wasn't superstitious or anything, but one viewing of a dead body was enough for her.

"How about the funeral tomorrow?" Bill was actually reaching for civility.

"I wouldn't miss it," she told him.

Later she tried Harry's home. His wife, Carol, answered the phone promptly.

"Mrs. Weinstein. It's Sergeant Woo. Harry isn't picking up his cell. Do you know where he is?"

She laughed. "Never. Harry could be in Florida, or out west, for all I know. People were out here this morning looking for him. What's going on?"

"What people?"

"Cops. Not anybody I know, though. What is it this time?"

Oh, so there were other times. "Didn't they tell you?" April asked, playing with the phone cord.

"No. It isn't about Bernardino, is it?"

"Yes, it's about Bernardino."

"Poor Bernie; he was such a *nice* guy." Carol's sympathy gushed out in a powerful Long Island accent.

"Yeah, he was. What time did Harry get home Wednesday night?"

"Oh, God, they already asked me this. Oh, I don't know when he came in. In time for breakfast Thursday, I think. Or maybe lunch. I don't remember. I told him first thing. Why are you asking this?"

"You told him about Bernardino?" April was surprised.

"Well, you know. Harry doesn't sit in front of the TV like I do. I always turn on the news first thing when I wake up to see if someone killed him in the night. Ha ha." She paused for a laugh but didn't get one from April.

"Harry, I meant. Not Bernie. See, I was shocked anyone would hurt Bernie. He was such a straight arrow, a real family man. Let me tell you, I can vouch for Harry. He didn't know a thing about it. Another cop was attacked at the same time; who was that?"

That would be me, April didn't inform her.

"What did you say your name was?" Carol asked.

"Sergeant Woo."

"Sounds familiar. Are you that famous Chinese?"

"I worked with Lieutenant Bernardino," April said smoothly.

"Well, it's a terrible thing. What do you want Harry for?"

"We're hoping that he can fill in some blanks for us about Bernardino's last few weeks."

"I wouldn't know where to look for him. I'm the last to know anything."

"Mrs. Weinstein, did Harry tell you when he was coming back?" April asked.

"No, he didn't even tell me he was leaving."

"Is that usual for him?"

"Well, he's been working pretty hard lately. We're moving to Florida, you know." She said this proudly.

"No kidding. I love Florida. Where are you going?" April wondered what Harry's hard work was, and if Bernardino's Florida files tied in somehow.

"Real soon. He could be there now, for all I know."

"When did your husband leave for Florida?"

"Friday or Saturday. I never said he went to Florida."

"Saturday was yesterday. Did he leave yesterday?" April persisted.

"Could be. The days all run together for me now. I'm in a holding pattern." She sounded as if she'd been in a holding pattern for some time.

"Look, when you hear from Harry, tell him I'd like to talk to him." April gave the woman her name and numbers.

"I'm sure he'll go to the funeral. He wouldn't miss that. Honey, you should do something for that cold," Carol added. "Your voice sounds terrible."

That Sunday was a quiet day for some people, but

nobody working the Bernardino case. After April's early calls from home, she felt well enough to start running again. Forest Hills wasn't as much fun as Astoria. Here the expressway cut through the neighborhood, and there weren't as many stores to look at, just blocks of brick apartment buildings and houses that she and Mike couldn't afford. For a little while she turned her mind off and let her body take care of itself. Mike had left early for the gym. It was a cool day, a beautiful day. She ran four miles. Mike returned about the same time as she. They showered together and fooled around just long enough to remind each other there was life after murder. Then they got dressed and drove into the city.

Mike went to the Sixth, where dozens of detectives were working overtime. April went to the tae kwon do studio on University Place. It was in an old building that smelled of ancient plaster, not unlike a police precinct. Up a steep and sagging staircase with green linoleum treads the door was open to more than one activity. Early Sunday afternoon had a step class going on in one room and ballet going on in another. Females mostly, in a variety of ages and shapes. It certainly didn't look as if this were the place a serious empty-hand fighter would come to bulk up or spar.

A skinny girl with a long rope of dark hair, a red bindi between her eyes, and a piercing in both eyebrows sat at the front desk. She was reading a book and seemed oblivious to the disparate music coming from opposite directions.

"I'm interested in tae kwon do," April told her. "How many members do you have?"

The girl gave her a blank look. "Gee, I couldn't give you a number. It's pretty busy. The classes are always filled."

"Do you have sessions every day?"

"I'll have to check the schedule." She riffled the pile of papers that covered her work space.

"How about advanced classes?"

The girl gave up the search. "Jooooe, need you," she called.

The sweet classical music ended and the ballet class broke up. The pop music in the step class thundered on. April turned to watch an overweight, middle-aged male with a jiggling tummy struggle with the moves.

"Well, hello. What can I do for you?" Joe was a buff male of the Dudley Doright school—six feet tall, a hundred and sixty pounds of solid muscle. His profile was godlike, his hair was blond, and his eyes were a striking azure. April preferred dark-haired men, but why quibble? He was grinning at her, and she felt the heat.

"I'm interested in martial arts," she said. "Do you have an active membership?"

"We have whatever you want. Would you like my credentials? A demonstration? Are you a beginner?"

April smiled. "No, I'd be interested in your advanced classes," she said. "How much practice can I get in?"

Joe nodded. "You want some juice or something? We could set something up for you."

"That would be nice. And I'd like a little background on the styles of all your best practitioners."

"You're really into it," he said.

"Oh, yes, I am. I'd like their names and addresses, too."

She stayed there for quite a while. She checked out what they had in the way of training equipment. They didn't have a lot. No scoreboard, either. It didn't look like a killer's playground, but you never knew. Joe was happy to talk about the personalities of his members and didn't have a class until four.

"Do you know anyone with a mastiff?" April asked her last question.

Joe laughed. "You do dogs, too?"

"Very funny."

After April identified herself as a detective, the girl with the bindi gave her the names and addresses of ten black belts. All of them lived in the neighborhood. None of them were women. Frank and Fred from the Fifth hadn't been there yet. Score one for April, but who was counting? She was out of there.

Twenty-six

On Monday morning Bernardino's funeral was covered by all the papers and TV stations in the area. With all the family secrets still in the freezer, the Department came through with a full police blowout, a bagpipe unit, the chief of police, chief of detectives and all—if not the actual police commissioner himself, who was with the mayor in DC on NYC business.

Four detectives from Bernardino's unit helped carry the coffin with his son and nephews. Some walked with the family, and some surreptitiously photographed every mourner in attendance. Nothing unusual about that. Investigators always photographed the crowds around crime scenes and funerals. Some killers became attached to their victims and returned again and again to relive their triumph. Others hung around to offer help. And a surprising number came to their victims' funerals to say a last good-bye.

Harry Weinstein's wife was right about his being sure to come to his old friend's funeral. April was the one to spot him at the cemetery. The same mustard-colored jacket he'd worn to Bernardino's retirement party stood out against a sea of gray headstones and the smaller throng of diehards wearing black and gray who'd taken the extra time to follow the hearse to Bernardino's final resting place in Queens right next to Lorna's brand-new mound that didn't have grass yet. Harry had missed the pomp and the eulogies up in Westchester, but was there to see his friend's coffin lowered into the ground.

April skirted the sad flock and caught up with him as he was sidling away. "Didn't you get my messages, Harry? I've been trying to reach you all weekend."

"Hey, April. How ya doin'?" Harry gave her a quick once-over the way cops do. Arrogant, checking things out.

"Not so great." April had a new trick. She could make her voice crack whenever she wanted to. She did it now.

"What's the matter with you? You got a cold or something?"

"Yeah, feels like someone tried to choke the life out of me. What about you? You hiding from something?"

His wide shoulders climbed up his neck. "I lost my cell. You know how it is. . . . What's on your mind? You're not on the case . . . ?" The question hung in the air as he gave her a sly smile that showed off big nicotine-stained teeth.

"Oh, I'm just trying to track a few things down for the family. Kathy and I go way back," she said.

"She's a good kid." Harry turned his head to stare out at the stalled traffic on the Long Island Expressway nearby.

April followed his gaze to nowhere. "What did you do after you left the retirement party?" she asked.

Harry's eyes snapped back to her in surprise, as if this were the very last question he expected to hear from her. "Me?"

"I'm talking to you, aren't I?" she rasped. Out of the corner of her eye she saw Mike approach.

"Hey, what's going on?" Harry looked at Mike, who nodded for April to continue whatever she'd been saying.

"Harry's been out of the loop. He doesn't know we're looking for a killer," she told him. "Funny, huh?" She scrutinized the old-timer and didn't make the introductions.

Harry was six-two, a hulking guy, slightly hunched over. He moved like a turtle, but bulk on an old cop could be deceiving. They were used to moving when they had to. Harry didn't smell of camphor or spearmint. He smelled like a bundle of very old clothes that had spent a century or two in a trunk full of cigar butts.

"I had some business out of town." Harry lifted one side of a long, untamed eyebrow at Mike. *Who are you?* it demanded.

"Lieutenant Sanchez, Homicide task force," Mike introduced himself without offering his hand.

Harry nodded, friendly. "Okay. I'll talk. But I'm hungry. Want to buy me lunch?"

Twenty minutes later they were sitting in a grungy pizza place in Elmont. Harry didn't want to go there, so he placed a defiant order of a meatball hero even though it wasn't on the menu. The waiter wrote it down without blinking. Mike ordered an everything pizza. April rolled her eyes because Mike refused to believe she didn't like cheese. She asked for hot tea.

"Red Rose is all we got. That okay?" the waiter asked.

She wrinkled her nose and nodded. All teas were not created equal.

When the ordering was done, Harry's shoulders relaxed a little and he leaned back in his metal chair. "I'm going to tell this to you, no one else, okay?"

Mike shook his head. It didn't work that way, and Harry knew it.

"Why are you looking at me like that? I loved the guy. I was the shlepper, never made more than detective third grade. Bernie made good. I would never hurt a hair on his ugly head. I worshiped him, okay? What do you got?"

"We got a few questions," Mike said.

"Okay, so ask." Then he started answering before Mike had time. "I came to the party. I wasn't feeling so good after all that heavy food. I didn't want to go home so I stayed in Manhattan with a friend, okay?"

"What friend?" Mike asked.

"This isn't for public consumption, so keep it quiet, okay?"

"What friend?" Mike raised his own eyebrows.

"Her name's Cherry. Hey, a little respect. Don't laugh; she's a business associate."

"What kind of business do you have with Cherry, Harry?" April coughed out the question through a bad case of the giggles and avoided Mike's eyes. Even so, she could see his shoulders shaking. Cherry and Harry. Everyone was going to have fun with this one. And poor Carol didn't have a clue.

"I'm in the horse-racing business." Harry stretched for some dignity and failed.

"Has Cherry got a number, Harry?" April asked.

"Look, she's a breeder, okay? This is completely legit."

"Cherry is a breeder? She's breeding for you?" This was another new one. Bernardino was gone and buried, and Mike and April were cracking up with the comic relief of Cherry breeding for Harry.

"Cut it out. She breeds thoroughbreds for racing."

"So what's your involvement with Cherry?" Mike couldn't help repeating the name and drawing out the two syllables into three.

"I've been looking at a horse. In fact, I bought one." He beamed with the pride of ownership.

"You bought a racehorse?" It took a second to digest this. April and Mike eyed each other, the laughter gone. "How much do thoroughbreds go for these days?" Mike asked.

Harry squinted, considering the question. "Not a lot, a few hundred thou. But we think he's promising. Warlord is his name." Harry's one long eyebrow did a dance. He was beginning to have some fun of his own.

"Harry, where did you get a few hundred thousand dollars for a horse called Warlord?" Mike inhaled on the absurdity.

"I got it from Bernie, God rest his soul." Harry crossed himself.

"Yeah," April cut in.

The pizza and meatball hero came. The hero was huge. Harry was in no hurry to wolf it down. For a suspect in the interview game there was pretty much only one trick: Keep mum on the important stuff, and nobody could do a thing about it. Detectives could bring a suspect in, keep him, let him go, then bring him in again. Fishing expeditions were annoying and time-consuming for a person being examined again and again but couldn't hurt anyone with the nerve to hold out. Lawyers could stop the questions, but only for a while. If cops had no secrets on a guy, no muscle in the form of jail-time threats to use against him, there wasn't a thing they could do short of beating him up to get him to give.

Harry Weinstein had been a cop for a long time. He didn't need a lawyer to help him obfuscate. Eight hours after Bernardino was finally laid to rest, he was still cruising for a bruising, completely comfortable with the situation. He was retired, on half pay for life. No one could fire him or put him in jail or hurt him in any way he cared about. He wasn't going to give.

After lunch Mike and April put him in the car and drove around for a while, taking turns hammering away at him. Then Chief Avise had a little chat with him downtown at headquarters. He didn't talk for the chief of detectives either, and didn't have to miss his bedtime. Everyone was tired. Around ten P.M. he went home wagging a tail he pretended not to see. He had an appointment to come back to the Sixth Precinct but didn't know it yet. His mood was high.

Twenty-seven

The next morning bright and early Harry had a surprise visit from two uniforms in a squad car, and got a free ride downtown to where April and Mike were waiting to do it all over again.

"You know we slept on your story and it's just plain disrespectful," Mike said. "You hurt our feelings."

"How so, my man?"

"We're not your man. We're your only hope here. You expect us to believe that Bernardino gave you a suitcase full of cash to buy a freaking horse? Come on." Mike had had a good night's rest and didn't give a shit how long it took to break Harry down.

"It's what happened, pally." Harry shrugged.

"No paperwork, nothing? What a friend!"

Harry shrugged some more.

"Listen, I heard different. I heard you and Bernardino were on the outs."

"Who said that? I never heard that." Harry feigned amazement.

"The way I heard it, he blew you off a long time ago, so what happened to change his mind?"

"What can I tell you? We went back a long way together. I gave him all the particulars on Warlord. He started slow, but he was picking up. A real beauty. It was a good deal."

"Who started slow? Bernardino or the horse?"

"The horse started slow. He was a late bloomer."

"So Bernardino gave you money for a slow horse. Why would he do that?"

"Bernie was like that, real heart-of-gold kind of guy. He believed in dreams. You know that about him, right?" He locked eyes with April.

"When did he fulfill your dream, Harry?" she asked.

Harry smiled. "I don't know, a couple of weeks ago. I don't remember what day."

"You can't remember getting a suitcase full of money. Can't remember when your dream came true. Come on." Mike laughed. "You're an insult to the field."

"Honest. I'm retired. I don't know one day from another."

But Mike knew they had a problem, and so did April. There was no mention of any meeting between Bernardino and Harry in Bernardino's daily calendar, and certainly no file on horses. Not any kind of horses. Bernardino had been a careful man. If he was going to spring for a racehorse, the odds were his files would be full of horse statistics, or spreadsheets—whatever they did with horses. But there was none of that. Bernie didn't have horse pinups in his file like his house pics. So many houses, all in different styles, different locations. Bernardino wouldn't purchase an item cold. He wasn't that kind of individual. Mike figured Bernie hadn't known about any horse. He changed tack and hammered the other subject.

"We need to talk to your girlfriend, Harry. Clear up a few things."

"Talk to her. Who's stopping you?" Harry lifted his shoulders, saw his hands fly up in front of his face, and took the opportunity to examine his nails. He could hardly control his grin. He was enjoying himself. No one could touch him.

"I would talk to her if I had a last name, a number," Mike said.

"I'm old. I forgot."

"Harry. Be easy on yourself. Give us a name. We're going to find her anyway. Down the road it's going to get nasty. You know how it is. If everything's on the up and up, nothing can hurt you. You got a gift horse. Okay we'll forget the gift tax. I give you my word. This is not about the money, you know that. Money . . ." Mike lifted his own shoulders and let the word trail off. "Money between friends. That's sacred. We won't touch it. Just give us the name." Mike glanced at April. She tapped her wrist. She was going out for a break.

"Mikey, I've been married forty-five years. Cherry's just a friend, but my wife is everything to me. You know how it is; I just can't do it."

Mike did know how it was. He'd hit a brick wall. But he had a method for finding people, and pretty much it always worked. "Yeah, pally, I do know how it is. See you later."

"Can I leave now?"

"What do you think?"

Mike and April left the interview room together. Mike called Marcus Beame on his cell. "I need you to find someone," he told him.

"No problem, Lieutenant, who?"

"Female known as Cherry. Breeds horses. I'd guess around fifty, maybe a little younger, maybe a little older, but not much. I don't have much more than that. She's a known associate of Harry Weinstein."

"Harry's girlfriend?" Marcus laughed.

"You got it."

"You got a place to start looking for Harry's Cherry?" Beame joked.

Mike clicked his tongue. "You know, he said he'd spent Wednesday night with her in the city, but I'm thinking she doesn't live here. Try upstate somewhere. Horse country. Nothing fancy, though. Harry's a lowlife."

"Okay. I can do that. Work back from Harry."

"You might try checking horse-breeding records, too. I think thoroughbreds are registered with the racing association—I don't know, some association. Cherry's got a horse called Warlord. See if she sold it to anyone."

"Anything else, sir?"

"That's it. And I don't want to know how you do it—whatever you have to do, just get her in here."

"Do I have twenty-four hours, boss?"

Mike checked his watch. "Yeah, sure. Before noon tomorrow would be real good."

April met him on the stairs a few minutes later. He was on his way to the men's room. "Something odd has come up."

"Oh, yeah."

"The same number came up on both Bernardino's and Jack Devereaux's caller ID list."

Mike frowned. "What does that mean?"

"Beats me," she said.

Twenty-eight

Jack Devereaux was an angry man. The press and the cops had made him a prisoner in his own home. He was stuck on the sofa with his sweetheart plying him with food he didn't want to eat, antsy as hell. He wanted to go out to eat. He wanted to walk, and he wanted out of where he was. His bruises were healing, and his broken arm itched. He was beginning to think of fleeing but felt he was too famous to move. It was not a good situation.

His father had left him a town house on Sutton Place, and another house in California. Both had heavy security, but he resisted moving into a world from which he'd been excluded for so long. To be sure the Manhattan house was amazing. The classic four-story brick building on Fifty-seventh Street had been gutted and redesigned for a contemporary sensibility. The rooms flowed one into another and even from one floor to another. Staircases seemed to be suspended on air.

He and Lisa had visited there exactly once. Lisa had been intrigued by the huge kitchen, the mirrored ceiling in the master bedroom, the terrace on the East River, and also by the obscenely large master bathroom. The bathroom took up half a floor and was tiled in three different colors of marble. The shower had no walls. The Jacuzzi was a custom design; its faucets looked like real gold. The attention to detail in the house was so opposite to the lack of attention paid to him that Jack reacted to the tour by vomiting in his late father's powder room toilet. He hadn't gone back. But now the idea of having resources was beginning to jell. He wanted some of that money so he could hide.

But it wasn't so easy. He couldn't exactly get a billion-dollar check and suddenly become the head of a giant corporation. It didn't work like that. There were little things like procedures, probate. Everything took time. He knew that from when his mom had died. In a huge estate like this, the feeding frenzy among the lawyers would drag it all out. Probate hadn't been filed yet, but Jack had been informed that he could take his trusteeship in the company foundation immediately. He could also request a deposit or something, a few mil to tide him over until the estate was settled. Since his visit to the hospital, he was getting calls from his new "friends," the lawyers at the firm of Gibson, Frank, and Field urging him to get out of town, and he wanted to go. But he was resistant to leaving the only life he'd ever known. He didn't want to lose himself.

On Monday after the murdered cop's funeral, he was wavering. On Tuesday when he got an early-morning call from Al Frayme, he still hadn't moved. Lisa wasn't quitting her job anytime soon. She was back at work, and he was alone again, bummed out, glad to get a friendly call.

"What's up, Al?"

"How are you holding up? We're worried about you," Al said. "Anything we can do?"

"Thanks, but as I told you Friday, there's nothing to worry about. I'm fine."

"Good. Then business. You're not going to let me down next week, are you?"

"About what? You know I can't do gifts yet."

"No, no, nothing like that. You're speaking at the reunion, remember? You're going to be okay for that, aren't you?"

"Oh, yeah. With all this I forgot about it. Gee, I'm not sure. I might have a conflict out of town next week." Speaking on any subject was the last thing in the world he wanted to do now. No way.

"Oh, God, don't welsh on me. I'm counting on you."

"Look, Al, what can I say? I got hurt last week. I just don't know if I'm up for it."

"But it's so fucking impressive. Everyone is dying to hear about it. What a New York story. Saving a cop, fighting off a killer . . . it's amazing."

"Oh, I really did a job on him," Jack said bitterly.

"Oh, come on, don't be so modest. I heard you hurt him bad."

"It's all a crock. I didn't get anywhere near him."

"Not what my sources say. We're going to write you up in the magazine. Billionaire alum, New York hero. What kind of Good Samaritan story is that?"

"It's great, but I'm not interested."

"Oh, come on, it would be so good for both of us."

"Al, I'm spooked, okay? I'm not interested in being described as a hero when there's a killer out there."

"I'm sure he doesn't read the alumni magazine."

"Very funny."

"Come on, lighten up. People like you are exactly what the university desperately needs. Don't let us down."

"Not right now, okay, Al?"

"What can I do to change your mind? How about a limo for the event?"

"I'm only a few blocks away. I could walk. That's not the issue." Jack was trying hard to be nice.

"Then what's the issue?"

"I told you I'm nervous. Call me a wimp, whatever.

I don't want to do the event. It's not safe." Jack gazed out at the reporters downstairs. He had a lot of trouble going out.

"The university could protect you, I promise."

"Don't make promises. That's not the issue."

"What's the issue, Jack? You're one of us. I want you to know we're here for you. It matters to us that you're happy, feeling secure. The president, everybody. We want you happy. We can keep you safe."

"Well, tell everybody I'm happy, but I have another call coming in." Jack cut him off. He didn't want to hear any more people telling him how important he suddenly had become. He wasn't doing the reunion, period.

His call waiting kicked in.

"Hi, it's April Woo."

"Oh, hello." That was all he could manage even for her.

"Listen, can you come in today? I need you to look at somebody."

"Who?" Then he got excited. Maybe it was over.

"A guy." The pretty cop was noncommittal.

"Look, I'm under siege here. Is this for real?"

"What's going on?"

"The reporters won't go away. Don't these guys have anything else to do?"

"Everybody's trying to flush you out of your little pond into the big sea where you belong. You're the only guy in the world who prefers a walk-up to the Ritz. And you're a hero. It's all news. Do you want me to send a car for you?"

He wasn't a hero, but everybody wanted to send a car for him. Why wasn't he impressed?

"Well, it would be nice to get there without a confrontation in front of the building," he murmured. On the other hand, it wouldn't be so nice to see a clip of himself getting into a squad car on the evening news.

The detective read his mind. "How about an un-marked car?" she said.

"That would be great. Do you have the man who attacked you? If you had him, it would be a huge relief."

"Yeah, for all of us. The whole city. A car will be there in ten minutes, maybe eleven if the traffic is bad. Officer Maureen Perry will be your driver."

Seven minutes later a black Buick pulled up in front of his door building. The driver was a blond woman in uniform. The uniform blew his cover.

"Good morning, sir," she said, a little surprised when he charged out of the building, dove into the front seat next to her, and slammed the door. After that she didn't say a word, only nodded when he got out and thanked her for the ride.

As he headed into the Sixth Precinct his arm itched badly in its cast, and he had the feeling of rage that had been flashing on and off in him like painful power surges ever since his father died and stole his identity. Now absent fathers and murderers were all mixed up in his mind. Maybe the absent father was the murderer. All he wanted was to be normal again—to watch the Yankees battle the Mets, to make love to Lisa, to build his little business his own way. Normal.

Instead he couldn't get out of being an item on the news. His photo, inset next to a larger one of his father, had been on the cover of *Time* magazine two weeks ago. He was followed around by reporters. Yesterday the cop's funeral had dredged it up again. And now he was in the center of a murder investigation. Every talk-show host wanted him on TV talking about it. He didn't see how rich was good. It got him into this, but it couldn't get him out.

Inside the precinct, the desk lieutenant gave him a quick glance and knew right away who he was. "Mr. Devereaux?"

"Yes."

"They're waiting for you upstairs. First door."

Jack found the stairs and took them two at a time. There was nothing wrong with his legs, and he was in a hurry to see who was in custody. At the top of the stairs the door to the detective unit was open and people were spilling out. With them came a cloud of cigarette smoke. So much for the law against smoking in government buildings.

"I'm looking for Sergeant Woo," he told a skinny man with a pencil mustache and a gun at his waist who was sitting on the first desk with his cell phone pressed against his ear.

"You can wait in here." The man got up and led him through a maze of detectives and desks to a room with a window. The blind on the window was up, and April Woo was in the room beyond. He could hear her talking with a man who was definitely not the person who'd attacked him. He was too big, too fat, and too old. Jack sat down, disheartened. He'd hoped it would be over.

After a few minutes Mike Sanchez came into the room and shut the door behind him. "Thanks for coming in," he said. "How are you doing?"

"I'm okay. It's not him."

"Are you sure he doesn't look familiar to you at all?"

Jack's memory of Wednesday night had jelled solid. It didn't vary with the time of day, and he didn't have to study the man sitting at the table in the other room to know he wasn't the one. The man he'd seen gripping April in the fog had been catlike, a dancer. The man in the room with her now had a soft belly that doubled over his belt. He was a bear with big flat feet and fingers like sausages. A bear crushes with his weight. Jack touched the cast on his arm. The man who'd attacked him had not been a bear. Not a polar bear nor a grizzly bear. He'd been snake thin, snake quick, and snake agile. Too fast to grab hold of. He shook his head.

"Are you sure?"

"I'm dead sure. Who is he?"

"Someone who borrowed a lot of money from the deceased."

Jack shifted his attention to Sanchez. "Why do you call him the deceased?" he asked.

"Sorry. No disrespect intended."

At that moment, a large woman in a red jacket went into the interview room and whispered in April Woo's ear. She got up and left. A few minutes later she joined them and nodded at Jack.

"Thanks for coming. The traffic wasn't bad?"

Small talk. "No, not bad. Thanks for the ride," Jack told her, smiling a little because she was so pretty, and pretty in a cop still surprised him. Call it male chauvinism. Sanchez was what he would expect. Sergeant Woo was something else. She acknowledged his smile with a little one of her own. She knew.

"How are you doing?" she asked.

"I'm doing okay."

"Good. How about our pal in there?" The smile disappeared, and the sergeant's face went blank. It was kind of eerie the way she wiped it clean.

Jack glanced at Mike, then shook his head. "You know it wasn't him," he said, studying her flat expression.

She shrugged and repeated her question. "How are you doing?"

"You already asked me that. What's going on?" Jack frowned.

"Well, the case is coming together." The detective sat down and took out a notebook and a pen.

Something about the way they were acting made him nervous. Sanchez sat down and took out a similar black-and-white speckled notebook. Now they were all sitting at the table. The notebooks were out. Jack had no idea what was happening, whether it was good or bad. His viable hand began to tremble. He wasn't doing well.

Woo turned some pages, checking her notes, then looked up. "Last Friday when I visited you, you told me someone was calling you, someone whose voice and phone number you didn't know. Have you had any more of those calls?"

He exhaled and realized that he had been holding his breath. "No. No. That situation seems to have resolved itself. Why do you ask?"

"Something odd came up this morning. I want to run this by you." That flat look was so unsettling.

"What?"

"There was a match between a number on the victim's caller ID list and yours."

Jack's heart jumped like a fish on a chopping block. Now Bernardino was the victim. "What does that mean?" he said softly.

"It means there might be a link between you and the killer."

"What do you mean, *might be* a link?" The air in the room was so heavy Jack felt as though he were breathing through a thick wad of cotton. How could he know a killer?

"It could be a coincidence, but we always work on the premise that there are no coincidences in police work." She said this with no expression.

"Whose number is it?" he asked in a small voice.

"It's a number in the York U phone system. Do you know anyone at York?"

Jack inhaled, taking a moment to digest the question. "Well, sure. I'm an alum. I know lots of people there. Al Frayme, in the development office, Wendy Vivendi, the vice president. I know the president, too,

Dr. Warmsley. Marty Baldwin. Some of my professors are friends now. Professor Callum is on the board of my company," he said slowly. "All kinds of people have my number. It's in the donor data bank. I get calls all the time. Whose number is it?"

"The number comes from the School of Social Work."

"The School of Social Work?" Jack placed it near Washington Square. He passed by the building every night on his walk with Sheba. But not since the incident. Now, because of the reporters, they had a dog walker taking Sheba out. He shivered at the way the two cops were looking at him.

"Do you know anybody in the social work school?" Woo's pen was poised for the answer.

"No, not a soul. Whose phone is it?"

"Dr. Foster."

Jack shook his head. "I've never heard of him."

"It's a woman. She's a professor, and she's been out of the country for several weeks. Ring a bell?"

Jack shivered again. "No."

Woo glanced at Sanchez. "We'll need a list of everyone you've been in contact with at the university, everyone you know. That okay with you?" he said.

Jack nodded. "Of course, but I have a question—is it all right to ask? What was the connection to the . . . deceased?" His tongue faltered over the word. He hadn't been on the block where Bernardino had died. He didn't know him. How could there be a connection between him and a murder victim? Lisa would be terrified. Sheba wouldn't like it, either. His arm started to throb for the first time since the weekend. And April Woo was busy taking notes. She didn't answer the question.

"The connection is just the fact that I was there when it happened, right?" Jack said, figuring that the murderer got in touch after he saw him on the news.

People who appeared on the news were at risk; he'd known that from the get-go.

"No, the number on your phone predates the murder," she said. Matter-of-fact.

His eyes widened as he tried to absorb the possibility that a murderer knew him and maybe he knew a murderer. The detectives let it sink in, and he wondered how long they'd known. It was an eerie sensation, more than eerie. As he flushed under the unfamiliar feeling of real fear, his eye strayed to the man behind the viewing window. The man who looked like a bear was getting restless. He was tapping his huge feet, eager to get out of there. Jack wanted to flee, too. He glanced back at Woo and Sanchez. Their faces didn't tell him a thing.

Twenty-nine

Late Tuesday afternoon Bill Bernardino bowed under heavy pressure and finally agreed to allow a search of his house and car without a warrant because he didn't want the media attention that the serving of a search warrant would bring on him and his family. The Department had given his father a good send-off. He owed them. Mike and two detectives proceeded to his home in Brooklyn, where they took the spacious family house apart as neatly as possible.

The three men did the search with a minimum of fuss and conversation, and Mike was the one to come across Bill's workout bag and sweaty gym clothes from which a strong odor of camphor and spearmint emanated. When he searched the inside pocket, he found a half-used bottle of Tiger Liniment. He seized it and a second bottle of Tiger Liniment, this one unopened, that Bill had stored in his medicine cabinet. Mike showed no reaction whatsoever to either of the other two detectives or to Bill about his find. But he was excited. They were a step closer.

Of all analgesics for muscle pain, Tiger Liniment was about the messiest. It was packaged in little bronze-colored glass bottles for an old-fashioned look, and some of it had spilled out into Bill's gym bag. The oil seemed an unusual choice for a no-nonsense kind of guy like Bill. As Ducci had pointed out on Saturday when they visited him in the lab, the newer patches with some of the same ingredients were easier to use and just as readily available. There wasn't a huge market for this.

Bill watched them packing up the contents of his medicine cabinet with a puzzled expression but didn't say a word. They dumped his gym bag and unwashed workout clothes in a carton. Not a word. He started protesting when his laptop computer full of files on the cases he'd been working for the DA's office was removed from the house. Then, practically frothing at the mouth, he called the office from which he had been suspended to see what could be done about it. The answer came back—nothing. His boss was furious because he hadn't thought to cleanse the computer before he left.

Thirty

Tuesday afternoon while Mike was in Brooklyn nailing Bill, April played it safe and followed up on the phone call to Jack Devereaux from York U. It was a halfhearted effort. She didn't expect much when she paid a visit to the brick building that housed the York University School of Social Work. It was a former mansion just off Washington Square with a center hall and a lounge on one side, offices and classrooms on the other side. In the middle was a tall staircase leading to the second and third floors. Professor Foster's office was at the top of the stairs, first door on the left, where anybody could walk right in if the door were left open. But the door was always locked and Foster was away for the semester, so she was told.

April met with the dean in her office to discuss the matter of the telephones and the locked door. Diane Crease was a tall woman who looked a lot like the first female attorney general of the United States. A string bean with a pleasant expression, Dr. Crease wore no makeup, had short, wavy, graying hair, and was wearing a springy pink-and-black tweed suit. On one lapel was a stiff pink plastic rose with a black center.

"What is this about, Sergeant Woo?" she asked, careful to see that the door was shut before she spoke.

"I'm investigating the homicide near the university last week," April told her.

"Ah, yes." The dean's eyes flickered. "Yes, I remember. A police officer, I believe. How can I be of assistance to you?" She stayed smack in the middle of her office, far from the safety of her desk.

"We're trying to follow up on a phone call that was made from Professor Foster's office to the murder victim." April was tired. Out of loyalty to the family, she hadn't wanted to be involved with Mike's search of Bill's house. But this scut work of looking for some phone caller was hardly a satisfying alternative. She coughed to clear her dry throat.

"Oh, my." The dean came to life with the cough. She turned her back on April to circle her desk for the carafe of water sitting on the credenza behind it. She poured out a glass and passed it to April. Then she sat down and gestured for April to do the same.

"Thanks." April swallowed gratefully and sat.

"This is very strange. Are you sure it was Dr. Foster's phone? She's been out of the country for several weeks. It couldn't be her. But I know she would be happy to talk with you when she returns."

"Who has access to her office?"

The dean leaned back in her desk chair. "I have no idea. I doubt if she would allow access to any of her students. But possibly her assistant might have a key."

"Who is her assistant?"

"I believe it's Margaret Eng. Dr. Foster's voice mail would have the contact number. Did you try it?"

"Yes, she didn't call me back."

"Well, she may have left for her internship. Classes are over for the term."

"Would the maintenance staff be able to get in?"

"Oh, of course they would." Dr. Crease frowned.

"I'll need a list of names," April told her.

"I can get that. We could also give you a list of classes and events that were taking place in the building on the day in question. Other people from the university do come into the building for meetings and talks and such. What day are you looking at? One day or more than one?"

"Only the tenth of this month."

"Okay. I'll check."

"If you have a record of repairs made in the building, that kind of thing would be useful, too."

The dean nodded. "I'll have my secretary work on this for you. But, you know, those locks are not very secure. Anyone could get in. There have been thefts in the offices in the past. But nothing serious." The dean was finished. April thanked her and gave her a card with her numbers on it.

Later she was not gratified at all to find out that her instinct about Bill had been correct, and he was their killer. When they met back at the Sixth, the noisy strategy meeting for the next step went on for hours. They had a lot more work to do on Bill to make a solid case, many more answers to get. With dozens of people involved and many voices coming from the top, the conversation went on a long time. April and Mike didn't get to bed until late.

Wednesday morning Beame called the apartment before seven. "I have her in less than twenty-four," he said. "Do I get the brass ring?"

"Cherry Packer, good for you. Bring her in," Mike said sleepily. Here was a loose end that had to be tied up. For sure Harry was involved somehow. Bernardino had given him all that money, or he had stolen it. Mike wasn't going to let that go.

Thirty-one

At eight-fifteen Cherry Packer was full of bile, and Mike was there for her dramatic display of pique.

"Just wait a little minute, will you? What's your freaking hurry?" She parked herself in the interview room of the Sixth Precinct, pulled a bunch of cosmetics out of her purse, then calmly began putting on her makeup in the mirrored viewing window as if this were something she did all the time.

"Drag a lady out of her home before she's put together," she grumbled, casting a furious glance at Marcus, who sat next to her at the table. "What's your problem?"

Marcus twiddled his thumbs and paid no attention, so she turned to Mike. "He pulled a freaking gun on me. I should put in a complaint on him. Police brutality. Your name's Beame, right?"

Marcus snorted comfortably.

Mike smiled at her. "You look great. A woman like you doesn't need makeup. I'm sorry you were inconvenienced."

"That's putting it mildly."

"We appreciate your coming in," Mike tried to soothe her.

"Fuck you." Cherry eyed him from top to toe. "You're a nice-looking guy. What's *your* problem?"

Mike straightened his tie. It was one of his many silver ones. He wore it over a dark gray shirt. Over that was a black-and-white tweed sports jacket. On his feet he had new black snakeskin cowboy boots. April preferred colors, but he liked a jazzed-up black-and-gray look. "My problem is I got a dead person to take care of," he said. "And that dead person is your boyfriend's ex-partner."

"Jesus. That's not *my* fault." She squirmed a little in her chair as if her pants were too tight, then made a big show of putting her makeup back in her purse.

She was quite a sight, pretty much what Mike would have expected in a girlfriend of Harry's. Cherry was a big blowsy blond with a bad haircut and a terrible dye job. She was built like a brick from shoulder to hip, with a shelf of bosom in front like two pillows on a four-poster bed, but her legs were as long and trim as those of the colts she supposedly trained. She definitely made an impression.

"Mrs. Packer, what is your relationship with Harry Weinstein?" Mike asked.

"He's a business associate." She pulled herself together on an expected question, extracted a pack of Marlboros out of her purse, and held it up. "Do you mind if I smoke?"

"Yes. Do you always sleep with your business associates?"

She dropped the cigarettes on the table. "Look, don't make a big deal out of this. I've known Harry for a long time, like fifteen years, okay? Totally on the up and up. He helped me out when my husband died."

"How?"

Cherry's crumbling was a subtle thing, like a fault line in the earth that doesn't show on the outside until the earthquake strikes. She was not as tough as she looked. She put the cigarettes away and dug around in her purse for her glasses. When she could see, she made a horrified face. "What's that?"

"Video camera," Mike told her.

"Is it on?" she demanded.

"No."

"Are you sure?" She regarded it suspiciously.

"Yeah. How did Harry help you?"

"It's a long, boring story." She took the glasses off and twirled them around her finger.

"Well, I got time." Mike checked his watch. "Let's hear it."

"Fine. My husband had gambling debts. He got in some trouble. You know . . ." She jerked her head toward the ceiling, as if the trouble were up there.

"He got beat up." Mike finished her sentence.

She nodded, clamping teeth onto her bottom lip. "Harry's been a good friend."

"How did you meet him?"

"We met at the track. Saratoga." A little smile came to her face. "We used to run a lot of horses up there. . . . We had a good business." She lifted a shoulder. "You know how it goes."

"No, how does it go?"

"Things change," she said wearily.

Mike guessed her husband had his weaknesses. Gambling and drinking kind of went together. "So how did Harry help you?"

Up came the shoulder again. Cherry heaved a sigh, deep into nostalgia. "He talked to the guys. He fixed it for us." Clearly she was proud to have a friend who could do that.

"The guys who beat Bobby? Or the guys he owed money to?"

Cherry looked surprised that he knew her husband's name. "Whatever."

Mike stroked his mustache, then started tapping two fingers on the table. This was an irritating habit he'd developed recently. He wasn't as patient as he used to be. He figured Harry was a gambler, so he'd probably known all the players. A cop, even one from down in New York City, could help out his friends. Maybe

Harry had been involved in the gambling himself. He'd probably always had the hots for Cherry. And she must have looked a lot better fifteen years ago. But who didn't? He got the picture and nodded, then glanced at Marcus.

Marcus had told Mike that Cherry had been hiding out in a crummy apartment in White Plains. He'd gone up there early this morning to get her. He didn't say who'd told him, and Mike didn't want to know. Marcus reported that she'd been sleeping when he knocked on the door and had tried hard not to let him in. Apparently they'd had some harsh words. Clearly Harry had his reasons for keeping his honey out of sight. Marcus was flush with accomplishing his mission under deadline.

"How did your husband die, Mrs. Packer?" Mike asked.

"You can call me Cherry; everyone else does." Cherry sniffed.

"How did Bobby die?"

"He had a heart attack," she said flatly. "They killed him anyway."

"He had the attack at the time of his beating?"

"No, about a month later."

"That's too bad. When was that?"

"Five years ago." She teared up and reached for a tissue.

"All right, so Bobby died. Then what happened?"

"Look, I didn't kill anybody. I don't even know who died. What does he have to do with me?"

"Do you know what an accessory is, Cherry?"

"Yeah, hat, bag, belt. Necklace." She laughed at her own joke.

"No, the other kind, when you help someone who committed a crime. You don't tell the cops something important because you don't want to hurt someone who helped you out a long time ago."

"I don't know anything, and that's the truth. I don't

know why you want to talk to me. I have nothing
to say."

"You know, if you're an accessory to a crime, you
can go to jail for almost as long as the guy who did
the crime. The law says you're a crook, too." Mike
tapped his fingers.

"Harry's a good guy," she said softly. "He wouldn't
kill anybody. He told me that."

"Then what were you doing in White Plains, honey
bee? Why did Harry call you and tell you to get out
of your house?"

"He didn't. I went to visit friends."

"Oh, yeah, what friends?"

"Her brother got sick. He had to go to the emergency room." Cherry looked at herself in the viewing-
window mirror, not at Mike.

"What are you talking about? You're not making
sense. Come on, you're heading into the racing season,
and you left your horses to visit imaginary friends in
a run-down dump? Nobody shows any respect for
my intelligence."

"It was tough. We'd already lost a lot of business.
We had a few horses left. I wanted to keep the
stables."

Mike frowned. Where was she going now? "Whose
stables?"

"Mine. Well, they were my dad's. He passed on in
'sixty-eight. They've been mine since then." She
heaved another sigh.

"Cherry, you're digressing." Mike checked his watch
again.

"I'm not undressing," she said angrily. She didn't
have much of a vocabulary. Mike suppressed a smile.

"Harry gave you some money." He tried to lead
her back.

"He didn't give me any money. He invested in a
very promising three-year-old," she said defensively.
"He's going to get it back in spades."

"I'll bet. Did Harry tell you how he got the money?"

Cherry squirmed a little. "No, of course not."

"Oh, come on. He's been your close friend for fifteen years. He's helped you out of trouble—I'm guessing here—over and over these past fifteen years."

She lifted a shoulder.

"Then suddenly out of nowhere he comes up with the money to buy one of your horses and doesn't tell you where he got it? Harry, who's always a little short himself? Come on, you can go to jail for lying to me."

"Look, he told me a friend won the lottery."

"Cherry, that friend was murdered last week. Your boyfriend is linked. We need answers to tie him in or let him go, understand?"

She nodded. "I do. But Harry didn't give me the money last week. He gave it to me a month ago, before Harry's friend died."

"A month ago?" Mike was flabbergasted. If that checked out, then Harry was telling the truth. A first!

"Yeah. What's the matter?"

"How about some breakfast, huh? Marcus here will get you whatever you want, okay? See you later."

Mike was out the door before she could say another word. A month ago. The money had changed hands almost as soon as it had come in. That meant Bernardino had given it to his friend, but why? The rest of the day April and Mike worked on Harry and Cherry, trying to get at why so they could eliminate Harry as a suspect, but Harry and Cherry weren't saying. With Bill still the prime suspect, maybe the why didn't matter. Maybe it was just one of those things: Bernardino got generous; Harry got lucky. End of story. April didn't believe it. Mike didn't believe it either.

Thirty-two

By the time Birdie Bassett's York U dinner came up, she had already lunched with the president of the Museum of Modern Art and the chairman of Lincoln Center, both friends of Max's, who were suddenly eager to acknowledge her as a friend. People were moving on her fast, and she was getting a sense of how the giving game was played. If she had five million a year to give away, that made her a very desirable acquisition to anyone's donor list. She was getting a crash course in having the power to decide where a lot of money was going to go. It meant jobs and careers and programs, prestige, and it was entirely a personal thing, just as Al Frayme had told her it would be.

Much of the time grant making was about connecting with the person who made the ask, and not about the cause itself. Since all kinds of people were bothering her with their impassioned requests, Birdie couldn't evaluate whose cause really appealed to her. People were pushing her in all directions, and it was a little scary. Voice mail was a step away from the human voice, but that didn't afford much of a buffer. On the computer, the list of begging e-mails grew every day.

"How do these people find me?" she wailed when Al called her over the weekend.

"People read the obits," he told her. "They target the heirs."

"But why do people give?"

"Cultivation. It takes time to break down a natural resistance." He laughed.

"What's funny about it?"

"Everybody wants to be loved, Birdie. And believe me, rich people feel guilty about being rich. They need to unload some of their good fortune."

Birdie knew that Al had been cultivating her for years, hoping for some of that Bassett money. "Giving money away responsibly is not as easy as you might think," she'd murmured, aware that she sounded a little like Max, just a little pompous.

"Whatever happened to loyalty, Birdie? You know it wouldn't hurt you the tiniest bit to send a few mil our way." Al's response came in a flash of anger.

She wasn't surprised. The truth was, all fund-raisers felt that way. It wouldn't hurt her, so why didn't she just do what they wanted? Well, in this case, she just didn't believe that York U needed money as badly as Al Frayme said it did. So there. She knew the university was very well off. With all the prime real estate it had, she was sure her alma mater was doing just fine.

And the truth also was that something about Al Frayme had always annoyed and irritated her. And because of *that,* she'd decided that ten thousand was quite enough for the university—enough to get her into the President's Circle, where dinner was served on a regular basis. It was personal, after all: She just didn't want to give it to him. But she didn't tell him that on Wednesday morning. She'd told him the ten was all she had at the moment. He tried to talk the figure up, but she remained firm.

"Nothing more for this year. We'll see how it goes. Maybe next year."

He seemed to take it graciously, but now it was evening, and he hadn't come to the dinner. She thought his behavior was just plain rude. Ten thousand wasn't chicken feed. She kept looking around for him. She'd expected to sit next to him, but he wasn't there among the company in the special dining room that consisted of a number of potential heavy-hitting donors, alums like herself, various members of the university's board of directors, the new president, John Warmsley, his new vice president, Wendy Vivendi, several old deans and two new ones: Diana Crease of the School of Social Work and Michael Abend of the Law School. Wendy Vivendi, who turned out to be the head fund-raiser of the university, was gracious and unreadable. But Al himself was simply not present.

After a glass of wine Birdie found herself not minding that much. She was with the kind of expensively dressed people she'd come to know and understand in her years of marriage to Max. This group conversed earnestly about important subjects like their summer traveling plans. No one talked money. They talked possessions—houses, boats, trips. Name brands, but never money.

As coffee was served, President Warmsley stood up to lecture long and passionately about all the admirable contributions the school had made to the city and the world, and all the new contributions it would make in the future with support from the donors in the room. Birdie was seated next to a tall, slender gentleman called Paul Hammermill, who was impeccably dressed in a navy double-breasted, pin-striped banker's suit, a pale yellow shirt, and a Ferragamo tie with tigers on it. He was not wearing a wedding ring and seemed interested in her. She couldn't help feeling just the tiniest bit gratified.

From the moment they'd sat down he'd started talking nonstop into her ear as if he'd known her all his life. He talked while the salad was served, while the wild salmon and garlic mashed potatoes were consumed, and all during the president's speech. Although Birdie was certain they had never met before, Paul was certain they had. When coffee was served he was still playing the where game.

"Are you sure you don't go to the Hamptons?" he asked.

"Absolutely." She sipped her decaf daintily.

"Martha's Vineyard?"

"Not there, either."

"Nantucket?" He cocked his head, flirting.

She shook her head.

"You must go somewhere in the summer," he prodded.

"Maine when my husband was alive," Birdie said, lowering her eyes with sudden genuine distress because he was no longer her protector.

"Ah, yes, so sorry." Paul waved over the server to pour her some more wine to bolster her spirits. When she demurred, he requested a refill for his own glass even though the wine-drinking part of the dinner was long past.

"And the winter, I believe you were in Boca?"

"No, Palm Beach." Under the table she checked her watch. It was time to go home to her empty Park Avenue apartment. Suddenly she was overwhelmed by her loss and had a powerful feeling of having to swim alone with sharks that could eat her alive if she wasn't careful.

"I know a lot of people in Palm Beach." Paul smiled, leaning farther into her space. "This has been very pleasant. Can I give you a ride home?"

She knew he was a lawyer in a prominent firm. He seemed to know a great many people, seemed to like her. Even though he'd had a bit to drink, he was still quite attractive, and lawyers could be useful at times. But she wasn't in the mood. Tomorrow she would meet with Jason Frank, Max's psychiatrist friend.

Then she'd learn more about Max and, she hoped, the reason he'd left her in such an unpleasant situation with his children.

"Thanks very much. I have a car," she murmured.

"Maybe another time," he said.

"That would be nice." She rose quickly. People were beginning to leave, and she didn't want to talk to anyone. Without seeking out Wendy Vivendi, or any of the deans or the president, Birdie slipped out of the room. She hurried down the stairs and out of the building. It never occurred to her that anyone might be interested enough in her to follow her. She didn't watch her back.

Outside on the edge of Washington Square, the night was wrapped in a warm and heavy mist. Fog had grabbed hold of the city for the second Wednesday in a row. Birdie was touched by the beauty and mystery of it. Then she was annoyed by the empty space where the black limo should have been waiting for her. Briefly she searched up and down the street but didn't see it. Other limos were dotted along the curb, but not hers.

"Damn." She didn't want anyone to catch her floundering, or have to accept that ride from Paul Hammermill.

She crossed the street and entered the square, teetering a little on her high heels. It occurred to her that since she had put in two orders for a car, and not requested that the first one wait for her, a different driver might have mistakenly parked on the wrong side of the square. Or worse, the second order might not have been processed at all. It had happened before. She resolved to get a new car service, one that didn't leave her stranded whenever the weather worsened. Max hadn't believed in keeping his own car and driver. Too much trouble, and often he'd preferred to walk. Birdie buttoned her jacket and glanced up at the sky. It looked as if any minute the fog would give way to rain.

Her heels drummed the sidewalk as she marched deeper into the square. The street people were pulling up their sweatshirt hoods. The chess players had long since gone home, and the dog walkers were scattering. The square was nearly empty.

"Come on, Junie, you're done for tonight." A dog walker opened his umbrella and urged his huge dog off the grass.

She listened to him as she peered ahead of her, searching through the fog and the trees for the car that was supposed to be waiting for her. More than halfway across the square, she heard the first clap of thunder and set her feet to sprint. The dog, on the other hand, chose to stand still. She heard impatience clip the owner's voice.

"Junie! Hurry up. It's going to rain."

Birdie's last easy thought was that the dog was not unhappy out there. Dogs didn't mind the rain. Then a hand dropped on her shoulder and without any warning she lost control of her limbs. She was in a spin, an inexplicable free fall. She didn't have time to protest or defend herself. She hit the ground and was stunned by the jarring impact. The man reached for her arm to pick her up.

"Sorry, my mistake."

"Oh, Jesus, what'd you do that for?" Fury sounded in Birdie's voice.

"Oh, come on, don't be like that." He hauled her to her feet, looking contrite. "I couldn't help myself."

"Junie!" The big dog began to howl. "Quiet!"

"Let go. What's the matter with you?"

"You didn't keep your promise."

Birdie tried to move her feet to get away but couldn't. It wasn't funny. "That's ridiculous."

"Don't call me ridiculous."

Birdie was less than a dozen paces from help. She reached out to the barking dog. "Help!"

Thunder drowned out her voice. The dog strained against its leash, but its master was the one controlling the choker collar. The dog obeyed the command for quiet as it disappeared into the downpour.

Then Birdie was really scared. He had her by the throat. Her heart felt as if it would burst with fear, worse than when she'd heard that Max was dead. She tried to knee him in the crotch, but he just caught her foot and twisted it until she yelped. Then he caught her before she fell.

"Don't play like that, and I won't hurt you. I *promise*. Let's dance. You like to dance."

The rain started in earnest as he spun her around, brushing the soles of her shoes against the pavement, then lifting them off again. Men had been doing that to Birdie ever since she was a little girl—lifting her off the ground—but never in a way that prevented her from breathing.

Her eyes bulged. *Okay, I'll keep my promise.* Fireworks exploded in her eyes as she fought against her own weight. His hands were around her neck, choking her. Her own weight was killing her. Panic rose with the agony. She kicked again and missed again. As she sank into darkness, her thoughts drifted to Max. He'd left her to swim with sharks. She lost consciousness.

She was almost gone when her feet touched the ground, and air suddenly came in. She sucked it in, saved. *Thank you.* She was breathing. Saved. *Thank you.*

"I'll keep the promise." She gasped.

"Too late!" The powerful strike at her throat came so fast she didn't see the hand retract, then fly at her like a launched missile. A sharp crack sounded on impact as the cartilage gave. Like Bernardino, Birdie was dead before she hit the ground.

Thirty-three

At ten-thirty-five on Wednesday evening Mike and April returned home from a long and unsettling day that ended with a hamburger dinner at the Metropolitan, a heavily cop-frequented restaurant close to headquarters. The energy level was rock bottom among the bosses gathered there. Ebullience at having resolved a sticky case within the week had turned to bitter disappointment late in the day when the Manhattan DA won the first round in the game of Pin the Tail on the Donkey.

No one in the Department wanted to hang a prosecutor for a cop murder, especially if the prosecutor happened to be the son of the dead cop in question. But between the two possible suspects on the table—a prosecutor and a retired cop, working alone, with each other, or Harry working with an unknown third party—the most comfortable choice was the prosecutor and no third party. The Tiger Liniment in his gym bag and on the victim was good enough for them.

Marvin Cohn, the Manhattan DA, however, wasn't buying. "I don't fucking care where you found stink oil. I don't care if it matches the oil on the victim's shirt and jacket. I don't give a shit. This isn't physical evidence. This is madness." He'd gone ballistic.

"Listen to what you're telling me! Nothing! We already know Bill had been in contact with his father that evening. The two men could have hugged. Traces of the oil could have rubbed off on him at the party, or at some earlier time. Drop it, unless you can do a lot better. What are you, stupid? Are you crazy? You have nothing but circumstantial. And that's fucking nothing."

And he'd said worse things to just about everybody. Bill's wife had confirmed that he was home at the time of the murder, and she passed a lie-detector test. That would be tough to fight in court.

"Give me a fucking break," Cohn had shrieked. It was the same thing that Bill himself kept saying.

Avise didn't like Cohn's attitude, which he considered nothing more than politics. But without the prosecutor's green light, the task force was back to Harry, working with a third party, because Jack Devereaux wouldn't ID Harry himself as April's attacker. There was no question that Harry was in deep, was connected somehow. According to Cherry and her bank records, he'd given her two hundred and fifty grand at least two weeks before Bernardino was murdered.

Harry had received the money right after Lorna died, just about the time four million was withdrawn from Bernadino's brokerage account. How much more of that Harry had come away with was anyone's guess. For all they knew, the two hundred grand might be just a drop in the bucket. If Harry didn't have the rest of it, maybe he knew where it was. He was It now. Every corner of his dusky life was under the microscope. Mike figured if he had more dough, he'd be spending it somewhere. They were checking Harry's every known associate for leaking money.

But April kept being teased by the karate thread. Every cop in the world could kill with a choke hold, but there was more to this than the choke hold. There was the need to kill in public, almost ninja style, the need to show off. You couldn't separate that aspect out. A little niggle about the competence of the two karate fans from Bernardino's own unit made her uneasy. If they were tracking a karate expert close to Harry, they had to be good. She knew them, but were they good enough? Were they going to the right places, talking to the right people, asking the right questions? The karate thread suggested she should take over the search herself, bring her own people in, figure it out her own way. Going it alone in investigations was a little problem for April. She didn't like being a team player. She didn't trust anybody else to get it right. She wanted to solve the cases fast. She didn't want to wait while the primaries dicked around with endless speculations.

As soon as she got home, she ran the water in the bathtub and started stripping off her clothes. She'd been the only woman at the table that night, and her gift for being there was a dry throat and smoky hair. She wanted to wash the male experience off as fast as possible. As a sergeant she was permitted to sit down with the big boys only because of her relationship to Mike. It always made her want to sink through the floor. That night she'd spent the time turning the pieces of the Bill and Harry puzzle around and around in her head to make them fit. They wouldn't fit unless Bill and his father's old partner were working together, or Harry had another friend.

"You don't need to look further. You've got your man right there," Bill had screamed at April in the late afternoon. "And tell Mike I want my fucking computer back." It didn't seem likely that Bill would be pushing for a partner's arrest.

April let her hair down and slid gratefully into the hot tea rose–scented water. She knew the answers would come to her if she let the questions go, if she loosened up her mind and relaxed a little. She breathed to slow her racing heart and was just begin-

ning to calm down when the phone in the living room
rang. She could hear Mike pick up.

"Sanchez." Then, "Shit." Then, "Give me thirty
minutes."

She was out of the tub at "Shit." Shit always meant
more than shit. She grabbed the towel and the pair of
slacks that she'd hung on the back of the bathroom
door, then dashed into the bedroom for some clean
underwear and a blouse. She had a towel wrapped
around her head and was zipping up trouser boots
when Mike's face appeared in the doorway.

"There's been another homicide in Washington
Square," he said.

The familiar sick feeling sucked air out of April's
lungs. "Who?"

"A woman called Birdie Bassett. Rich widow. She'd
been at a dinner at York U. She was a donor."

York U! She was stunned. "Did he get away?"

"Yeah. You coming?"

This was the moment April always needed reassur-
ance and never wanted to let on. The moment when
they found out a case they'd been working wasn't
going to be an isolated case, when someone died because they'd been moving too slowly. That was when
she felt the worst.

Mike read it in her face and moved toward her to
give her a quick hug. It wasn't her fault. That was
what the hug said. "Look, you don't have to go."

"Yes, I do. I want to see her." April put her face
in his shoulder and inhaled his scent, sweet and com-
plex even after a long, hot day. His body held hundreds of memories of passion and good times. It was
tough to shrug off her own wish for love and sleep.
But, shit, she did want to see this Birdie before they
took her away.

She unwrapped the bath towel and let her wet hair
hang down on her shoulders. "Let's go."

Thirty-four

This time they took the Camaro, and no one grumbled about the muffler. The gas was low in the Chrysler, and noise didn't matter to them now. April combed her wet hair with her fingers, feeling guilty for her quick soak in the tub.

"You're quiet; are you okay?" she asked.

"It could be a copycat," Mike muttered. He didn't like the possibility of losing Harry, his second-best suspect.

April flashed to Jack, the alumnus of York U. Neither of them were happy.

Mike accelerated, and the Camaro thundered through the Midtown Tunnel. When they came out on the Manhattan side, the city was still very much awake and alive. Warm weather always drew people to the streets and kept them out until late. Rain scattered them to dry spots under store awnings for a few minutes, but they often emerged again before the sky stopped spitting. Tonight the sidewalks were wet, but the rain had stopped.

As always on her way to a homicide, April was beset by Chinese demons. This time it was worse than usual. The repeater they had on their hands could have murdered her. Almost dying had humbled her. After nearly a year of being engaged, she and Mike would have missed their chance to marry, to buy their house and have a baby. She hadn't even changed her address. At her not-quite-real home, they were still sitting on Mike's hand-me-down sofa, living in a partially furnished apartment and driving worn-out cars. What were up-and-coming careers in the face of the gaping failure to take some time for living? Suddenly it seemed as if they were living an unfinished life on borrowed time. Lorna was gone, Bernardino was gone, and now someone else was gone. *Shit.* She touched Mike's upper arm and reflexively he made a muscle for her to grip.

At the crime scene the Camaro joined more than a dozen vehicles with flashing lights that roadblocked the streets around the east and south sides of Washington Square. Mike parked behind one of them and killed the engine. From a distance April could see that someone had hung lights in the tree above the body, and yellow crime-scene tape roped off the area. Her heart beat in her throat as she clipped on her ID, swung her heavy purse over her shoulder, then got out of the car.

They walked without being challenged to where detectives from two precincts and brass from downtown stood away from the body, talking, smoking, holding on to their cigarette butts. The local news vans with their satellite dishes were also showing up. April didn't join the crowd. With her makeup in the drawer, and her hair hanging down like a wet mop, she was in no mood to socialize. She wanted to see the woman who hadn't gotten away.

"Sergeant Woo."

April turned around and saw Chief Avise beckoning her with his index finger. She put her hand to her wet hair and walked over.

"You interviewed a Dr. Crease yesterday?"

"Yes, sir," April said. He knew that already. She had the dean's list. And so did everyone else.

Chief Avise jerked his head at a park bench close

to the south side of the square. "She wants to talk to you."

"Really? What's *she* doing here?"

"The vic had been at a York University party. One of the guests saw her come in here. He thought she was going to get caught in the rain and drove around to pick her up. When she didn't show, he came to look for her."

April frowned. "Is that guest still here, too?"

Avise nodded. "He left his driver with the body and went back for help. Dr. Crease was inside the building waiting for the rain to stop."

"How long did it rain?"

"Five minutes, more or less. She's over there." The chief didn't say anything else, just walked away toward the permanent cement chess tables, where Mike was now talking to the crime-scene team.

April took a wide path into the grass around the yellow tape and came out behind the bench where the dean was waiting for her. Dr. Diane Crease was sitting primly with her knees together, still wearing the same pink-and-black tweed suit. She stood up when she saw April.

"I'm glad you're here," she said quickly, then swiped at her eyes. "This is terrible. The president lives night and day for this school. It's been his whole life for twenty years."

April tilted her head, thinking of the victim. It was worse for her. "Who is Birdie Bassett? Does she have another name?" Birdie was a name for a sparrow.

"I don't know. I didn't know her. I just met her tonight. She was new."

"New?"

"New to the circle. I don't know anything about her. I'm new to the circle, too. I don't know the ropes yet. I've been here only six months—since Dr. Warmsley took over. He recruited me."

"You wanted to talk to me," April said.

"Yes. You were asking about the tenth. Several things were going on that day. But one in particular in the afternoon. If you can pinpoint the time of the call, it might help. I didn't think it was particularly relevant until this happened."

"How does it relate?"

"Well, some of the names I gave you were for a development meeting. This was a development dinner." She looked so uncomfortable. "Dr. Warmsley is going to be so upset."

"Development of what?" April asked.

Dr. Crease gave her a look. April read it as the dumb-cop look. She didn't know what development was.

"Fund-raising," Dr. Crease explained. "Dr. Warmsley has a goal for each department. The pressure is on us all to bring in resources to raise each department to the highest level, both academically and in services to the community. That's my mandate."

"Oh." April got it. With five first-rate schools in the immediate area competing for students and funds, Dr. Warmsley was putting on the pressure for York.

Dr. Crease was badly shaken. "I just wanted you to know."

"You told me Dr. Warmsley was here for twenty years," April said.

"Yes, but he just became president. He's going to be very upset."

Well, who wasn't? One retired cop and one university donor were killed within a block of each other. And April had the strong feeling that Jack Devereaux was somehow targeted, too. She swallowed the lump in her throat. "Thanks. You can go home now. You know where to reach me if you have anything else."

April finished her good-byes and found Mike interviewing a tall man in an expensive-looking suit.

"The only person I saw was a man with a big dog," he was saying as April joined them. Mike made the introductions.

"Sergeant Woo. Mr. Hammermill."

He nodded. "Pleased to meet you."

As April nodded, her attention strayed to the CSU unit, now dressed in their white Tyvek overalls and white booties. They were talking with the ME, who had come to the scene himself. Unusual for him, but she seemed to remember that Dr. Gloss lived somewhere in the neighborhood. She watched them as they moved toward the taped-off area. Hammermill kept his eyes averted.

"Can you describe the man with the dog?" Mike asked. He was doodling down the side of his notebook.

"He wore a Yankees hat," Hammermill said. He looked at April again; then his eyes glazed over. Maybe he'd had too much to drink. He was a very elegant man, out of his element.

"Anything else?" Mike asked.

"He had a Chase Bank umbrella. I didn't see his face."

"What kind of dog?" April asked.

"I don't know. It was big and hairy."

Uh-huh. "Would you recognize the breed if you saw it again?"

"I don't know. I don't notice dogs much."

But he had noticed the dog. People always noticed dogs. April checked her watch and followed the ME to where the victim was still lying where she had fallen over an hour ago. The CSU team lifted the tarp that had been covering a beautiful young woman wearing a snug black cocktail dress. The dress was hiked up high enough to reveal long legs and smooth thighs. Suddenly open to view, she looked like a mannequin from an expensive department store, posed in a party dress on the ground with her head twisted and her face frozen in a fake expression of emptiness. She was lying on her side. One leg was straight and the other bent. April was shocked. Somehow she'd expected a Birdie to be old.

She caught her breath and coughed, then moved closer to get a better view of the expensive sling-back heels with the open toes that revealed the nail polish on the woman's toenails. Her fingernails were a matching pink, and her hands, curled in death, looked soft and appeared to be without any defense wounds. But first impressions could be deceiving.

Sometimes when the medical examiner removed victims' clothes, puncture wounds were discovered, knife wounds, gunshot wounds. Even hair sometimes hid deep depressions in the skull from blows to the head. Tissue from the killer could be found under the victim's nails. A broken nail from the killer could be caught in the victim's clothes. Many things not visible to a viewer at a scene could be hiding somewhere on the victim's body. It was clear that this kill was cold and calculated, like an expert hunter killing a deer. And the most macabre thing about the scene was that rain had fallen for at least a few minutes after the victim died. Droplets of water still hung from the soaked blond hair. Rivulets had run down her arms and her legs and puddled in spots in the pavement around her. April stepped back and watched the ME go to work.

Thirty-five

Early in the A.M., after a late night and very little sleep, Mike and April traveled back into Manhattan to the edgy Sixth Precinct. The rain had started again before dawn and held through the night. It was a wet morning. Fog from their warm breath steamed up the car windows, and traffic was already beginning to bunch up around the bridges by seven-fifteen. April hadn't slept enough and hadn't had enough tea to get her voice going. She wanted to talk, but they didn't have a chance in the car.

Mike was on his cell phone, taking a call from the branch supervisor of the FBI. The FBI had an instant response to serial killings. Two killings of a like kind pushed the button, and special agents were coming in to help the NYPD, like it or not. For April and Mike it meant there would be more toes to avoid, more people to keep in the loop.

As Mike talked, his voice was low and calm. He was supposed to be on his way out of Homicide, no longer engaged at this level on the front lines of murder investigations, but he did not show any sign of irritation. He was at home under the gun, still good at keeping the sharp edges off his Bronx machismo. Mike was a born negotiator, never at a loss. April could almost be lulled by his confidence, his assurance to the Feeb that everything was under control, even though it wasn't at all.

Before they hit the Midtown Tunnel, she called her boss, Lieutenant Iriarte. Like everybody else in the department who'd had enough sense to get out of the boroughs, where the population was too dense and the apartment prices were too high, he lived up in Westchester. She knew he was on the road by six-thirty.

Iriarte picked up his cell on the third ring.

"It's April," she croaked, letting her voice do its cracky thing because she hadn't been in to work in a week and didn't know how well he was taking her absence.

"Oh, nice of you to call in, Woo. Feeling better?" Iriarte asked sarcastically.

"Yes, sir. How's it going?"

"With us? I'd like to say it's been a madhouse, and we're swamped without you. But the truth is it's been quiet," he admitted. "I hear you caught another one downtown last night."

"Yes, sir."

"I hear it's bad."

"Yes, sir," April repeated, because that pretty much covered it. Two killings in the same place a week apart had about the same odds of occurring as lightning striking the same building twice. It wasn't exactly an advertisement for an area with the highest concentration of students in the city—including CUNY, the New School, the School of Design, NYU, Pace, and York University. One murder in a location considered a quality-of-life safe zone might be considered an unfortunate anomaly. Two murders there could only be deemed careless. Not enough uniforms on the streets, yada, yada, ya. The unlucky commanding officer of the Sixth Precinct, Captain Jenny Spring, was on the carpet big-time. Nobody envied her unfortunate situation.

"What do you have on this karate nut?" Iriarte asked, sounding satisfied that his own detective unit wasn't going to be a mob scene for the duration.

"You seem pretty well informed already, Lieutenant," April croaked out.

"No, all I heard is he's right up your alley. That why you're on it?"

With this remark, he reminded her that the killer was better and smarter than she, and also that Iriarte knew things he wasn't supposed to know.

"No, sir. Doesn't seem to be my alley at all." April hesitated.

"How can I help?" he asked.

She could feel him settling back in his Lumina, letting his hostility melt. She could tell he was beginning to like her. Maybe she should stay out of his sight more often.

"I need somebody," she said slowly.

"Don't we all? Who do you need, Woo?"

"Woody, sir."

Lieutenant Iriarte broke out in laughter because he considered Woody Baum the worst detective in his unit, which was one of the reasons April could rely on him. Loyalty always came easily to the underdog.

"Oh, sure, take him and never send him back." The lieutenant laughed some more.

"I'd also like Hagedorn to check a few things." Hagedorn was the computer whiz in the Midtown North unit. He was a real yin character, with a pudgy body and a soft moon face, but the fastest detective at pulling a back story out of the Net.

Iriarte snorted, pleased to be useful. "Fine. Whatever you need."

April thanked him, and they both hung up. Mike hung up, too, and they headed into the tunnel for the second time in less than twelve hours.

Thirty-six

Dr. Jason Frank was a morning person, always up at first light in a race with his two-year-old toddler, April, who was a morning person, too. They both wanted to be the first to greet the other. Jason's wife, Emma, slept in an hour longer. What drew her out of bed and into the kitchen every morning was the aroma of coffee, toasted waffles, bagels, or corn muffins— whatever Jason offered up in the way of breakfast. His culinary competence was limited to freshly squeezed orange juice, fresh fruit, and toasted whatever, and Emma was always appropriately grateful for whatever he served.

On Thursday April won the first-up race. Long before six, she'd climbed up on her parents' bed, put her face about an inch from her father's nose, and breathed on him until he grabbed and tickled her.

"Orange juice, Daddy," she demanded. "Please."

After he got up to supply it, she sat on the closed toilet seat while he went through his shaving routine. Sometimes Jason wore a short beard for a year or two. But now he was back into the routine of scraping his cheeks and gabbing with his little nonstop talker, who liked to lather her own cheeks and play-shave herself.

By seven he'd finished showering and was dressed in a white shirt, lightweight blue suit, and one of his dozen boring blue-and-red-striped ties. He'd already checked his e-mails and his phone messages, and thought that nothing terrible had happened in the night. Patients needed prescriptions refilled, they wanted to change appointments. Colleagues had to re-schedule meetings. At that moment everything appeared normal in his world, and that was enough to make him happy.

Despite the endless round of terrors expressed daily by his patients about world war and the precarious state of the stock market in addition to their own private tragedies of death and life-threatening events, the rebirth of spring was reviving his hope. He loved his wife and baby and worked hard every day to balance fear against normalcy.

In fact, life's urgencies post-9/11 had taken on a new poignancy for him. Just having the privilege of being alive and present for his family and patients felt like a gift. Every day was a new gift. Today, when Emma came into the kitchen with a sheet crease on her left cheek, her lovely hair still a little messy, wearing one of his T-shirts, and yawning her sleep away, he felt it again. Blessed.

"Hey, baby," she murmured to Jason.

"I'm not a baby," April replied.

Jason laughed. "Hey, gorgeous." He moved close to cuddle his beautiful wife, nuzzle her neck.

"No way." Emma made a grumbling noise at the idea of beauty in the morning, so he hugged her and kissed her some more until she stopped protesting. Then he poured coffee with hot milk into a large mug and handed it over so she could climb out of the sleep pit.

"Thanks." Her first smile of the day.

After that first smile had warmed him all the way up, Jason finally turned on the news. The first thing he saw on NBC was a fast-breaking news alert that Birdie Bassett, his most important appointment of the day, had been murdered last night.

"Oh, no." He felt the blast of another human life

wasted and gone. What was it with him and homicide?
He'd had respite from violent death for more than a
year, but now it was back. Someone on the fringe of
his life had a violent death the night before he was to
meet her to discuss important business. *Damn!* Reflexively, he moved the plastic syrup container out of
April's range. She already had a lake of it on her plate
and was squeezing out more.

"No, Daddy!" She tried to retrieve it from him.

"You've got lots," he pointed out.

"What's the matter, honey?" Emma responded to
his body language. She always knew when he crashed.
April didn't.

"Yum," she said, eating her waffle with both hands
and dripping all over the table. "Yum, yum."

"Somebody I was supposed to see today died last
night," Jason said softly.

"Goodness. Who?" Emma's eyes opened wide.

"Remember Max Bassett?"

"Of course, your lifesaver. But didn't he die weeks
ago?"

"Yes. This is his widow." Jason was too depressed
to pour more coffee for himself, and he needed it now.

"I'm sorry," Emma said. "Was she old?"

"No, she wasn't old."

"What did she die of?" Then she got it and stared
at him questioningly.

Jason shook his head. He didn't want to go there.
Emma herself had been stalked and almost killed a
few years back. She was still suffering nightmares
from the experience. Only months later, her best
friend had been stabbed to death. Their lives were
changed forever, and baby April was the result of
their need to love each other and have a family.
Their precious daughter was named for April Woo,
the detective who'd handled both cases, and baby
April reminded them of her in some way or another

nearly every day. But Jason didn't want to face another murder.

"No, sugarplum. That's enough." A few seconds ago Emma had been sleepy and out of it. Now she was on active toddler duty with a wet towel at the ready to swab sticky syrup out of April's adorable blond curls as soon as she finished covering them with it. And Emma was on that other alert, too. The murder alert.

"What happened?" she asked as soon as Jason muted the TV.

"Later." He clicked his tongue. He *really* didn't want to talk about it now. The sudden death didn't bode well for the institute, and that was upsetting, too.

Jason was a prominent psychiatrist/psychoanalyst who taught and supervised candidates at the Psychoanalytic Institute. He also chaired about a hundred thousand ineffective committee meetings there a year. Max Bassett had helped the institute emerge from several decades of decline and finally enter into the modern age. With Max's death, chaos among the dinosaurs was certain to reign again.

It was a selfish thought, but Jason couldn't help it. The whole mental-health field was suffering from HMO-itis, but psychoanalysts most of all. Psychiatrists had become closely aligned with drug companies and were reimbursed nicely for heavily medicating every kind of emotional distress. Psychoanalysis didn't qualify for reimbursement by HMOs and was scorned by drug companies. To make matters worse, analysts had trouble accepting the fact that they had to fund-raise to support their institutions just like everybody else. Soliciting funds from their patients and patients' families was considered taboo. It was a catch-22. With the loss of an important advocate like Max Bassett, so much had been at stake for the institute that Jason had been looking forward to meeting his widow.

He pushed away the selfish feeling of loss for the institute with the same motion he used for his breakfast plate. Then he remembered the tremor in Birdie's voice when she'd returned his call a week ago. Something had been bothering her about her husband's will and about his death. She had questions. Jason hadn't thought much of her concern at the time. No one ever believes death is a natural consequence of living. But now that she was gone, he was sorry he'd taken so long to see her. His week could not have been that busy. What had he been thinking? He began to torment himself about it.

At eight he said his good-byes to Emma and April, then traveled the long distance to his office in the apartment next door to begin his patient day. Several hours later, during the time he was supposed to be at Birdie Bassett's apartment, he'd brooded long enough to call April Woo on her cell phone.

"Sergeant Woo," she answered right away.

"Hey, April, it's Jason. Long time no talk."

"Jason! I thought you dropped off the end of the earth. How's my namesake doing?"

"Talking up a storm. Emma's great, too. How's Mike?"

"Oh, being promoted to captain any day. We're doing okay. What's up? I never hear from you unless there's trouble."

"Well, there's trouble. Birdie Bassett, that woman who was murdered last night . . ." He sighed. "I had an appointment with her today."

"I'm sorry for your loss, Jason. How can I help you?"

"Well, her husband was a donor at the institute. I didn't know her, but she called me last week."

"I see. Do you have some information that could help us?"

"Her husband died recently and she voiced some concern about it. I'm calling about that."

"What kind of concern?"

"She knew him well, of course. She said he was in perfect health, but you know, people have trouble accepting the fact that sometimes no one is to blame. We're a blaming society."

"For sure. What are you suggesting?"

"I'm not really suggesting. . . . You just always told me there are no coincidences in police work. And Mrs. Bassett was troubled last week. I don't know the full extent of her suspicions. I'm just reporting what she told me in the few minutes that we talked. She'd inherited a lot of money, and she gave me the impression that her stepchildren didn't get what they expected, and they were contesting the will. She definitely had her concerns. Last night she was murdered. I just wanted you to know."

April was silent. She wondered about Mike's copycat speculation. Maybe Bernardino's death presented an opportunity to Birdie's enemies. It had happened before.

"Are you there?"

"Yeah, I'm here."

"Can you talk to the detectives handling the case?" he asked.

"Oh, sure. I guess I could do that," she said.

"Are you the detective handling the case?" he asked after a beat.

"One of them."

"So you know everything about it?"

"There was another homicide in Washington Square last week, a retired police lieutenant, my old supervisor, in fact. This is the second one," she said slowly.

"What does it mean?"

"I don't know. At the very least it means there's a sick person out there who kills rich people with his bare hands."

"Rich people. I thought you said your supervisor was a cop."

"Bernardino was a cop with fifteen million dollars in his pocket. Thanks for the tip, Jason. I'll get back to you."

Jason hung up the phone more distressed than he'd been before.

Thirty-seven

When April hung up with Jason, the sun was out and the city was heating up. It had gone from rain to shine without her noticing, and she felt she'd missed something, missed a lot.

"What's going on, boss?" Woody Baum was heading uptown in the unmarked unit, away from the mob scene at the crazed Sixth Precinct. He was driving with one hand, playing tag with civilian cars, running red lights, all his usual antics to keep things interesting.

Woody had been in a rough-and-tumble anticrime unit for three years, driving around with a bunch of tough guys on the third tour in the earliest hours of the morning, looking for bottom feeders to lock up before they got impatient and shot someone. There had been a lot of shootings among the dealers back when Guiliani was cleaning up the city block by block. Since then Woody had hung up his spurs, cleaned up, and cut his hair real short. He was a good-looking, almost preppy kind of guy now, trying to be a nice, quiet detective. It wasn't so easy for him. His life on the streets had made him somewhat unpredictable. April thought of him kind of like Dim Sum—a bad dog with some training that didn't always stick. The poodle squatted in the kitchen when she was thwarted. And Woody kept testing his limits, too.

Right now April was too preoccupied to chastise him or answer his question. Jason's call had caught her off guard. Cops rarely made friends with people whose lives they'd saved. They didn't like to be reminded of their traumas. But Emma and Jason had been different. They trusted April, had even named their daughter after her. It always made April laugh to think that a little blond angel was carrying her name. But she was proud of the child and secretly wanted to return the favor. A dark-haired Emma, or maybe a Jason. Why not?

She'd consulted Jason on many cases. In return, Jason seemed to feel that April and Mike were his own private police force he could call on whenever something was off in his world, which was too often for comfort. He treated many different kinds of people and was no stranger to the dark side of human nature. Woody finally got her attention when he ran a light on Forty-second Street while a bunch of car horns blared in protest.

"Hey, slow down, Woody!" April closed her eyes as a bus hurtled toward them.

"No problem." Woody chuckled as they made it across the street unharmed.

April turned her attention to her cell phone and called Mike. "Yo. Sorry to bother you," she said when he answered.

"What's up?" He sounded stressed.

"Jason Frank knew Birdie Bassett's husband. He was a donor at the institute. The funny thing is, Jason was supposed to meet her today."

"Jesus. Okay, thanks for the heads-up," Mike said hurriedly.

"She thought her husband was murdered. She wanted Jason to look into it."

"No kidding." Now he was interested.

"And I got a hold of Brenda and Burton Bassett. Guess where they are?"

"Their father and Birdie's apartment."

"Yes, in one. It looks like they'd planned to raid the place before the IRS could get there. Can you get up here?"

"Give me an hour. I'll try."

"Right." She hung up as Woody plowed up the Park Avenue ramp to circle the Hyatt Hotel and Grand Central Station. Her cell rang again before they got to the top. "Sergeant Woo."

"It's Kathy. What about that second homicide in Washington Square last night?" She sounded stressed, too.

"Oh, you heard," April said a little guiltily.

"Of course I heard, but not from you. Why didn't you call me last night? You promised." Kathy was peeved.

"Sorry. I tried you yesterday afternoon." But then April's plate got full, and she forgot.

"Who's the vic?" Kathy asked.

"She's the widow of a richie, a big philanthropist. You can look him up. Max Bassett. Two Sams, two Toms. Birdie was attending a dinner at York U. Seems she was an alum there. A donor." April paused at Kathy's sharp inhalation of breath.

"York U?" Kathy said.

"Yeah, does that mean something to you?"

"Well, yeah. Dad went there," Kathy said slowly.

Bingo, a third connection. "Your father attended York University?" April said excitedly.

"Yes, ma'am, he got his BS there. He went at night when I was little. I think he got most of the credits he needed for a master's degree, too. I don't know why he didn't finish." She paused for breath. "York U. Humph."

"That's good, Kathy. Thanks." April was elated and wondered why it hadn't come out before.

"April, do you still think my brother is involved in Dad's murder?" Kathy's voice was cool.

"Kathy, I'm going to be honest with you. Bill wasn't forthcoming about a number of things. Right off the bat he made himself suspicious. He left the party early. It seemed odd, you know. Other things, too. I don't want to go into it. But we have to eliminate the family first in every case; you know that. And he's looking clean now."

"I know," Kathy said softly, but her voice was still icy.

April let it pass for the moment. "Look, we gave Bill every opportunity to help us out. He came downtown a few times. He invited a search of his house, and some detectives went over it and his car pretty carefully. I'm sure you know he was present at the time of the search. This was on the advice of his lawyer; you know what I'm saying?"

"I know what you're saying. I don't know anything about a search. When did you do it?"

"Tuesday."

"What did they find?" Kathy asked.

"Look, your brother is a prosecutor. He knows as well as you and I do how to hide an elephant."

"Are you saying you didn't find anything?" Kathy was still on the search.

"You know I can't answer that. All I can tell you is that Bill knows how to handle himself. And his team is on his side."

Suddenly April felt very tired. She couldn't talk about Tiger Liniment or missing millions or anything else with Kathy. For a second she let her thoughts wander to last night, when she'd taken her turn at examining Birdie Bassett's body. The staggering thing about this murder was that the killer had choked his victim—there were bruises on her neck—but that wasn't the cause of death, and he hadn't yoked her as he had Bernie. It was clear to her what he'd done because she knew the move. He killed Birdie with a

karate technique few black belts had the deadly
strength to execute. One punch, one kill. This time he
signed a clear signature. Now she was sorry she hadn't
asked Gloss whether Bernardino's killer was left-
handed or right-handed. As soon as they knew that,
they'd know if there was one killer on the loose, or
two.

She shook her head. One punch, one kill. The move
everyone practiced, and that looked so great on TV,
came with the caveat of "Don't try this," along with
a bunch of other moves it was stupid to attempt when
a mugger held a knife to your throat or a gun to your
head. The truth was, karate only worked to give a
potential victim a second or two. Ninety-nine out of
a hundred amateurs could not gain enough time to
get away from an opponent with a gun or a knife.

Dr. Gloss had sniffed the body for the odor of Tiger
Liniment, but Birdie Bassett's body had smelled only
of its own waste that she'd excreted at the moment
she'd died. And she'd smelled faintly of perfume,
blood oranges and roses.

Kathy made an impatient noise, and April changed
the subject. "Can you add anything to what we know
about Harry?"

"Forget Harry. I want to know what's the link between the two victims?" Kathy returned to the question that prompted her call. She wanted her brother
well off the hook. That was all she cared about right
now.

"Both victims had a spouse die recently. They'd
both inherited big money." April's voice cracked on
the words *big money* because she didn't want this bit
of news to surface in the media. "Keep this to yourself, Kathy. Let's not make it a circus, okay?"

Then April shivered with excitement. No one in
the investigation had copped to the fact that both
victims had money and both were alums of York

University. Marcus didn't know it, and Mike didn't
know it. Only she and Kathy knew it. April loved
having an edge, even if she'd keep it for only about
ten seconds. There was nothing overtly competitive
about her.

"Tell me about Harry." April was back on Harry,
relishing the few moments of relative peace in the car
with her maniac driver before she'd have to move into
the murk of the new victim.

Kathy clicked her tongue. "Bill told me about the
racehorse. That's a crock, you know."

"You mean, your dad wouldn't give Harry a few
hundred grand to buy a horse?"

"Not a few hundred anything!" Kathy exploded.

"Even in special circumstances?"

"No!"

"What about Bill—would he give money to Harry?"

"Are you nuts?" The suggestion made Kathy
ballistic.

April paused to give her another moment to specu-
late. *Come on, Kathy, don't make me hurt you,* she
thought.

"Look, I've been thinking about it a lot," Kathy
admitted finally.

"Uh-huh." April was sure she had.

"I don't know. The truth is, Dad had been acting a
little off before he died."

"How off?"

"I told you this before. Obviously he was secretive.
You know Mom was into the lottery, but I didn't
know how it works. Call me crazy. I didn't know it
came in so fast, and I didn't know what he did with
it. I know he was depressed about his future. He
kept talking about living in a hotel, sitting on a park
bench. Crazy stuff. I didn't know he was looking for
a house in Florida. There was a lot of stuff I didn't
know."

"Do you think he was feeling guilty?"

"For surviving Mom? I'm sure. He thought he'd neglected her."

"What about that *and* distributing money to Bill and Harry? Maybe guilt for excluding you was what you heard in his voice."

"Jesus, April. Don't go there. I knew Dad. He was my buddy. Why would he do that to me?" But Kathy wasn't sure now. April could hear it in her voice.

"Maybe your dad had a plan for you, too," she said. "Maybe the check was supposed to be in the mail and just didn't get to you."

"He would have told me," she said quietly. "He was a careful man. I'm sure he would have told me."

April had planned to save this for a time when the two of them were sitting face-to-face, but she went ahead because she didn't know when that time would be. "He didn't tell you everything, Kathy. He had your mother cremated."

"Oh, Jesus. That's a crock, too. Where did you hear that?"

"We know he did," April said softly. She didn't have to offer proof. It was in the computer if Kathy cared to look.

"Oh, sure, and where are the ashes? She had a funeral. I saw her buried. She didn't have an open casket because of how bad she'd looked. But I did see her buried."

"I know you did. What did you see her buried in?"

"A casket, of course. Where are you going with this?" Kathy was furious, but she sounded nervous, too.

"Okay, good. She was buried in a coffin. Maybe our information is wrong. Look, Kathy, I'm sorry about all this. We'll straighten it out, okay?" Lorna was buried in a coffin? April shivered. Something wasn't right; she could feel it.

"Where are you *going* with this, April? I need to know what you're doing," Kathy demanded.

"I'm doing whatever I have to, Kathy. Your father was a friend of mine." April was puzzled. What picture was she seeing?

"Fuck you. It doesn't sound like it," Kathy muttered before she hung up.

Thirty-eight

April's stomach knotted up as they continued north on Park Avenue. She felt bad about Kathy. Something was way off between her and her dad, also between her and her brother. It appeared that Kathy had been out of the loop as far as the family finances were concerned, and she sounded concerned about the murder rap threatening her brother. But April knew her distress went a lot deeper than that. Now she had to worry about her mother's ashes. What was that all about? April was getting a creepy idea, but she pushed it away as traffic slowed them down in Midtown.

By the time they got to Fiftieth Street, she'd stopped brooding about the Bernardinos. Ten minutes later, when she and Woody got to the tenth-floor Bassett apartment, she had other things to be concerned about. For one thing no uniform was there to secure the victim's home. Here was another unsettling parallel with the Bernardino case. The heirs had gotten here first.

"Okay, okay. I heard you. Come in if you're coming in." Brenda Bassett opened the door for the two detectives, then quickly turned her back on them.

April stepped inside and was stopped dead by the magnificence of a rose-colored marble floor in a gallery hung with oil paintings of horses and dogs in various hunt modes and dead animals in small still-lifes. Also portraits of richly dressed people picnicking on flawless lawns in front of grand houses. A huge chandelier lit the hall. Under the chandelier was an ornate table inlaid with tortoiseshell, mother-of-pearl, and brass. Under that was a thick Oriental carpet in bright blues and reds. Way over the top, it was just the sort of place to which a cop from a string-decorated house in Queens could really relate. It was the kind of display that only big money could swing.

Brenda Bassett walked around the center table to a mahogany door on the other side. She was a tall woman, probably close to six feet in high heels, and thinner than a healthy person should be. Ms. Bassett had no bosom and no fanny, and it struck April as perverse that someone with so much money wouldn't eat. To the Chinese, food was pretty much everything. Most memories of luxury and excess were of eating, never of going hungry.

April blew her breath out as Brenda led the way through a door into a dark wood-paneled library where the walls were lined with a collection of books that looked as old as the paintings in the hall. Ms. Bassett turned and seated herself in one of several leather wing chairs, and April got to see her face. Her features were all angles. She had a long, straight nose, slab-sided cheekbones, a sharp chin, and razor-blade lips—the kind that couldn't be improved with lipstick. Her hair was black and blunt-cut.

The man, who stood near the desk, was five-eight, and had a heavy build, no chin, little hair, and moist pink lips set in soft round cheeks. April didn't have to examine him closely to catch the dazed look of an all-night drinker who'd been forced out into the daylight way too early. Boyfriend, brother, lawyer? A messy pile of papers and other small items on the desk indicated that a search had been in process. The man put some space between himself and the desk and sat gingerly in another wing chair.

"I'm Sergeant April Woo. And this is Detective Baum," April said. Woody took his at-ease position by the door, and she waited for a cue to sit. It didn't come.

"Well, this is my brother, Burton Bassett, I'm Brenda Bassett. What do you want?" the woman asked bluntly.

Burton put a hand to his head. "Gently, sister," he said in a pained tone.

Not a lawyer. Brother and sister. April quickly formed the impression that the genders of the Bassett siblings had been reversed. Brenda was the strong and pushy yang; Burton was the passive, yielding yin. Neither appeared to be in mourning for their father or stepmother. Suddenly new links between the Bernardino and Bassett murders occurred to April. Both victims' names began with B, both spouses of the victims had the money and had died first of natural causes. Both had two adult children, a boy and a girl. What else?

What, boss? Woody's body language told her he was trying to read her orders. "Do you need something to drink, Sergeant?" he asked out loud. Their code for, *Do you want to separate them?*

"Thank you, Detective. In a minute," April replied.

Neither Bassett offered her any water.

"I was at home last night," Brenda said, "if that's what you want to know." She smirked.

"I was out with friends, till . . . quite late." Burton actually yawned.

Brenda glared at him suddenly. "Birdie was a nice woman. She didn't deserve to die like that." Her mouth shut like a clamshell, then opened again. "Do we need a lawyer? You're not reading us our rights, are you?"

April smiled. People always jumped to conclusions. "We just need some background about your stepmother."

"Well, I don't know how much we can help you. We weren't close."

"When was the last time you saw Mrs. Bassett?"

"Dad's funeral. She was pretty out of it." This came from Burton, who looked pretty out of it himself.

"That would be when?"

"A month ago, something like that."

April frowned. Lorna died a month before Bernie was killed. What did the length of time between the natural death and the murder tell them about the perpetrator? "What day?"

"I don't remember." Brenda turned to her brother. "What day did Daddy die? I'm so upset with this—"

Burton shrugged. "Thursday? No, I was playing golf Thursday. It had to be Friday."

"Yes, it was Friday. But I can't remember the date." Brenda Bassett's mouth made an astonished O. "I've lost track of time."

"We'll need the time frames," April told her, as if they wouldn't know pretty much everything about them by dinnertime. Hagedorn would hack into their lives until nothing was secret.

"For God's sake, why?" Brenda made some noise with her breathing.

"How was she doing with your father's death?" April didn't bother to answer the question.

"I have no idea," Brenda said indignantly. "It's not like I knew her. I didn't *know* her. I mean, I'd seen her a couple of times a year. At family events. Thanksgiving, things like that . . ." Her voice was strong and angry. Maybe she hadn't liked being excluded.

"Did you speak to her after the funeral?" April asked.

"About what?" Brenda made a face, then lifted a shoulder.

"Your father's will, arrangements for . . ." April let her hand reference the rifled desk, the contents of the apartment.

"No, is the correct answer," Burton told her. "We did not speak to Birdie. She didn't speak to us. We don't know who her little friends and associates might be. We never knew what she did from day to day. We don't know why she would go to a dinner at York U. None of *us* went there; we didn't support the place."

"How do you know it was a York dinner?" April asked.

This time Burton made the O with his mouth.

"Someone called us," Brenda said quietly. "Someone from there, a dean or someone."

"That's how you heard?" April took out her notebook and began to write.

"Of course that's how we heard." Brenda frowned at her brother.

"How did they know to call you?" April asked.

Brenda blinked. "I have no idea. It wasn't me. Burton got the call, didn't you, Burr?"

"Well, I didn't *speak* to anyone. Someone left a message. I was out at the time. I didn't get in until late."

"What difference does it make?" Brenda said impatiently. "You called me in the middle of the night. After that I didn't sleep a wink." She sniffed over the lost sleep.

"Did you save the message?"

"No, why should I?" Burton said.

"What did you do then?" April asked.

Silence. The siblings locked eyes.

"You know, I think I would like that water," April said, but no one made a move to get it for her. "Detective, would you like some water?"

"Thanks, water would be great." Woody was enthusiastic. Now he'd get a chance to question Burton alone.

"Miss Bassett, would you show me the kitchen?"

Brenda remained motionless in her chair. Even when April reached the door, she still resisted getting up.

"It's not like I live here," she protested finally. "I haven't lived here since I was thirteen."

"You still know where the kitchen is," her brother pointed out.

Brenda pulled herself out of the wing chair. "Follow me," she said coldly.

She led the way into the gallery with all the paintings, then through a doorway to an inside dining room that wasn't very cozy. All it had in it was an old table and some wooden chairs. When she turned around, the fluorescent light from the ceiling fixture made her look old. "The servants' dining room," she said.

"Does someone live in?" April wouldn't mind knowing what had been taken out of here since last night.

"Not anymore."

"How about daily help?"

"I wouldn't know Birdie's arrangements." Brenda moved through a doorway into a kitchen April's chef father would appreciate. It wasn't one of those new overdone ones.

This kitchen was all utility and about the size of April and Mike's one-bedroom apartment. Half of it was equipped with a huge old restaurant stove, miles of stainless-steel countertops, and high glass-doored cabinets full of crystal glasses and delicate china. The main area boasted two refrigerators, two sinks, and two dishwashers. Another section had more miles of counters, with heat lamps set into the cabinets above and a third sink and dishwasher.

"Butler's pantry." Brenda waved her hand toward the area with the heat lamps near the dining room. An open silver closet revealed felt-lined shelves, heavily laden with silver casserole dishes and plates and serving trays and salt and pepper cellars, the gamut. An elaborate coffee and tea set on a silver tray, four large candelabra, and an open chest full of flatware on the counter had already been removed.

On the question of the water, Brenda seemed stymied by the three sinks, as if each one might dispense a different flavor. April pushed open the swinging door and went into the dining room.

This, too, was like a room from a museum. The door swung closed again as April tried to absorb a level of magnificence she'd never seen before. A huge table had sixteen English-looking carved mahogany chairs set around it. A beige-and-gold Oriental carpet matched the gold trim on navy brocade drapes. The drapes were tied back with golden ropes, and the sheers underneath were closed to shield the silk-covered Queen Annes around the table from the sun. But maybe the chairs weren't Queen Anne. Who knew what they were. But April did recognize the Chinese porcelain. Valuable pieces had been removed from the display area on either side of a huge marble fireplace. A large Tang camel, an even larger Tang ram, three stunning export chargers from a much later period, and a bunch of teapots all different ages. April noticed that the marble fireplace was inlaid with brass, or maybe even gold, and above it hung a painting of a rosy-cheeked girl that April knew was a famous one. *Auguste Renoir,* read the brass plaque on the frame.

"I thought you wanted water." Brenda pushed the door open and grimaced at the dining table loaded with expensive goodies. "They were my mother's," she said defensively.

"Very nice," April said. "But please don't touch anything else or take anything out until we're finished here."

"Why?"

"Your stepmother was murdered last night. We need to go over the apartment," April told her.

"But the police were already here."

No doubt they were. Soon after the body had been identified, someone would have come to the apartment to notify the next of kin. But there had been no next of kin, and no one had stayed behind to guard the place. If Birdie had died there, the apartment would still be overrun with cops. April couldn't even guess how much the contents of the apartment were worth. But if Birdie Bassett had made a will, then her estate probably owned them. Who owned what, however, wasn't her department.

"Maybe, but there's still a lot to do. I'd like to see her bedroom," April said smoothly. Did she ever, and Birdie Bassett's jewelry box, and her closet and the contents of her medicine cabinet and her cosmetics, and the messages on her answering machine, and pretty much everything else.

Brenda gave her a truly hostile look. "What about that water?" she asked.

"Maybe later," April replied.

Thirty-nine

Jason returned many of his calls, but he delayed returning the urgent phone call of Sid Barkow, president of the institute. At four P.M. he felt he couldn't in good conscience wait any longer. He dialed the number in a fifteen-minute break between patients, fervently praying that he'd reach Sid's voice mail and be spared talking to Sid himself. Sid must have been screening his calls, because he picked up immediately.

"Hello."

"Hi, Sid, it's Jason." Jason tried not to sound disappointed.

"I know who you are. But I'm with someone. When are you free to talk?" Sid let his breath out in a long whoosh, as if he'd been holding it in all day.

"I'm free now, Sid," Jason told him.

"Okay, well, I'm just finishing up. I'll call you back in five minutes." Sid hung up. Five minutes later he called back, and right away his hysteria spewed out. "For God's sake, Jason, did you hear about Mrs. Bassett?"

"Yes. I saw the story on the news. Very sad," Jason murmured. The more he'd thought about it all day the sadder it became.

"Jesus, it's just such bad luck. Did you have a chance to talk to her about the institute?"

"You know, Sid, you're a—" Jason almost let his mouth say *sleazy bastard,* but he stopped himself in time. What was the point in antagonizing an old colleague? "No, I was supposed to meet with her today."

"Oh, God, that's just terrible. Who gets control of Max's foundation now?" he asked.

"You know, Sid, I wouldn't know that." Jason was distressed by the one-track mind. Institute, institute, institute. Couldn't anyone take a break? Poor Mrs. Bassett. She'd sounded like a nice lady.

"I thought you knew Max so well," Sid started whining. Now that the legacy was gone, he must feel very threatened.

"I didn't know him *that* well." In fact, Jason had met with Max dozens of times over the years and they'd talked about many things, but never about his dying someday, or the details of his foundation.

"Well, what were his plans for the institute when his wife died?"

"He didn't tell me, Sid. He didn't think his wife would die. She was only thirty-seven." Max hadn't thought he would die either, for that matter. Jason pondered the two deaths so close together and wondered what he'd missed in that conversation with Birdie.

"Will you find out, Jason?" Sid's voice had that panicked tone that always irritated everyone in board meetings.

"Yes, Sid, I'll find out," Jason promised in his most soothing tone.

"How soon?" Sid demanded.

"Well, I have to check my notes, talk to a few people. It may take a week or so."

"Can you hurry it up, so I can add it to my report for the June meeting?"

"Sure thing, Sid. I'll get back to you soon. Got to go. My patient is here."

As soon as Jason hung up, his doorbell really did ring. And it was Molly, who happened to be a lovely woman, ironically thirty-seven years old. When she'd come to Jason two years ago, she hadn't had a date in ten years and suffered from so many phobias that she couldn't leave her apartment for anything but food. Now she was working and dating like a maniac, even talking about getting married and having children. One of his success stories. But today he couldn't get interested in any of her exciting plans for the future.

He was distracted by remorse for having put Birdie Bassett off for a week. He should have met with her that evening. It really bothered him.

"What's the matter?" Molly gave him a funny look. He came to and smiled benignly.

"You were frowning at me," Molly accused. "You don't think I mean it?"

Jason had no idea whether she meant it or not. He hadn't been listening. "What are your feelings about that?" he asked. A shrink could turn anything back onto the patient. While Molly thought about important people in her life who had frowned at her, he pondered his relationship with Max Bassett.

Max had wanted to understand the failures of his first marriage. At the time, Jason had encouraged him to talk to a good analyst and formalize his query into why he'd been so passionately loyal to a woman who'd caused him and his children so much damage and pain. But Max wouldn't hear of it; he didn't want to pay to tell a stranger the terrible secrets that made him feel squirmy. So Jason had let Max talk to him for free. He'd been an important donor to the institute. If he'd wanted a little free treatment in return for his largesse, Jason complied. It was one of the services he donated to the institute that no one knew about.

When Molly's session ended, she left with a smile and surreptitiously wiped the doorknob of his office only twice before touching it. Two hours later, his last patient, a lawyer who booked two double sessions a week but rarely came to both—and sometimes didn't show up for either—canceled yet again. Jason was secretly glad to have the free time. He called April to ask if she could see him, and she came right over.

At seven forty-five she gave him a real hug, then took a seat in his patient chair. He was impressed. She looked even prettier than the last time he'd seen her many months ago. Her hair was longer now, and she was wearing a stylish navy suit and red blouse. In fact, she looked better than good. She had metamorphosed from an insecure and prickly female cop who knew pretty much nothing else, into a confident, competent executive who was comfortable in any situation.

"I'm glad to see you," he said, putting a world of meaning into the simple greeting.

"Well, thanks for calling. I'm glad to see you, too." She gave him a rueful smile. "I'd like to see Emma and the baby later if they're around, but business first. I need your help."

Jason smiled. "So what else is new?"

"Look, we've got our own profilers. The FBI, they've got theirs, too. Everybody's got a profiler, and everybody's in this."

"Of course. So how can I help you?" These were the words Jason said to every potential patient who came to him. Just the way the cops said to each other, "What do you need?"

"How much time have you got?" April crossed her legs and relaxed a little in the chair.

"I'm done for the day; take as much time as you want, as long as it takes."

"Okay, did you read that piece about coincidence and terrorism in the *Times* a few months back?"

Jason frowned. "About the confluence of a dozen weird and weirder deaths of people involved in biomedical research following the anthrax scare?"

"Gee, anybody ever tell you that you speak in full paragraphs, Jason?"

He laughed. "My wife."

"But yes," she said. "The idea was that the world is big enough for lots of very odd things to happen at the same time, but the world is also small enough for people to take note of odd occurrences and study them. And that even though it seemed logical that terrorists were killing off the experts, in fact, their dying the way they did was really just coincidence. Do you believe that?"

"I don't know. It's a very profound concept, but what's your point?"

"Last week my former supervisor—the man who'd promoted me to detective—was murdered in Washington Square on the way home from his retirement party. He'd left without saying good-bye, so I followed him out. I was the one who found his body." She put her hand over her eyes for a second, then went on. "I was supposed to call for help, but I didn't. I ran after the killer and ended up in the hospital. So did another man. He saw me being throttled and risked his own life to save me. New York isn't so bad, right?"

Jason frowned and started to say something, but April held up her hand. "That's not the weird part. Last night Birdie Bassett was on her way home from a York U dinner, and was murdered in a similar way in pretty much the same place. Coincidence?"

Jason opened his mouth, but again April held up her hand.

"They both had come into money very recently. They both had been alums of York, and they both had known their killer."

"Not coincidence. Someone from the university," Jason said. Being a detective wasn't so hard.

"Not necessarily. Berardino's wife died five weeks ago of natural causes. He inherited her lottery money.

Now four million of it is missing. He's murdered exactly thirty days after his wife's death. Circumstantial
evidence points to his son, who maybe didn't want to
wait for his dad to die of natural causes to get it, and
his former partner, who gave two hundred thousand
away to a girlfriend."

"Interesting, but you already told me some of this.
How much money did Bernardino get?"

"Fifteen million. Now Birdie. When her husband,
your friend Max, died, she inherited more than thirty
million, his houses, and his foundation. The lawyers
won't give the details yet. Anyway, she got hit the
same thirty days later. Sounds like the same killer is
working a pattern? A natural death, wait a month,
then kill the heir?"

"Yes, sounds like a pattern."

"Maybe it is; maybe it isn't. In both cases the children of the deceased had something to gain by the
deaths, and only one of the four has an alibi."

"Does one of the children work at York U?"

"No, but that is a good question."

"So what's troubling you, April?"

"The third coincidence. The man who tried to save
me and ended up with a broken arm is Jack
Devereaux."

Jason drew a blank. "Who's that?"

"Don't you read the newspaper, Jason? He's Creighton Blackstone's son."

"I don't know who that is." Jason's head was beginning to swim with this.

"Oh, for heaven's sake, he was one of the billionaire
founders of the Internet. He left a son no one knew
he had."

Jason brought his lips together. "Oh, yes. Now I
remember. This is a little out of my depth. Where are
you going with it?"

"Jack Devereaux walks his dog every night in the

square. He was there the night Bernardino was killed. He's an alum of York U, and the same caller at the university called both him and Bernardino."

Jason frowned and finally let his breath out. "Before or after he intervened with you?"

"Another good question. Before."

"Well, who's the caller?" Jason asked.

"We don't know yet. York U is a big place."

"April, I'm a little lost. What's your question for me?"

"Probabilities, Jason. Bernardino and Devereaux happen to be connected by calls from the university, but the perpetrators of the two murders could still be the children. You following me?"

"Right."

It had been a long, nerve-racking day. Jason was hungry and wanted to see his girls. For the first time he thought April was acting like a nut. Her voice was scratchy. Maybe she was sick. He gave her a speculative look. "So you're saying that just as the anthrax cases seemed to be connected to Arab terrorists because they occurred directly after 9/11, one of the murders appears to be linked to York University by a phone call, but in fact both murders might have been committed by the children in the end."

"Yes." April looked pleased.

Jason blinked. "Okaaay. Now what about your Jack Devereaux, who happens to be a billionaire himself now, and was walking his dog on the night of your supervisor's murder—did I hear you say he's a York U alum, too?"

"Yes, Jason, you did."

Jason blew air out. "Then you'd better tell him to stay home at night. What do you need from me?"

"I need everything you have on Max and his children. You said he wasn't a patient, so you have no confidentiality issues here. And I need to know everything about Birdie and her relationship with her stepchildren."

"That's easy. Is that it?" He glanced at his watch.

"No, Jason. I also need a profile. What kind of person in a university would target alums who became millionaires?"

"Somebody with a grievance." Jason lifted his shoulder.

"Maybe. We have the hows. Now we need the whys. Will you help me?"

Now Jason really was puzzled. "Well, sure, I'll help you. But you just said you suspected the children."

"I do, but what are the probabilities of that?"

Jason rolled his eyes. *Cops.*

Forty

By evening, NYPD brass had been informed of the York U connection between the two murder victims, but it was one of only a few facts they had under wraps about the cases. The talking heads were all over the Washington Square chop murders. Connie Chung, Larry King, and the rest of the gang were deep into their ritual prime-time dance with people in the know.

Just under twenty-four hours after Birdie Bassett's death, her mother was on TV talking about the tragic loss of her daughter, Martha. The police commissioner appeared live to make some general remarks about beefed-up security in the Washington Square area. When pressed for more information on the two murders, he hedged.

On the TV in the war room, Mike, Chief Avise, and some other important bigwigs watched their boss do business as usual. They thought the PC did pretty well until he was followed by former LA medical examiner Henry Lao. Lao always made everyone in law enforcement from coast to coast foam at the mouth with his pronouncements about high-profile cases he knew nothing about. Tonight, from three thousand miles away, Lao spoke authoritatively about retired lieutenant Bernardino's and Birdie Bassett's cause of death from karate blows. The detail with which he described what happened to the two victims happened to precede the New York City medical examiner's preliminary report on Birdie Bassett, and made both the detectives on the cases and the PC look like idiots. In fact, in the case of Bernardino, he was dead wrong. Birdie had been choked and chopped, but Lao didn't know that.

Compounding the problem, Larry King followed Lao with karate master Ding Ho, who demonstrated the one-punch-one-kill method by breaking a brick and a two-by-four with the side of his hand. This party trick hadn't been a subject of interest on TV for quite some time and further infuriated the detectives. New York City was topping the charts for the freak-of-the-week crime story.

Lightning had struck twice in the same place in the same unusual way. Now everyone in the entire world knew about it, and everyone from the PC on down was embarrassed. Embarrassment on top always passed the gas along to the ranks below. When April met Mike at his car in the garage of headquarters, his face was gray. She'd been with Jason and didn't know about the TV fiascos.

"What happened?" she asked.

"Henry Lao was on *Larry King* right after the PC. Made him look like an asshole."

"Oh."

"How did you make out?" He gave her a distracted kiss.

"Good," she said, and hugged him back hard. "What did he say?"

"Lao? He talked karate chops. Then someone came on to break bricks with his pinkie. After the PC had refused to talk cause of death, it was humiliating," Mike told her.

"You okay?"

"Oh, yeah. A lot of asses on the line, but not mine. Or yours. You got some points for the York U connection." He gave her a quick smile, then drove up and out of the garage, waved at the uniforms on guard around the barricades that kept civilian cars and vans far from the building, and took his first easy breath in sixteen hours.

April took a breath herself and settled down. It was a clear, clear night. A beautiful spring night with the kind of low humidity that gave a piercing clarity to the air and made the lights on the Brooklyn Bridge look like sparklers. Some New Yorkers had long since finished dinner and were easing toward sleep. Others were just on their way out on the town or heading to work.

"Jason and April and Emma are fine," she said slowly. "He knew Max Bassett well, Birdie not at all. Birdie was Max's secretary before she became his wife. She didn't get along with the stepchildren. They're older than she. Seems they clung to Daddy. The son never married. His father thought he was a poof. Those two are quite the pair. They were busy looting the place when Woody and I got there and probably continued after we left. Woody checked out the son's alibi. Burton was drinking at Player's Club last night. A lot of people remember him. Nothing on the daughter. She's very thin."

"How does that pertain?" Mike asked.

"Doesn't. I just like to count the anorexics. It seems the richer they are the thinner they get. Makes me glad to be poor."

"You're not poor, *querida*; you're rich in love. And her name is Martha," Mike added.

"Birdie's?"

"Uh-huh. Martha Mandelbaum. I saw her mother on TV."

"No kidding. Martha Mandelbaum." The name was no poem, but Birdie Bassett wasn't much better. The whole family was full of Bs. It was a B case. Everywhere Bs—what was the probability of that? "What's the mother like?" she asked.

"A mother." Mike was noncommittal about mothers. "What else?" he asked.

"Martha's late husband was a big giver at Jason's institute. When he called her last week to set up a meeting, she told him she thought her husband had been murdered."

"What did Jason have to say about that?"

"Nothing at the time. Late this afternoon he checked with Max's doctor, Paul Perry. Dr. Perry said there was nothing to his suspicion. Max was eighty-one. He had a massive stroke."

Mike stopped at a red light. The car was making a lot of noise. He tried to ignore it. "What about the apartment?"

"It's a museum. So much stuff there you wouldn't believe it. The vic had gorgeous clothes, beautiful jewelry, but she couldn't sleep at night. I'll check with her doctor tomorrow. There was Xanax, Valium, a whole pharmacy in there. She also liked enemas. There were dozens of them in the vanity under her sink. Some people do that to diet," she said softly.

Unlike Woody, Mike chose not to make any smart remarks.

"I listened to her messages, but who knows if any were erased by the stepchildren before I got there. I have her calendar and address book," she finished.

"What was on her schedule?"

"I haven't had time to study it. . . . What do you think are the odds of two offspring killing a parent the same way in the same place a week apart?" she asked.

"Oh, about two hundred and fifty million to one."

"About the same odds as winning the lottery, probably. But think about it. In the lottery, someone's number always comes up."

Mike groaned. "Oh, don't start with the numerology."

"I'm not kidding. What about the odds of Jack Devereaux's being in that square at the moment I ran in chasing Bernardino's killer?"

"Oh, that's an easy one. Jack was in the square every night. There was a hundred-to-one chance that he would be there."

"His father died three weeks ago."

"So?"

"Mike, we have a killer who's murdered two heirs on the thirty-day anniversary of the wealth holder's death. Is that a coincidence, or what?"

"Oh, give me a break." Mike came off the Brooklyn Bridge and hung a left on the ramp for the BQE.

"You picked it up, though, didn't you?"

"Yeah. I did, and Harry got his money the day after Lorna's funeral. Numerologist, how does that add up?"

Mike put some speed on the Camaro, and the tires squealed as he understeered around a turn. He didn't say anything the rest of the way home.

Forty-one

In the old days when April had lived at home, Skinny Dragon Mother used to show her love by force-feeding her daughter before she went to bed. Didn't matter what time April dragged herself home after work. There was always food waiting for her. One, two, three in the morning. The poodle Dim Sum would be waiting and so was the real dim sum. Pork and shrimp and vegetable dumplings, steamed rolls. Crab in ginger sauce, lamb and scallions. Succulent chicken and vegetables in the clay pot. Skinny was a big nag and threatener, but a great feeder. April sometimes got nostalgic thinking of home.

By the end of the week, the refrigerator in her kitchen was usually empty. She didn't have time to shop or cook. Mike didn't care what he ate during the day, but she was picky. If she didn't take the time to find something she liked, she went to sleep hungry and almost missed her mom. That night she missed her. After they'd settled in for the night, she lay in Mike's arms for hours listening to the steady beat of his heart and thinking about love and food and telemarketers all over the country, armed with the tools for the most insidious kind of home invasion— telephones.

People called from real companies like AT&T and Sprint, and Chase and Citibank, from charities like heart and cancer organizations, from the Special

Olympics, from Channel Thirteen. And they called for phony charities, like police and state police funds that didn't help the police. They called from chiropractors and dentists. And they called alums from universities, where they knew how old you were, where you lived, and what you looked like.

Her restless dreams were full of probabilities. Armies of black-belt wanna-bes practicing one punch, one kill against herself, naked and out of shape. Horses stuffed with thousand-dollar bills. And the approaching thirty-day anniversary of Jack Devereaux's father's death.

At four-thirty A.M. thunder struck in the distance, forecasting another rainy day. April climbed out of her bad dreams and out of her bed. Mike never knew she left. In a T-shirt and a pair of NYPD shorts, she foraged in the kitchen for food. Way at the back of the freezer she found two ancient heavily frosted roast pork buns under a half-filled ice tray. She defrosted them in the microwave and boiled some water for tea. A few minutes later as the buns were steaming, she found the calendar of the woman she still thought of as Birdie Bassett.

Detectives were forbidden to take any kind of evidence from a homicide. April knew that it was a serious breach for her to have any items from a victim's home in her possession. The calendar should be in the file along with everything else relevant to the case—the tape that Woody had made of Birdie's voice messages, the list of the last hundred numbers dialed to her phone that had been on her caller ID, the notes and receipts from her various purses, the recent mail and correspondence on her desk and in her files—the whole panoply of bits and pieces that compiled a paper trail through her life.

April didn't dwell on the infraction as she drank her tea slowly and turned the week-at-a-glance pages

of the last year of Birdie Bassett's life. Before her
husband died, when the couple had been in New
York, she'd spent her days mostly on maintenance.
Once a week she'd had her hair and nails done and
had visited Bliss Spa for aromatherapy and massage.
She had standing appointments. Twice a week she'd
played tennis at East Side Tennis in Queens, and three
times a week she'd exercised at Pilates on Fifty-sixth
Street. From time to time she'd visited doctors and
had fittings for her clothes, some of which appeared
to be custom-made. Why anyone would need to do
that in one of the fashion capitals of the world, April
couldn't begin to fathom. But the really rich were
different.

In the evening, Birdie had attended benefits and
dined out with her husband. During her winter in
Palm Beach, the drill had been pretty much the same.
The woman didn't appear to have many friends of her
own, and her routine seemed set in stone. Some life
for a woman not very much older than she was, April
thought. She poured herself more tea and thoughtfully
chewed on the soft, tasty buns, which were none the
worse for the ice crust from the freezer. She reached
the recent past in Birdie's life. After her husband died,
her routine had changed. She abruptly stopped playing
tennis and going to Pilates. New names appeared on
her calendar. She'd lunched nearly every day.

On a legal pad, April wrote down all the names and
dates, then turned to the list that Dr. Crease had given
her. Not counting the as-yet-unknown number of students who had been in the building the day of the
calls to Bernardino and Devereaux, twelve university
staff members had been at meetings there.

The dean had categorized the list. Beside each name
was a title and the location of the person's office in
the university and their reason for attending a meeting. She was a thorough person. She'd also included

a list of maintenance people who had access to the professor's office and the duties they'd performed the day in question. Diane Crease would have made an excellent detective.

As the sun rose, April began cross-checking names of people who'd attended the president's dinner, people Jack Devereaux knew at the university, names from Bernardino's private files, people who'd been in contact with Birdie Bassett after her husband died, and people who had been at both the meeting and president's dinner last night. Only three people had attended both the dinner and the meeting: Wendy Vivendi, the vice president for development; the dean herself; and Martin Baldwin, the head of alumni affairs. None of them had been in contact with Birdie Bassett. However, one person on the dean's list had been in contact with Jack Devereaux, and had spoken with Birdie Bassett many times and had had lunch with her only a week ago. His name was Al Frayme.

Forty-two

April and Mike were at Devereaux's apartment before nine Friday morning. A warrant check on Al Frayme had come up negative for past arrests. They knew where he lived and where he worked, but a deep background had not yet been done. So far he seemed clean as a whistle. Jack buzzed them up and opened the door before they reached the top of the stairs.

"It must be important if you're here yourselves."

"We wanted to be sure to get you," April said.

He laughed. "Yeah, as if everybody in the world doesn't know where I am."

"That's an issue."

"Tell me about it." He closed the door, locked three locks, two of which looked new, then led the way into the living room where a collection of cuttings from stories about him and his father was piling up on all the surfaces. It looked as if he was going off the deep end with his celebrity.

Mike raised his eyebrows. "How ya doing?" he asked, leafing through the top few clippings on his table.

"Oh, don't get me started. I'm going nuts with this. You have no idea. None of the facts about me and Lisa are true. Lisa wasn't pregnant with my baby. She never had an abortion or a miscarriage as a result of this. I'm not having a nervous breakdown over my crippling joint disease."

"You have a joint disease?" Eager to help, April flashed to ginger broth, good for rheumatoid arthritis.

"No. And although my mother did die of cancer, we weren't homeless my whole young life." Jack leaned over the back of the sofa and peeked his head around the curtain to see what was happening outside. Nothing. The fact that the press had moved uptown to Park Avenue didn't seem to reassure him.

"Well, don't take it to heart. Nobody gets the crime stories right, either." April saw two half-filled suitcases through the open door to the bedroom. He and Lisa were going someplace. That was great news.

"That's exactly the point. Look at those clippings. They say I'm a witness. You think I'm a witness. You got me under surveillance. He's killing other people right under your nose. How do I know I'm not next?"

April nodded. He was right. "Where's Lisa?" April asked suddenly.

"Oh, she's really pissed at me. She wants to get out of town." He waved his hand toward the suitcases in the bedroom. "She went to work. She works for a literary agent; did you know that?" Finally satisfied there was no one lying in wait for him on the street, Jack threw himself on the sofa. His big dog dropped to her hindquarters on the floor next to him, whimpering and nuzzling his knee. It reminded April that the detective working on dogs had not been successful in finding the dog she was looking for. Another tiny detail she was going to have to take care of herself.

"Frankly I'd go, but I don't know where. No mom, no dad to run to. It's inconvenient," Jack went on.

"You sound sorry for yourself," Mike remarked.

"I'm a little down. This second murder has pushed me over the edge," he admitted. "Now I know how women feel when there's a serial rapist out there. I have the same feeling. I can't help it. I think the press is targeting me for him, calling me a witness and everything. It may be silly, but I think that. Maybe the press wants me dead."

Suddenly he focused on the detectives. "Why are you here? Is there someone else you want me to look at?"

The small talk was over. April sat in the club chair beside the sofa and crossed her legs. Mike turned the desk chair around. They both took out their notebooks. When they were all settled, April took the lead.

"You told us the other day that you're an alum of York U."

He nodded. "Well, sure. 'Ninety-four."

"Are you a member of the President's Circle?" she asked.

"Ah, no. Should I be?" The question seemed to surprise him.

"Maybe. It's a club for people who give ten thousand a year or more to the university."

Jack snorted and glanced around his little living room, all the extra space taken by just three people and a dog. "Does it look like I do?"

"You're a rich man now. You might have started."

He shook his head.

"You haven't started giving yet?"

"No. I haven't even met the players," he said almost angrily.

"Who are the players?"

"At the Creighton Foundation? I have no idea. . . . You know, real life is not like the movies."

"Gee, that's amazing to me. What's the difference?"

Jack snorted again. "Hello. In the movies, when the prince who grew up in a humble hovel never knowing he was a prince finds out he's rich, he collects his billion dollars that day, and moves right into the palace with no backward glance at his past.

"And guess what else, the press and his public adore him. He has no problems getting a fabulous beautiful princess whom he marries on TV. Then he rules the land in a benevolent manner and lives happily and wealthily ever after."

April's face didn't change as he spoke. "So what's wrong with that picture?" she asked.

"You don't get over the past so easily, for one thing. No one gets that. Not even Lisa. My father never spoke to me once in my whole life. When I was desperate for work I applied for a job at his company and got rejected. He probably didn't know it, but maybe he did. That's not the way dads are supposed to act. Now I'm not sure I want his money. I want to smash his face in. And he's dead, so I can't do it." He made a face. "And all these clippings say I'm a weird phobic like Howard Hughes."

"So what?" Mike said. "What do you care?"

"There you are. Get over it. That's what I'm supposed to do. Shit, I don't know why I'm telling you all this."

"Because we're here," Mike laughed. "It's okay. Say whatever you want."

Jack cradled his cast with his good arm. "And then there's the little detail that some madman wants to kill me."

"How do you know he wants to kill you?" April this time.

He gave her a weird look. "You told me, remember?"

She shook her head. "I didn't say he wanted to kill you. I just said you got a phone call from the same person who called Bernardino. It could be a prank call, a coincidence."

"But now there's another murder." Jack exhaled, blowing air loudly out of his mouth. "I don't want to be paranoid, but it's freaking me."

Neither detective had a handy reply for that. "We wanted to talk to you about Martha Bassett," April said after a moment.

"I didn't know her," he said quickly.

"But you know Al Frayme pretty well, right?" April asked.

"Well, sure, he's the alumni guy at York. He called me to speak at the reunion." Jack cheered up at the mention of Al. "It was my first request."

"How much do you know about him?"

"I know he's a nice guy. After everything came out about my dad, he called to tell me my old buddies at York were thinking of me. A friendly voice from my old school. I thought it was a very decent thing to do."

"Then what?"

"Well, then we went to lunch a couple of times. York has been my family for years. You know how it is."

"What did you two talk about?"

"We have a lot in common. His dad abandoned his mom, too. Married someone else. The dad's rich, has a new family. He and his mom have nothing. He knows what I'm going through. He asked me to speak about my York experience at the reunion. He said a lot of people would be interested."

Mike nodded. "What about his private life? Do you know anything about that?"

"He mentioned karate a few times," Jack said, uncomfortable for the first time.

Mike and April locked eyes. Now they were cooking. "You didn't tell us that before."

Jack made an impatient gesture. "We were talking about stress and anger. He told me it's great physical training, and good for channeling anger. I didn't think anything of it." But he didn't look easy about it.

April put her notebook down and leaned forward in her chair. "Think hard, Jack; is Al the person who broke your arm?"

"Well, actually, I have been thinking about it. The whole karate thing made me think of him immediately. But that's because he's the only one I know who does karate."

"Why didn't you tell us?"

"It seemed too far-fetched. I felt stupid raising the issue. There must be thousands of people who do karate . . . and I didn't want to implicate a friend." He looked as if he felt really bad about it even now.

Mike and April didn't show their feelings. Maybe if he had told them his suspicions sooner, Birdie would still be alive. But Jack was still equivocating.

"And I know what he smells like. He didn't smell like the killer."

"The killer was in karate mode. He would have been full of adrenaline. His personal odor would have been different, sweaty. You may have smelled fear." April tried to stay calm. Jack had edited his comments. Witnesses were not supposed to do that. The whole case against Bill had rested on his nose. The smell of Tiger. She felt like smacking him now. Instead she remained patient.

"What does he smell like normally?" she asked.

"Lime. He smells like lime. And I wouldn't say he's big enough to take me on."

"Size can be misleading in the martial arts," April murmured. Every judgment Jack had made had been wrong. "Could you say for sure it wasn't Al?"

"No. I just didn't think it was he."

"I'm going to ask you one last time. Don't hold back. Do you have any other thoughts on Al Frayme or anything else?"

"Yeah." Jack scratched his stubbly chin. "Am I next?"

"Let's put it this way. How do you feel about taking a little vacation?" April asked.

"You mean you'd like me to get out of here?"

"We would," April said softly. "Let us do what we have to do."

Mike nodded. "Go someplace only you know about."

Jack scratched his chin. "Okay," he said. "I hear you."

Mike and April were finished and got up together. It was time to rock and roll.

Forty-three

The alumni office of York University was housed on the second floor of the main administration building on Fourteenth Street, right next to Admissions. Beyond the small reception area, Albert Delano Frayme had a small cubicle without a window. When April and Mike arrived there at noon and flashed their gold, he was busy strewing his napkin-spread work space with crusty crumbs from a French-bread sandwich.

"Lieutenant Sanchez, Sergeant Woo," Mike said.

He took a moment to chew and swallow. "Oh, excuse me. I didn't have time for breakfast today. I was just taking an early lunch." He put the half-eaten baguette down and flashed an apologetic smile. "Marty isn't in right now. Is there something I can do?"

"We'd like to talk to Albert Frayme," Mike said, eyeing the name plaque on his desk.

"Oh. That would be me. How can I help?" Al smiled again, totally benign and relaxed.

It was a little disconcerting. He did not even remotely look like a killer. He looked like thousands of midlevel employees in companies all over the world. He had a soft voice without any discernible accent, wide shoulders on a slender build, a small head with a round face, a button nose, and an eager-to-please expression. His almost-blond hair was short in the back and long enough in front to dip into pleasant gray eyes. He looked like a very nice man, until he brushed away the crumbs on his desk and showed the flat, callused blades of his big-knuckled hands.

"We're investigating the murder of Lieutenant Bernardino last week." Mike's eyes flickered at the size of the hands, but Al didn't seem aware of their interest.

"What a loss. The lieutenant was a great guy." He shook his head and brushed his palms together.

"How well did you know him?" Mike asked.

"I wish I could offer you both seats." Frayme indicated the one chair in front of his desk. "I don't rate two chairs." He laughed.

"No problem. We can stand," Mike replied.

April didn't say anything. She was standing close to the door, inhaling deeply as if the air itself could tell her this was the man who tried to kill her. The space smelled of newly baked French bread, the citrus aftershave that Jack remembered, and something else, a rotten something.

"What did you want to know?" Al frowned as if he'd forgotten the question. He looked from one to the other with no apparent recognition of April. She would work on that.

"How well did you know Bernardino?" Mike repeated the question.

"Very well. He was an alum, of course. This is the alumni office. It's our job to keep track of them." Al shrugged.

"How do you do that?"

"We send out postcards for them to fill out their news for the alumni magazine. If they don't keep in touch, we go to their parents, ask their classmates. Then, of course, we have a press service. Every time the university name pops up in any kind of article, we get a clipping of it. Same with alums. When their names come up anywhere, we know it. God bless computers, right?"

"How did Bernardino's name come up?"

"Oh, his name has always been on the front burner. He's spoken here many times. He was a local hero, you know. Everybody tried to get him to fix their parking tickets." Al laughed again. "Not that he'd do anything to help," he added quickly. "But he was useful with security issues. He helped us out . . . and, of course, a few years back when that girl was murdered in Chinatown, we did an article on him in the alumni magazine."

April flashed again to her first big case, the one that had made Bernardino notice her. She'd been the link to the family after the little girl was kidnapped by a neighbor for ransom. She was the only one in the unit who could speak Chinese.

"Then we had a theft here. It wasn't even Bernie's territory, but he helped us out with it. A real nice guy." Al Frayme nodded. "A good cop."

"When was the last time you saw him?"

"Oh . . ." Frayme scratched his chin. "Let's see. Hmmmm. I don't know that I saw him. I called him a few times."

"Why?"

He grinned. "His name came up when he won the lottery. He was a big winner. You knew that."

Mike shifted from one foot to the other. "And?"

"Well, it was a natural progression. He's always been a great friend to the university. My job is to make the ask. I knew him the best, so I was the one to make the ask."

"You called him up?"

"Oh, yes, several times."

"Where did you call him?"

"I called him at the precinct before he left. I called with my condolences after his wife died. Let's see." He pursed his lips. "I called a few weeks later to see how he was doing. We were going to have lunch, but—"

"How do you make the ask?" Mike broke in.

"Why do you want to know all this?" He looked bewildered by the interest.

"Two of your donors and personal friends were murdered. Struck with a karate chop." Mike demonstrated.

He laughed some more. "A karate chop? I don't think so."

"Why not?"

He looked at his hands for the first time. "From what I've heard it's not that easy. You might be able to disable somebody for a little while. But kill, no. Maybe a child," he amended.

"You seem to know a lot about it."

"I just use it for balance. Am I a suspect?" he asked, stroking the blade of his left hand.

April guessed he was left-handed. It was time to pin down the ME on which arm the killer had used to yoke Bernie. The death report hadn't come in yet, and not even the preliminary death report was in on Birdie. Gloss was being thorough. He had speculated on the scene that a blunt weapon, maybe the side of a hand, *could* have made the artifacts on Birdie's neck, but he wasn't sure. He wanted to photograph the bruises and try to make impressions of different possible weapons to see what matched. He hadn't speculated about which-handed the killer was.

"You do karate?" Mike asked.

"I think you know I do. Or you wouldn't be here. It doesn't make me a killer. Lots of people do it."

"True, but probably none of them know both victims." Mike and April did not look at each other as Al laughed comfortably.

"Well, you can rule me out. I love God's creatures. I couldn't kill a cockroach."

"That's good to know. Then you won't mind telling us where you were the last two Wednesday evenings."

"Oh, that's easy. I was right here. This is our big

season. Graduation, reunion. I'll be working pretty much twenty hours a day until the end of June. Our office has a big goal this year."

"What kind of goal?"

Al made a face. "Ten million."

"Is that unusual?"

"It sure is. The alumni office does not traditionally go after the big donors. We're on notice, like everyone else."

"Did anyone see you?"

"When?"

"The last two Wednesday nights?"

"Oh, I don't count them, but I'm sure. There are plenty of people around here all the time."

Mike made a note, then changed the subject. "Tell me about making the ask."

Al lifted his eyes to the ceiling. "Oh, God. It's an art, and I love it. People don't always know that they need to give back. But they really do. The fun part is opening their eyes to the need. They're so happy when it comes together for them."

"What do you mean, people need to give?" April spoke for the first time. He shifted his eyes to her and gave her an odd smile.

"Have you ever noticed how messed up rich people are?" he asked.

"More than nonrich people?" Mike asked solemnly.

"Oh, of course. Rich people have a limitless amount to give. They buy their wives, have a kid or two, spoil them all with indulgences you wouldn't believe." He let his eyes crinkle at those indulgences. "Then they leave them for prettier women who smell good. I see it all the time." He dropped his eyes to his half-eaten sandwich, which was beginning to smell.

April's nose twitched. Brie cheese, that was what it was. Warmed by the hot bread, it was beginning to soften around thin slices of prosciutto ham. And reek.

Many old-style Chinese, who could tolerate any odor of garbage, were totally repulsed by the smell of cheese. Thousand-year-old eggs (buried for weeks in crocks in the backyard) and a whole host of other fermented foods that stank to heaven were considered lovely and fragrant, but cheese products? Disgusting. April was first-generation American with old views stuck deep in her psyche. She swallowed her aversion to the rank smell and thought about Brenda and Burton Bassett.

"How do they need to give?" Mike echoed her thought. This question put Al in an expansive mood.

"Most of the money that comes to us isn't old, you know. The students who come here don't have anything. It's not like Harvard and Princeton, where families go way back. This is a down-to-earth kind of school. A lot of our kids work their way through. Frankly, we make them what they are. Down the line they become big earners. A surprisingly large proportion of our graduates make big money."

"And where does guilt fit in?"

"Oh, you want to be educated."

"Of course. What happens when they don't give?"

"They feel bad, really bad. You have no idea. People who don't give are selfish. They hurt other people." He tapped his head. "Psychology. If they give back, they feel better."

"What if they don't want to feel better?"

"I feel sorry for them, I really do."

"Did you feel sorry for Lieutenant Bernardino and Martha Bassett?"

"Very sorry," he said sadly. "I'll miss them."

Forty-four

April left Mike with the suspect and went down-stairs to make some calls. Woody Baum showed up in the unmarked unit she'd requested and waited in the car. Two good-looking uniforms borrowed from the Sixth idled by the front door of the building. Three bigger ones guarded the room where Mike was show-ing muscle while getting educated by a nut. April was on the phone for close to an hour. She called Hage-dorn at Midtown North to check on his progress with the Bassett heirs. He'd done his homework.

"Wednesday evening Brenda walked her dog at nine-thirty and didn't leave the apartment the rest of the night. Confirmed by her doorman. She would have to pass him, and he would have to unlock the front door for her to get out," he said. "She's been married twice. Two nasty divorces, came out pretty well. She owes two million on her apartment, but pays off her credit card debt monthly. She has nearly eight figures in a brokerage account. A standard credit check comes up with no financial difficulties, no other debt. She winters in Santa Fe, votes Republican, plays golf at two private clubs where she's a full member. She likes to go on cruises. Crystal Line. Two or three a year. She's clean, no arrests, no troubles in the past. I've just started, though."

"What about the brother?"

"He bought land outside of Denver for development twelve years back. Turned out there was no water there, and the zoning changed. Lost his shirt. He's down to a couple of mil, drinks like a college freshman, golfs at a club in Connecticut where he has a restricted membership. Votes Republican, had a couple of DUIs in the past. No driver's license at the moment. That's it."

"And he has an alibi for Wednesday."

"Yes. In plain sight at a bar at the time of the murder. But he could have hired someone. We need to subpoena bank records to get more. Cherry Packer is a small-time horse breeder and trainer, née Olivia Brancusi. Not even a parking ticket on her. Lot of financial problems, though. She's had to refinance the stables several times. The property is maxed out, so are her credit cards, and she owed almost nine months on her mortgage until a month ago. She does have a three-year-old called Warlord, but it's never run any race.

"Pretty horse, but probably a hacker. She's had a longtime association with Harry Weinstein. They talk on the phone every day, traveled to Florida twice together last winter. She still has two hundred twenty-five thousand in her account—didn't pay off the credit cards yet, nor has she gone on any spending sprees since the money came in. She's acting as if this is all she's getting. Do you want me to work on Weinstein?"

"That's terrific. Thanks, Charlie. I owe you. But that's a no on Harry. Mike's people are on it."

"Give me a few days and I'll come up with more," he said hopefully.

"I've got a bigger fish for you. I want you to work on a guy called Albert Delano Frayme. He's in the alumni office at York U. He's a karate freak. Hands like sledgehammers. He might have been a competitor. See what comes up on him."

"How are you spelling that?"

"Sorry. Frank, Robert, Allen, Yankees, mother, Ellen."

"That's frame with a Y?"

"You got it."

"How are you feeling?" he queried before she hung up.

"Better, thanks for asking. I didn't know you cared," she said.

"See ya."

She dialed Kathy Bernardino's number at one P.M. "What are you up to?"

"I'm going through the shit, cleaning up. No one else will," Kathy replied.

"Looking for the money?" April couldn't resist saying.

"Maybe. Your people didn't help in the mess department, and I'm sure Bill tossed the place, too. I miss Weenie, but the kids want to keep him. Dad and Mom left me the house; did you know that? It was in the will from years ago after they helped Bill buy his house."

"It must be nice to know your parents were thinking of you. The place will be great once you get it cleaned up. Are you going to live there?"

"No, I'm selling it."

April had no comment for that. Too bad. "What do you think is the significance of the number four?" she asked after a pause.

"As in million? I have no idea." Kathy's voice sounded weary. "No idea at all. Does it tie into the murder?"

"Still working on it. Have you heard of a guy called Al Frayme?"

"No, the name doesn't ring a bell. Who is he?"

"He's a fund-raiser in the alumni office at York U. He knew your dad from way back. Our guess is he started putting the arm on him for a contribution as soon as the lottery money came in."

"Him and everyone else."

"Yes, but he knew Birdie, too. Neither one gave him any money."

Kathy whooped. "I knew it wasn't Bill!" Then she was quiet for a moment. "What's the motive? He killed them because they didn't give money to a *school*?"

"This is very early days. We think he didn't want them to have a guilty conscience."

"What?"

"It's a little unclear why, Kathy. But he knew their movements well, and he had opportunity."

"Do you have anything else on him?"

"Not yet. We're still in the process of subpoenaing the wills and financial records of Birdie and your dad. The paper is coming in. In the Bassett case we don't know yet who stands to gain."

"What can I do?"

"It's Frayme I'm interested in at the moment. If you see anything with his name on it, any notes your father may have made, anything to connect the two recently, that would help. I don't want to jump the gun, but at the moment he's looking good."

"I'm sorry I haven't been more help," Kathy said after a pause.

"No problem. I'm still on your side. We'll find that money. Give me a call on my cell." April hung up. She didn't have anything else to add.

Al Frayme's name wasn't on April's list of black belts at the nearest tae kwon do studio on Twelfth Street. That didn't surprise her. She called Marcus Beame to alert Fred and Frank.

"Hey, April. I'm going nuts here with no news. What's going on?" He sounded more than glad to hear from her.

"I have a question for Frank and Fred on the karate angle."

"Shoot."

"We have a suspect. His name is Albert Frayme, with a Y. He lives in the area, East Eighth Street." She gave the building number.

"That's Frayme with a Y," Beame confirmed.

"Yes. Mixed-fight expert. He has the hands. I don't know about the feet."

"Is he the one? You'd know, you fought him, right?"

The question made her uncomfortable. Mike had given her the look in Al's office. Before that, she and Jack Devereaux had given each other the look in his apartment. Jack couldn't be sure; her memory was faulty. It was pitiful. She just didn't know.

"We're just fishing at the moment, Marcus. Just ask them if the name has come up."

"Will do. Anything else?"

"You know, yes. I'm getting a funny feeling about a guy seen walking a dog near both homicides. We've been thinking of him as a witness, but maybe he was a lookout."

"How would that play, April?"

"I'm getting some expert help on this. But I'm guessing it might be someone who was on the scene but didn't actively participate—like someone riding shotgun in a car. Frayme may be one of those guys who wouldn't kill without a friend to egg him on. Check the name Frayme, his known associates and sparring partners. If we're real lucky, one of them has a dog."

"Yeah, I got it," Marcus said excitedly.

"Call me back right away." April was sweating with excitement. That dog piece of the puzzle had been driving her nuts. Now it was beginning to play.

She caught Marty Baldwin coming in the front door of the administration building. "Mr. Baldwin. I'm Sergeant Woo from the police. I'd like to ask you a few questions." She showed him her ID.

Marty Baldwin glanced back at the two uniformed officers and nodded. He was a short, round-faced cherub with a balding head and a bulging muscle in his neck that masqueraded as a double chin. He wore a yellow-and-blue tattersall shirt and a brown suit with a red silk handkerchief in the breast pocket. "Okay. Let's go to my office," he said.

April followed him up the stairs to where the three big officers hung out in the hall.

"Did something happen?" he asked anxiously.

April didn't answer. She took the lead as they went into the alumni office, where Mike was sitting in Al Frayme's only guest chair.

"Oops, getting crowded in here," Mike said cheerfully. "Mr. Baldwin, I presume. I'm Lieutenant Sanchez, Homicide."

Marty nodded again. His eyes slid over to Al. "What's happening?" he asked again.

"Just clearing up a few details about Wednesday night. Al, let's give your boss some privacy here."

"Where are we going?" Al asked.

"To the station."

Al made a farting sound with his lips. "Sorry, Marty, looks like I'll be out of the office for a while." He glanced down, then carefully started wrapping his half-eaten sandwich to take with him.

"You won't need that," Mike jerked his head at April. She went out into the hall and beckoned the officers. They filed into the office.

"It cost nine bucks," Al protested.

Mike tossed it in the trash, and Al's gray eyes grew stormy.

"Sir, would you go into your office, please," April directed Baldwin. He complied without a word.

When Mike, Frayme, and the three officers were gone, April sat down in Baldwin's office and took out her notebook.

"Is this about Birdie Bassett?" he asked quietly.

"Yes, it is, Mr. Baldwin. On the tenth of this month you went to a meeting in the School of Social Work. Do you want to tell me about that?"

"Huh?" He was startled. He glanced up as Woody Baum came into the room.

April nodded and Woody took a seat next to her. "This is Detective Baum."

"Sir," Woody said.

He looked from one to the other.

"What was the nature of the meeting?" April asked.

Baldwin cleared his throat. "That was a while ago. I'm not sure. We've been meeting in all the schools. There are fourteen of them at the university." He made a face. "President Warmsley read the riot act when he took over, so each school has to stand on its own financially now, raise its own money." He licked his lips. "How is this relevant?"

"What time was the meeting?"

"Ah, I don't recollect much about that week, much less that day. It's the end of the school year. We're pretty pressured right now. I'd have to look it up."

"That would be good."

He didn't move. "Ah, I think the one you're talking about was pretty much a meet-and-greet. The dean there is new. Her alumni traditionally give little to nothing, so she has a problem. Going into the social services, as you know, is not the way to make money in this world."

"What was discussed in the meeting?"

"We were trying to come up with some alternative fund-raising strategies. Going to private foundations interested in vulnerable populations, to the state, and so forth."

"Is that part of your job description?"

"No. It was a waste of our time."

"Did you stay all the way through it?"

"Of course."

"How about bathroom breaks?"

Baldwin blinked. "Everybody takes bathroom breaks. What is this about?"

"What about Al; was he there?" She scribbled some notes.

"Oh, Al is everywhere."

"Does he take bathroom breaks?"

"He's in and out. I don't know why you're asking this. He's terrific. I don't know what I would do without him. He does most of the writing for the magazine. That's a quarterly. And he's great on outreach. He answers the phone, never gets annoyed."

"Mm-hmm." April wrote that down. "Tell me about the outreach."

Baldwin hesitated. "He does the reunions, follows up on careers. Thousands of them. He was very upset to hear about Birdie's death. She was an undergrad classmate of his."

That was news. So that was the reason for their lunches and talks. They went way back. Frayme hadn't mentioned it. "Did he come in on Thursday, seem normal?"

"He was upset. We all were."

"Was she one of his targets?"

Baldwin stared. "I don't know what you mean."

"As a giver."

"Oh. Yes, I guess so." He looked down as the phone rang. April shook her head.

"Did you talk about her?"

"Well, sure. We talk about everybody. They all promise to come up with the big bucks as soon as they have something to spare. With her husband out of the way, Al thought the time was now with Birdie. He's not a violent man, if that's what you're asking. Once a mouse got in his desk. He couldn't even kill that. He caught it and gave it to Maintenance."

"Thanks for the anecdote. But maybe he didn't hate the mouse," April remarked.

"I don't think he hated anyone," Baldwin said angrily.

"How long has he been with you?"

"Well, let's see. I've been here for three years. He started here after college, a decade before that."

"How come he didn't get your job?"

Baldwin checked the ceiling. "I wouldn't know that."

"Take a guess."

He lifted a shoulder. "He's great at what he does, but he's not a closer. He oversells, and that makes people nervous."

"That must be death in the getting world." April made a note of it. "Tell me about Wednesday night."

On safer ground, Baldwin exhaled and began describing the dinner. He'd left the office at four-thirty to set up the cocktail hour and talk place cards with Wendy Vivendi. It took forty-five minutes to get through it. Except for the president, they were the very last ones to leave. He was not able to verify Frayme's whereabouts on Wednesday after four.

"Thank you, Mr. Baldwin. You've been very helpful. If you think of anything else about that night, would you give me a call?" She left him a card with all her numbers. On the way downstairs Woody spoke.

"When the maintenance man came by to lock up the building Wednesday night, Al was in his office. They close down at eleven," he said.

"Anybody see him between eight and ten-thirty?" April asked.

"Not yet. Where to?"

"Wendy Vivendi," April said.

"She's on the fourth floor," he said.

Forty-five

Ever since April's visit, Jason Frank had been thinking about Max Bassett's first wife. Cornelia had been a spoiled narcissist with an arctic temperament and a scorched-earth policy toward her husband and children. She'd frozen them out of her heart, then ignited their jealous rage with her other passionate relationships. Brenda's and Burton's characters had been formed in the cradle of their mother's volatility. Neither had ever worked or ever wanted to. Neither could love or connect with anyone. And Birdie, his second wife, who'd come from a loving middle-class family and had made their father happy for the first time in his life, had been their nemesis.

One thing about Birdie's murder was crystal-clear to Jason: Her killer was organized, and the two siblings were not able to plan anything. Burton had been missing doorways and walking into walls all his life. Burton couldn't remember his own phone number and was too pickled most of the time to keep track of movable objects like his wallet and credit cards. For Burton, optimism, not regrets and rage, lived in the bottle. Drinking had never made him want to kill. For Brenda, happiness could come only in the form of a wealthy man who would love and tolerate her as her daddy had loved and tolerated his wives. Her revenge would be in making such a match. So far she hadn't been able to do it, but she was an aggressive seeker. She didn't have time to kill her stepmother.

Jason was screening his calls when April phoned late in the afternoon. "Do you want to meet someone?" she asked when he picked up.

"I haven't even located my notes yet," he said. He had his opinion, but he wasn't ready to make pronouncements. He wanted to make sure he hadn't missed anything.

"Are you free?"

"For ten minutes. What's the story on Birdie's will?"

"Don't have it yet. The lawyers have not been responsive. It's not clear she had one," April said.

"How about Max's will? Does Birdie's legacy revert to his children upon her death?"

"It's early days, Jason. I don't have that yet."

"Well, I haven't had time to do a profile on your killer," he said slowly.

"May not matter now. We have a lead. Will you come down to talk to him?"

"Who is it?"

"A fund-raiser. Looks like a nutcase to me. I want you to talk to him."

"Why me? Why not your people?"

"I have my reasons," she said.

"They are?"

"You're not threatening. I have a theory."

"A lot of people aren't threatening."

"Okay, you're not one of us."

"What else?"

"Three more things, Jason. This is between us. I want to know if he recognizes me. I want to know his feelings toward Jack, if he was targeted. But I can't go there directly. Jack is freaking out already. Maybe you could talk to Jack, too. He doesn't want to be rich."

Jason sighed. "That's it?"

"Well, one more little thing. From a psychological perspective, could this squirrel do two such bold killings on his own? Or did he have someone with him—

not actually doing the kill, but serving as a kind of commander or validator? You know what I'm saying?"

"That's very interesting, April. Ah, tonight I have a meeting at the institute until nine-thirty," he said slowly. "But for this I can cancel."

"Well, that's not necessary. Ten will be absolutely perfect. I'll send a car for you."

"Don't make it a squad car." Jason groaned. He hated traveling in a blue-and-white.

Forty-six

A l Frayme had to pee. Mike could see it in his
face. He was sealed away in the same small room
where they'd parked Cherry Packer for two days while
they'd tried to nail either Harry or Bill Bernardino.
Cherry was back upstate feeding her horses. She had
orders not to flee. Harry was home with Carol, still
on warning, too. Neither was deemed a flight risk at
the moment. And Al Frayme was all alone in the
hot seat.

Two teams of detectives were taking turns with him.
A confession would be preferable to the thousands of
man-hours it would take to make a case, but Al wasn't
the scaredy-cat type. So far he hadn't had any trouble
containing his temper or his bladder. He'd refused
soda and coffee, but spent the afternoon guzzling bottles of sparkling water without any concern about vol-
ume. Only now was it looking as if his full bladder
was getting to him. That was good. Detectives came
and went from the room, had their sandwiches and
cigarette breaks. Frayme's requests to take a piss were
ignored. He was beginning to get the idea.

When April returned from three interviews at York
and caught up with Mike outside the viewing room,
she was starved. "Have you eaten?" she asked.

"Hours ago. It's practically dinnertime now. What
do you want?"

"Club sandwich," she said.

A uniform took the order and went away to have it filled. As they waited for it, they sat outside the viewing room watching the suspect squirm in his chair.

"How's he doing?" April asked.

"He's had about four quarts, so we know he's got a lot of control. You first."

April opened her notebook and turned the pages. "Wendy Vivendi doesn't have this guy on her radar screen. He's a nonentity as far as she's concerned. He isn't asked to any of the important functions, doesn't know the president to shake his hand. The big donors are not even handled through the alumni office. Two independent teams work the donors. Under a hundred grand is the development office. Over a hundred is handled on the executive level. Vivendi does it herself. If she knew that Bernardino was a target for fund-raising, she certainly didn't tell me. Same with Birdie. Jobs are on the line for sure, but it turns out Baldwin is the one on notice. He's got the quota to fill."

April glanced up and saw Frayme all alone. He was checking his watch, tapping his foot. He had to pee.

"He's been unhappy for an hour," Mike said. "What else?"

"Let's see. The dean of the social work school remembers meeting the alumni people. She says that Baldwin pretty much nodded through it, and Al Frayme was in and out of the room."

"Clearly not to pee."

"Maybe not. Crease doesn't know either of them well and understood from the get-go that they were not interested in helping her out. Social work is pretty much the bottom of the food chain. There are plenty of students who want to do it, but the field doesn't bring in research, state, federal, or private money. No one wants the poor, the addicted, the homeless, the mentally ill. I got the whole litany. She's a desperate woman."

"So you have nothing."

"Well, maintenance doesn't clean private offices, and there was no scheduled work on the floor that day. We went in and dusted the phone. It had been wiped. We checked the desk, chair arms, doors, and doorknobs and lifted a bunch of prints just in case. Do you have Al's prints?"

"Yes, he parked them all over his water bottles. We're running them. What else?"

"The boys down in the Fifth do not have Frayme on anybody's dojo list. But he has to be training somewhere. He has to be sparring with somebody. You don't do this alone. It's a partner thing, like tennis. Since his own name hasn't come up, I'm guessing he has an alias for this aspect of his life, maybe a code name. We're getting a poster made up now. I have Hagedorn checking on his background."

The sandwiches came. April took a few delicate bites, then gave in and gobbled. When she'd finished half of it, she shifted to Baldwin's input.

"Frayme was a classmate of Birdie's. We can try him with that. Maybe she blew him off back then, and he nursed a grudge. Maybe she blew him off again with the money, and this time he couldn't take it. Baldwin said Al's a schmoozer, not a closer. He was passed over for Baldwin's job three years ago."

"A loser, then! That would play." Mike reached for her uneaten French fries.

Frayme got up and pounded on the door. "I need to fucking urinate. What do you want me to do, piss on the floor?" They'd reduced him to begging.

April and Mike slapped each other five.

Forty-seven

Jason left his institute strategy meeting early. The eight committee members had been contentious and nonproductive as usual, and the prospect of police work was far more exciting. He had plenty of experience evaluating new patients for himself and the institute. He'd worked in psychiatric hospitals, and occasionally did family and marital counseling, although couples therapy depressed him because the sessions were bitter and it was sad when people had to break up their homes. The occasional opportunity to do some forensic psychiatry was a bracing treat.

He made his excuses to his colleagues, grabbed a cab, and headed downtown, relishing the prospect of being on task in a dirty police interview room. With all those cops around, he got a testosterone high, almost as if he were one of them. And suspects were a pleasure to work with. Unlike patients, he had no loyalty to them and didn't have to stick to the truth. Whenever he had the opportunity to help nail a killer, he always felt like Bogey in a trench coat. His job was just to catch them out. It was a real nice change from having to cure them.

When the taxi pulled up in front of the Sixth Precinct, it looked familiar somehow, but he didn't know why. A lot of people were gathered there. Even at nine-fifteen it felt as if he had to push through a hundred individuals carrying guns to find April and Mike.

He made his way upstairs and through the crowded detective unit.

When he opened the door to the CO's office, where Mike and April were presently camped, Mike looked happy to see him. "Hey, Jason, thanks for coming in so late. We appreciate it. Close the door, will you?"

"No problem. I'm happy to help." Jason shut the door and relaxed. His own day was over, and for a moment he considered loosening his tie. Then he remembered that everybody here was still on duty and abandoned the idea.

Mike stood and stretched his arm across the desk to shake hands. "You're looking good. How's life?"

"Couldn't be better. You?" Jason got his second hug from April in two days, a reward for coming in.

She didn't speak, but her eyes said it all. *Thanks.* He sat down in the chair next to her, basking in the warmth. "Okay, I gather you want an evaluation. That's a relief. I'm not a profiler."

"You'll do."

For the next half an hour they filled him in on the case, discussed April's buddy theory involving the mystery man with the dog who'd been on the scene in both cases. Then they blocked out areas of interest they'd like him to cover with Frayme. Jason was a fresh face on the scene with a new role to play.

A few minutes after ten he entered the interview room, where Al had been getting his first taste of the business end of criminal law enforcement. As on previous occasions Jason was shocked by the grunge.

The small room, like so many others of its type in precincts all over the city, didn't appear to have been cleaned in some time, but maybe the mess had only accumulated since morning. It smelled of sweaty feet and spoiling food. The wastebasket overflowed. Plastic cups littered the floor. Some coffee had spilled out of one of them and not been cleaned up. There was graffiti on one wall: *Cops are dicks*—a bit of poetry that no one had bothered to erase. The lack of amenities was meant to intimidate, and it did. Jason took a look at the suspect and pasted on a smile.

"Mr. Frayme. How are you doing?"

Al was in a position of repose. His head with its light-colored hair was cradled in his arm on the table. He didn't bother to acknowledge the new visitor by lifting it up.

"I'm Dr. Jason Frank. I'm a psychiatrist," Jason added.

Then the head came up. If he'd been dozing, he was wide-awake now. "Are you a cop?" he asked.

"No." Jason laughed comfortably.

"The FBI?"

"No, no. None of the agencies. I've had a request to make sure everything is on the up-and-up. I'm neutral."

"Did the university send you?" Frayme said hopefully.

"I'm not at liberty to say. But I do want you to know I'm here to protect your interests. Are you having any problems you'd like to put on record?"

"Yeah. I was kidnapped out of my office. A fucking SWAT team—excuse my French—took me out right in front of my boss. It was humiliating. I've been cooped up here for ten hours, prevented from doing my job. They won't let me pee or call in. You are a cop, aren't you?" He eyed Jason warily.

"Absolutely not. Do you need to go to the bathroom now?"

"No," Frayme replied angrily. "Before. I had to go before."

"Are you comfortable now? Do you need anything?"

"I need to get out of here. I need to get back to work."

"Well, the workday is over now; you don't have to worry about that. But maybe I can help get you home."

"Why doesn't the university send a damn lawyer? They have a whole fucking law school—excuse my French." He said it automatically. "They could get me out of here in a snap. You know the FBI is here, too. It's been crazy."

"I understand where you're coming from. But you seem like a reasonable guy. You know what they're up against. This is an important case." Jason pulled out a chair and sat down.

"Well, I am a reasonable guy."

"That's what I heard. You're a reasonable guy, and the police are interested in you. You know what that means, right?"

"A dozen fucking cops and FBI agents tried to confuse me about the facts of my own life. Excuse my French, but do they think I'm stupid?"

Jason smiled. "As long as you know them, you'll be fine."

"What?"

"The facts of your life," he said.

"Oh, ha, ha. What's the university doing for me?" Frayme propped his chin on his hand and tried to look boyish.

"I believe their position at the moment is that a clean bill of health will go a lot further than aggressive saber rattling. Raising hackles won't cut it with them. Got it?"

"Oh, Christ, don't give me that humanities shit."

"Yeah, well, play ball or lose sympathy, that's the word. You're up against the Feds, here, too. A very important case."

"Yeah, and the victims were friends of mine. This is doubly hard on me." Frayme sighed hugely. "Okay, I'm on my own. What if I want a lawyer?"

"I'm sure one will be provided if you need it down the road. For now we're asking for your help. This is a critical time for everybody. You don't want to embarrass anybody, do you?"

Frayme made a noise in his throat. "Tell me about it. I'm pretty embarrassed myself." But he didn't look embarrassed saying the words.

"Okay, then let's prove they got the wrong guy." Jason scratched his chin. "Why don't you start with the fighting."

"They're making a mountain out of nothing. It's a hobby, that's all. I told them that. There's nothing more to it." Al rubbed his hands together.

"I hear it's a hobby you can get into pretty deep."

Al dipped his chin. "It's interesting. There's a lot to it, like chess."

"You ever tell anyone it was a religion to you?"

"Hell, no! I never said that. I never talked about it."

"Are you sure?" Jason sat back on the uncomfortable chair. He was having fun already.

"Of course I'm fucking sure, excuse my French. I did it for balance, that's all. Like dancing school."

"Did you tell them what school you go to?"

"The detectives or Devereaux?"

Oops, there was a name. Jason was careful not to look in the viewing window. "The cops, of course. Did you tell them what school you go to?"

"No, because I don't go to school. I work at home," he said without blinking.

"You said before it was like chess. Don't you have to play with someone else?"

"Not really."

"What about training? Doesn't someone have to teach you how to do it?"

Frayme shook his head. "I don't like the slants. I never wanted to get into it."

"Slants?"

He made a face. "You know, the whole Oriental thing. They give me the creeps. Why are you asking me all this?"

"Oh, I thought you might have a sparring partner, a school, where the people can vouch for you." Jason lifted a shoulder.

"Oh." Al's face froze. "I told you I work alone."

"You just bang away at the bricks in your living room?" Jason sounded doubtful.

"That's right. That's how I train."

"Must be dusty," he remarked.

Frayme shook his head again. His face held a blank expression. "Not at all. I wrap them in napkins. I told you. I don't fight. I just do it for balance."

"How do you get the balance if you don't practice with anyone?"

He didn't answer.

Jason made a clumsy karate chop with his hand. "What does this have to do with balance?"

"I don't use it to fight."

"Okay, if that's the truth, it's the truth," Jason said. "But what about the witnesses?"

"Oh, Christ. Come on, you know they don't have witnesses." He put his wrists together and raised them over his head. "If they had witnesses, they'd have arrested me already. Anyway, they were my friends. Why would I hurt my friends?"

"Well, that's a good question." Jason tilted his head. "Sometimes friends piss each other off and they're not friends anymore. Then one might have to take revenge."

"Not me. I'm a sweet guy."

Whenever a man claimed he was a sweet guy, Jason always knew he probably wasn't. Nice guys didn't have to advertise for themselves. "Well, that's good to know. I want to talk about karate some more. How long does it take to get good?"

Al made a noise with his lips. "A long time."

"What level of skill do you have?"

Al shook his head. "I wouldn't know. I'm not into competition."

"Okay. When these murders occurred, you were working a big donation with both of the victims. Isn't that a little suspicious?"

A little anger erupted in Al's eyes. "No. This is a personal tragedy for me," he said.

"You hoped it would get you out of the alumni office, away from your do-nothing boss, right?"

Frayme shifted in his metal chair. "How do you know that?"

"Oh, there's a lot of change happening. It was time for a change for you. You do all the work. He does nothing. Clear as crystal. All you needed was one little break on the donor end, and you'd be golden in corporate. That's what you wanted, right?"

Al nodded. "I deserved it. I've given everything for this school."

"Well, maybe your friends refused you, and you lost it," Jason suggested.

Frayme shook his head. "It wouldn't happen like that. I used to get mad, but I don't anymore. I've grown up."

"Why did they refuse you?"

"I didn't say that. I said if they *had* refused me I wouldn't have been hurt or angry. I'm way over that. I've learned a lot."

"You've learned a lot from your karate. And you're a sweet guy. Maybe you didn't mean to hurt them, just a slap on the cheek."

"You'd have to prove it," he said, looking down at his hands.

"Okay, I understand. I can see how it might happen. That lottery cop coming along the night of his retirement party, a little high and loose, celebrating his good fortune right in your neighborhood. Maybe it was just a chance meeting. He told you he was going to Florida, was taking off without giving you any of his money. So you hit him, just a little tap."

"That's not the way it happened." Frayme slammed his fist on the table so hard it jumped off the floor. "I didn't hit him. I wouldn't do that."

"So how did it happen?"

"I don't know. I was in my office."

"But no one saw you there."

"Doesn't mean I wasn't there."

"Okay, so you're a bit of a loner, no one to practice with. Maybe you don't know how strong you are. The cop pissed you off . . . an accident. We could work with that."

"I'm not a loner," Frayme said sullenly. "I have people."

"You just told me you practice your religion alone. Doesn't that make you kind of a loner?"

"Marty sits all day playing chess with a fucking computer. If no one sees it, what kind of win can that be?"

"I see your point. Now, Birdie told you she was giving ten thousand to the university the day she was murdered. That must have been a disappointment for you."

"Listen, I don't know where you heard that. It's a crock. I was getting a couple of million from each of them. B and B were doing it for me. I'm telling you it was a sure thing. You just said I was on the way up. Why would I kill my future?"

"Do you have anything to support that, something in writing?"

"Who wants to know?" Frayme's chin quivered. "Maybe I could document with my notes. The pledges were made on the phone, but I don't have tapes. We're not supposed to do that."

"Did Baldwin know about it?"

"Not the amount. He would have tried to handle it himself, and the man couldn't squeeze dick out of the mint." He paused. "Do they think we could go to the estates?"

Jason raised a shoulder. "Maybe."

"I could take a crack at it," Frayme said with an engaging smile.

"How about Jack Devereaux?"

"Oh, God. Don't get me started on Jack." Frayme looked at the graffiti without seeing it.

"What about him?"

"A sad story! I know what it's like. My dad left me, but at least I know where he is. Jack's dad wouldn't even admit he had him. I feel real bad for him."

"Well, you don't need to feel bad for him now. He's on top of the world now. A wonder boy."

Frayme laughed. "Oh, you don't know him. He's a real kook. Afraid of his shadow—crazy-in-the-head paranoid. Look at what he told you about my fighting. A lot of paranoid lies."

"Jack is paranoid? I didn't know that."

"Well, it's common among them. You can't imagine what it's like working with those people day after day. They get some money in their hands and they start treating you like shit."

Jason flashed to his rich banker client who often treated him like shit. "I bet it's tough," he said. Then he got down to it and began questioning the suspect in earnest.

Forty-eight

By midnight Jason had covered all the subjects on his list more than once. He thanked Al for his help and told him he'd see what he could do to get him out. A few minutes later Albert Frayme was quietly released from the Sixth in spite of the many inconsistencies in his story and incriminating statements he'd made. A uniform came in and told him he could go.

By then the squad room had emptied out, and practically no one was there. Only a few people from the second tour were left. Al carried his last water bottle with him as he skipped down the stairs to where Mike and Jason were waiting by the front door of the building.

"Thanks for coming in, Al; you've been a big help," Mike said.

"Am I done?" he asked.

"Yes. You're done for now. We may need your help down the road. You want a ride home?"

"No, thanks. No more hospitality, please. I'll walk." Al glowered at the heavyset lieutenant at the front desk, then put the water bottle right next to his hand.

"Garbage," he said, and gave Jason a triumphant look.

"Don't leave town, and don't get in any trouble," Mike advised him.

"I don't get in trouble." Al stuffed his hands in his

trouser pockets and walked out the front door, whistling a happy tune as if all his business there were taken care of.

"Why didn't you let me crack him?" Jason asked when the door closed and he was gone.

"We still have some details to pin down. If we can't place him on the scene, we've got a problem. He won't give on his sparring partner. That may be the missing piece. If we can get him and persuade him to testify, we can make an arrest. Come on; we'll drive you home."

"Are you sure you want to? It's out of your way."

"No problem."

April came out of the muster room. "Ready to go?"

The men nodded. Mike disappeared for about sixty seconds behind a closed door, then came out jingling somebody's car keys. He'd snagged a nice unmarked vehicle that was conveniently parked out front.

"Let's roll." He got in the front seat of the shiny Lumina. Jason took shotgun, and April sat in the back.

"So I thought that went very well," Jason said as soon as they were settled.

Mike fired up the engine and pulled out. "Yep, we've got a scrambled egg, all right."

"He's got the perfect job for his mission," April murmured.

"Absolutely," Jason said. "He's surrounded by the kind of people he hates. He's a perfectionist, but not a visionary. He doesn't hear voices. He has an idea what's going on around him, but has trouble reading people and computing the meaning of their actions. He's a narcissist. He actually believed he was important enough to merit an emissary from the university with the power to get him out." Jason paused for breath, then went on.

"He likes to be in control. In the next interview, if

you tell him you need his expertise on martial arts and ask for his help, he'll talk your ear off and give you some specific details about the killing. He said he didn't hit Bernardino. He knew the killer hadn't hit him and was angry when I gave a wrong detail."

"Would you have been able to predict who he was?"

"I might have gotten a few things, maybe. The fact that he did so many things right out in the open— used the phones to call his victims, had lunch with them. I'd guess he probably followed them around. He feels personally close to them. Calls them B and B. I wonder if that's his favorite drink. Of course, he never thought anyone would connect the dots. I'd have guessed someone who was powerless but felt invincible. Had reason to feel that way. Was maybe thirty to thirty-five years old. How old is he?"

"Thirty-six."

"Ha. And his core feeling would be chronic rage."

There was very little traffic, and Mike sped up Third Avenue. Jason still felt the high.

"He must have been cooking for a long time. These murders are the act of someone who's been building up to it. I'd say he's been able to contain his rage at his position, both at the university and in life, because of a profound feeling of superiority that he's developed from his karate and his identification with the powerful and successful father who rejected him long ago."

"And then a new president came in," April said.

"Yes, a new dad to please. And some good luck for a change. Some of the alums he actually knew had a dramatic change in fortune. B and B. Here's your coincidence, April. Bernardino and Birdie unexpectedly came into money. Frayme finally had his chance. He acted like a long-lost friend to them, called them frequently until they rejected him. This happens to be a repetition of the story of his life. No one thinks he's important. No one takes him seriously. I wonder if he's hurt anyone in the past."

The three of them were silent for a moment.

"And of course the murders were displacement of his rage against his siblings, who were born and took his place after his father remarried. When B and B held out on the cash and love that he needed to move up with the wealthy people he identified with, he did to them what he never had a chance to do to his real brother and sister. He throttled them."

"Transference is all," April murmured.

"And he's a narcissist. He doesn't think anyone exists except as his friend or his enemy. You noticed that he projected his own paranoia onto Devereaux," Jason added.

"He thinks Devereaux told on him. That pissed him off."

"It's his need to be in control of people that consistently alienates them. When his charm fails to win people, he has to annihilate them. In the past he just did it in his head. Now he's moving on to killing. He's a mission killer. Rich people."

"Did you hear him complain about the Asian students?" April murmured.

"Yes. He didn't recognize you because you all look alike to him."

"I wondered," April said.

Mike took Seventy-ninth Street across town. It was a beautiful night. The trees in Central Park were fully dressed for summer, turning the street into a leafy bower. The perfume of spring was heavy in the night. On the West Side he came out on Eightieth and Central Park West, only a hop away from the Twentieth Precinct, where they all had met. The cross street changed direction at Columbus. Mike had to go south on Columbus to get farther west.

"Two things bother me," Jason said as they rejoined Seventy-ninth Street and cruised closer to his home on Riverside Drive.

"Only two?" Mike said.

"How good are Frayme's fighting skills?"

"He took Bernardino with no trouble at all, and Bernie was a big guy," April said.

"What about you?"

"And he took me," she said quietly.

"About Marty, he said what was a win if no one saw it. I think you're right that he has a fighting partner. He kept saying he'd learned. I think what he learned was how to channel rage into fighting power. He's very organized, very tied to his work. I'm sure he isn't traveling far. Convenience matters to him; the gym would have to be close."

"Yeah, that's what I'm thinking. What's the other thing?"

"It's related to your theory, April. He's a careful guy. How did he know that no one would come along and stop him?"

"Are you thinking his friend might actually have lured Birdie into the square?" Mike mused.

"Maybe. The more I think about it the surer I am that he didn't act alone."

Mike drew up in front of Jason's lovely prewar building on Riverside Drive. "April?"

"Good night, Jason. Thanks for everything," April said.

Jason grunted and got out. "Keep me informed," he said.

Forty-nine

April's heart was racing. "We need to talk to Hammermill again," she said excitedly as soon as Jason was out of the car. "If we could just nail the dog down, we'd have something solid. If the dog I saw on the street when Bernardino was killed and the dog Hammermill saw when Birdie was killed are the same dog, we have that accomplice. This is coming together."

"Maybe if we showed him some photos it would help," Mike suggested.

"He told me it was a brown dog."

"There are a lot of big brown dogs, *querida*. Labs, all the sheepdogs and shepherds, retrievers. Weimaraner. Dozens."

"Weimaraners are gray," she said, "and I know it wasn't a German shepherd or a Doberman or a rottweiler. But photos would help me, too." She plucked her phone out of her purse and dialed a number, then put the cell on speakerphone so Mike could hear. "Woody, it's me," she said. "Get me some flip charts on dogs."

"And hello to you, Sergeant. It's one in the morning; where am I going to get that kind of thing now?"

Mike shook his head.

"Not now. In the A.M., Woody."

They heard him sigh. "Okay. What do you need?"

"I need dog pictures."

"Can you narrow that down?"

"All the big brown ones."

"Yes, sir. And Sergeant, Frayme was at the funeral."

"Bernardino's?"

"Yeah, his picture came up several times in the crowds. He was at the cemetery."

"Thanks, Woody." She hung up and turned to Mike. He was talking softly on his phone while she dialed another number. Now they were cooking.

"Jack, am I waking you up?" she asked.

"Who is it?" came a sleepy voice.

"April Woo."

"Oh, Jesus, April. What time is it?"

"Sorry to bother you so late. This dog question is still really bothering me. Did you give any thought to other dogs when you were walking Sheba in the square that night?"

"Jesus, there are always other dogs."

"I know, but we have to nail this down. Sheba was barking. What was going on before you became aware of me?"

"Gee, do I have to do this now, April?"

"It's important."

"Yeah, there was somebody with a big dog. The dog barked at Sheba, but I got distracted when I saw you. Listen, Al called me a while ago. What's going on?"

"What did he say?"

"He said you interrogated him all day, and he's helping you with the investigation. Is he cleared?"

"Did he say anything else?"

"He was upset that I told you about the karate thing. He said he'd told me about it in confidence. It caused trouble for him, but it's all cleared up now, and everything is fine. Is that true?"

"Did he say anything else?"

"No, he was very open about the whole thing. He

told me he was treated like a suspect, everything but the fingerprints and the lie-detector test."

April snorted—another stupid criminal. They got the fingerprints and the DNA (should they need it) from his water bottle. Only the molds of his handprints were left to do, and they wouldn't do it until the ME told them they had a mark on the body they might be able to match with it. "Was he disappointed about that?" she said.

"No. Completely secure in his innocence. He was excited. He wanted to make a lunch date to tell me all about it."

"What, at midnight?"

"He sounded a little high, April."

"Interesting."

"It was a little creepy. He didn't seem to mind being a suspected murderer."

"Well, people like attention," April told him. "What did you say about the lunch?"

"I don't know where you're going with this, but I can't be sure he didn't break my arm, so I said no to the lunch. I told him I was going out of town for a couple of weeks."

"Good. I'm going to want you to look at some dog photos in the morning. See if you recognize any of them from the neighborhood. What time are you leaving?"

"Noon. Can I go to bed now?"

"Sweet dreams."

"Help me out, *querida,*" Mike said when she hung up. "I told Marcus we need the list of martial-arts studios in a twenty-block radius of Fourteenth Street, especially the ones on the East Side with professional sparring partners and non-Asian masters. He wants to know what system Frayme favors—karate, tae kwon do, judo, tai chi, kickboxing, hapkido, kung fu. There's a mess of them."

"Put him on speaker. Marcus, hey. The serious practitioners learn more than one system. Bear with me while I fill you in. The Chinese claim that karate derived from kung fu. They're both unarmed methods of combat with all parts of the body used to punch-strike, kick, or block. Karate itself means 'empty' or 'China hand.' Judo, jujitsu, and go ti are wrestling forms and considered the art of the gentle. That's out. Tae kwon do is the Korean method—probably the most popular form of martial arts these days, called 'way of the hands and feet.' There are tournaments for all the systems, but the belt grades and many terms derive from the Japanese. And everybody has to learn the kata, the moves and maneuvers. Kenpo may be what Frayme favors, since he's a fist man. Kenpo comes from Hawaii and the Americas, introduced by a guy called Ed Parker. Most people learn several mix-fight methods, bits and pieces of several systems."

"Can you narrow this down a little?"

"Frayme probably goes to a place called Tiger Strike, or Praying Mantis, or Silent Warrior—as you said, no Korean or Japanese or Chinese name. Maybe U.S. professional, something macho without a particular accent." April lifted a shoulder.

"That's what I told them. What about the brick thing?"

"Okay, my take on this is he doesn't break bricks at all. That's too old-fashioned. A clumsy party trick. He was talking about doing it for balance. That means not standing there and pounding something but moving. That means he'd be working with kick mitts and striking pads, coaching pads. I believed him when he said he did that at home. You can get sandbags and platforms and various kinds of striking pads to practice at home, but it wouldn't be enough. He certainly had the ridge hand of a fistfighter, which means he could fight without a protective mitt, but I wonder if he was wearing one when he killed Birdie."

Mike slowed in front of the precinct, where they

had to switch cars. It was one-thirty. "We need to clear this up with Gloss. This may be what was bothering him. The bruise on her neck might be wider than the blade of a hand," he said. He turned off the headlights.

"Want me to call him?" April asked as he went inside to return the keys.

"I already did. He's not picking up the page."

"Well, he'd better get to it if we want to resolve it before the funeral." April yawned and got out of the car. She could hope, couldn't she?

Fifty

After April and Mike switched cars and drove home, it was both a long night and a short one: long on worry, short on sleep. Bernardino's case was a little like lightning. The one strike sent down more than one deadly streamer and left some unresolved issues. Even if they indicted Frayme for the murder, four million dollars was still missing, and Harry Weinstein had briefly been in possession of two hundred and fifty thousand of it. So far there was no trail that led to Bill or Kathy. But for Bernardino's sake, April was not going to be able to let go of that. Launching further assaults on a tough old cop was not going to be easy. More important at the moment, though, their only really viable suspect was still walking around, making late-night phone calls and working out with his unregistered weapons. Mike and April were too wired to calm down.

April was up again at five-thirty, drinking hot water and scanning the yellow pages for martial arts. She was not surprised to find some of the names that had come to her on the spur of the moment. Silent Warrior would be a natural. It was there. So was Praying Mantis. She was also attracted to the strongly American typeface of Professional Prepare at Twenty-second Street and Broadway.

Mike was up at eight, on the phone again trying to reach the ME. More than forty-eight hours after

Birdie Bassett's murder, the preliminary death report on the cause of her death still had not left his desk. Her funeral was set for Sunday afternoon out in New Jersey, and he was determined to have some resolution before then. Dr. Gloss didn't pick up the second urgent page and return the call until nine-thirty Saturday morning. By then, Mike and April had already visited Ducci in the lab for the second Saturday in a row and were on their way into the city.

"Yeah, Mike, what's up?" Dr. Gloss said.

"How about Birdie Bassett? We're at a critical juncture here."

Gloss sighed. "Yeah, I know. You'll have the prelim as soon as I do. I'm still working on it."

"By now you should already know pretty much everything you're going to know."

"What's your hurry?"

"The funeral's tomorrow, and we need some specifics to move forward."

"Well, nobody told me there was any particular rush," Gloss said.

"I'm telling you. Aren't I good enough?"

"Don't get huffy. I can give you generalities. What do you need?"

"How about the murder weapon?"

"Look, that's what I'm working on. I want to be sure. She has some deep premortem bruises on her neck. It looks like he roughed her up a little before he killed her. The bruising on the neck is consistent with manual strangulation, the kind from his squeezing and her struggling that would take place in that circumstance. There's a bruise at the base of the neck possibly caused by pressure from the killer's hand."

"But . . . ?"

"But there are no petechiae in the mucosa of the lips and lids of the eyes. And, of course, you saw her face. It wasn't the dark red that would be consistent with the slow bleeding that occurs with strangulation. And her neck is broken."

"So the blow killed her. Tell me about the blow."

"Okay, the blow. More force was used than would have been necessary to kill her. The neck is broken, as I said. The spinal cord is crushed. All this indicates that she did not ultimately choke to death slowly."

"Okay, we know that. So he started to strangle her and changed his mind."

"It looks that way. He changed his mind and hit her. Maybe somebody interrupted him. Maybe she did something to infuriate him."

"Okay, could be either. But what did he use?"

"That's what I'm working on. We know it's some kind of blunt instrument. He could have come at her with his hand, but I want to be sure it wasn't a pipe or a baseball bat. We're measuring, okay; we're trying to make a match with different things. It's too easy to go for the karate stuff. It's possible he hit her with something else."

"Lao really hit a nerve, huh," Mike said.

Gloss grunted angrily. "Look, it's not that easy to kill someone with a hand. Arm yoking, absolutely. Break their neck, easy as pie. You have to be strong, but a lot of people are strong. Crushing a spinal cord with a hand"—he clicked his tongue—"that's another story . . . but on the other hand, if he had used a pipe why not just bash her on the head? You see, it's not such an easy call."

"His psychology is the key to this."

"Whatever makes the case."

"If he's a kung fu nut, he'd want to use the hand in the traditional way. Are you telling me it wasn't a hand?"

"All I'm saying is, it could be. We're still trying to get an impression, work backward."

"What about a protective mitt?"

"No, a mitt would have spread out the bruising."

"All right, can you tell me which hand the killer used?"

"Oh, that I can tell you. The killer was facing her. The blow was on the left side of her neck. That makes him left-handed."

"And Bernardino?" Mike said excitedly.

"Bernie was yoked from behind. Pulled from right to left. The guy's still left-handed."

Mike whistled. "Thanks."

"Well?" April asked when he hung up.

"A lefty, just like Ducci predicted, and he wasn't wearing a mitt."

"A purist. That son of a bitch Ducci. Amazing how somebody who never even saw the body could be so sure."

"He saw the photos. Home sweet home, *carita.*"

They pulled up in front of the Sixth, where Woody was waiting outside in the sunshine, turning the pages of a book.

"Look at these cuties," he said when they parked the Camaro and got out. "I used to have one like this." He pointed at a little white hair ball with two black ribbons on its crown. A real man's dog, with a fringe so long its paws were covered.

April glanced at the photo. "Jesus, Woody. A Maltese?"

"Did you locate Hammermill?" Mike asked.

"Yeah, he's out in the Hamptons. Want me to drive out with the pictures?" he asked hopefully. It was a nice day for a drive.

April took the book out of his hand. It still had its Barnes and Noble price sticker on it. Woody had done things the easy way, as usual. He'd paid thirty-five dollars for *Choosing a Dog for Life,* and would put in for the refund. Still, it had good pictures of 166 breeds. Should do it. They went inside where the task force was assembled for the morning meeting.

Fifty-one

Breakfast was Krispy Kremes. A couple dozen detectives gobbled them up as if there were no tomorrow on fat, talking the case and drinking extra-large cups of coffee. The ones who never learned were smoking, too. April studied the dog book, something she should have done in a much more focused manner a week ago.

"You want me to run out to the Hamptons and interview that guy Hammermill?" Woody whispered in her ear. As usual, he'd do anything to get out of that room and out on the road.

"Not right now, Woody." She turned some pages, hoping some canine posture would loosen up her blocked memory.

"That's a cute one." He pointed to a bloodhound. "He's got a nose like Harry's. Ha, ha. Get it, a nose for money?"

"Is that a Jewish joke, Woody?"

"Of course not." Woody was Jewish, so he looked offended.

She noted that bloodhounds were twenty-six inches tall, a pretty standard size for lots and lots of brown, and tan-and-russet, and black-and-tan dogs. How could she remember which one she'd seen among all these haulers, herders, hunters, chasers, retrievers, sniffers, swimmers, guiders, and savers? There seemed to be a dog bred to do just about anything. She wanted to stand up and measure how high twenty-six inches was but didn't have a tape measure with her. She was pretty sure it was a mastiff, but there was more than one kind. She smiled. Shown at different stages of maturity, these dogs were pretty much all cute. It was hard to look at them and pay any attention to the task force meeting.

The big boss had been right when he'd said back at the get-go that this case was too personal for her. Right now she was ahead of everybody else in her thinking, so she couldn't even pretend to be interested in the catch-up going on. Charts up on boards showing the last twenty-four hours in the lives of the victims and the suspects. Albert Frayme, Harry Weinstein, Bill Bernardino, the Bassett siblings. What they'd been doing then. What they were doing now. None of that was important now.

When it came time for the playback segments of Frayme's taped interviews, she gave up and went to the ladies' room. She'd heard almost all of it before and didn't want to revisit Frayme's Asian phobia. He didn't like slants. He'd said it when she was sitting right next to him, as if she didn't exist. How to win friends and influence people.

In the ladies' room, she gazed at herself in the mirror, then washed her hands and her face and reapplied her makeup. She had to prepare for war. When she was ready she went downstairs, took out her cell, and listened to her messages. She wasn't going back into that room. Mike could yell at her later. She didn't care. She was going to find the place where Frayme trained. In the end, she always had to do everything herself.

She listened to her four messages. Skinny Dragon, Devereaux, Marcus Beame, and Charlie Hagedorn. Skinny Dragon wanted to be taken out for a ride. Saturday was her shopping day, and Astoria where she lived didn't have the best stuff. The dragon wanted worm daughter to pay attention to her, take her to Flushing. April called Skinny back and told her she couldn't play chauffeur; she had to work.

"Half day enough. Your father don't feel good." Skinny stuck in the knife. "Better come at three."

The parry struck home. Did her dad have a big hangover or did they need a lightbulb changed? "We'll see how it goes, Ma." April had learned a long time ago never to give her mother an absolute no. Then she called Devereaux.

"Are you coming over or not? We're getting ready to leave," he said the minute she identified herself.

"Yeah, I'll be there before noon, promise. Where are you going?" she asked.

"Lisa's parents have a house on Martha's Vineyard."

"Nice place, I was there once." She was relieved he was still determined to get out of town. She was just finishing up with Devereaux when Woody appeared with the dog book.

"Where to, boss, the Hamptons?" he said, looking relieved to have found her.

"No, not the Hamptons. What took you so long?" she demanded.

"What am I, a mind reader?" He gave her a look, then opened the precinct door for her.

At least he'd learned some manners. Outside he opened the passenger door of the unmarked vehicle from Midtown North that he'd brought for her. She was gratified that old dogs could learn new tricks. As soon as he'd closed the door for her, she ignored him the way her bosses always ignored her.

She strapped herself in and dialed Hagedorn. "Sergeant Woo," she said when he came on.

"Finally. Okay, I got the skinny on Albert Delano Frayme. Frayme took his mother's name after the divorce, so I went back and found the court records. His father's name is Alberts. His birth name was Albert Delano Alberts, Junior."

"A.A.," April said.

"Is there some significance to that?"

"Only that the two victims were B.B.s."

"Okaaay. So I checked further. Frayme has a double identity with credit cards and a social security number in the name of Albert Alberts. You want me to subpoena the credit card records?"

"Very good, Charlie!"

"Is that a thank-you?"

"That's a dinner at your favorite eatery."

"Check. What about the subpoena?"

"Go for it. Everything you can get on him."

"Anything else?"

"That's peachy for the moment," she said.

"Where to, boss?" Woody was playing with the car keys like a six-year-old.

"Devereaux's home," she told him.

Then she dialed Beame. "Sergeant Woo."

"Hey, April. Mike isn't picking up. You wanted likely dojos, right? I got Praying Mantis. It's 16 East Thirty-second Street. Professional Prepare is on Twenty-second Street at Third Ave. I have three more. You want addresses? You were right on the Silent Warrior call, but it's too far uptown."

"How far up?"

"Two Hundred Thirty-second Street in the Bronx."

"Too far."

"We were checking for more Caucasian gym owners. But that requirement cut the list way down. There are a few more on Bowery. All the suppliers are down there. We could check with them. They'd know who's who. A lot of others are on the West Side and Midtown too. How wide do you want to go?"

"I have an a.k.a. now. Alberts is his father's name. Al Alberts."

"Okay. This is good. Then your first choice is Professional. They didn't have a Frayme on their members list. But Albert struck a chord when we spoke with them. They have an Al. We were going back there with the photo today. You want me to do that now?"

"Uh-uh, Woody and I are in the neighborhood. We'll go."

"You like to do everything yourself, don't you, Sergeant?" Beame said. "I'll bet you knew the locations already."

"Nope, I didn't," she lied. "Thanks, Marcus. I'm going to remember you on your birthday."

"It's July nineteenth," he said.

"Woody, turn right here; we're going to Third Avenue."

"Yeah, boss." He hit the siren, and the tires screeched as he cut across two lanes of oncoming traffic.

Fifty-two

Ten minutes later April and Woody located Professional Prepare's building on Third Avenue and left
the car in front of a fire hydrant. The gym was on the
fifth floor of a five-story commercial building, and the
stairs getting up there were steep. April could hear
Woody panting a little as she stepped back to let him
go through the door first. Clearly he'd never practiced
his *chi kung,* the breathing so vital to physical power
and control in all martial arts. She snorted and stared
at the door in front of her when he leaned against the
wall to catch his breath.

As Jason had predicted, no Chinese or Japanese or
Korean calligraphy was exhibited next to the name.
No yin/yang or mystic symbols were displayed either,
no front-kicking silhouettes. The gym's door was
painted black and had a simple sign with *Professional
Prepare* in block letters. It looked like a no-nonsense
kind of place with a greater emphasis on the fight than
the philosophy.

Finally Woody stopped wheezing, grasped the door
knob, and opened up. Bright light from a skylight
shone down on an entry formed by movable screens
that blocked any view of the activities beyond. In the
small space was a metal desk; on top of it were an
open appointment book, a leafy bamboo cutting in a
vase full of water, and a telephone. At eleven-thirty
on Saturday the place sounded busy.

On the other side of the screens, kumite sparring commands and training grunts came from both directions. No one was seated at the desk, so April paused to examine three walls of photos covering every inch of the rice-paper panels. The photos showed buff white males in various tournament settings, dressed in traditional gi and caught by the camera in appropriately impressive maneuvers with their black belts flying. Vertically along one screen was a row of members who were of the eighth- to tenth-degree black-belt rank that designated them honored masters. Five big guys with blank expressions and black tengui wrapped around their heads indicated this was a serious place. They looked between thirty and fifty years old. Albert Frayme was not among them. In a line next to them were fifth-degree-black-belt-ranked members, then fourth, and the ranking went down to the beginner level. Albert Frayme was not pictured at any degree.

Disappointed, April stepped around a jog in screens into a place that was both intensely familiar and completely unfamiliar. Unfamiliar was the sight of two Caucasian white-haired instructors sitting up front on the traditional Japanese kamiza, divine seat of honor, and a group of slightly younger but like-looking males sitting cross-legged below them on the floor, while on the main mat two practitioners demonstrated Gake, a hooking action used for ankle and sacrifice throws. Nearby was a kumite scoreboard with the Japanese word card commands that were used in matches. It was a karate center.

Those things were familiar, and the odor of sweat was familiar, too. But the lack of any Asian practicing what April considered the one uniquely Asian sport gave her an uncomfortable feeling. The martial arts had been developed over millennia by Japanese, Koreans, Chinese, Malaysians, Indians, and Filipinos. Each believed their system was the oldest and best. April didn't know why she reacted so strongly to the exclusion of females and Asians here, for certainly Chinese and Korean and Japanese all had their exclusive training gyms, and some still passionately excluded women and girls.

Also unfamiliar at Professional Prepare was the training area that contained a wall hung with protectors and training devices that were far more expensive and modern than any she had ever used. Here, the face shields and fist, body, and leg protectors all were made of expensive white molded plastic and leather. The variety of striking pads, sand bags, iron clogs, kick mitts, focus targets, and coaching mitts was a far cry from the "hand sticking" and "penetration hand" Chinese exercises of her youth. Back then *hand sticking* meant she had to plunge her soft fingers into bags of powder, then rice, then beans, and finally pebbles to condition her hands for striking. The Chinese exercise tools she'd used consisted mostly of chashi, blocks of cement with handles for one- and two-hand exercises to strengthen the wrists and arms, and black canvas shoes with iron weights in the soles for feet. Tradition. The training area also had five posts designed to toughen up various parts of the body. Each had a striking pad shaped to receive the strike of a specific part of the anatomy; hand, foot, shin, shoulder, head.

A gi-suited practitioner with a black belt tied around his waist and a black tengui wrapped around his forehead quickly separated himself from the others and stepped forward to talk to them. April had both her badge and plastic ID in her hand by the time he reached them.

"Hi, I'm Mel. How can I help you?" Mel was a dark-haired giant with friendly blue eyes, who didn't seem fazed by a visit from the police.

April's head came almost to his shoulder, but maybe closer to his armpit. She had a sixth-degree-black-belt ranking and was used to sparring with normal-sized people—Chinese males with compact musculature and far less bulk. She didn't think she could take him.

The sparring partners bowed, and a new pair moved to the mat. "*Randori. Hajime,*" said the white-haired master. "Begin free sparring."

April stepped back behind the screen. Woody stayed to watch.

"I'm Sergeant Woo, NYPD," she said politely.

He glanced at her picture, then at her. "A pleasure. How can I help?"

"Are all your members posted up here on the rogues' gallery?"

Mel's blue eyes followed her hand indicating the photos. "No, the masters have to be there. Some of the others practice for tournaments, so they're always looking for sparring partners and don't mind being called at home or work. But a number of our members don't participate in the classes. Some train on their own and just come in when they have time, take their chances getting someone they like to spar with." He adjusted his headband.

"Do you know a man called Albert Alberts?" April reached in her purse and pulled out the photo of Al Frayme in a gray suit, looking very somber at Calvary Cemetery in Queens just ten days ago.

"Yeah, I know Al. He used to come a lot, not so much anymore. Is there a problem?"

"What's his ranking?"

Mel twiddled his belt in his fingers. "He's pretty good, not the most graceful practitioner I've ever seen, but he makes up for it with determination. I'm not sure about his rank."

Woody joined them. "He ever hurt anybody?"

Mel laughed. "That's a funny question."

"What's so funny about it?"

He laughed some more. "We live to hurt each other.

That's the fun of it. No, no, no." He reacted to April's disapproving expression. "Just kidding. Of course, we don't mean to do harm. But let's face it, we've got serious pros here, and sometimes somebody does get hurt. Mostly pulled muscles, sprains. Occasionally a snapped tendon. Once in a long while a broken bone. We train to fall light, know what I mean?"

April nodded.

"But no trouble. If there's an accident, no one complains." He shrugged. "And people get hurt in every sport, don't they? Was there some report of trouble with him?"

Woody smiled at April and held up a photo of a redheaded guy in street clothes with a black-and-tan dog on a chain lead. "Who is this guy?" he asked.

"Humph," he said musingly. "Where did you get that?"

"It was on the other side of this. Someone stuck it in a corner." Woody tapped the screen.

"Nice picture. That's Rick. Rick Leaky."

"And the dog?"

"That's June, Junie. Nice, isn't she?"

Bingo. April now remembered. The guy was tall, wore a hat. She recognized the dog now. It was a mastiff with powerful jaws. A hunter, a drooler, a fierce protector of its master. "Is Rick here today?" she asked.

"No, he comes in on Sundays. On Saturdays he helps out in a dojo in Queens."

"Is he a friend of Al's?"

"I guess you could say he's Al's trainer. They've been working together for years. Is there a problem?" He looked concerned for them.

"Do you have a name for that dojo in Queens?" April asked.

Mel pressed his lips together as his forehead furrowed with thought. "Of the dojo? Not offhand."

"How about a contact sheet?"

He breathed in through his nose, still thinking. "Yeahhh, we have a contact sheet, mostly phone numbers."

"You want to give me his phone number?" April said, a little annoyed by now.

"Is Rick in trouble?"

She tossed the question back. "Has he been in trouble before? Has he hurt people?"

"I have no idea. We don't talk about our personal lives here," Mel said. He went to the book on the table for the number, then showed the page to April. Rick Leaky's number had been crossed out.

"Oh, yeah, I remember now. He moved," Mel said.

"You want to go in there and ask if anyone has the new one?" April smiled. "I need it right now."

"Sure thing." Mel trotted around the screen to comply.

"Good job, Woody." April was exuberant. She slapped him five. It was the least she could do. She would have missed the photo.

Mel returned a minute later, flipping his huge palms up. "No. We were going to update his info when he comes in tomorrow. Do you want to leave a message?"

April thanked him for his help and gave the task force's number, not her own. Her cell was a private number, but there were times a person couldn't be too careful.

Fifty-three

Mike wasn't too happy when she reached him on his cell. "Where the hell are you?" he demanded.

"I have a name on the guy with the dog."

"*Querida,* whatever happened to communication?"

"How about a thanks?"

"I'm the primary on this, okay? I need to know where everybody is. Get back here right now."

"You're welcome. His name is Rick Leaky. L as in 'love,' E as in 'ever,' A as in 'after,' K as in 'kiss,' Y as in 'you.'"

"Very nice, *querida.* Leaky as in 'faucet,'" Mike said. "Where are you?"

"I'm outside an all-white, all-guy gym called Professional Prepare. Frayme goes there. Leaky goes there. It's quite a place; the members like to hurt each other. There's been some kind of trouble there, but I don't know what."

"S and M?" Mike asked.

"Only the karate kind."

"How did you find it?"

"Frayme has an a.k.a. It's Alberts. Al Alberts is his father's name."

"Get back here right now." There was some pretty heavy tension in Mike's voice.

"Okay, boss. I'm on my way to Devereaux's. I've got a photo to show him. He has a flight to catch.

Look, I got your a.k.a. I got your witness. What's your beef?"

"What ever happened to teamwork?" Mike was seriously pissed.

"Look, we've got this down really well, *mi amor*. You're doing the team. I'm doing the work." She heard his intake of breath at the smart remark. To anybody else he would say, "Fuck you."

"Do you have an address on Leaky?" he asked angrily.

"No. How about your team does that?"

"What about the dog?"

"It's a mastiff."

"Okay, get right back here and bring us the photo. And I mean now."

April checked her watch. "I'll be back at twelve-thirty, one," she promised, a little miffed at his lack of enthusiasm for her initiative.

At eleven forty-five Woody pulled up behind the limo waiting in front of Jack Devereaux's building. It was a busy Saturday in Greenwich Village. The car was idling in a no-standing-anytime zone, but no traffic cop was around to give the driver grief. April got out.

"I'll be right back," she told Woody.

This time she was able to identify the plainclothes cop sitting in a Corvette in front of the limo, also in a no-parking place. But she didn't take the time to stop and talk to him. She hurried across to the building's entrance and stabbed the intercom button. She stared at the officer in the Corvette until he raised one finger off the wheel to acknowledge her. The buzzer sounded. She pushed the door open and took the stairs two at a time.

When she reached Jack's floor, he was holding his door open and looking cheerful for a change. He was wearing khakis and a lightweight V-necked sweater.

French blue, April's favorite color. His arm was still in its cast, and he hadn't shaved in ten days, but he looked as if he was finally getting a grip on his life. Lisa came to the door, and she was smiling, too.

"I hope this won't take long. We have to go," she said.

"I'm just going to stay for a moment. I just want to show you something."

April stepped around a pile of luggage to follow them into the living room, where the light was better. "What made you decide to get out of town?"

"You did." Lisa brushed her dark hair back. "Last night when Al called after you let him go, Jack looked at me and said, 'I must be crazy. What am I doing still here, still talking to a killer?' "

Jack nodded. "It's time to move on. Nothing like a life-threatening event to goose a person into reality. This is my life now. I have to deal. We're on standby on US Air. If we don't get on, we're taking the shuttle to Boston, then driving down to the ferry. When are you going to arrest him?"

"Probably today. We have a few things to clear up."

"Yeah, well, let me know when it's over. This has been . . ." He sat on the sofa, shaking his head. Lisa perched on the arm of the sofa. "We have to go," she reminded him.

April pulled the photo of Rick Leaky and his dog out of her pocket.

"And guess what—he called me again this morning." Jack couldn't quite let go. "It's so fucking creepy."

"Oh, yeah? What's he want now?"

"Same thing. He wanted to make sure I was coming to the reunion next week."

"What day is that, Jack?"

"Helloooo, it's Wednesday."

"Okay, Wednesday isn't a good day for either of us."

"No, and he asked about you."

"What?" April felt a little stab of concern. "Me cop?" *Or me victim?* she didn't ask.

"He recognized your picture in the paper. You'd better watch out."

April's tongue darted to the corner of her mouth. *Never underestimate an opponent,* she thought. "I have people with me," she said. And she was in a car, had a gun, was a cop.

"He's already killed a cop." Jack read her mind. "He's crazy. He thinks you're after him."

"Well, he's right. And I'm going to get him, too. Don't worry; we know where he is. He's not going to hurt anyone else." Still, she felt a second prickle of anxiety. Hell, she was furious, and worried. A second later she brushed off the fear. He wasn't Superman. He was just a crazy squirrel with a friend who got off on hurting people, seeing people hurt. Two nuts who probably egged each other on and weren't even smart. She'd found them, and they couldn't find her.

"What did you want me to look at?" Jack asked.

She passed the photo of Leaky and his mastiff called June. "Have you ever seen this guy before?"

Lisa and Jack studied the man and dog for a long minute. Lisa shook her head. "Who is it?"

"Someone who works out in a gym around here," April said vaguely.

"That's some powerful-looking dog. What is it?" Jack asked.

"She's a mastiff. Her name is June; have you seen her?"

"Maybe." He covered the man's red hair with his hand.

"Maybe isn't good enough. It's an unusual dog."

Lisa pointed at her watch. It was five to twelve.

April didn't move. She wasn't hurrying through this. What was time to them now?

"Okay, I have seen him, but not with the hair," Jack said finally.

"The night of the murder?"

"No, I saw him before that."

April's heartbeat spiked. "When?"

"I saw him with Al, a couple of weeks ago, maybe the Saturday before. Yeah, I remember. It was a Saturday. The press was still following me around, taking pictures wherever I went. There are a lot of pictures of me and Lisa with Sheba around. I wouldn't be surprised if someone took a picture of us. I was with Sheba. This guy was with Junie. Yeah, I remember. He was wearing a Yankees cap and called her Junie. Al introduced us. Those two looked very connected. Are they a couple?"

April shook her head. "Just the karate thing. Were they in the square the night of the attack?"

"I'm not sure. Maybe Sheba would know." Jack cracked a smile.

"Where is Sheba?" April asked.

"She's with my girlfriend Sharon. Can we go now?" Lisa asked.

"There's a guy in a Corvette downstairs. He's going to follow you to the airport and make sure you get on the plane. Do you have a number where you can be reached?"

Lisa wrote it down and gave it to her. Then she jumped up and did something unexpected. She reached out and gave April a hug. "Thanks. You saved our lives. I guess you're one of those heroes they write about."

"No, no." April shook her head. She hadn't saved anybody. Bernardino and Birdie Bassett were still dead. Al Frayme and his buddy were still walking around. "Get out of here, and have a nice flight," she told them.

Fifty-four

Mike exhaled noisily as he examined the photo of Rick Leaky. "We got them now. This puts Leaky at the scene of Bernardino's murder. You sure this is the guy you saw, *querida?*"

"Where's my medal?" April burst into a grin. She figured she'd done most of the work here, and now she wanted to be there for Frayme's arrest. "When are you moving?"

Mike shook his head. "You're something of a management problem," he said angrily. "Why did you take off like that?"

"I don't know what your problem is. I had to pee. When I was finished peeing, I had messages. We wanted Devereaux safe. Well, he was leaving town, so I had to see him before he went."

"How about consulting with me?" Mike didn't like these answers. His fuse was getting shorter.

April delicately lifted a shoulder. "I was downstairs. You were busy. You didn't pick up on your cell." *Thank you, Beame,* she thought. "Be reasonable."

Mike's fingers drummed on the desk. He wasn't buying the excuse. He was looking like Lieutenant Iriarte, April's boss from Midtown North, accusing her just because he could. It was a familiar scene in her life, a superior who happened to be her fiancé, chewing her out in the CO's office.

"Excuse me; you left something out," he fumed.

"Well, I already had the name of the gym. I got Frayme's a.k.a. It would have been a waste of time not going over there." He had her on the defensive big-time, and she didn't like it one bit. What was his problem?

"Look, we have a plan going here; you messed us up," Mike said sharply. "I'm the boss here."

"Well, you have no concept of time," she snapped back, surprised at her vehemence in telling the truth. It was taking time. Everything had to be done just so, and everything took forever, preparing the search warrants, waiting for rulings from the judges on the warrants, serving the warrants, doing the searches. The hours and hours of back-and-forth with the DAs, chewing, chewing over every little detail. Dotting the Is, crossing the Ts, and all the time the suspect was free.

April glared back. Only she seemed to be in a hurry. How could he expect her to sit there while they played with themselves hour after hour? She'd saved them a couple of days at least. Messed them up! How about broke the case? Her face froze into a Chinese wall of (number forty-two) silence as she tallied all the days of this case when she'd been up hours earlier than Mike, doing the kind of grunt work that he didn't do anymore. She was the one who had cross-checked the phone lists and the names and found Frayme in the first place. She was the one who had ordered the dog book, who had located likely karate studios, who was on the phone with Kathy and Bill and Beame and Hagedorn.

This was exactly what happened with commanding officers! They thought just being the head was enough. But the head of a snake couldn't move without the tail, and the head of a man couldn't think without a beating heart. And she was the beating heart of this case. Her heart hammered out her resentment, and also warned her to keep her mouth shut. The tongue was the enemy of the neck. And she didn't want her head to roll.

"We have a team here. An ABC kind of schedule going," Mike said slowly.

April concentrated on her actions. She'd shortened the lead time. What was the fault in that?

"You've lost your perspective here. You're too personally involved. The chief was right."

April kept her mouth shut.

"You're acting out. You're acting as if you're alone in this. And you're wrong not to step back."

He was pushing all her buttons. Her face was shut down. She inhaled through her nose, exhaled through her nose, letting *chi* reinfuse her body with all the vitality Mike was trying to strip away.

"Oh, Jesus," he said. Not Chinese spirit breathing.

She breathed. He swore some more.

"You've had it," he said. "You're too personally involved. And you're my wife. You'll have to go home now. I can't put it any softer than that. We can't have it like this."

His wife! She was not his wife. She finished breathing and felt much better. "What's going on here? What's your real problem?"

"I told you. I wouldn't put up with this with anybody else."

"I don't know what you're talking about."

"You mishandled this from the beginning. You didn't go by the book. You almost got killed. After that, you disobeyed me. You wouldn't take no for an answer. You never back off. So stubborn. You had to be on the team. I trusted you, and now you've drawn attention to yourself. Again. You make me nervous, April. I don't like you out there on your own. And that thing you always said. You were right: Couples can't work together."

April's features unfroze. He got her where it hurt, and he was right. "You work too slow," she said meekly.

"It doesn't matter. In this I have to be the boss." He put his foot down.

"I can't make the arrest?"

"No."

"I can't even be there?"

He shook his head.

"Is this a punishment?"

"No, *querida*. This is right. You don't want to be in the paper. You don't want to stick out in any way. You'll have to testify in court. Okay, you're going home, right?"

April swallowed hard, then nodded. At least she'd get to testify in court.

"I'll have Woody take you home. If he doesn't take you there, he's fired, okay?"

April nodded again. She felt like a kid called on the carpet. Her cheeks were flaming. She was busted. "You have everything you need to know?" she asked.

"I think we're just fine. Thanks." His eyes softened, but only a little. "Ciao."

Fifty-five

April trudged back downstairs and got into the car without looking at or saying anything to anyone—not to the uniforms enjoying a break in the sunshine in front of the precinct or the detectives heading in from lunch. She wasn't talking. Lucky for her no press was around to see her banished. Not that anyone would know, she told herself. No one on the task force, not even the primary, was allowed to comment on the case. So all the reporters were camped in the press room at headquarters, waiting for news. No one else knew she was out. It was her burden to carry. *Shit.*

As far as she knew, the only good thing right now was that the crucial info she'd supplied about Frayme and Leaky was still secure. Politics was the only real constant in life. At that moment she wasn't looking around, wasn't vigilant, and didn't feel she needed to be. Who else was going to stab her in the back but her own people? She brooded as she waited for Woody to return from receiving his instructions from Mike. *Son of a bitch.* Everything she'd always warned him about couples working together—and that he'd always pooh poohed—was coming true. The female always got screwed in the end. It was a fact of life. Woody was *her* person, from *her* precinct, and Mike was giving him orders. She and Mike had driven in together this morning in his car. She didn't even have her own car to drive home. So many mistakes every step of the way.

Nothing about what was happening now felt right. The only really positive thing coming out of this was that nobody had even once hinted at the possibility of using Jack Devereaux as bait to catch Frayme. She had to hand it to Mike for that. Soon Jack would be safe on Martha's Vineyard, learning how to be a gracious prince.

Her head turned and her eyes scanned people walking on the sidewalk. Nobody but cops around. She was jiggy for no reason. A little paranoid. By then it was way past lunchtime, almost two P.M. Maybe it was the fact that she wasn't a team player, so she hadn't been invited to lunch with the team. Pushed out of the action, she had no choice about being a good sport. Oh, she was feeling paranoid.

She shifted uncomfortably in the warming vehicle. The window was open, but it was hot in there anyway. And it was taking Woody way too long to come back. She felt like killing him for keeping her waiting. Angrily, she flipped open her cell to see what was going on there. She was surprised to find a bunch of new messages. Jason Frank. Oh, God, she felt bad about him, too. After putting him to work on the case, it was only fair that she call him right away to thank him and let him know they were both off it now. Kathy Bernardino had left two messages. What could she say to Kathy?

This is the story, Kathy. Al Frayme may have killed your father; just a little mission killing, nothing personal. But—either your brother stole your dad's money, Harry Weinstein stole it, or your dad hid it very well. April didn't think any of that would go down well. Another call she wasn't going to make.

She considered revisiting the missing-cash possibilities and decided that Harry most certainly knew where the money was. Getting him to give it up was another story. Maybe he was waiting for everything to blow over to retrieve it for himself. But how could she get to him now that surveillance on him had been lifted? She debated driving out to Westchester to check out that house again. Maybe she and Kathy could come up with something no one else had thought of. *I'm smart,* she thought. *I cracked this case. I can crack that one.* She pondered the number four million—minus a quarter. She didn't want to go home. She wanted to accomplish something.

She was feeling really whipped when Woody climbed in beside her. "Where to, boss?" he said.

She shook her head at herself. No, she was definitely not up to telling Kathy that she'd landed in the same boat as Bill. In exile, excluded. And four was a problem number, not a lucky number to the Chinese. Chinese lucky numbers were three, five, seven, uneven numbers. She wouldn't look at Woody. Her impulse was to smack him for following orders of the enemy, her former almost husband. The best she could do was ignore him for a moment longer. Oh, well, she decided she needed an ally. And what the hell, she was hungry. She'd go home and get some food. Skinny Dragon would be happy to see her. "Astoria," she said.

"Yes, ma'am."

For once Woody had the good sense not to share his feelings. He drove in silence without automatically cutting off all the other drivers on the road whose cars he didn't like. Or even a bus or two just for fun. He took First Avenue and cruised almost slowly up to the bridge. Then he took the upper level, which was flowing pretty freely outbound at this time of the day. Off the Fifty-ninth Street Bridge ramp, he followed the signs to Northern Boulevard. Nice and quiet and smooth as could be. April didn't feel any less jiggy out of Manhattan, though. In fact, she felt worse the farther away they got.

The Woo house was a few blocks south of Hoyt

Avenue, the Queens-side exit of the Triborough Bridge. Woody turned into her block and everything was copacetic here, too. But why not—Queens didn't have a lot of crime, like sections of Brooklyn and the Bronx. There were plenty of stores and commercial enterprises in Queens and both airports, but essentially it was a residential area. April's *qi* was as low as it got. She'd done good, but Mike was angry at her. Her ego and dignity were wounded. She didn't know which was worse, hearing his disapproval for her taking independent action, or feeling hurt at being kicked out like a cowboy cop. Frankly, she wasn't sure how they could recover from this.

Out of habit she checked the street for trouble. Saturday afternoon was quiet. She didn't know why people didn't sit outside around here, but they didn't, certainly not in the front yards of their houses. Nobody was gardening, hauling groceries inside. There were plenty of parking spaces and no sign of anything wrong anywhere.

Woody knew which house it was because he'd taken her there before when she'd been stranded without a car. Bloodred azalea bushes lined the walk to the front door. They'd burst into bloom since April's last visit. An arch of purple wisteria around the front door was blooming, too. The botanical display was a nice touch for a family that wouldn't upgrade the plumbing. But it didn't cheer her up. She couldn't banish the feeling of paranoia. Something was wrong.

"What?"

"Nothing." April's heart hammered out a warning.

"You okay?"

She frowned. Her street looked normal, but her house did not. Skinny Dragon was like a dog that knew at least an hour before its owner showed up that the master was on the way. Skinny had yelled at April to be there at three. It was after two-thirty now, and her mother's frizzy-haired head was not framed in the window. Where was she? April shrugged off the feeling that something was wrong. There could be a million explanations. Skinny could be in the bathroom, the kitchen, even the backyard. April got out of the car.

"You want me to take you somewhere?" Woody asked.

April considered the shopping trip to Flushing her mother had requested. She considered asking Woody to drive her over to Forest Hills to get her car. Why hadn't she thought of that on the way? She needed the car. What was wrong with her? She shook her head.

"You sure?"

Something was bothering her. Maybe it was the way Mel didn't know where Rick Leaky was. Maybe it was the fact that everyone was so casual about Frayme's status. She wished she could make sure that Lisa and Jack Devereaux had gotten on that plane and were gone. She wanted to call Mike and make sure—absolutely sure—that Albert Frayme was exactly where they thought he was: pinned down in his office on the second floor of the York U administration building. If she were in charge, she'd make sure, but she wasn't in charge.

It wasn't her problem. Mike was the head of the team, and it wasn't up to her to second-guess him. Skinny would say her *qi* was low, all yin and nervous for no reason. And she was not used to the feeling. She could have told Woody to wait, to drive her and her mother anywhere they wished. But she was demoralized and just wanted to go home.

"Thanks for the ride," she said.

"No problem, boss." And Woody drove off.

Fifty-six

April took the house key out of its zippered pocket in her purse and did not look back. She walked slowly to the front door of the brick house. By then it was nearly three, but the Dragon was still not waiting for her in the window. April turned the key in the lock and pushed the door open. From the kitchen came no sound of Chinese TV. All was quiet until she closed the door and the dog came alive, barking its head off as it ran out to meet her.

"Shi wo," she called. It's me.

"Wa wa wa wa!" the dog yapped excitedly. April dropped her purse on one of the uncomfortable carved wooden Chinese throne chairs and squatted down to pick up the dog.

"Hey, baby, where is everybody?" She put her nose in the apricot coat that was still puppy-soft, and the dog went nuts, wiggling in her arms, licking her face. Then abruptly she wanted to get down again. April put the dog down and headed into the kitchen. "Ma!"

"Shhh." Skinny Dragon came out, waving a dish towel like a matador with a red cape. She looked like a Chinese version of those overdone Hollywood stars on the *People* magazine worst-dressed list, a crazy lady in plaid trousers—brown and yellow and black—with a psychedelic twinset with a design of red, purple, and pink flowers on it. *Whoa.* With the furious expression and the inch-too-long, ink-dyed, freeze-dried hair sticking out of her scalp like a fright wig and new oversize purple glasses, Skinny was quite a sight.

"*Ni hao,* Ma," April said.

"*Bu hao,*" Skinny replied angrily.

"Oh, yeah, what's wrong?"

"Dad has upset stomach. Not up yet," Skinny scolded in Chinese. The dog jumped up on those awful pants. Skinny picked her up and patted her furiously. The dog didn't seem to mind the rough treatment. Like April, she was used to it.

"Oh, the usual," April said. A hangover. In that case she didn't have to go in and say hello.

Skinny rattled on cantankerously in Chinese. Lots of things were wrong in her world that she had to report. "People calling for you all day. Don't they have your number?" she complained.

April felt a chill. All day? "Who called?"

"People from work, wanted to know where you were."

Uh-oh. People from work knew where to reach her. April moved to the side of the front window and cautiously looked out. Nobody in front. The house was attached. Nobody could be in the backyard without going straight through the house, or over a lot of fences. Reassured, she moved away from the window. "What did you tell them, Ma?"

"Said you were coming at three. And now those gas people are here." Skinny didn't look too happy about that.

What? April's stomach did a somersault as she crossed the room to protect her foolish mother. "What gas people?"

"There might be a gas leak. The whole block could go—"

April's heart thundered in her throat. "How many?" she asked softly.

"Two. Something wrong?"

Yeah, no Con Edison truck was parked out front.

"Is Gao here, or his friend?" April asked.

Skinny shook her head.

Okay, just the three of them. Two old people and her. But she had a gun. She swallowed a thousand questions because she already knew the answers. "Where are they?" she said.

Skinny looked confused. "In the basement, of course."

The basement door was outside in the backyard. The gas line came up through the kitchen. It would be easy to rig the house. Just start a fire and it might go up. Nothing fancy. She'd seen it happen before. Just thinking about it made her hand tremble.

"Is the back door locked?"

"No. What are you doing, *ni*?" Skinny's eyes widened as April unholstered her big gun and started hustling her toward the bedroom, using her body as a shield.

"Go get Dad, Ma. Get out of the house, quickly. Call nine-one-one," she whispered. She handed her mother the cell phone from her pocket and pushed her toward the door.

"Jiu yi yi? Weishenme?" Nine-one-one, why? Skinny grabbed her daughter's arm, freaking out. "What's the matter?"

April tried to shake her off. "Just get Dad and get out of the house. When you're outside call nine-one-one. Say there's an officer down and give the address."

"Why? What are you doing, *ni*?" Skinny was a real management problem. She didn't want to do it.

April had her back to the wall that separated the living room from the kitchen. She was in the ready position with the gun, covering the door so her parents could get out of there.

"They're not from Con Edison," she said hissing.

"No?" Skinny was having a problem with this. "Why not?"

"Listen to me. Get out of here now before the house blows up." All this in Chinese.

Then Skinny's expression changed from confusion to rage. "My house? My house?" She started screaming, "Dad, get up. Get up. The house is going." All *this* in Chinese.

April's ears popped with the noise and she took her eyes off the target for just a second. That was when Al Frayme leaped through the door with one of those Japanese fight yells intended to terrify an opponent. It terrified her, all right, and it roused her father.

Shouting himself at all the noise, Ja Fa Woo chose this moment to stagger out of his bedroom in his underwear.

To April's right were her precious parents, to her left the enemy who'd killed Bernardino. She swung left and fired. The gun discharged as he knocked it up and out of her hands. Swearing, she sprang away from him as he moved forward to attack her vulnerable middle.

"Get out," she screamed to her parents.

Now she remembered what had happened that terrible night! Frayme had come up from below with his shoulder, aiming for her *tan tien*—the psychic center of the body right below the navel that protects balance and produces the reservoir of force needed to fight. In one blow she'd lost her breath and her sea of *chi,* and spun like a top, kicking at him again and again until he caught her. Instead she should have let her mind turn to water. She should have spun away and away each time he came after her.

Now there was no hope for a more powerful weapon. Her Glock was on the floor in the corner. Her Chief's Special was in her purse. Her mother and father were screaming at each other in Chinese. *Do something. Do something.* Useless.

A second man followed the first through the kitchen door. And then there were two martial-arts maniacs circling around her with no soft mat to spar on and a new mission in their eyes: Kill her for fingering them. All she had were calm thoughts and labyrinth arts. Karate versus *mi tsung i*. Not very much.

But she did it. She let her mind turn to water and fake-danced on the walls of her childhood living room, making so much motion with her body and the heavy Chinese chairs that the two men were trapped with their fist weapons striking air. Monkey child danced up the wall, spun, and struck and spun away. Enraged, Frayme grabbed a chair and smashed it against the wall, missing her by inches. Leaky grabbed one leg as she came down but caught an unexpected fist in his mouth before he could drop her. His head snapped back, and pain ripped through her arm as her knuckles connected with breaking teeth.

Skinny screamed as Frayme sprang at April from the other side. Mind like water, April spun again, moving toward the front door. Her plan was to get them out of the house.

Fifty-seven

His assignment completed, Woody Baum cruised slowly to the end of the block. He was free now, and there were a lot of things he could do. He had the unmarked vehicle and was working on the chart. He'd copied the photo of Rick Leaky and his dog. One thing he could do was take that drive out to the Hamptons and get a positive ID from the lawyer, Paul Hammermill. Save the task force some time. It might be what April would do if she were still on the case. He wanted to do what she would have done.

He slowed the car down to a crawl, thinking about other things his boss might have done in the remaining hours of the day. And he also considered things his boss never did. One thing she never, ever did was strand herself without a car. This thought pulled him to a complete stop. He knew his sergeant's Le Baron was in Forest Hills. Why hadn't she wanted a ride there to pick it up? Maybe she hadn't asked because she felt bad. Lieutenant Sanchez must have knocked the starch out of her, and Woody knew that scenario too well from his own career. He worried about her.

A car behind him honked, and he realized he was blocking an intersection. He shot the driver the finger and remembered that he hadn't fulfilled his assignment. Sanchez had told him not just to drive April home, but to see her all the way into the house and make certain it was secure before leaving. It was just a routine precaution, but he hadn't done that. The car behind him honked again. Woody made a U turn in the intersection and headed back.

Fifty-eight

April did not make it out the front door. Chaos reigned over the calm lake of her fighting spirit. She could not lure both attackers out the door. Blood poured from Leaky's bleeding mouth and a cut on his forehead. Skinny Dragon was shrieking with pure terror as he tried to get a killing hold on her slippery daughter. April's father had disappeared into the kitchen and was now trapped inside.

In a second of clarity, Skinny reached for a soapstone smiling Buddha from the dining room shrine, stepped across the room, and whacked Leaky on the back.

"Arrgggh." Bellowing like a bull, he turned and in one fluid motion grabbed the old woman by her scrawny neck.

The game was over. April's heart almost stopped when she saw the Dragon she'd thought all-powerful transform into an old woman in a giant's choke hold.

That was it. She lunged for the gun in the corner of the room, kicking away the table that blocked the kitchen door. Frayme flew to block her. She rolled away from him, and the gun skittered under the sofa. As she dove after it, the kitchen door swung open and her father came out with a butcher knife in each hand. Stunned, Ja Fa Woo saw his wife of forty years caught in a killing hold.

"No!" April screamed. Her father had bleary eyes

behind his thick black frames. He was a cook, and not entirely a sober one. His watery eyes seemed puzzled as he tried to choose in a nanosecond which knife to throw at the bloody-faced man holding his wife.

"Ma," April screamed. She did not have a chance to say "duck." She was distracted. In that second Frayme grabbed her and twisted hard. She felt searing pain as her shoulder dislocated. Then her mind cleared, and she came up with her head, bashing him under the chin. His body jerked up. As he straightened and became a clear target, Ja Fa Woo moved like a ninja in his underwear. One hand, one knife. The biggest one, his hacking knife, he wielded like a hatchet, striking Frayme between the shoulder blades.

April dodged the falling body as Frayme crashed on the sofa. Then Ja Fa turned to a stunned Leaky.

"Aieyeee," he yelled, and launched his second knife. This one had a very thin razor-sharp blade and was his favorite. It was the one he used for boning duck and chicken.

Leaky screamed as the knife sliced into his chest only an inch from the top of Skinny's head. He reached to pull it out and her knees gave way.

At that moment, Woody Baum charged into the house with his gun drawn yelling, "Police—freeze!" at the bloody scene.

Fifty-nine

April had a headache that wouldn't let up. Long after her shoulder and other bruises had healed, important Department people were still dragging her through every move she'd made in the weeks since Albert Frayme had first tried to take her down in Washington Square. She felt terrible. The terrible feeling was constantly reinforced by everyone.

The questions IA investigators asked over and over sounded to her as if they actually believed it was her fault for not immediately linking Al Frayme with karate after his name came up as a caller on both Bernardino's and Devereaux's phones. No, she had not been holding out on them. No, she could not have acted sooner to identify Frayme as Bernardino's killer and save Birdie Bassett. It was an insulting idea. Still, she felt bad. The killer had been an expert at locating disappearing graduates. He had known exactly who she was and where she lived (or used to live) as soon as her name appeared in the press following Bernardino's murder—long before he decided he had to kill her and her parents in their home. She hated to think about missing that.

She told herself that it was not her fault that Frayme had known ways to escape from his office, and had done so many times when people assumed he was there. Before the unfortunate incident in her home, she had told Mike everything she knew about Al

Frayme. It had not been on her watch when he took a subway to Queens to meet Leaky after she and Woody had fingered him as an accessory in the case. Nor was it her fault that they set out to convince her parents into thinking they were Con Edison workers so they could get into the house to rig an accident. But she felt that it was her fault. They all could have died. All the Woos.

IA's job, of course, was to deconstruct any and all failings occurring in the system. Why had the case ended in a spectacular mess in an officer's private home? How could they prevent such a disaster from happening again? It wasn't a hard one: Keep cop victims away from their own cases. That was their conclusion. Even though she had solved the case, she hung her head.

Like Harry Weinstein and his story about the quarter mil from Bernardino's lottery money, April had her story about what had happened in the Woo house. She stuck to it. The knives got into the perpetrators' bodies . . . she had no idea how. The dead couldn't speak, and Ja Fa Woo could speak, but only in Chinese. She didn't want him under any kind of scrutiny, so she took the Department hit for a thousand mistakes. It was her filial duty.

So many faults gave her a bad headache, but there were a few compensations. Mike couldn't apologize enough, couldn't do enough to atone for sending her almost to her death with only the useless Woody Baum to protect her. He'd do anything to win back her love and trust, and April had quite a list of tasks toward that end. Paint the interior of her parents' house, buy new furniture for the living room. Renovate the awful avocado bathroom. Promise never, ever to thwart her again in any way. *Ha.* That was the big one, and he was taking it pretty well. After all, it was his fault that Frayme had gotten away. They should never have released him in the first place. There were lots of should-haves and should-not-haves in the case, but who was counting?

In the middle of her interview ordeal, when April was holding back one of several hundred little details about the case that she didn't want known, she had a surprising insight that was so obvious she couldn't imagine why no one had thought of it before. On her first day of freedom she called Kathy Bernardino.

"Thank God you're still there," she said when Kathy answered. "I was afraid you'd left already."

"Soon. But April! I'm so glad you called. I hear you're getting it bad," Kathy replied.

"There's never any mercy for the innocent, but I'm okay," April told her. "When are you leaving? I want to talk with you before you go."

"That can be arranged. Bill and I want to thank you properly for what you've done for us."

"Your father was good to me. I owed you," April said. But she had more to do.

Bill was wearing a crumpled gray work suit and was in his usual hurry to get back to court when they met in Chinatown for lunch. April had the day off, and Mike had been promoted to captain but not yet reassigned. Kathy was returning to Seattle in less than a week. She'd had her hair done and looked good in a lucky red suit, April's second-favorite color after blue.

April ordered the lunch in Chinese. Dumplings, Ants Climbing Tree, Peking Duck, Noodles for Long Life, Golden Coin with Broccoli. Too much, but so what?

Everybody was in a good mood. Bill slapped Mike on the back a few times, and the two talked about how his messy Tiger Liniment had almost put him on trial for murder.

April poured the Chinese tea for health and began.

"Mike and I were talking. Loose ends were bothering us," she said, "so we have a few details to clear up."

"Oh, yeah?" Bill laughed uneasily. "With you guys it's never over, is it?"

Mike shook his head. "This is just between us."

"Okay, what?" Kathy looked a little nervous, too.

"What's your mother's date of birth?" April asked.

"Four, four, forty-four. She was younger than Dad. Weird, right?"

April knew that because she'd checked it out. "Anything strike you about that number?" She glanced at Mike and smiled.

"Of course, Bill and I talked about it a lot. It's the amount of missing cash. And, you know, those numbers came up on her winning lottery ticket. She used them every time." Kathy shook her head.

"Kathy, I'm sure you looked into your dad's files and found the receipts that showed he had your mom cremated."

She locked eyes with her brother. "I did look after you brought it up," she admitted. "Mom would never have wanted that. Why did he do it?"

April took a deep breath, then let the air out slowly. She glanced at Mike again, and he nodded for her to take the lead. Figuring it out hadn't been hard once she'd had time to give the mystery some thought. For Kathy and Bill, she took it one step at a time.

"You know, the Chinese burn fake money at funerals to help their loved ones in the afterlife."

"Interesting." Bill glanced at his watch.

"And the Egyptians filled the tombs of their pharaohs with everything they'd need in the afterlife, including their wives and servants. In many cultures people send loved ones off with the things they valued most."

"Oh, shit!" Bill said, getting it. "You're not suggesting Dad buried money with Mom!"

"Oh, my God. I don't believe it." Kathy put her hand to her forehead. She did believe it. All of a sudden it made sense.

"What got me thinking, Kathy, was when you insisted you saw your mother buried in a coffin. Why would she be buried in a coffin if she'd been cremated? The cemetery accepts cremated remains, so he didn't need to fool them with a coffin. The only people he needed to fool were you two."

"Jesus, Joseph, and Mary!" Kathy was so agitated that she broke a chopstick. "I understand. Dad wanted Mom to take it with her. I guess he thought four million was her share." She shook her head. "Unbelievable."

"What troubled us," Mike said, "was that no one believed you didn't know where it was. Anyway, one of you did. Harry did." The dumplings arrived and he tucked in, delighted by the reaction they were getting.

Kathy and Bill looked at the food blankly.

"Dad didn't tell me because I wouldn't have let him," Bill said.

"But this is just the kind of thing Harry would enjoy doing. What a hoax, and two cops could pull it off easily. They put the cash in the coffin. Dad gave Harry his piece and knew that as long as he was alive the money was safe in the grave. Jesus, I'll bet Harry was just waiting for Dad to leave for Florida to go and get it," Kathy said.

"Eat," April ordered.

Kathy laughed nervously. "How can I eat when we don't know he hasn't already taken it?"

"I gave him a little warning," Mike told her. "When I told him we knew everything, he confirmed. Eat; we have all the time in the world."

Kathy's face turned the color of her jacket with the excitement of revelation. "Look, with Bill as my witness, I'm going to make you two a promise. If that money turns up where you say it is, I'm going to give you Dad's house for a dollar and see you married there." She sounded so positive about it that April had to laugh.

"What if I don't want to marry him?" she said, rolling up a Peking Duck pancake and handing it over to him.

"You will," Kathy said.

Bill lifted a shoulder, then started to eat. "It's only fair," he said. "The whole thing could have gone a lot worse."

Bernardino's lovely house in Westchester, for April and Mike and maybe a couple of kids? The two of them were enjoying the food and the occasion. The promise made them look at each other and just laugh. A reward for doing their job? That would be the day. But it sure felt good.

If you enjoyed *A Killing Gift,*
be sure to look for Leslie Glass's
next thrilling suspense novel,
which takes April Woo into the bedrooms
and nurseries of Manhattan's
wealthiest young families
as she tries desperately to stop
a killer before another child
is left motherless. . . .

Turn the page
for an exciting sneak preview. . . .

Coming soon from New American Library

Everyone has a favorite place and a favorite time of day. For Maddy Wilson, mornings in her private spa in the garden at the back of her town house were her salvation. Every day that she had to endure the pressure of living in New York with her famous husband, Wayne, and hyperactive little boys, she spent the hours between eight and eleven in her gym to get away from them. At thirty-four, in the prime of her life, Maddy had never experienced violence in any form. She had never wished real harm on anyone. All she wanted was the kind of peace and contentment she felt while working out in her spa. Never in a million years would she have believed that a bloody fight to the death would occur there, and she would not emerge the victor.

Wayne had taken the trouble to build the gym for her, Maddy now believed, as a salve to his guilty conscience for ignoring her exactly the same way he had his previous wife. The gym had a glass-roofed exercise and massage room, a hot tub, and a shower that was studded with a bunch of pulsing jets and could also be used as a steam room. Sometimes she slipped away there in the afternoon, too. The spa was her haven, the only really private place she had to indulge herself and soothe away the nagging irritations of a glamorous existence that had come with a very high emotional price tag.

On June fourth her morning started in the usual way, with a spike of rage. In his typical hurry, Wayne had inched out of their bed before she'd even thought of opening her eyes. She felt logy, not quite herself, and was hit with a renewed annoyance that her husband, a restauranteur of some renown, had the ability to slip in and out of the bed they shared without her being aware of it. He never woke her when he came home from work very late, but even when he went to bed at the same time as she, he was never there when she awoke in the morning. This was a chronic hurt. And so was the fact that he could eat and drink all night and still be up before she, hungry for more, while she couldn't eat or drink much and needed her full eight hours of sleep.

In the early days of their marriage, Maddy had considered his stealth in the bedroom a blessing. She'd thought he was considerate to be so careful not to bother her with the demands of his job—all that coming and going for the early staff meetings and the endless rounds of late-night parties. She hadn't wanted to give credence to the myriad bitter complaints of his first wife, Jenny. First wives were by definition evil hags. Jenny still harassed him, and often Maddy as well. It wasn't a pleasant situation.

She used to think Jenny was just crazy, but now that she knew better she was more sympathetic to her former rival. Wayne's bedroom stealth was just sneaking around, a trick he must have mastered with Jenny, or even before.

Maddy had been twenty-seven and rather naive when she'd met the handsome forty-two-year-old. They'd been on a daredevil ski trip in which a group of wealthy friends flew in small planes to a remote area way up in Canada to ski fresh deep powder on a virgin slope. Right away Maddy had been attracted to him, had appreciated his appetites, and like numerous women before her, she'd ended up pursuing him as much as he pursued her. He was backing out of a failed marriage at the time and the father of two nice children, but she believed every word he said about Jenny's shortcomings as a wife.

Maddy had been sure she was a woman of the world, up to anything. She'd been a champion skier, after all. All legs and pretty enough to be a model. With her huge blue eyes and lots of blond hair, she'd been photographed many times for ski magazines and had plenty of boyfriends in the sports crowd. Her past popularity and athletic prowess were painful to remember now because Wayne had turned out to be no sportsman. He was just a very handsome foodie. Seven years ago she didn't even know what foodies were. Now she was buried in them—that special breed of human beings who devoted their entire lives to the art of the meal.

Never mind what meal, never mind where it had been taken, how, or when. A foodie could spend hours discussing the merits and demerits of a meal consumed a decade ago in a country that had been annihilated since. Breakfast, lunch, dinner, even tea—it didn't matter. All kinds of meals were worthy of long savoring and even longer debate. Life's other events and the passage of time had no relevance whatsoever to the memory of an excellent meal.

When the two handsome people had met in a tiny plane in a very cold place where Maddy felt very much at home, she had no way of knowing that history, even Wayne's own personal history, was significant to him only in the context of some dish or some ingredient of some dish. He remembered Jenny through the itinerary of their meals.

And then, almost worse than being foodies, Wayne's friends were winies, too. Or maybe winos was a more fitting description. When wine was added to the menu of foodie conversation, they talked all day and all night. They knew which wine went best with each and every course, which slopes and caves in every country were best for the grapes, which years were the best vintages and when every vintage should be drunk, as well as the perfect temperature at which it should be served. Not to mention the shape of glass required to give every wine the very best nose.

Maddy Angus Wilson was raised in Jackson, Wyoming, where she grew up on Cherry Coke, beef, French fries, and not a lot else. Maddy preferred a different kind of physical life. Her friends were skiers, skaters, sailors, golfers. Unfortunately, however, there were a great many women who shared Wayne's passions. Maddy had become an angry woman, and who could blame her?

At seven thirty she dragged herself out of bed and studied herself critically in the mirror. She was still a beautiful woman, but for some reason not as sharp this morning as she should be. She washed her face, brushed her hair, dressed in sneaks and almost see-through pink leotards that showed off her magnificent figure. Then she hurried into the kitchen, where Wayne was finishing breakfast with the boys and their nanny, Remy.

"Remy made pancakes, Mommy. They're sooo yum." Bert was five and a half. Towheaded and smiley all over, he was a happy puppy of a boy who looked just like her. At the moment, the bottom half of his face was smeared with bright red raspberry jam, and so were two of Maddy's favorite French blue toile napkins. Maddy's mouth tightened.

"Hi, Mommy," little Angus chirped from his special high chair. He was three and a half but still had a throne of his own, and he, too, was covered in red, likewise his napkin.

"Hi, sweetie," she cooed, and gave both boys careful kisses on the tops of their heads. She did not kiss Wayne.

"Hey, they're not just plain old pancakes, boys—they're crêpes. Didn't Remy do a great job?" Wayne said.

"Yay, Remy!" Angus said.

That did it. Maddy wanted their nanny out of her house. Out of her life. Today. She was gone, fired. Maddy picked up a jam-smeared napkin. "The boys are going to be late for their first day," she said coldly.

Remy checked her watch and jumped up. She hoisted Maddy's little Angus angel down from his chair, took both boys to the downstairs bathroom to remove the kid-sized chef's aprons that had been protecting their clothes, and got them washed up for the beginning of day camp.

"Where are you going?" Maddy snapped as Wayne headed for the garage.

"I'm taking them to their first day, then Remy's driving me to work," he said.

"I thought you weren't going in until noon." Maddy frowned. He was wearing a polo shirt, no jacket. He never went to the office that way, never took the children to their first day of anything. She glanced at Remy, smiling and laughing with the boys as they returned, gathering their backpacks and kid stuff for the day.

"A little problem came up that I have to look into." Wayne was scratching his nose, the clear sign of a lie.

"Yeah, well, there's a problem I have to take care of today, too." She leaned in and spoke softly in his ear so that he could not mistake her meaning or her intent. "I'm calling the agency for another girl. I've had it with this one. She's history. Say good-bye, Wayne. Remy won't be with us tonight."